HEARTLAND

The great agricultural center of America, where spacious skies overarch mile upon mile of amber fields of grain.

HEARTLAND

The Russians want it. They'll stop at nothing to get it.
  This year they've found their weapon.
  It will destroy far more than the target—unless one man can stop them.

HEARTLAND

A novel as real as today's headlines—
As terrifying as the end of the world. . . .

Also by David Hagberg
Published by Tor Books

LAST COME THE CHILDREN

HEARTLAND

DAVID HAGBERG

TOR

A TOM DOHERTY ASSOCIATES BOOK

HEARTLAND

Copyright © 1983 by Sean Flannery, Ltd.

A Tor Book

Published by Tom Doherty Associates, 8-10 W. 36th St., New York City, N.Y. 10018

First printing, January 1983

ISBN: 0-523-48051-2

Printed in the United States of America

Distributed by Pinnacle Books, 1430 Broadway, New York, N.Y. 10018

This book is for my children;
Tammy, Kevin, Justin, Travis and Gina.

Foreword

The world is not running out of food, contrary to popular belief. There are vast surpluses of grain in the United States, Canada, Argentina, and several other countries. The United States and the European Common Market don't know what to do with their mountains of dairy products. But surpluses are concentrated in only a handful of countries; most of the world must import at least part of its food from those few.

We are heading at breakneck speed toward a disaster on another front.

All of the world's commercial corn is of a series of hybrids. These varieties are used precisely because they are so successful: they grow fast, produce wonderful yields, and have resistances to most diseases bred into them. What cannot be prevented by genetic engineering is controlled by chemical pesticides. As long as each variety is grown in the environment for which it was developed—particular soil, temperature, and moisture conditions—these hybrids are among the miracles of our time.

But hybrids cannot reproduce themselves, so farmers turn every year to the seedsmen who, in effect, control what varieties will be available to them.

If a new, virulent disease were to occur in one of the surplus-producing countries—and I've been led by agronomists to believe that such a possibility does exist —the results could be devastating. It's possible that most of the world's commercial output of that crop would fail. The consequences are hard to conceive.

Corn is not a major foodstuff to most of humanity. Its importance lies in its use as feed for animals. Our standard diet—beef, pork, chicken, milk, eggs, butter, cheese—relies on corn-fed animals. A catastrophic failure of our crop would surely result in the almost complete disappearance of these items from the dinner table. And could we live with the fare of starches and vegetables that would have to take their place?

My thanks, for the intriguing idea, to Tom Doherty and Harriet McDougal, who believed not only in me but in the basic human ability to pull ourselves up by our bootstraps; to Dan Morgan, who wrote the fascinating book *Merchants of Grain* (Viking Press, 1979); and to a number of grainmen in my home city of Duluth, Minnesota, who showed me the practical side of all this.

September 1982

HEARTLAND

THE DAWNING

A Book of Verses underneath the Bough,
A Jug of Wine, a Loaf of Bread—and Thou
Beside me singing in the Wilderness—
Oh, Wilderness were Paradise enow.
—Rubáiyát of Omar Khayyám

Michael McCandless stuffed the last of the computer-enhanced photographs in his already bulging briefcase, snapped the catch, and walked out of his office on the third floor of the Central Intelligence Agency complex near Langley.

"Your car is ready, sir," his secretary said.

"Right," he mumbled, preoccupied as he passed her desk. He emerged into the corridor, took the elevator down to the subbasement, and was processed through the security post.

McCandless, a tall, thin man in his late forties, was deeply worried. But those who knew him would not have been surprised. He always seemed to be worried about something. This evening, however, his concern went deeper than usual, for reasons even he could not completely define.

Slipping his plastic identification card in the key slot at the door marked TELEMETRY AND ANALYSIS, he waited impatiently for the lock to cycle. When the door buzzed, he pushed it open and stepped inside.

The room was very large, and plunged three stories deeper beneath the building; equipment-filled balconies ringed what was called the pit on three sides. Dominating the far wall were two huge displays. One was an electronic map of the world over which were superimposed a dozen satellite tracks. The Agency's spy satellites. The other was an identical map of the world, superimposed with the computer-enhanced photographic images of the earth as seen from the satellites whirling far overhead.

"Anything new?" McCandless asked, approaching the chief analyst's console.

Joseph DiRenzo, a young man with flowing mustaches and deep, penetrating eyes, turned in his chair. "Are you all set, then?"

"I have a few minutes yet. I thought I'd stop down to see if anything else has come up."

DiRenzo glanced over at the maps. "SPEC-IV is just coming up on Novosibirsk," he said. "You've got the entire package, along with our best estimates. I haven't seen anything to modify what we already know."

McCandless set his briefcase down and pulled out his cigarettes, offering the other man one. DiRenzo declined. McCandless lit up and looked at the huge photographic display.

To the east of the central Soviet city of Novosibirsk, dawn had come to the land. To the west it was still night. As the satellite continued beaming its photographs down, widely separated pinpoint groupings of lights indicated cities still in darkness. But as the dawn came, the lights went out.

It was a strangely lonely, nearly empty view of the world. And McCandless caught himself thinking morosely that they had not come much further than cavemen. The world was still essentially uninhabited. Populations, for the most part, were centered around major rivers, along coasts, or within areas of natural resources. The oceans, and most of the land mass, were barren of people.

DiRenzo smiled. "If all of our problems were like this one, we wouldn't have much to worry about." He glanced again at the maps. "I mean, it isn't as if they were building new missile bases, or moving troops. This isn't going to amount to anything more than a social and perhaps minor political problem."

McCandless stubbed out his cigarette, his taste for smoking suddenly gone, and shook his head. DiRenzo was called the whiz kid around here, but he had no real understanding of geopolitics. None whatsoever.

He picked up his briefcase. "Anything comes up, you know where to reach me."

"Sure thing," DiRenzo said, and McCandless turned on his heel, left the pit, went up to the ground floor and signed out with the Marine guard at the front door, and went out into the early May evening.

As he was being driven into Washington, McCandless worried that the President would take the same off-handed view that DiRenzo had taken. He tried to marshal his arguments, fighting his underlying fear that he was missing something. Some vital element that would make certain sense of all this.

As an assistant DCI, he had had no problem in getting an early appointment with the President. General Lycoming, the director, was away, speaking before the California Bar Association, so there had been no one else to take this information to the top.

But now he was almost beginning to worry that he had overstepped his bounds. Paranoia, every Agency officer's constant companion. He sighed deeply, then lit another cigarette.

Lycoming would certainly hear about his appointment, but not until tomorrow, after the fact. The seed would have been planted in the President's mind.

At the White House, the President's appointments secretary showed McCandless immediately into the office in the West Wing, where he greeted the President, opened his briefcase, and laid out the photographs and bulky report he had prepared.

"I'm not going to read this tonight, Michael. You'd better give me an overview of what you've come up with," the President said. He was an old man, and although he normally looked years younger than his age, this evening he seemed wan, tired.

"In a nutshell, Mr. President, the Russians are preparing seemingly every square inch of their land for planting."

"Planting?" The, president looked up from the dozens of photographs.

"Yes, sir."

"I don't mean to seem cavalier about this, but so what? Don't they do that every spring?"

"Not to this extent, Mr. President. What they are doing amounts to the most massive agrarian reform in the history of mankind."

The President ran a hand across his forehead. He seemed vexed, and McCandless suddenly was very uncomfortable. "Give me the upshot."

"The results could be devastating not only to our farmers, but to the entire world economy. If the weather holds, they'll have massive surpluses."

The President sat back in his thickly padded leather chair. "If the weather holds. If they actually plant the acres you say they've prepared. If they can harvest such a massive crop. If they can distribute it." He shook his head.

"I'm worried, Mr. President. We've had our troubles in the Middle East and now in Central and South America. Such surpluses could be a political bombshell."

"I'm worried, too, Michael," the President said, getting to his feet. *"And I want to thank you for coming to me with this. I'll look it over in the next few days and get back to you. We'll probably get Curtis Lundgren in on it. Meanwhile, I want you to keep on top of things."*

"Yes, sir," McCandless said, disappointed. He had tried.

When he was gone, the President's National Security adviser, Sidney Wellerman, came in.

"What was McCandless all het up about this time?"

"The Russians have given their farmers carte blanche, and he's worried about surpluses."

Wellerman's right eyebrow rose as he slumped down in a chair across the desk from the President. He eyed the photographs and report. *"Ship it over to Lundgren. He'll love it. Meanwhile, have you had a chance to look over the material I brought you this afternoon?"*

The President nodded tiredly. *"Do we get the rest of the Cabinet in on this?"*

Wellerman shrugged. *"Not yet, I don't think. But something big is happening, or is about to happen. Lycoming tells me that the Russians haven't had such a run on hard Western currencies since 1981, when they needed operational funds to hit Afghanistan."*

"Give me the bottom line, Sid."

"No way of telling for sure, but the run'll be in the billions of dollars, unless I miss my guess."

"What the hell do they need it for?"

"The sixty-four-dollar question, Mr. President."

1

No one had all the pieces to the puzzle, certainly not that summer. Afterward, though, when conversations came around to Kenneth Newman's response to the summons from the Russians, there were those who said it was due in large measure to his frustration at the time.

Other, less charitable souls, who perhaps didn't know Newman quite as well, simply shrugged it off, saying that Newman was "the Marauder" after all. The man could hardly *not* respond as and when he had.

Some people who did not know Newman at all, except by reputation, maintained that Newman's response wasn't significant. Anyone could have done what he had. The fact that the Russians called at all, was the sole important factor.

The people who were charged with picking up the pieces didn't give a tinker's damn about the puzzle.

They were more interested in repairing the damage.

But the very few who were in the know pointed to a certain dark, brooding Friday evening in Moscow, when two incidents inseparably bonded the lives of two diametrically opposed Russians with that of Newman.

The weather had been almost too warm all week, culminating in a record high for June second of eighty degrees Fahrenheit. It was still in the seventies, with a humidity to match, when Colonel Vadim Leonid Turalin stepped outside the service entrance and cautiously sniffed the air. He was a small, intense man, not given to hurrying under any conditions, especially in such warmth, so he lingered by the door for a moment. His eyes were large and very dark—penetrating, his peers said—and his complexion swarthy. He was dressed in uniform.

The two guards on the door snapped to attention, but he ignored them. He strode across the Lubyanka courtyard and passed the black statue of Felix Dzerzhinsky, the founder of the Cheka, which was the forerunner of the KGB.

Turalin was in a foul mood. Over the past weeks he had been getting the distinct impression that his department was being interfered with. And he did not like it. From the beginning of his career with the GRU, and more recently with the Komitet, Turalin had always been a hard man, in the parlance, but an accurate one. He brooked absolutely no meddling by outsiders, either above or below him in rank.

In his mind at this moment was the nagging concern that whoever was looking over his shoulder was doing so as a direct result of the operation he had begun putting in place more than two years ago.

"From flights of fancy to the harshness of reality is often an unbridgeable gap," they had been taught at 101 School. "Often the simple idea, put in place with ease, will have the most telling effects."

The rear door of a Zil limousine opened as he approached, and a tall, heavy-set man, dressed in civilian clothes, climbed out.

"Good evening, Comrade Colonel," he said. His voice, like his manner, seemed oily.

One of Brezhnev's aides, Turalin thought, but he wasn't sure. "It was you who telephoned?"

"My office, but permit me to introduce myself. I am Shumayev. Anatoli Andreyevich." He held out a pudgy hand. Turalin ignored it.

"What do you want with me this evening?"

Shumayev smiled, then stepped aside, motioning for Turalin to get in the car.

When a summons came, one never refused it. Turalin nodded and climbed in. Shumayev joined him, and a few minutes later their driver was heading briskly out Yaroslavskoye Road. An army jeep joined them as an escort.

Shumayev poured a small glass of vodka from his flask and handed it to Turalin. Then he poured himself one and raised his glass in toast.

"To operation . . ." He hesitated a moment. "Is there a name for your plan?"

Turalin drank his vodka and put the glass back in its slot on the seatback rack. "What is this all about, Comrade Shumayev?" he snapped. "Why have you come for me like this?"

As chief administrator for the KGB's First Chief

Directorate, Turalin enjoyed a certain power within the Soviet hierarchy. But his long, hard years with the Komitet, and his reputation for being an unpleasant man, lent him even greater power.

It was said of him, although certainly never to his face, that he was a man with an iron will, steel muscles, a heart of granite, and the mind of a computer.

His wife had never been seen at any Party functions, nor had his three children, who were stowed away at school in Leningrad all but the summer months.

Shumayev, as close to Brezhnev and the reins of government as he was, had power too. But for this moment he bowed to Turalin.

"There is someone who wishes to speak with you," Shumayev said.

"Then we will proceed?"

"It would appear so. But it depends upon you. Do you feel convincing this evening?"

Turalin shook his head in exasperation. The man was a pompous, arrogant fool.

"I'm with you, Vadim Leonid, in other words," Shumayev said. He leaned closer. "And no matter what you may think of me, I am a man to have as a friend in this."

Shumayev's chauffeur drove fast but skillfully through the deserted Moscow streets. The smell of the lovely spring that had been and of the summer that was approaching lay thick in the air. And a haze, or a light fog, had settled in over the great city. Turalin wondered who he was supposed to meet tonight.

If too many people knew what he was involved in, it would ruin everything. There were bound to be leaks. And it was such a delicately balanced operation, that even the slightest leak could be deadly.

As First Directorate chief, Turalin was responsible for all Soviet clandestine activities abroad, and he ran a very tight ship, accepting absolutely no excuses from those beneath him. An operation either succeeded brilliantly, as planned, or he knew the reason why, and heads rolled.

But in dealing with those outside the First Directorate his control was less than absolute, and then he often became frustrated. He was frustrated now.

"How did you come to learn of this operation?" he asked sharply.

"Comrade Brezhnev asked me to look in on it."

"As a control?" Turalin asked, concealing fury. He knew that he should maintain civility. But he found it difficult.

"Don't overstep your bounds," Shumayev said harshly.

Control. Turalin sank into his own thoughts. Control was everything within the Soviet hierarchy, from the lowliest corporal stationed on the Chinese border to Brezhnev himself who answered to the Central Committee.

Control in itself was an intrinsically sound idea. But in practice the bureaucracies it spawned were monstrous, and often self-defeating.

Control, he would accept. A committee he would not. And yet . . . another thought came to him. Brezhnev himself did not know all of the pieces of this puzzle, nor would anyone until the operation was firmly in place. By then it would be too late. Far too late, he thought with satisfaction.

As they passed the All-Union Agricultural Exhibition

on the north side of town and continued out into the country, Turalin turned the operation over in his mind.

It was all a vast game of chess. Only the pieces were real men, and the stakes actual life or death. But, as in a game of chess, the king played no part in the attack. Other pieces, such as the knights, were far more powerful.

A dangerous game, he cautioned himself. The risks were high, but the rewards. . . . He smiled.

It was dark now in the car. Through the haze outside he could see the sparse birch forests on both sides of the road, white on black. And he imagined that he could hear the wind sighing through the upper branches. A sound that was at once lonely, yet comforting; cold, yet gently warm.

Indeed, he thought. The board had been laid out, the chess pieces set in place. This evening would see the opening moves.

The dacha was set on several hundred acres beside a small manmade lake. It was a large, very old house, with etched-glass windows, a half-dozen massive brick chimneys, dormers, and a large porch, the roof of which was supported by ornately carved wooden pillars.

There were no other automobiles in sight when the Zil pulled up in front and the chauffeur jumped out to open the rear doors. Turalin stepped out, his boots crunching on the loose gravel of the driveway.

It was quiet out here. The fog's wispy tendrils among the trees, and low across the lake, lent the place even more isolation and detachment than it actually had.

Turalin stared up at the house. He recognized this place. He had seen it before. But when?

"Lovely old place, isn't it?" Shumayev asked good-naturedly.

"Lovely," Turalin agreed absently.

Shumayev took his arm, and as they mounted the steps to the porch, the memory suddenly came to Turalin. He did know this place; he had seen photographs of it. And the realization was startling.

"*He* requested your presence here," Shumayev said, sensing Turalin's sudden understanding and emphasizing the first word, almost as if he spoke of a god.

Inside they went directly into a large room with floor-to-ceiling bookcases along three walls and a massive fireplace in the fourth. A fire blazed in the grate, making the room almost unbearably hot.

Several deeply padded leather chairs were grouped around a massive oak coffee table. Shumayev directed Turalin to take a seat.

"Vodka?" he asked. "Or perhaps a little cognac?"

"Cognac," Turalin said sitting down.

Shumayev poured his drink and then set down.

There was a large painting above the mantel, a Van Gogh perhaps, and the bookcases held numerous statues, medals encased in frames, and other bric-a-brac as well as books. The floor was covered with a huge Persian rug, and in a far corner was a standup writing table, such as accountants might have used long ago.

"You have done a fine job with your directorate, Vadim Leonid," Shumayev said almost casually.

In the light now Turalin could clearly see the man. He was large but shapeless, like a sad lump of clay. His eyes were set deep beneath a simian ridge of bone, and his puffy cheeks were crisscrossed with broken veins. He was disgusting.

"We manage," Turalin grumbled.

"I have an admission to make to you."

Turalin said nothing to the man's inane prattling. Instead he was listening to the sounds of the house. Somewhere in the distance, he thought he could hear someone talking. From elsewhere came the sound of an electric motor running, and he also thought he could hear music.

"You have been presented for promotion twice in the last two years. Each time I've recommended no. You have been doing such valuable work where you are, it would have been a shame to remove you."

"Promotion to what?" Turalin asked.

"To the third floor, of course."

"As a Komitet deputy?"

Shumayev flared. "You would do well to curb your tongue . . ." he had begun, when the library door opened and the First Secretary of the Communist Party of the Soviet Union walked in, bringing both Shumayev and Turalin to their feet.

He was a tall man, husky, with a wide face and large peasant eyes set beneath bushy eyebrows. He was not smiling.

"Leave us now, Anatoli Andreyevich," he said. His voice came from deep within his chest. But it was soft.

"Of course," Shumayev said, and he left the room, gently closing the door behind him.

"Have a seat, comrade," the First Secretary said, his voice cold. He poured himself a small cognac. "Your family is well?"

"Yes, they are, Comrade First Secretary. I will tell them you asked."

"You will not," the First Secretary said, sitting down

across from Turalin. "No one will know that we have spoken."

"Of course," Turalin said, looking the man in the eyes. He felt as if he were very near a high-tension line. The slightest wrong move on his part would be instantly fatal.

"It is not too warm in here for your liking?"

"It is fine, comrade."

The First Secretary shook his head, then took a small, delicate sip of his drink. "We must not begin on the wrong foot, Vadim Leonid. I am an old man, and not well, but I still have full use of my faculties, unlike poor Shumayev who is afraid for his own skin."

Turalin was silent. That the First Secretary admitted weakness was disappointing.

The First Secretary spoke again. "What is it exactly that you hope to accomplish?"

"I don't understand, comrade."

"Come, Vadim Leonid, let us not play games. Please. It is late and I am tired. I want to know what you are up to in your dark building. What are you doing? What is your operational goal?"

"Revolution on the North American continent," Turalin replied.

"You are either incredibly naive, or you have something up your sleeve. Something that you have omitted from your daily summaries. Something even that ferret Shumayev cannot discover."

"Yes, comrade," Turalin said.

The First Secretary sat forward and very carefully set his glass down on the table. His hand shook as if he had a slight palsy.

"You have stetched many rules, Vadim Leonid. That in itself is no mean feat. You have been a difficult man to watch. But watch we have.''

Turalin found that he was becoming angry with this old fool who obviously was on his way out. Angry that something might be going wrong and a scapegoat being chosen.

He had worked so hard, these past twenty-four months, with a dozen bureaucracies in a dozen regions, each of them independent of the others; with a hundred ministries; with a thousand factories and distribution networks for cover; and with thousands of people who all were made to feel that Turalin's ideas were their own.

He started to speak, but the First Secretary held him off with a gesture.

"It may take us years to come to a complete knowledge of how you have operated, so that such a thing cannot happen again. From what I understand, you have single-handedly created at least three hundred conduits for Western funds.''

"It is for the Party, Comrade First Secretary. Certainly not for personal gain.''

"Nothing you have caused by your ingenious manipuations has occurred without the tacit approval and cooperation of your chairman, of the Politburo, and, indeed, of me. But, Vadim Lenoid, you failed us. You neglected to reveal your ultimate goal.''

The First Secretary looking longingly at his unfinished drink. He shook his head. "The American workers shall rise and a new socialism will sweep the land, all because of the Soviet farmers' willingness to believe a new promise.''

"No, comrade, nothing like that.''

The First Secretary's eyebrows rose. "You do surprise me. What then?"

"An economic revolt of the consumer."

"And how will this come about?"

"When American food prices rise, as oil and gasoline prices have risen, there will be a revolt of the American people that will demand a change in their government. A change in their government's basic structure."

"Nonsense."

"No, comrade, not nonsense. Hard, true fact. We almost accomplished it in the early seventies, when my predecessor manipulated the grain market. There was chaos worldwide."

"Is that what you desire? Chaos?"

"The breeding ground for revolution."

"Explain then to me. Explain it well, because you have caused us to embark on a path that is fraught with danger."

"There are three vital elements to my operational plan, Comrade First Secretary. The first is the creation of a surplus of wheat and corn."

"Such a mundane beginning," the First Secretary said with some sarcasm.

"Yes, comrade. The second is a surplus of Western currencies. We will have the grain and the money."

"Certainly nothing in comparison to the wheatfields of Kansas or the pampas of Argentina."

"By the time we are finished, perhaps."

"And the third?" the First Secretary asked.

Turalin had to smile inwardly. Even now he would not reveal the third corner of the triangle. He had his deceptive answer ready.

"And the third is the ruination of the American farmer by the manipulation of the market."

For a long time the room was silent, except for the music still playing somewhere in the house and the crackling fire on the grate.

The First Secretary reached out for his cognac and drank it in one swallow. He slammed the glass back on the table, then got to his feet.

"Rubbish, Turalin. Pure rubbish! You are maneuvering us into madness."

Turalin looked up at the man. At that moment he felt very much alone. There was no one to turn to.

"I'm giving you a choice, now, of either abandoning your scheme, or returning here within forty-eight hours with the details for its implementation."

Turalin got to his feet. "I will return in forty-eight hours, Comrade Secretary."

"See that you do. And the next time we meet, there will be no lies. No half-truths. Nor will we be alone."

Outside, alone as he waited for Shumayev's car to take him back into the city, Turalin tried to think out his next moves. It seemed almost chilly outside after the oppressive heat in the study, and he shivered.

He had done well over the past two years, and would probably have continued to do well if not for Shumayev's snooping. There were leaks within his own directorate that would have to be plugged. And yet the next phase of the operation would of necessity have to be expanded outward. More people would have to be included. More resources committed.

He turned and looked back at the house. Had he underestimated the First Secretary?

The car came, and the driver jumped out and opened the rear door. "Comrade?" he said respectfully.

Turalin looked at him, then shook his head. "I will not be returning just yet," he said. He went back to the house and let himself in, just as Shumayev was coming from the parlor.

"Vadim Leonid. You forgot something, perhaps?"

Turalin nodded. "Will the First Secretary see me again?"

"Of course. I'll just tell him you've returned."

The truth, Turalin thought. Or at least enough of it to insure Brezhnev's cooperation.

2

Delos Fedor Dybrovik closed the file he had been staring at for the last hour, lit an American cigarette with shaking hands, and got up from behind his desk. He went to the window and looked out across the dark rear gardens to the Polytechnic Museum, which was brightly lit from the front. It was very late.

He shook his head in sadness. The spring had been lovely and the summer, less than a week away, promised to be wonderful. But the fall. The glorious fall harvests were only four months away, and then Exportkhleb would shine as it hadn't since the seventies.

There were some who would call him poetic. Others would classify him as a maudlin fool.

Dybrovik was unlike most Russians, in that although he was a large man, almost fat, his hands and especially the features of his face were light and delicate. Western,

his closest friends called him, a remark that pleased him
greatly, because he loved the West.

The Soviet Union was, in his estimation, a magnificent country—from sea to shining sea, as the Americans
might say. From the awesome steppes of Siberia, to the
Ural Mountains, and finally European Russia, the
Soviet Union was as varied as her people.

But once a man traveled outside of the country, to the
gaiety of Paris, the hustle of New York, the charm of
New Orleans, the cosmopolitan atmosphere of Rome or
Montreal or Buenos Aires, Moscow paled to a dark in-
significance.

He had been born in Leningrad, and he should never
have been given schooling or promotion. His father, a
carpenter, had spent more time criticizing the Revolution than building cabinets. And it was rumored that his
mother, a white Russian, had been more of a lady of the
evening than a wife.

But schooling had come, nevertheless, possibly
through some contact of his mother's, and at Lomosov
University Dybrovik distinguished himself in business
administration and finance.

From there he had gone to work for the Soviet Economic Council, one of his most important early projects
being the turnaround of the department store Glavny
Universalny Magazin: GUM. It was only a couple of
blocks away from his present office, but seemed a
million years ago in time.

Actually, it was only fifteen years ago that he had
been assigned to Eportkhleb, the Soviet grain-trading
bureau. At first he had languished there. "What does a
poor carpenter's son from Leningrad know about grain
trading?" he had cried more than once. He had learned

though, and learned well, and had in fact risen spectacularly in the ranks. Now he headed the bureau, much of his rapid rise due to the Soviet reward system. Those who did well, who learned their jobs well, were allowed to travel abroad. At once a simple and stunning idea.

Less than a year after he had started with Exportkhleb, Dybrovik had seen Paris, spending two marvelous weeks there with the trade mission. Then Buenos Aires the next year. New York, London, and Paris all in the third year. And, in the next years, every major Western capital.

He smiled now with fond memories, not really seeing the Polytechnic Museum. He had always loved Mother Russia, he told himself, almost as if he had to tell himself in order to believe it. Yet he loved his country better from afar. While in Paris, he often lunched at Russian restaurants. While in New York, he would extravagantly telephone his wife, Larissa, to tell her how much he missed her and their tidy apartment on Kutuzovsky Prospekt.

After those little nationalistic indulgences, Dybrovik would invariably dress in his finest Western suit, dine at the finest Western restaurant, and hire an escort for an evening of dancing and then pleasure.

This double life in no way affected his performance for the bureau. On the contrary, he often told himself that he did so well precisely because of this dichotomy in his personality and tastes. He could at once understand the solidity and comfort of collectivism and yet see the obvious merits of capitalism. He understood his peers and loved his wife, while at the same time he felt a certain kinship with Western grainmen such as the McMillans of Cargill, the Louis Dreyfuses, the Fri-

bourgs of Continental, and of course the mavericks like
Ned Cook and Kenneth Newman.

He laid his forehead against the cool window glass
and closed his eyes for a few seconds. His father, who
had lived with his share of strife, had told him once that
being a man was nothing more than the willingness to
accept responsibility. But what happens when the responsibility is killing you? His father had never been
able to answer that question. And his father's responsibility had eventually killed him.

A truck rumbled distantly up the street and disappeared around the corner. Dybrovik turned back to his
desk, bundled up the files he had been studying, and
stuffed them in a lower drawer. Then he locked the
drawer.

If all went well, if the weather held, the grain harvest
in the fall would top 250 million metric tons. The largest
in the history of the nation. A glorious achievement of
the collective farm system, the posters would proclaim.
A triumph of Soviet knowhow, the radios and tele-
visions would blare.

But he would not be here to participate in the sale of
the twenty to thirty million tons of surpluses expected.
He would no longer be a part of the system. He would
no longer even be a Soviet citizen.

They had been watching him over the past year or
more. His personal mail had been tampered with, and
there always seemed to be new staff members underfoot. And three months ago, in Montreal, he was certain that he had been followed.

Degeneration, they would call it. They always had
names for everything. He had succumbed to Western
decadence. He smoked American cigarettes, drank

Scotch whiskey, preferred steak to borscht, drank coffee instead of tea with lemon from a glass. He understood free enterprise too well. And he had been unfaithful on more than one occasion. In Paris with Marie Genarde. In New York with Marilyn Morgan. In Montreal, just three months ago, with Susanne Armor.

"For those and other crimes against the state, against the sensibilities of good morals, we find you unfit for further travel abroad."

Dybrovik left his office, walked past the darkened rows of empty desks in the main trading and posting center and down the two flights to the ground floor.

The evening smelled warm and moist, a fog forming from the Moscow River a few blocks away. It was the kind of evening that most people preferred to spend indoors, but it suited Dybrovik's bleak mood.

Unlike Paris or New York, cities that never slept, Moscow was a dark, forbidding city after nightfall. There were very few cars on the streets, no pedestrians in this section, and only the occasional streetlight to provide any illumination.

Stuffing his hands deep into his pockets, he turned east and headed toward his apartment building half a mile away, the soft slap of his heels on the pavement keeping time with his fears, with the nagging worry that had been with him for months. Had he made the wrong decision?

The buildings here were all old, with baroque exteriors, and stained, it seemed, with the sweat of the city; windows like blank eyes, blind to the tribulations of the people who passed. Doorways locked now, but in the daytime opening to shops and offices and a clinic. Busy people here by day, but by night they were all at home, locked away with their own fears and guilts.

Maybe he was going insane, he thought, stopping momentarily at the corner. Only this morning Larissa had planted that seed in his head.

"What's wrong with you lately, Pasha?" she had asked from the bed where she lay bundled under the covers.

He had opened the windows in their bedroom last night and had forgotten to close them before he went to bed. Larissa had spent a restless night cuddled next to him. It was chilly in the room.

"What do you mean by that?" he asked, coming from the bathroom.

"Look at you, you're getting fat, and you don't care. You eat greasy food and smoke disgusting cigarettes. Who would want you, except for me, I ask?"

Dybrovik stared down at his wife. Her face was plastered with a mudpack he had brought back for her from Montreal; her hair was done up with French curlers and wrapped in a scarf from Finland, blue and green.

He loved her, there was no doubt about that. But he loved the West and personal freedom as well. And he never hated them, as he sometimes hated her.

Across the street and down the block Dybrovik turned onto Kutuzovsky Prospekt, his step slower now that he was nearing his building.

In less than twenty-four hours he would be on an airplane for Geneva, where he would pick up the money he had hoarded there (another of his crimes against the state), and continue west. Paris the day after, and then New York City and finally Washington, D.C., where he would ask for political asylum.

It was time, he told himself again. It was time to leave. Time to expand. Time to change—or more accurately, to shed—his old skin, and become, in the light of day, what he had always been.

"Larissa," he cried out loud, stopping once again, his own voice startling him. It was too late to go back. There were no simple Leningrad days to return to. No Black Sea vacations to pine for. Only freedom in the Western sense of the word.

Years ago he had been in Gaborone, Botswana, with a trade delegation to the capital city, and he had watched from his hotel balcony as five thousand blacks gathered in the city square shouting the one English word "Freedom!" Only in their chanting it came out as two words: *Free Dom! Free Dom! Free Dom!*

He could almost hear them now. Shouting, screaming for something they had no earthly conception of. Free enterprise, and voting, and telephones without taps, and butcher shops without lines (supermarkets, they called such places). *Free Dom.*

All day he had vacillated about saying something to Larissa—some small word by way of a gentle goodbye. He would never see her again. But did he really give a damn? No children to worry about. Just twenty years of marriage, stretching backward like a littered path through a dense, troubled jungle. Vacillated between that and maintaining a stoic front. Another trip. Be gone for a week. Bring you back something special.

Without realizing it, he had begun walking again. Brezhnev himself lived on this street. Several blocks away, in a less shabby stretch, but on the same street nevertheless.

It had been the proudest moment of Larissa's life

when her husband had been promoted to chief of the bureau and they had been assigned this apartment on the Prospekt.

At length, Dybrovik arrived at his building. He checked his empty mail slot, then walked down the corridor to the back stairwell. They had been having problems with the elevator for the past several months, and the OUT OF ORDER sign was still on the door.

Why was it, he thought as he started up the dirty stairs, that his countrymen never seemed able to get telephones or elevators to work? Rockets to space, deterrent nuclear missiles, and world-girdling nuclear submarines. Triumphs of technology. But when it came to telephones and elevators, all science and technology seemed to break down.

At the top floor he walked down the corridor to his apartment as he pulled the key from his jacket pocket. Once again he hesitated.

If he tried to be tender with Larissa, she would either mistake his intentions for desire and would rebuff him, as she had for the past several years, or she would read right through him, another trick she had developed over the past few years, and would understand that he was leaving.

Either way he would come out the loser. Better not to say a thing. Later, when he was out, he could write her a very long letter, explaining what he had learned in Africa.

He unlocked the apartment door and stepped inside the tiny vestibule, where he took off his sweat-stained jacket and hung it on one of the hooks. He looked at himself in the mirror beneath the hat rack. He had been sweating profusely. His forehead was wet, and his hair was plastered against his skull.

He did what he could with it, with his fingers, then turned and, bracing himself, marched down the short corridor and around the corner into the living room.

Only the light on the small table in front of the window was on, and it illuminated the features of a dark, very intense-looking man who fairly exuded officialdom, although he wore civilian clothes. His three-piece gray suit, although out of date by Western standards, looked very modish here.

"Delos Fedor Dybrovik?" the man asked politely, his voice soft.

"Yes?" Dybrovik said. His knees were weak; his stomach churned and he felt the urgent need to relieve himself. This was trouble. Very big trouble.

The man uncrossed his legs, got slowly to his feet, and shook his head sadly. Dybrovik was surprised at how short he was. His features too, were small, almost delicate.

Silently, the little official crossed the room to the bathroom door, which was between the bedroom and the kitchen. It was ajar, and the little man reached out with his right foot and eased it the rest of the way open.

"We have much to talk about, Pasha," he said.

Something was hanging from the ceiling of the bathroom, but for several seconds Dybrovik could not understand exactly what he was seeing. It was pink, with mottled splotches of red and blue. But . . .

Suddenly he understood what it was hanging from the ceiling. Hanging nude, her toes just inches above the tiled floor, her buttocks dimpled with overweight and strangely colored with blue.

"Larissa." Her name choked at the back of his throat.

3

The night had suddenly become cold, the fog thick and malevolent, the darkness empty. Dybrovik, walking closely beside the official who had not bothered to identify himself, had no real sense of time or of what was happening to him. Larissa was dead. She had hung herself. But why? The question kept hammering in his head. And almost more important to him: Why couldn't he feel sorry for her, or feel the loss? He was in a dream.

"I'm really very sorry for you, Pasha," the little man said softly.

"Who are you, what do you want of me?" Dybrovik asked. Everything he had worked for—his apartment here on the Prospekt, his position, and his travel to the West—it was all gone.

"I came to see you, and when no one answered the

door I opened it and went in. I was just going to wait inside in comfort, you see, rather than out in the corridor. And I found her like that.''

"How do you know I am called Pasha?'' Dybrovik asked stupidly.

The little man smiled. "Ah, Pasha, we know many things about you. Many things. You have been a naughty boy these past two years. Perhaps, and please, it is merely a suggestion, perhaps your behavior drove your poor, overburdened wife to take her own life.''

"No,'' Dybrovik cried, raising his right hand, almost as if warding off a physical blow. "What do you want of me? What have I done to you?''

"It is not so much what you have done, my dear Pasha. It is what you can and will do for us.''

They had stopped, and Dybrovik looked at the other man. Perhaps *he* had killed Larissa. Perhaps *he* had hung her to make it look like a suicide. Things like that happened. It wasn't beyond possibility. But why?

Geneva and the West seemed so far away now, so unobtainable, and yet Dybrovik felt a certain sense of relief. The question of Larissa had been solved for him, and as heartless as it seemed even to him, he could feel the mammoth guilt he had carried with him these past months begin to bleed away. But what did that make him? A heartless monster, who was dancing on his wife's grave?

"I have worked hard for the department . . .'' he started, breathlessly, but the expression on the other man's face stopped him.

"Of course you have, my dear friend. And you will continue to work hard. Harder than you have ever worked. But with elegance, Pasha. With an elegance that will earn you a medal. You'll see."

The little man took Dybrovik's arm, and they started down the deserted street again, almost as if they were lovers out for an evening stroll.

Larissa was dead. It was an amazing thing to contemplate. At once frightening and yet somehow relieving. No longer did he have to face his wife—face the problem of loving her and hating her at the same time. But he was tied up with another, deeper guilt now, because of those complicated feelings. His mind seemed disjointed. It was difficult to focus on one thought, let alone follow a train of ideas.

"I know what is going through your mind, my poor fellow," the official said. "Believe me, I know and understand, and sympathize with you. But it is a terrible thing, nevertheless, don't you agree?"

Dybrovik found himself nodding. "Yes," he mumbled. "Yes, comrade."

"Yes, comrade," the little man said softly. "I understand, but alas, I do not think your colleagues would. Nor do I believe the Presidium would understand, and they have been taking notes of you these past months."

A cold wind passed through Dybrovik's soul, and he shivered.

"Don't you know, Pasha, that we have been disappointed with you? Deeply disappointed. We had such high hopes."

The fog seemed thicker now, the night more intense, the deserted streets even more lonely, the West more distant.

"It is why we began to look very carefully at you. It is why we wanted to know more about you, to see if you were of the necessary caliber."

If there was a choice at this late hour, which would he pick? He had wanted the West, still wanted the lights and the freedom. Yet this was home, this was comforting. He had never felt lonely here.

"And then, when we all began to realize what you had done, what you had been doing, we were deeply disappointed. Heartsick, if you will." The little man's voice was almost like an aphrodisiac, but the words he spoke were painful. "Still," he said on a more positive note, "all need not be lost."

Dybrovik turned to him. Was it possible?

"I'm talking about redemption here, Pasha. Do you understand that?"

Dybrovik nodded, the saliva gathering suddenly in his parched mouth. Maybe he had never wanted the West. Maybe he had never wanted anything more than what he already had. Moscow as home, the West as a plaything. A bauble.

"It could take years, you know. But you could redeem yourself. You could become a useful citizen once again."

They had turned the corner and were heading down the final half-block to the bureau, and Dybrovik had the sudden terrible thought that whatever was asked of him, he would be incapable of doing. All his life he had lived with the fear of being unable to manage whatever was expected of him. And now he was terrified.

"If you are worried that you will not be able to do what I ask, banish that from your mind," the little man said, as if on cue. "You are the right man for the job. None of us ever doubted that."

"Thank you," Dybrovik said simply.

"No, it's never been your abilities under question,

Pasha. It has been your willingness that we have wondered about."

A tentative sense of hope filled Dybrovik's breast. "Anything," he said, the word sounding hollow to him.

"Splendid," the little man said. "I told them we could count on you. I told them just to leave everything to me, that you were right for this."

They turned into a doorway, then went down a hall and up two flights of stairs that were familiar to Dybrovik and yet, in his present state of shock, strange.

"You will have to begin immediately," the little official said, his voice echoing hollowly in the stairwell. "Tomorrow, as a matter of fact."

"Yes."

They had reached the second floor, and the little man unlocked a door and stepped inside, waiting for Dybrovik. Only then did Dybrovik recognize that he was back in his own building, in his own office, and he stopped short. The rows of desks in the dark trading and posting room were like soldiers in ranks, all staring at him, accusing him of his crimes past and present. It was an embarrassment to be here now like this.

"In Geneva," he began, "there is a bank . . ."

"I know, Pasha," the little man said comfortingly. "I have the funds, and no one here will ever be the wiser. Your trip to Geneva will simply be postponed for a few days, perhaps as long as a week."

They had known everything after all. He felt even more foolish that he had tried to desert his country. Yet he felt a certain sense of pride and comfort in the knowledge that such capable, all-knowing people were in charge.

Across the large room they entered Dybrovik's office,

where the official motioned for him to sit behind the desk. When they were both settled, the only light in the room coming from the outside, the little man delicately crossed his legs and lit a cigarette. He did not offer one to Dybrovik.

"You have done well for yourself, you know. Some might argue, too well."

"What about my wife?"

"The civil police are at your apartment. It will all be quietly taken care of. Believe me when I promise you that."

Dybrovik nodded. There was nothing he could say, nevertheless he shuddered at the image of her gross body hanging from the bathroom ceiling. He had had the thought at the back of his mind that Larissa would end up married to some minor Party official or perhaps an engineer; someone more precise than he had been. That was it. She had always needed accuracy in her life, a crispness that he had never been able adequately to provide.

"I would like to talk about grain, Pasha," the little man said.

Dybrovik blinked in surprise. "Grain?"

"Corn and wheat."

"To sell?" Dybrovik asked. His heart accelerated. "This fall there will be surpluses."

"The harvest will be nearly three hundred million tons."

The figure took Dybrovik's breath away. It was much more than he had been told. Yet he did not think to question it.

"But we need more, Pasha. I want you to buy grain futures. Immediately."

"But what would we do with it?"

The little man smiled, his eyes flashing in the darkness almost as if they had a light of their own. "What nations provide the largest surpluses these days, Pasha, can you tell me that with certainty?"

"The United States," Dybrovik said immediately. "Corn, wheat, soybeans, barley, even rice."

A nod. "And corn? Who else provides corn?"

"Argentina."

"Wheat?"

"Canada."

"No Warsaw Pact countries?" The question was almost sad.

Dybrovik shook his head. He had no idea what was coming.

"Tell me, Pasha. How much grain could you manage to buy in complete secrecy?" His voice was still very soft, but even in his present confusion Dybrovik could sense that the little man was excited. But such a question.

"In secret?" he said, drawing it out. "It would depend upon how much grain was needed."

"As much as could possibly be purchased."

"It would take money. Hard Western currencies."

"An unlimited amount would be at your disposal."

Dybrovik stood up, suddenly very excited with what he was being asked to do. It had almost happened back in the seventies. They had bought mammoth amounts of grain futures, and then, when the market suddenly destabilized because of their massive purchases, they were left holding huge grain reserves whose prices had shot up to unusual levels. The Western press had dubbed it the Great Grain Robbery. But these days there were closely monitored international regulations to stop just such a thing. And yet. . . .

"This would be for me, Pasha," the little man said, looking up at him. "Your expertise would become your path to redemption. But there could be no mistakes."

Dybrovik's mind was far ahead now: leaping to personalities, because that was what the international grain market was all about, after all.

Six family businesses controlled more than ninety percent of the industry. The McMillans of Cargill in Minneapolis; Michael Fribourg of Continental out of New York; the Louis Dreyfus conglomerate in Paris; Georges André, the Swiss; the Hirsches and Borns in Brazil; and largest of all, E. Vance-Ehrhardt, Ltd., in Buenos Aires.

In each case, the company was privately owned; its finances were its own concern and highly secret. Yet such huge conglomerates always suffered leaks of information because of the sheer number of persons involved.

Still thinking, Dybrovik lit a cigarette, unmindful for the moment of the man sitting quietly, watching him.

No, he told himself firmly. It could not be one of the conglomerates. Rather, it would have to be one of the independents. Ned Cook in Memphis would have been perfect, but he was gone now. His business ruined. Which left Newman, the Marauder, the one man in the business whom Dybrovik feared and respected most. The one man who could pull this off. Who would do it.

"Are we purchasing world grain, or are we targeting the United States?" he asked, suddenly turning.

The little man smiled, the expression totally devoid of humor. "You can be perceptive, Pasha," he said. "The United States."

"For what end?"

The little man stood up. "It is not for you to ask. Can it be done?"

Dybrovik nodded, a new strength seemingly pouring into his veins. He was on his own territory now. He knew what he was doing. "There will of necessity be travel abroad."

"I understand."

"A lot of it. This will take time. Months, perhaps."

"Yes."

Dybrovik moved around his desk. "Do I report to you on my progress?"

"It will not be necessary."

"How about the funds? We will need Western currencies."

"A conduit has been set up for you with a bank in Geneva."

"My passport?"

"Unlimited external travel."

The little man smiled again, then started to the door.

"And afterward, comrade?" Dybrovik asked on impulse.

"Afterward, Pasha? There is no afterward, only here and now. And always there will be the question of poor Larissa." The little man looked directly into Dybrovik's eyes. "Did you kill her, or did we? Which would the civil police want to believe?" And then he was gone.

The call to Kenneth Newman went out the very next day, but it was a full twenty-four hours later, on June 17, that he got the message. That was due in part to the fact that in the interest of secrecy Dybrovik had initiated the contact through a low-level Exportkhleb clerk as a routine telex to a Newman subsidiary, Abex, Ltd., in

New York City. From there it was shuttled to Newman's main office in Duluth, Minnesota, and finally down to Buenos Aires where Newman was a guest of the Vance-Ehrhardt family. The delay was also due to the fact that no one wanted to pass on any kind of business message to Newman on the day of his wedding. Thus it was only later, after many hours had passed, that Newman became aware that he was being summoned by the Russians. And his reaction then, according to those who knew him well, was understandable. To those who didn't, it was outrageous.

4

It was a few minutes after 8:00 A.M. on a lovely South American fall Saturday. The Vance-Ehrhardt estate stood at the center of two thousand heavily wooded acres just to the northeast of Buenos Aires along the Río de la Plata. The house was huge: three stories, with gables and dormers, and bristling with chimneys. It had been copied after the original Vance-Ehrhardt estate of the 1700s in Austria, but was not out of place here. Many Germans, Austrians, Swiss, and even Belgians had immigrated to Argentina over the past hundred years, especially during and after the Second World War. The German-speaking peoples had their own residential areas and styles, their own hospitals, churches, schools, and shopping centers.

The house fronted on a paved road that meandered three-quarters of a mile through the forest to the government highway. On either side of the road were rose gardens, well-tended lawns, fountains, statuary, and innumerable trees of dozens of different species.

To the rear of the house, however, a much shorter section of tended lawn gave way rather abruptly from the pool and patio area to a thick tangle of jungle undergrowth that led down to the river. It was cut through by a wide flagstone path that led, to the right, to the river and boat docks; and to the left, one mile away, to a well-lit paved runway that could handle all but the largest of business jets.

On this morning Kenneth Newman stood at the balcony window of his third floor bedroom, looking toward the airstrip as he drank his first coffee of the day and smoked his first morning cigarette.

He was a large, good-looking man in his early forties, with a broad, honest face, wide blue eyes, and a thick shock of wavy brown hair. "The face that has sealed a thousand deals," *Time* Magazine had once called it.

"Eyes that inspire trust, and a personality that requires all who come in contact with the man to open wide, to hold absolutely nothing back," *Newsweek* had written.

At this moment he was dressed in a soft velvet robe. His hair was tousled and his eyes still somewhat clouded with sleep, although he had not slept well last night. The same dream that had been plaguing him for weeks had bothered him again. In it he was dressed for the wedding and was walking slowly down the aisle. Lydia waited for him at the altar. Only he knew somehow that the woman behind the veil wasn't her, and yet he could not resist going to her side and continuing with the ceremony. Each night, at the point where he was supposed to raise her veil and kiss her, the congregation began to hiss and boo and throw things at him, and he awoke in a cold sweat. Some nights he would have the dream several times. And each morning on awakening, he would wonder if it had been a dream at all, or some kind of portent of something disturbing to come.

The distant roar of a Learjet, approaching from the northeast, broke him out of his thoughts, and he looked that way, shielding his eyes against the sun as the plane came in low and very fast for a landing.

It had been like that for the past forty-eight hours. Guests had been arriving from all over the world, some by limousine up from the city, but most by private jet. And yet it was not the festive, happy occasion that it should have been. There was a lot of animosity toward him from the Vance-Ehrhardts, as well as their guests.

Newman smiled, stubbed out his cigarette in the ashtray on the small wrought-iron table at his side, finished his coffee, and went inside to the marble bathroom. He stepped into the shower, and turned on the spray as hard and as hot as he could stand it.

Except for Lydia, he would be friendless at his own wedding. He had been the one to insist they marry here in Argentina. Lydia had wanted simply to get married by a judge somewhere in a civil ceremony, and the hell with her parents. Another in a long string of defiant acts. But he had insisted. And because of his insistence, he had not felt right about inviting any of the people from his business.

It didn't really matter. Newman was a loner, had been a loner all of his life. His parents had died within months of each other when he was nineteen and in college. He took a couple of years off to work in the wheatfields of Kansas, near his father's boyhood home, before he went back to school at the Polytechnic in Berne, Switzerland.

His father, who had been a small American name in the oil-tooling industry in France, had given his son two important things. The first was absolute honesty ("Your word is the only thing you cannot lose, so don't give it away"). The second was an inheritance of slightly less than one million dollars.

Newman had parlayed both into a reputation as a tough but honest grain dealer and a fortune approaching the fifty-million-dollar mark.

For a time, after college, he had worked in his father's business—which was finally taken over by Arlmant-Genard, S.A., a gigantic French steel, oil, and shipping conglomerate—as a common laborer, and later as an ordinary seaman aboard the A-G fleet, which included grain ships.

It was there he met Jorge Vance-Ehrhardt, through a shipping contract, and a working friendship had resulted. Within a year the friendship had developed into a job for Newman as personal assistant to the great man himself.

From that moment on—it seemed a million years ago to Newman—he had learned the grain business. He had learned about weather, which was vital to grainmen the world over. Sunspot cycles of eleven and twenty-two years, which affected the weather, therefore crops and as a result prices, became second nature to him. Shipping tonnages and contract rate schedules were music to his ears. New hybrids, new planting methods, new tractor designs, elevator construction, and dock workers' union business became his front-page news.

Balance of trade, international currency exchange rates, the gold and silver standards were all important. And finally there were personalities, dealing with people on a one-to-one basis. That was the most important of all.

In the seven years Newman worked with Vance-Ehrhardt, he learned his lessons well. And his own specialties began to emerge.

Early on, Newman developed the uncanny ability to sense a grain deal in the works. A run on shipping tonnages here; there the emergence of an African leader who understood that his people had to be fed; an adverse weather report in one section of the world, with bumper crops in another—all became signs to Newman that a deal was in the making.

This ability, combined with the backing of the Vance-Ehrhardt conglomerate, allowed him to undercut competitive grain dealers even before they knew what hit them. Corn to Johannesburg at two-ten a bushel? He could turn it into two-fifty. Canadian wheat languishing in the fields? He bought at fifty cents a bushel discount, held for three months, and resold it at a ninety-cent profit when everyone else was screaming for a quarter higher.

Thus he became known as the Marauder.

Then, eight short years ago, Newman had branched off on his own, taking with him not only the expertise Vance-Ehrhardt had taught him, but several of the conglomerate's most lucrative contracts.

For that Jorge Vance-Ehrhardt had never forgiven him. The term Marauder was not used as an endearment in that household, rather as an obscenity.

It didn't matter, though, he kept telling himself. Today was the wedding, and by this evening he and

Lydia would be gone. After a brief honeymoon he would be back at work.

He turned off the shower, dried himself, and went back into this bedroom, tying the belt of his robe.

Lydia was standing there, her back to the hall door. She was clad in a black bikini, a light robe over her shoulders, sandals on her feet. She jumped, a surprised look on her face that turned to a seductive grin.

"What are you doing here?" he said mildly.

"I was getting set to join you in the shower," she said. Her voice was soft and very pleasant, with the slightest trace of a German accent. She was a tall, willowy woman, with small breasts, a flat stomach, and a small, almost boyish derriere. Her skin was deeply tanned, which accented the long blond hair that cascaded around her shoulders.

"Your mother will have a fit," Newman said, not moving from the bathroom doorway. He was conscious of his heart beating in his chest. Lydia was a lovely woman.

"Screw it," she grinned. She undid her bikini top, tossed it and the robe aside, stepped out of her sandals, and slipped off her bikini bottom. Her pubic hair was nothing more than a light tuft of blonde. She came across the room to Newman, put her arms around his neck, and pressed her body against his.

"Hmmm," she sighed luxuriously. "I've missed you, Kenneth."

Newman resisted for just a moment, but then he pulled her even closer, and they kissed deeply, her breasts crushed against his chest, her long legs soft against his, and he could feel himself responding despite his determination to do absolutely nothing here that could be criticized. But he loved her. Despite her faults, which he knew and understood all too well, he loved her.

He had watched her develop and mature during the years he had worked for her father. At first he had called her the snot-nosed kid. But then, one day, he had suddenly seen her in a new light. She was not a kid, snot-nosed or otherwise, but a beautiful woman, though headstrong, petulant, and spoiled. A woman he had fallen deeply and irrevocably in love with. Nothing had happened to change that in the two months since he and Lydia had announced their engagement. Not her family's animosity, not her shenanigans (as her father called her defiant acts), and certainly not any second thoughts on his part. If anything, he had fallen even more deeply in love with her.

If he was a marauder, then she was a pirate. Uncompromisingly selfish, but lovely.

They parted, and he held her at arm's length as they looked into each other's eyes.

"Not now," he said firmly.

"Don't be a boor, Kenneth," she said.

He laughed, pulled her closer so that he could kiss her tiny, upturned nose, then spun her around by the shoulders, and slapped her on the bottom.

"Your mother and aunts are probably having fits right now trying to find you. Don't disappoint them. Just this one time."

She wheeled back to him, her hands on her slim hips. "You son of a bitch," she shouted.

Newman laughed again. "Hell of a thing to call your groom on your wedding day."

For just a moment it seemed as if she wouldn't back

down, but suddenly she grinned. "It's one of the many reasons I love you, you know. You're such a bastard, I can't get around you."

"And you're a spoiled-rotten little bitch. A hell of a relationship we've got ourselves here."

She laughed as she gathered up her bikini and threw on her robe, but then she turned serious. "You'll rue the day you met me, Kenneth. You do know that, don't you?"

He nodded. "It's one of the reasons I love you. I like living dangerously."

"I will hurt you."

"You already have."

"Bastard," she said. Someone knocked on the door. She threw it open as her startled father was raising his hand to knock again.

She reached up and pecked him on the cheek. "He's a son of a bitch, Father," she snapped, turning around to smile at Newman. "But I love him." And she brushed past her father and was gone.

Vance-Ehrhardt looked after her for a long moment, shook his head, then turned back to Newman. "May I come in?"

"Of course," Newman said.

Vance-Ehrhardt stepped into the room, softly closed the door, and came across to where Newman was standing. He seemed ill at ease, almost embarrassed.

"I came to offer you money to quit this nonsense."

"It would have to be quite a sum to tempt me, Jorge," Newman said angrily. He had always respected the older man's wisdom when it came to business. But his judgment of the people closest to him had always been wanting.

"Five million."

"Dollars?"

"Of course," Vance-Ehrhardt said. He was a short, stocky man with thinning white hair, a double chin, jowls, and deep-set, hooded eyes. No one knew his real age, but Newman was sure he was in his late sixties at least.

"You value your daughter highly," Newman said.

"Don't play games with me, Kenneth," the older man said, a bit of color coming to his cheeks. "I don't want you as a son-in-law. I don't want you married to Lydia. I don't want you a part of this family."

"You're forgetting, Jorge, that Lydia will take my name. She becomes a part of my family."

"You have no family!"

"Does that mean you will deny your own grandchildren?"

Vance-Ehrhardt raised his right hand as if he would strike Newman, but then he lowered it. "Are you saying my daughter is pregnant?"

"No, unfortunately not. But I'll do everything within my power to make sure she is within the next few months, with or without your blessings."

A range of emotions played across the older man's face, which had turned a mottled red. "Why have you done this to me, Kenneth?" he asked at length. "Why have you singled out my family?"

"I've not singled out your family, Jorge," Newman said with feeling. He truly liked the old man. "In the beginning we were friends. You taught me nearly everything I know." He turned away and looked out the open doors toward the jungle, the airstrip beyond. "I had always thought you would be proud of my achievements."

"Proud?" Vance-Ehrhardt sputtered.

Newman turned on him. "Yes, goddamn it, proud. I was like a son to you."

"A son who turned on his father."

Newman wanted to tell him that Lydia had demanded they marry anywhere but here. He wanted to tell the older man many things, but he held his tongue. He could understand his feelings of betrayal, and although he could not help him, he would not make it any more difficult than it already was.

"I will not accept your offer, Jorge. Lydia and I will marry this morning, and afterward we will leave here and remain away for as long as you wish."

Vance-Ehrhardt stared at him a moment longer, then turned, stalked out, and slammed the door behind him.

For a time Newman remained still, listening to the sounds of the house and to the roar of yet another approaching aircraft, but then he turned away, took his cigarettes from the bureau, and lit one.

The wedding was scheduled for 11:00 A.M., and afterward there was to be a reception on the lawn beside the pool. Lydia had made him promise that they would remain only two hours, and then they would leave. It would be one more thing Vance-Ehrhardt would blame on him, but in the end it wouldn't really matter.

They had been friends once. Now they had become fierce competitors, not only in business, but for the affection of Lydia, Vance-Ehrhardt's only child.

A deep sorrow passed through Newman, because he knew that his marriage to Lydia would never work out. They were bound to fail. And if there were bad feelings all around now, they would worsen with time. And yet he could not help himself. Because he did love her.

5

The heat shimmered off the main east-west runway at Mexico City's International Airport as the gigantic Aerolinear Argentinas 747 came ponderously in on its final approach. Newman glanced past Lydia, who was seated by the window, his earlier agitation finally subsiding. They had flown all night, and a thick early-morning haze covered the city so that he could not see the mountains, and he was glad that they would not be staying here, as they had originally planned. The city was too depressing. They had only two weeks, and he wanted to relax and enjoy himself.

He sat back away from the window, and Lydia reached over and kissed him on the cheek. "It wasn't as bad as you thought it would be, was it?" she asked.

"Still, we should have stayed a little longer."

"So what?" Lydia said disdainfully. "You and he

would have gotten into an argument sooner or later. My mother would have cried. Pablo would probably have threatened you. And my uncles would have stormed out.'' She tossed her right shoulder and glanced out the window as they crossed over the end of the runway. ''We saved them all that grief.''

Newman reached for her hand, and she turned back to him. ''No regrets?'' he asked.

She started to laugh, but then she read the serious expression on his face. ''No regrets, Kenneth,'' she said softly. ''But I'm frightened.''

It was a rare admission for her, and Newman wondered if she was merely toying with him. ''Of what?'' he asked, nevertheless.

''Of myself,'' she said solemnly.

For several seconds they looked into each other's eyes, but then the aircraft touched down with a lurch and a loud bark of its tires, breaking the mood. Lydia smiled.

''I really don't know what married life is all about, yet. But as soon as I get you into our hotel room, I'll see what I can do about that.''

''There'll be a slight delay,'' Newman said, and before she could say anything, he added, ''I've got a little surprise for you.''

''Surprise? What kind of surprise?'' Lydia bubbled.

''You'll just have to wait and see.''

''What have you done?''

''Soon,'' Newman said. ''You're Mrs. Newman now, not Lydia Vance-Ehrhardt.''

Lydia's expression darkened for just an instant, and Newman felt certain she was going to flare, but then she settled back in her seat, a quiet smile on her lips. ''Mrs.

Kenneth Newman. Strange."

They were slowing down now, and as they turned off the main runway onto the taxiway, the stewardess came down the aisle. She was smiling. Newman looked up.

"Mr. and Mrs. Newman, you will be the first off the aircraft. There is transportation awaiting your arrival."

"Thank you."

"I hope you enjoyed your flight."

"Yes, thanks," Newman said, "Our luggage will be taken care of?"

"Yes, sir, it will be sent on."

"Sent on where?" Lydia asked sharply.

Newman glanced at her. "You'll see."

The stewardess went back up the aisle, and Newman watched her go. She was a plain girl, but she had a pleasant Spanish face and a warm smile. How different his life would have been, he thought, had he never met Jorge Vance-Ehrhardt. Had he never fallen in love with Lydia. How different, and how much less complicated.

Lydia squeezed his hand, and he turned back to her again. "Any regrets?" she asked.

"Lots," he said. "But not because I married you."

Lydia gazed down the aisle toward where their stewardess was talking with another. "You're not sorry you didn't marry someone less complicated?"

"Simple women bore me," he said.

"I'll never bore you."

"I don't think so."

The aircraft lumbered up to the terminal and stopped, but before the loading tunnel was attached, the stewardess came back to them. "You may deplane now, your car is waiting. And may I offer my congratulations?"

"Thank you," Newman said. He unbuckled his seatbelt, then got up, helping Lydia out of her seat. They went down the aisle, the other first-class passengers looking up curiously. Boarding stairs had been pushed up beneath the waiting tunnel at the front door, and the stewardess smiled at them again as they left the aircraft.

It was hot outside, and the air smelled strongly of burned jet fuel and automobile exhaust. Paul Saratt, Newman's business assistant, was waiting at the bottom, a huge grin on his face.

"Welcome to Mexico City," he said, as they came down the steps. "And congratulations."

Newman shook his hand. "Thanks, Paul, but don't say a thing to Lydia about our plans, she has no idea yet what's going on."

"May I offer my congratulations to you, Mrs. Newman," Saratt said gallantly.

"Only if you tell me what's happening here," Lydia retorted testily.

"My lips are sealed," Saratt said. He was a heavyset man of medium height, with white hair and a wide, pleasant face. He had worked with Newman for the past eight years and knew almost as much about the grain business as Newman himself, and certainly more about Newman's actual holdings. They had become great friends, and Newman trusted him more than any other person on the face of the earth. It had hurt Saratt that he was not invited to the wedding, but he said he understood. Newman had the distinct impression, however, that Saratt did not entirely approve of Lydia.

He led them to a waiting Rolls and, when they were in the back seat, climbed in the front with the uniformed driver. They headed rapidly across the field, toward the private aviation hangars and terminal.

"Will someone tell me what's going on here?" Lydia asked.

Saratt did not turn around, and Newman stared out the window, a silent grin on his face. Two weeks ago he had arranged all this with Saratt, and now he intended to play it to the hilt. As far as the Vance-Ehrhardt family knew, he and Lydia would be spending the next couple of days here in Mexico City, and then a week and a half at the family's estate near Mazatlán, before returning to the States. Several weeks ago, however, he had been offered the use of a lovely villa overlooking the Mediterranean just above Monaco, and he had accepted. Very few people would know where they had gone, which was the way Newman wanted it. He knew he would have felt uncomfortable in a Vance-Ehrhardt house, with a Vance-Ehrhardt staff watching his every move and reporting back to Jorge.

Despite himself, Newman found his thoughts drifting back to the business, specifically his relationship with Jorge. Had his and Jorge's positions been reversed, Newman had no doubt that he would have reacted much the same as the older man. He too would have been hurt, then angry. Yet it was part of the grain business. From the earliest days it had been a cut-throat enterprise. And after the Second World War, when many nations had suddenly found themselves very dependent upon their neighbors' food supplies, the business had become even more fiercely competitive.

"It is the survival of the fittest, Kenneth," Jorge had once told him. "The strong survive, the weak perish. As it should be." It was a lesson Newman had learned all too well.

The car pulled up by the front hatch of a 707. The plane was painted a muted gold color, with the Newman Company logo—twin eagles holding stalks of grain in their talons—in bright red on the tail.

"We're not staying in Mexico City?" Lydia asked, realizing what was happening.

Newman smiled. "How about Monaco?"

For a moment it seemed as if Lydia would flare again, but then she laughed. "Father will be furious," she said. "He wanted us in Mazatlán under his control for a couple of weeks. He probably had our bedroom bugged."

"I wouldn't put it past him," Newman said.

"Or me?"

Newman wanted to laugh, but something in her eyes held him back. Or her? It had happened before. Industrial espionage through a carefully arranged marriage. *The lady doth protest too much, methinks.* The vagrant line crossed his mind. It wasn't beyond Jorge. But Lydia?

The chauffeur opened the rear door on Newman's side, then stepped back respectfully. Saratt turned around in his seat.

"I'm going to hitch a ride with you two, and then take the plane. I have some business to take care of."

Newman started to ask where, but then held back as Saratt's eyes narrowed. Lydia caught the exchange of looks between the two men, but said nothing.

"Are we just going to sit here for the remainder of the day?" she asked.

"I hope not," Newman said, and helped her out. Saratt followed them up the boarding stairs.

"Good afternoon, sir," Jacob, Newman's steward, said, greeting them just within the cabin. He was a small, dark-skinned Arab.

"Are we about ready to take off?" Newman asked.

"Whenever you and Mrs. Newman are ready, sir." Jacob had been the chief steward aboard the grain ship *Pamplonas*, owned by one of Newman's subsidiaries, until Newman had been so impressed by the man's grace and abilities that he had hired him off the ship for personal service. Jacob had proved to be even better than Newman had hoped he'd be.

Saratt went forward onto the flight deck as Newman led Lydia back into the luxuriously appointed main cabin, equipped with several easy chairs, a couch and coffee table, and a wet bar. An aft cabin contained a bedroom with a queen-sized bed and a large bathroom.

When they had strapped into easy chairs, Jacob went forward, and moments later the jet's engines whined into life.

"I have a feeling something is going on," Lydia said.

"What do you mean?"

"Don't play games with me, Kenneth. I saw the look between you and Paul. He's got something cooking. You forget, I know the business too."

Newman nodded. "He probably does," he said. "But I'm on my honeymoon."

As the aircraft began to move slowly away from the terminal, Lydia reached out for Newman's hand, an intense expression on her face. "It's not going to be easy between us, Kenneth. We both know that. But . . ." She hesitated a moment.

"But what?"

"These next two weeks may be the only nearly normal time we'll ever have."

Newman started to protest, although he knew she was correct, but she held him off.

"No, listen to me, darling. I don't want anything to

spoil these next few days. I was going to suggest we not go on to Mazatlán, that we go someplace else. But whatever it is that Paul is going to tell you once we take off, don't let it change anything. At least not now.''

Newman didn't know what to say. At that moment he felt an overwhelming love for her. She was like a little lost child whom he would have to protect, not the willful, headstrong daughter of one of the wealthiest men in the world.

"I'll have to listen to whatever it is Paul has to say. But whatever it is, I'll talk it over with you,'' Newman said.

Lydia shook her head. "I don't want to hear about it. I don't want to hear about anything except us.''

Newman just looked at her.

"In fact, I never want to know anything about your business. I'm still a Vance-Ehrhardt. It's something you should never forget.''

"You're my wife . . .'' Newman started, but again she cut him off.

"Listen to me with your brain, not with your heart, Kenneth, because this is probably the only time I'll ever be this honest with you. I *am* a Vance-Ehrhardt, I'm Jorge's daughter. I love you, but I love my father as well. I never want to know about your business. That will have to remain totally separate from our world together. It's for your own protection.''

The aircraft's intercom chimed, and the pilot's voice came over the speakers. "Are you ready back there, Mr. Newman?''

Newman reached over and picked up the telephone. "Any time you are,'' he said.

Immediately they turned onto the runway, the engines

rose up the scale, and they were accelerating, pressed deeply into their seats.

Newman found himself thinking back to the stewardess on the flight from Buenos Aires. She had seemed like a simple, sweet girl. Uncomplicated, with no guile. He had always been a loner in his business, and yet he had wanted someone to share in it with him. A wife with whom to live his triumphs and defeats, his fears and regrets. But Lydia was telling him that that would be impossible with her, because whatever he told her about his business would of necessity get back to her father.

It was ironic, he thought, that he had hurt Jorge so terribly and now had placed himself in a position where Vance-Ehrhardt could gain the advantage. But such was life. Despite the difficulties, he was glad he had married Lydia. Despite the fact their marriage was doomed to fail, he was still happy at this moment.

Within a few minutes they had cleared the Mexico City Terminal Control Area and had climbed to cruise altitude. Jacob came back and offered them a glass of champagne, and a moment later Saratt motioned for Newman to join him forward.

"Be just a moment," Newman said to Lydia.

She squeezed his hand. "Remember what I said, Kenneth."

"I will."

Saratt stood between the main cabin and the flight deck. On the port side was a complete galley; on the starboard, a small but well-equipped communications station, including teletype and fascimile.

"This came from Abex while we were waiting for

you," Saratt said. He held out a short piece of yellow teletype paper.

Newman made no move to take it. Instead, he looked directly into Saratt's eyes. "I'm on my honeymoon, Paul, so I'm going to ask you to take care of this on your own if it's at all possible. I don't even want to know what it is, unless it's of the most extreme importance. Your decision."

Saratt nodded, grim-lipped. "You'd better look at it, Kenneth."

"No doubt in your mind it's that important?"

"No doubt."

Newman sighed deeply and took the telex from Saratt.

```
333xxxpd17882xxld
0803mct

Kenneth Newman
Abex, Ltd.
New York, N.Y.
ABEXLTD
```

GENEVA EUROBANK MONDAY PM STOP STRICTEST CONFIDENCE REQUIRED STOP EXCLUSIVE STOP END OF MESSAGE

```
1018est
EXPORTKHLEB
DYBROVIK


MGMCOMP   MGM
```

"He wants to meet with us," Newman said, looking up.

"With *you*," Saratt corrected. "He says exclusive."

"I can't. You'll have to go."

Saratt shook his head. "I appreciate your position, Kenneth, I really do. But when the Russians call—and it's an exclusive call—through Eurobank, they mean business. Business we cannot afford to pass up."

"We can afford it."

"Goddamn it, you know what I'm saying," Saratt snapped. "Last time something like this came up, you were with Vance-Ehrhardt, and he decided to pass on the Montreal meeting. And you know what that cost him."

His reputation and a lot of Warsaw Pact grain deals, Newman thought. He glanced back. Lydia sat sipping her champagne, staring out the window.

What the hell were the Soviets up to now? It had to be big, otherwise Dybrovik himself would not have been the signatory on the telex, nor would he have mentioned Eurobank in Geneva. That meant money. Hard Western currencies. It also meant immediate action was required, or, whatever the deal was, it would be canceled and someone else asked.

Newman had worked with Dybrovik on a number of occasions. He did not particularly like or trust the Russian, but he did respect the man's expertise.

"What do you think, Paul?"

Saratt shrugged. "There's been no glimmer of anything cooking with the Russians over the past month or so. At least nothing I've noticed."

"How about an estimate on their harvests?"

"Too early, really, for that. But from what I gather, it'll be a routine year, although Fairbanks is calling for an early winter across the plains."

"Could be they're running scared, and Dybrovik is hedging his bets."

"I thought so at first, but he mentions Eurobank. I'm assuming he's talking not only about instructions for the meeting, but about the availability of real money."

Newman reread the message and glanced again at Lydia. She was watching them. He smiled at her, then turned back.

"Get on the wire and have Sam dig up anything he can. Have Felix set up something in Geneva for me."

"Are we going first to Monaco?"

Newman nodded. "Might as well. Lydia can stay there while I meet with Dybrovik. Let's hope it won't take more than twenty-four hours."

"It lasted two weeks in Montreal."

"Three-fourths of the industry power was there. There was more infighting than work going on."

"Do you want to confirm with Dybrovik?"

"I think not, Paul. I have a feeling he wants to keep this very quiet. For now, we'll play it this way."

"All right," Saratt said. He glanced beyond Newman at Lydia. "What about her?"

"I'll take care of that problem."

"She won't be very happy."

"Don't look so smug," Newman said sharply. "She's a grainman's daughter. She'll understand."

6

The weather in Geneva was gloomy. It had rained all afternoon, and now, as Newman stepped out from beneath the awning in front of his hotel, a cold, windblown mist enveloped him.

He was tired from the nearly nonstop flying he had done, from Buenos Aires to Mexico City, from there to Nice, and then this afternoon here to Geneva. And he was disgusted with himself over his inability to arrange his life in proper priorities.

"You're a grainman, first and foremost," Lydia had said yesterday afternoon, over the Atlantic, when he had told her he would have to be gone for a day and a night.

He had not told her whom he was meeting, or where the meeting was to take place, but she had known that it had to be a grain deal—that was the only thing that would take him away from her on their honeymoon.

Beyond that, she had not been visibly upset. They had made love on the bed in the aft cabin, and later had taken a long, leisurely shower together.

It was late at night when they touched down at Nice, so Newman set aside his plans to go straight to the villa, and the three of them checked in at the Hôtel de Paris in Monte Carlo. He had left Lydia there early in the afternoon, and he expected that she had immediately telephoned her father with the information.

Saratt had driven with him out to the airport, and on the way he had seemed disturbed.

"Out with it, Paul," Newman had said.

Saratt glanced at him. "With what?"

"You've got a bug up your ass. Lydia?"

"She'll call Jorge . . . probably is on the phone right now."

Newman looked out at the city, and nodded. "Probably."

"Don't you care?" Saratt asked. He was exasperated.

Newman turned back. "Yes, I do care. Very much. But it doesn't change a thing. She's my wife."

"Despite what could happen to your business?"

"Leave it alone, Paul."

"Jesus! At least let me cover our—"

Newman cut him off. "Don't say what I think you're going to say. Don't ever say it to me. You're my friend, as well as my closest business associate. If you have to do something to protect our business, something I shouldn't know about, then do it. But don't ever tell me or Lydia what you've done. Clear?"

"Clear," Saratt said glumly. "But it's a hell of a way to do things."

Newman had not picked up on that remark, and they had dropped the subject, turning instead to the information the Newman Company's affiliates had gathered on Dybrovik and the upcoming meeting.

From their meteorologist at Fairbanks, Alaska, Saratt had received confirmation that the best prediction was for an early, cold winter all along the Soviet East European Plain, the Ust-Urt Plateau, and the West Siberian Plain, which could mean a shorter growing season for the Russians at best, or, at worst, a widespread disaster in which much of the Russian wheat and corn crops would be lost.

Saratt had sounded a cautionary note on that point, however.

"Bender stressed the fact that the long-range forecast was entirely his doing, and that there has already been quite a bit of heated discussion about it."

"They might have good weather?"

"Fifty-fifty."

"If Dybrovik is aware of that, he just might be hedging his bets after all."

"It's a possibility, but there's something even more worrisome. Everyone is mum about the Soviet winter and spring planting. We couldn't even get a non-committal statement out of them. Not average, below average, or above. Not even if the crops were in yet. Nothing."

"Another Great Grain Robbery?"

"It's a distinct possibility," Saratt said.

"I wouldn't think they'd have the hard currencies available to them. Not after Afghanistan, or their five-year revitalization project in Cuba. They've pumped a lot of money into those projects."

"We checked with Eurobank on a routine money-transfer verification. We tried once at a mil five American, and again at eight-point-seven million West German marks."

"Both were verified?"

"Immediately. Dybrovik has got at least four million American on call. Possibly a lot more. And even more significantly, there were no holds or blinds on his account. They didn't give a damn that we were obviously checking on them."

"He's in Geneva to do business, then."

"Exactly," Saratt said. "But what kind of business, and how much?"

"I guess we'll see," Newman said. "What about Dybrovik himself? Anything?"

"The usual. He's been screwing around again, this last time back in Montreal."

"Anything we can use?"

A sour look came over Saratt's face. "She's a young girl. College student, working nights to help support her expensive habits. Unless you want to upset her apple cart, there's nothing we can or should do."

"We don't do business that way."

Saratt grinned. "I didn't think so, but I put a loose watch on her to see if she heads to Geneva. So far, she hasn't moved."

"When did Dybrovik come out?"

"No one seems to know, although I didn't push it too hard. Things like this have a tendency to get out, and then we'd have half the world on our tails, especially the Georges André crowd."

"I don't want that. It'll probably get out fast enough as it is," Newman said. "How about State?"

"Not a thing from Washington, which also strikes a strange note."

"Good. Lundgren's one idiot I'd just as soon keep as far away as possible. We'll backtrack later for licenses if and when we make a deal with Dybrovik. Anything else I should know about?"

"Brezhnev is sick again. He'll probably be out within the next six months."

"We were told that three years ago, and the old goat is still going strong."

"Not this time, Kenneth. He hasn't been seen anywhere."

Newman thought about that for several moments. "We'll just have to watch our backs, then, on anything long range. Let's stay beyond a hundred and twenty days. If Brezhnev steps down, there's no telling what his successor might do with existing agreements."

"Especially if it's Andropov."

With those remarks in mind, Newman hunched up his coat collar and headed away from the hotel, which was on the Quai Mont Blanc, facing the inner harbor, and worked his way to the main post office.

He had telephoned the depositors' special night number at Eurobank, giving his name and the telex number, and had received the instruction to proceed on foot alone to the main post office just off the Rue des Alpes at 10:00 P.M.

It was nearly that time now, and as Newman walked he went over everything Saratt had told him, as well as what he knew about the Russian he was to meet. But ever present at the back of his mind was Lydia, and guilt that he had left her alone on their honeymoon. A shaky beginning to a difficult marriage; it did not portend a rosy future.

There was very little traffic, and even fewer pedestrians, because it was late, the weather was rotten, and the real tourist season had not yet begun. Geneva, besides being a business center, is a tourist town in July and August. In the off-season it resumes its usual Swiss flavor: quiet and somewhat stodgy.

The post office was housed in a large, very ornate building. As Newman approached the front entrance, guarded by twin lions flanking the stairs, and gargoyles above, a black Citroën DS 19 pulled up to the curb beside Newman. The rear door came open.

Newman looked both ways up the street. There was no one else in sight, no cars or buses or people.

"It is I," Dybrovik's voice came from the dark interior of the sedan.

Newman climbed into the back seat beside the Russian, who reached across and pulled the door shut. Immediately the driver pulled away, turned the corner at the end of the block, and headed toward the Cornavin main railway station.

"So," Dybrovik began, "you received my message, you were intrigued, and you came. All despite my understanding it is your honeymoon." There seemed to be a sadness about the Russian. His manner was not as light as Newman remembered it.

"At this time tomorrow evening, I will have returned to my wife," Newman said evenly.

"A time limit he now imposes," Dybrovik guffawed. But before Newman could reply, he went on, "It is just as well. When men like us gather, it is not very long before the wolves begin snapping at our heels."

"You are expecting surpluses and you want to sell grain," Newman said, taking a stab in the dark.

Even in the darkened interior of the car, Newman could see something flash in the Russian's eyes. But it was gone, covered up as rapidly as it had come.

"We would hope for surpluses, my friend. But, alas, such will likely not be the case."

Something wasn't right. "Then you wish to purchase grain?"

"Indeed."

"Why me? Why like this?" Newman asked, still fishing.

Dybrovik grinned. "The second question is so obvious, it demands no serious answer. But the first . . . well, then, that is serious. To that we shall speak at length. Soon."

"Soon? When? Where?"

"Do not attempt to manipulate me, and I shall not attempt to do so with you. Without that, it is possible that we shall have a fruitful association."

Dybrovik was probably in his forties, Newman figured, but he sounded like a sixty-year-old, his baby face looked twenty, and at times he acted like a naive teenager. Despite those outward appearances, however, the man was no fool, and had been around the grain business longer than Newman.

At this point, then, Newman decided he would play the Russian's game, at least until he had a better understanding of what was going on.

They turned north at the railway station and headed up the lakeshore past the Museum of Scientific History, toward Versoix and finally Coppet about ten miles away, where their driver turned onto a narrow, graveled driveway that led into the woods away from the lake.

Within a hundred yards the road entered a wide clearing in which stood a large, rambling house with a huge marble portico. Their driver pulled up beneath the overhanging roof and wordlessly jumped out and opened the rear door on Dybrovik's side. The Russian shuffled his bulk ponderously out of the car, and Newman slid to that side and got out as well.

"I've leased the house for one year, and it will be our operational headquarters for the duration, although I suspect we will have concluded our business by early fall," Dybrovik said.

Inside, a dim light illuminated the entrance hall; the stained-glass windows were dark. The wide stairs leading up were lost in darkness, as were the corridors to the left and right.

Without hesitation Dybrovik led the way to the right, into what appeared to be a large, luxuriously decorated drawing room. He flipped on a bronze table lamp, motioned Newman to take a seat, then went to a sideboard and pulled out two brandy snifters.

"Cognac or whiskey?" he asked.

"Cognac will be fine," Newman said, crossing the room and sitting down on the long leather couch. He lit a cigarette.

Dybrovik handed Newman his drink, then raised his glass in a toast. "To a successful business between us."

Newman nodded, took a sip of his drink, then set his glass down on the low coffee table in front of him. Dybrovik remained standing. Psychology, Newman thought. He had used the same methods himself. It was going to be a job, he figured, to hold Dybrovik to a reasonably short initial negotiation process.

"You mentioned you would like to return to your bride no later than this time tomorrow evening,"

Dybrovik said. "You will be able to return to her this evening, if you like, or certainly no later than tomorrow morning. Our business will be very simple. Your work will not be."

Strangely, for just an instant, Newman had a premonition of doom, and with it the urge to get up and leave before the Russian had a chance to say anything else. But then the feeling passed, and he held his silence.

"Simply put, my government wishes to purchase corn."

Newman wasn't quite sure he had heard the man correctly. "American corn?"

"It is of no consequence where it comes from."

"Routine," Newman said. "Why not just put through a simple order? Abex would have been pleased to handle it for you."

"You do not understand yet, my friend, which is entirely my fault. We wish to purchase a lot of corn."

"How much?"

Dybrovik shrugged. "Ten million tons. Twenty million. Thirty."

"Large numbers," Newman said cautiously, although his blood was beginning to race.

"Perhaps larger."

"Meaning?"

Dybrovik took another large swallow of his drink, then set the glass down. "We want to purchase, in absolute secrecy, as much corn as you can possibly supply us."

"What is the limit?"

"There is no limit."

Newman carefully held himself in check. "A hundred million metric tons?"

"More, if you can get it."

"At what price?"

Dybrovik laughed. "At the prevailing market price. But of course it must be done in secret, so your purchases will not inflate unit costs."

"Not until later, when the information is leaked by your government," Newman said, getting to his feet. "You'll buy on margin, drive the price up, and resell, as you did in the seventies."

"We will purchase on margin if we can," Dybrovik said unperturbed. "We will pay cash for the futures if need be. It is negotiable."

"You will guarantee that the grain is for internal consumption?"

"If you are asking me, internal to the Soviet Union, I cannot answer that with any degree of certainty. If you are speaking, internal to our Warsaw Pact nations, I can give you a qualified yes."

This was all wrong. Newman knew it; he could feel it thick in the air between him and the Russian. And yet it was food they were speaking of here. Food that would ultimately be used to feed people. Cubans in addition to Albanians? South Africans in addition to Poles? Did it matter?

"Licensing would be difficult if not impossible," Newman said cautiously, but he could see the glimmerings of triumph on the Russian's face. More psychology, or the real thing?

"Difficult, yes, but not impossible given a proper infrastructure, which is your particular area of expertise."

Multilevel dummy corporations, shipping companies, elevator firms, railroad cars. Newman saw every bit of it as one large picture, and it excited the hell out of him. It could be done. But what of the moral implications? What of the international ramifications? What of the political weapon a hundred million metric tons of corn could become? It was akin to selling the entire year's output of oil from all the OPEC countries in one fell swoop.

"It's a powerful thing you ask," Newman said, sitting down.

"It would make you a wealthy man."

"I'm already wealthy," Newman countered.

Dybrovik smiled, his grin feral. "You hesitate. You are afraid, perhaps, of another market manipulation? Your people called it the Great Grain Robbery. Amusing."

"It has crossed my mind."

Dybrovik laughed out loud. "Several dozen times in the last minute or two, no doubt. But so what, I ask you?"

"Neither I nor any other Western grain company would do business with you again."

"I think that would not be the case, Mr. Kenneth Newman. I think not. Money, after all, is why you do what you do."

The remark offended Newman, all the more because it was true. Like all grainmen, Newman feared and resented government meddling in what they felt was one of the last truly free international enterprises. Yet Newman personally felt a deep moral responsibility toward people. Not merely Americans, but people the world over.

"Two conditions," he said.

Dybrovik's eyes narrowed, but he nodded.

"A ceiling is to be set on the unit price at which your government will ultimately sell its surplus grain."

"Impossible."

"Just outside the Warsaw Pact."

Dybrovik went back to the sideboard and poured himself another drink. "I would have to get approval from my government before I could agree to such a condition."

"How soon could you have an answer?"

"Within twenty-four hours."

"That's acceptable. In any event, it will take me longer than that to begin."

"The second condition?" Dybrovik asked.

"Much of the corn I will be selling you will be in the form of futures, naturally, but a significant portion is already dried and in storage."

Dybrovik said nothing.

"I will want the majority of your grain moved immediately to the Soviet Union."

"If we were to resell the corn at a later date, we would pass the cost of transportation on to the end user."

"I assure you, there will be excessive storage charges at my end if it is not moved."

Dybrovik turned away again. "We will accept fifty percent of the corn now in storage, and negotiate later on movement of the futures as they come in."

"Ninety percent and negotiate on the futures within thirty days."

"Seventy-five percent," Dybrovik said. "And that is my top. But I will agree to on-the-spot negotiations for the futures."

It was Newman's turn to keep silent. It was better than he had hoped for. They both understood that storage the world over was at a premium. When the bins were full, the corn would have to be stored either in railroad cars or on the ground. Bad weather would ruin millions of dollars' worth of grain. Storage was, simply put, the biggest headache of the business. Dybrovik had agreed to shoulder the lion's share of that problem.

"Is it a deal?" Dybrovik asked.

"Contingent on your answer about the resale price."

"You will have your answer tomorrow. But if it is a no?"

"I'll have to think about that."

"Further negotiations would be possible, I would assume. If not, I would have to approach someone else."

"Like Georges André?" Newman said, again getting to his feet. "I think not. They would run you around in circles, if they would deal with you at all."

"Then your father-in-law."

Newman smiled. "I don't think he could keep it quiet."

"Probably not," Dybrovik said. He finished his drink. "Where may I contact you tomorrow?"

"Through Abex, as before," Newman said. "You mentioned that this place will become your operational headquarters?"

Dybrovik nodded. "Communications equipment will be brought in tomorrow, and my staff will be arriving by evening. But it will take a week or perhaps ten days before everything is ready at this end."

"Very good," Newman said. "We may have a deal, then, depending upon what your government has to say tomorrow."

"Excellent," Dybrovik said, and they shook hands,

which in the grain business was all the contract needed.

"And now, if you would ring your driver, I'd like to return to my hotel."

Alone again, Dybrovik stood by the window in the hall, watching Newman climb into the back seat of the Citroën. A great, almost overwhelming sadness overcame him. On the one hand, he wanted very much to be a man such as Kenneth Newman. A free-wheeling spirit who was at home in all the capitals of the Western world. But he was already beginning to miss Moscow.

He laid his forehead against the cool window as the Citroën pulled away from the house, and watched its taillights disappear into the darkness.

Newman would return to Monaco, to his wedding bed. Within a few days he would be back in Duluth, Minnesota, one of the major American grain ports, at work on his deal. The deal of his life. A deal so mammoth that its international repercussions would certainly last for years . . . even without whatever it was the little man had in mind.

He turned away from the window finally, went back into the drawing room, poured himself a stiff shot of the Glenlivet he had been drinking most of the night, and sat down on the couch with a cigarette.

He closed his eyes. Larissa. Where was this all heading?

ASHES TO ASHES

The Worldly Hope men set their Hearts upon
Turns Ashes—or it prospers; and anon,
  Like Snow upon the Desert's dusty Face,
Lighting a little hour or two—is gone.

—Rubáiyát of Omar Khayyám

It was late, and Michael McCandless was dead tired. He had worked through the afternoon and into the evening on the latest batch of field reports on the Argentine situation. The aftermath of the Falkland Islands debacle still lingered; would for years. Some of the reports were in the form of raw data, while several large boxes contained asessment and analysis files; all of them bulky and dull.

For the last few weeks he had been expecting either the President to call, or the DCI to come down on him over the way he had handled the Soviet crop forecast. But no one had called, and nothing had been said.

On the positive side, however, neither had anyone interfered with McCandless' continuing work on what he was calling the Emerging Soviet Agrarian Threat.

The CIA'S SPEC satellites continued watching the Soviet fields, and DiRenzo continued sending up his reports. McCandless continued collating them with the others, digesting and then filing them.

The Soviet farm fields had been plowed into furrows, dragged to pull up the rocks, and finally disked and planted. Corn and wheat mostly, in a wide variety of hybrids. If the crops came to maturity, and if they were harvested, the Soviet Union would not only become food self-sufficient (something it had been unable to manage for several decades), it would have mammoth surpluses. Which would, McCandless firmly believed, have far-reaching political consequences.

But no one would listen, he thought, looking up from his Argentine reports. Hardly an hour went by when he did not think about it. Yet he knew he was getting nowhere.

He had thought about going to the President again, or at least forcing the situation to a head through General Lycoming. But in the end he had decided against it. He had alerted the White House. He had done what his job demanded of him; he had provided hard intelligence to the President. Whatever became of that intelligence was totally outside his purview.

Swiveling around in his chair, McCandless stared out his third-floor window down at the woods behind the agency complex and let his mind drift, just as the SPEC-IV *satellite was at this moment drifting over the Soviet continent.*

His worry was very probably moot, he told himself. Most estimates from meteorology were for an early winter . . . possibly too early for a decent harvest over there. If that was the case, all the acres planted would amount to naught.

Yet, as much as he wanted to comfort himself with such thoughts, he could not. It simply would not work.

In the morning, he would telephone Curtis Lundgren, the Secretary of Agriculture, and find out if the President had indeed passed the first report and photographs along. If he hadn't, McCandless decided, he would personally meet with Lundgren and lay it all out.

Meanwhile, what would happen next would be up to mother nature and the Soviet farmer.

7

The dying sun was just touching the western horizon, its light reflecting deep red off the upper windows of the skyscrapers in downtown Buenos Aires, when Carlos stepped out of his hovel in the *villa miseria*. He was a short man, something under five foot five, but his dark-skinned, youthful body was muscular from his constant workouts and field training.

He looked nervously to the left and right, unconsciously fingering a long scar on his side. He proudly carried his training scars from the PLO camp he had attended two years ago outside of Beirut, as well as the slightly misshapen left arm which had been broken during training in one of Colonel Qaddafi's schools for terrorists in Libya.

Behind the tin-and-cardboard shack where he had lived for the past few months, he pulled aside a filthy piece of canvas, uncovering the only possession, besides his training, of which he was proud: a small Honda 125 motorcycle. He pushed the bike back around to the narrow dirt track at the front of the shack, kicked it to a start, and took off toward the city, several miles distant.

It was still warm, although the South American winter had officially begun. Before the cold came, however, he and the others would be long gone from here. Probably back to Libya for asylum, now that the Israelis had overrun Beirut. Perhaps even to Iran.

As Juan Carlos drove, he found that now that he was actually on his way, now that the months of planning were finally coming to an end, he was nervous. His stomach seemed empty, and the muscles at the back of his legs were tense, as if he had just run ten miles.

Their instructor in Libya had been sympathetic when he had displayed the same problems during the live-fire exercises.

"There is no shame in feeling fear, comrade. The only shame is in allowing your fear to control you."

Juan Carlos was frightened now. At the same time he was proud of going ahead.

Within fifteen minutes he had made it downtown to the Plaza del Congreso, alive with pigeons and old ladies and children, occasional lovers strolling arm in arm, and cars, motorcycles, and bicycles everywhere.

He threaded his way through the early-evening traffic around to the rear of the fountains, just across the avenue from the slim-domed capitol building, spotting Teva Cernades seated at the edge of the pool.

She jumped up as he pulled to the curb and nervously scanned the area behind and to the left and right of her. There was no one watching them.

"Did you have any trouble getting away?" he asked as she came up to him.

She pecked him on the cheek. "None whatsoever," she said climbing onto the motorcycle behind him. "You?" Her eyes were bright, and there was a smile on her delicate face. She wore designer jeans, a sweatshirt, sandals, and a bright red bandana to contain her long, light-brown hair.

"I circled around and came up from the university," he said. "Have you heard from Eugenio?"

"Not today. But he'll be there, don't worry about it."

"I worry about him."

"You worry about everything, Juan. Perhaps you worry too much."

Juan Carlos looked over his shoulder at her. She was very slim, almost emaciated, but he had seen her in action in the training camps, and they had been lovers for thirteen months now. He knew that her slender body was powerful and well muscled. She could outshoot, outfight, and certainly outlast most men in the field. Besides his work in the camps, and his motorbike, he was most proud of Teva. "Too much?" he asked. "Someone must be concerned. I do not want to throw my life away uselessly."

"Nor I, *estúpido*," the young woman flared. "But you know what the man told us."

"No, refresh my memory, my little dove," Juan Carlos said sarcastically. She hated being called his "little dove."

"The plan is a good one. It will work. We will see to it."

"The plan is a good one, because it is my plan. And

without concern for detail, even the little man could never make it work.''

Teva's nostrils flared, but she looked the other way, across at the capitol. "Pigs," she said half under her breath.

Juan Carlos slipped the bike in gear, revved up the engine, and popped the clutch, nearly spilling both of them before he managed to regain control. Teva's arms were around his midsection, and she jerked hard, causing him to wince in pain.

They rounded the plaza and headed north out of the city, up the coast, toward the railway station at Olivos. Conversation was impossible because of the wind whipping around their ears and the engine noise, and it was just as well, he thought. Just as it was for the best that very soon they would be going into action. It was already the end of June, and all of them were on edge. Each accused the other of worrying too much, of being too nervous.

"It is the pigeon in the park too frightened to eat near the well-intentioned passerby, who will starve," the Argentine homily went.

And it was true. Drink at the well, or die of thirst. Move forward, ever forward, or stagnate and die.

For years there had been order and stability in the country. Socialist goals were becoming a fact. But then, after Perón, nothing seemed the same. Of course Juan Carlos knew of those times only through books and political tracts, but he could see with his own eyes what was happening these days. The farmers were oppressed, little more than slaves. The government was rotten, a mere tool of the North American capitalists. And even the military was unable to do anything right. The loss in the Malvinas was a national shame that would sting for years to come.

A blow had to be struck. Now. And very hard. But with care, lest they fail. They could not fail, for if they did, it would set back their cause—Argentina for Argentines—by years.

Loyal but empty-headed women like Teva, and idiots like Eugenio, knew what had to be done and why, but neither of them had the slightest feel for the details.

The little man had taken him aside personally last night and told him that he was to be the leader, because he had an iron courage and a head for detail.

"You are a natural-born leader, Juan," the little man had said. "I trust you to be my field commander."

"I will not let you down," Juan Carlos had promised. Nor would he.

It was a few minutes after 7:00 P.M. when they finally made it into the small college town of Olivos. Juan Carlos drove directly over to the railway station, where he parked his bike behind the market stalls, closed now for the evening. He was careful to wrap his chain first around the bike's frame and then around a metal light pole, before locking it and pocketing the key.

Teva watched him, and when he straightened up, she shook her head. "Is that what you call your attention to detail?"

He looked back at his bike and shrugged.

"We are not returning here. Not for a very long time. Once we are finished we will be leaving the country. Or we will be dead. Yet you lock your precious motor-cycle."

"If they are to steal it, let the bastards work for it," he said, and he strode off around the corner, toward the front of the depot.

There was quite a bit of traffic around the station, mostly college students heading into the city, farmers going to market, and businessmen coming out of the city from work.

Eugenio was waiting for them, across the street from the taxi stands, in a battered old pickup truck. "Any trouble coming up here?" he asked, pulling slowly away from the curb. He was dressed as a farmer.

"None," Juan Carlos said. "How about you? Did you notice anyone watching you? Anyone suspicious?"

"There was an accident in front of the depot, and the stupid police had half the barracks there. Must have been someone important. There were ambulances too."

"When?" Juan Carlos snapped, looking back at the depot. It didn't smell right. That was how they could have brought in their snoops. Set up their watchers, maybe even taken photographs of stupid Eugenio.

"Half an hour ago. Maybe a little more. They just cleared it up a few minutes before you arrived."

Eugenio Mendes was a larger man than Juan Carlos, and although at twenty-eight they were the same age, Eugenio seemed ten years older in his face, his actions, and his speech. At first he seemed a thoughtful man who chose his words with care. Perhaps a scholar. But in actuality Eugenio was that rare person who was slow, yet recognized he was slow, so always took care with what he said and how he acted. As slow as he was mentally, however, he was quick on his feet. In school he had been a fine athlete, and now as a terrorist, he was a fearless fighter. A follower, not a leader.

They came onto a narrow secondary road that roughly paralleled the main federal highway back into

Buenos Aires. Eugenio drove at a steady forty miles per hour, a huge yellow dust cloud rising behind the truck.

Teva lit a cigarette with nervous hands and flicked the ashes on the floor. "Did you call your cell?" she asked Eugenio.

He glanced over at her and managed a thin smile. "Yes, I did. They will all be out of the city by morning, and ready the night after tomorrow. There is nothing to worry about now, Teva."

"All hell is going to break loose once we pull this off. You know that, don't you, Juan?" she asked, turning the other way.

"As long as everyone keeps his cool, and doesn't do anything he isn't supposed to do, it'll work out. Is it you worrying now?"

"Of course I'm worried, but about the proper things," she shot back.

"Don't fight," Eugenio said simply.

Teva started to say something, but then thought better of it and slumped down instead, staring out the dirty windshield.

Juan reached for her cigarette, took a deep drag, and handed it back. "Where is the meeting to take place?"

"On the boat," Eugenio replied, without taking his eyes off the road.

"When?"

"As soon as we get there. He is taking us up to Tigre; from there we will have to go on foot to the clearing."

After that it would be touch and go. But in the short time that Juan Carlos had known the little man, he had developed an abiding trust in him and his judgment. If the little man said such-and-such was so, and would work . . . then such-and-such was the truth, and it would go like clockwork.

He had known only a few men like that in his life: a professor at the university, who had introduced him to the group; two instructors in Libya; and then of course Colonel Qaddafi and Arafat.

All great men. All like the little man, who inspired trust and confidence. Anything that could be thought of as worthy of doing for the cause, could be done. Given the proper plan, the proper equipment, and the proper manpower, anything on this earth could be accomplished.

The Red Brigades, the Baader-Meinhof gang, the Sandinistas, the FALN—all of them lent credence to that philosophy.

Juan Carlos and his Montonero cell would go into the history books for their upcoming action. He could almost taste the victory that would be theirs. Soon, very soon.

Eugenio drove them into Buenos Aires, right through the downtown Federal District, and then to the commercial docks along the southern waterfront. There they entered a warehouse and parked the truck.

Without a word, the three of them climbed out of the truck, hurried across the warehouse, and slipped out a back door. They crossed the wide dock and went down a flight of stairs to the floating concrete dock, riding on the tides, where a sixty-foot sport fisher was tied, its diesels ticking over slowly, its bridge lit a dull red. Farther up the dock, a Swedish ship was unloading cargo. But here it was quiet, with no prying eyes to see the two men and the woman slip quietly aboard the local charter fisher *Santiago*, and move into the shadows along the port companionway.

As soon as they were aboard, several deckhands emerged silently from one of the aft hatches and slipped the docklines. The boat slowly headed away from the dock toward the breakwater and out into the Río de la Plata.

When they were under way, a steward came out onto the deck. "This way, please," he said politely.

They followed him aft to the well-furnished main salon. Its entire rear wall was sliding glass doors looking out over the fantail, beyond which were the lights of the city they were leaving.

Only the light from the outside provided any illumination. The steward left, closing the door.

"I trust you managed to make it here without attracting undue attention," someone said from the far corner.

Juan Carlos took a step forward. "Is it you, comrade?" he asked.

"It is I," the man said, and a soft light came on, revealing the little man seated on a high-backed stool before a wet bar. "But you have not answered my question."

"No one followed us," Juan Carlos said. He moved across the room, Teva and Eugenio right behind him.

"Your cell leaders have been alerted?"

"They will be leaving the city this evening, and all of them will be in position within forty-eight hours."

"Very good, Juan, very well done." The little man got off his stool and went around behind the bar, where he brought out a bottle of good red wine and a large bottle of carbonated water.

He was an intense-looking little man, with large, penetrating eyes, and a swarthy complexion. In a way the man almost looked Oriental to Juan Carlos, or perhaps even Indian, except that he knew the man was almost certainly a Soviet officer of some sort. He had come with the highest recommendations of Colonel Qaddafi himself, so from the beginning the Montonero leadership had not questioned his presence. Nor had Juan Carlos or the others.

They sat down across the bar from him. He poured them each a tall glass of wine, mixed half and half with carbonated water, then poured himself some of the wine straight.

When they all had their drinks, he raised his in toast. "To the liberation of your people."

"*Libertad*," Juan Carlos said, and Teva and Eugenio repeated the single word. They drank deeply.

Just outside the breakwater the ship rose to meet the larger waves, and the little man came around the bar to a long dining table in the center of the room where a detailed topographic map was spread out. He flicked on an overhead light. Juan Carlos and the others gathered around.

"We will have to be well away with this boat before the operation begins, which is why I am dropping you at Tigre so early," the little man began.

They had all seen this map before, but Juan Carlos leaned forward so that he could get a better look at it. He didn't want to miss a detail.

"How far is it from the drop point to the clearing?"

"A little less than ten miles. It will be difficult, but you should be able to manage it by morning."

"Our provisions are there?"

The little man nodded. "Along with your weapons, and the radio with which you will summon the helicopter. There's enough food for a week, in case we run into any delay."

Juan Carlos studied the map thoughtfully. "Another five miles from the clearing to the house. A ten-mile round trip. The most difficult part of the operation."

"Under cover of darkness and the diversion, you should not have any trouble. You should be able to make it well within the limits."

Juan Carlos switched his attention from their objective to the river where the other Montonero cell would be waiting with a very old, very large river boat. At the set hour, they would bring the boat up behind the main house and set it on fire. The commotion would, according to the little man, bring most of the house staff on the run down to the river.

"His personal bodyguard may be with him, but between the three of you, there should be no real difficulty."

"What if we meet with heavier resistance?" Eugenio asked.

Juan Carlos and the little man both looked up at him.

"You will have your radio. Channel A is the helicopter, and B will be monitored by the cell leader aboard the boat. He understands the contingency. If you run into unexpected trouble, he will lead his people up to you."

"Will we have time to get out of there?" Eugenio asked.

Juan Carlos was frustrated by the questions, because they were valid and well thought out. He, the leader, should have thought of those contingencies first.

"Timing will be critical, of course. We're assuming that, once the action begins, the authorities will be notified," the little man said. He turned to Juan Carlos. "If that happens, if you need help from the river, then your fallback code will be 'Helpmate one,' which will bring the helicopter directly to the airstrip behind the house."

"There may be more resistance there."

"Almost certainly there will be. But by then you will have been joined by the other cell, and the helicopter crew will be armed."

"There will be no other changes in that event?" Juan Carlos asked.

"None," the little man said. "You will be set down with your cargo at the interior point where the van will be waiting." He stabbed a blunt finger at a spot on the map about fifty miles inland and slightly north of Buenos Aires. "You only have to hold them for twenty-four hours, then you can release the ransom message and get out. The second cell will take over from there."

Juan Carlos nodded. Eugenio looked thoughtful. Teva was flushed.

"Transportation will be provided for you to Tripoli, but there will be absolutely no negotiations from there. The colonel was most clear on that point. All communications will go through Geneva. We have someone in place there at this moment. Once you get to Tripoli, instructions will be waiting for you."

Juan Carlos studied the map a bit longer, almost overwhelmed by what they were about to pull off. Their action would forever change Argentine history. And the blow to the morale of capitalist pigs the world over would be stunning.

He raised his glass again. *"Libertad,"* he said fervently. *"Libertad!"*

8

The weather had turned slightly cool this evening, causing a dense fog to rise up from bayous surrounding New Orleans, across Lake Pontchartrain, along the commercial docks, and among the grain elevators standing like proud, erect ghosts.

Traffic over the causeway toll bridge, and along the interstates and bypasses which cut through the city, moved at no more than 15 miles an hour. There was an eighteen-car pileup on Interstate 10 just west of Lakefront Airport. All flights were grounded, of course, and even the city bus service was running late on every one of its lines.

As one hip disc jockey put it over the air, not long before midnight: "You might just as well stay home, baby, and enjoy the soup, 'cause ain't nobody goin' nowhere nohow tonight."

Louie Benario, a long-time torch out of Detroit, only lately arrived in New Orleans, shuffled along the railroad tracks behind the International Trade Mart near the Bienville Street Wharf. He was a tiny man who all his life had been called the runt, or peewee, or short stuff, or midget. Terms he resented deeply, because he had always thought of himself as a big man.

In the old days, when someone called him such a name, he would puff up to his full five foot two and take a swing at his adversary, which more often than not landed him flat on his back beside his bar stool. His nose had been broken so many times he had lost count; his arms had been broken, his fingers snapped, his wrist half-crushed, his jaw dislocated, and his skull fractured. His ribs had been battered until they were soft to the touch.

Because of this, he was, at forty, a misshapen old man who walked with a stumbling gait and hardly ever raised his eyes in public. Louie had finally learned his lesson: In public, keep your mouth shut. Blend into the woodwork. Make no waves. Be inconspicuous.

But in private Benario shone. He was an expert. One of the best torches in the business. Those in the know never called him peewee or midget to his face, because they knew they might wake up the next morning in a burning house.

He had learned his trade from Studs Logan, one of the most famous of all Detroit torches, before Logan became a victim of his own handiwork.

For a few years afterward, Benario had worked Logan's territory, and in ten indictments he had been convicted only once, for setting fire to a warehouse for a client who needed the insurance money more than he needed his business. The boys hired Benario a crack lawyer out of Los Angeles, and in three months Benario was back on the streets, free on a technicality.

Eighteen months ago, Louie had burned down the home of a General Motors executive who had been putting the heat on a union-organized numbers racket. The executive was a fighter, and Louie had been advised by his friends to get out of Motown for a year or two until the smoke cleared.

Louie did just that, and had fallen instantly and deeply in love with New Orleans, whose mild winters and ultra-hot summers reminded him of a furnace. His kind of place.

He stopped for a moment, away from the railway traffic signals, adjusted the heavy pack on his right shoulder, and peered through the dense fog. He knew his objective was less than a block away. But he could see nothing except for the swirling mist, and after a bit he continued forward.

In his years Benario had set fire to no less than thirty warehouses, nineteen hotels, two nursing homes, a dozen or more private residences, and even a Chicago police precinct house for an irate out-of-town client. In those blazes, he had been responsible for at least ninety-five deaths and more than three hundred and fifty serious injuries, including a dozen or so firemen.

But Benario never thought of himself as a murderer. He was a torch, plain and simple; a man devoted to fire.

In the distance to the east, he heard a siren. He stiffened instinctively, a faint smile coming to his lips. There would be sirens after this job. Lots of sirens. The thought broadened his grin, and he chuckled out loud.

This would be his biggest job ever, made even more important by the sheer size of his target. It was the largest grain-elevator complex in the world, and brand

new. Owned by the Cargill conglomerate, it had been
put in service less than six months ago, to replace hundreds of antiquated elevators up and down the delta. It
would burn beautifully, the little man had assured him.
The hot yellow flames would reach hundreds of feet into
the sky. People for miles around would taste the smoke.
Newspaper headlines across the country would blare:
GREATEST GRAIN DISASTER IN HISTORY. LARGEST FIRE
IN THIS DECADE. THE WORK OF AN EXPERT ARSONIST.

Benario had to laugh out loud with the sheer magnificence of it all.

On top of all that, like frosting on a cake or the cherry
atop a sundae, was the fact that Benario had finally
come into his own as an internationally known torch.
The little man who had hired him for this job was a foreigner. French or Jewish or a Polak or something. Not
only was he foreign, he was a little man, not much taller
than Benario. They saw eye to eye.

He laughed even louder at his little joke. Eye to eye,
watching the flames that'd tower over the tallest man in
the world.

"Eye to eye," he sang a tuneless melody. "Eye to eye,
watching the pretty flames. My pretty, my pretty,
watching my pretty flames, eye to eye to eye."

A series of massive structures loomed out of the darkness to the right, toward the waterfront, less than a hundred yards away. Benario stopped in his tracks, hiccoughing as he choked off his song.

He could see now the dim halos formed around the
lights at the base of the grain elevator, and around the
red lights at the top.

He took a few steps forward, over the rail, and then
scrambled down into the ditch beside the tracks. There

was activity over there this evening beyond the chainlink fence. Trucks were coming and going with their loads of grain. He could hear the dull, deep-throated mechanical noises of a grain ship tied up at the dock, although he was unable to pick out the ship's lights from where he stood.

It was there, in front of him. Ready and waiting for his skills.

He climbed up out of the ditch, soaking his trousers to the knees in the wet grass, then crouched down at the base of the fence and fumbled inside his heavy pack for his large wirecutters. Within a couple of minutes he had cut a large hole in the fence and crawled through it. On the other side, he pulled the cut section back in place, so that nothing but a very close examination would reveal the hole.

Spittle was oozing from the corners of his mouth. He licked his lips frequently as he scrambled away from the fence, toward the edge of the blacktop driveway that surrounded the mammoth elevator complex.

Five days ago, the little man had supplied him with a complete set of working blueprints for the complex, along with totally self-destructive fuses and enough plastique to bring down ten such installations. Benario had worked with such materials only once before, up in Detroit, but he had read all the available literature and was certain it would be a piece of cake.

The problem, he had reasoned, would be to contain the initial explosion very low in the complex, in the conveyor system, where the explosive grain dust would be at the highest concentration. The explosion and fire would start, then, from the bottom and quickly work its way upward.

At the edge of the blacktop, Benario worked his way among the long rows of parked trucks, until he came to a grain-unloading bay that wasn't in use.

He slipped inside through a service hatch that led directly down into the mixing and delivery conveyor system. There he began placing his explosives, attaching each package with loving care, setting the fuses for 8:00 A.M., when, the little man had assured him, the grain would be moving through the system and the dust would be at its maximum concentration in the air.

It was a little after 6:30 on the morning of June 28 when Laura Conley's bedside telephone rang, the shrill noise bringing her instantly awake. She sat up with a start, the sheet falling away and exposing her bare breasts, looked down at Peter Rossiter still sleeping beside her, then reached across him and picked up the telephone on the second ring.

"Hello?" she said sleepily.

"This is Elizabeth Rossiter. I have to speak with my husband."

Laura's heart skipped a beat. She and Peter had been lovers for less than six months, and she had had no idea that his wife even suspected. Today he was supposed to be in Minneapolis, meeting with Cargill executives.

"Miss Conley?" his wife said. "Are you still there?"

"I'm here," Laura said. "I think you must have the wrong number."

"Cut the bullshit, I know my husband is there. I telephoned Minneapolis and there is no such meeting. Which leaves only your place. Now put him on the phone."

Peter was starting to wake up, and Laura began to

panic. "I don't know what the hell you're talking about . . ." she started, but Elizabeth cut her off.

"Goddamn it, there's trouble down at the elevator center. They need him immediately. If you don't want him to talk to me, at least pass on that message."

Laura slowly hung up the telephone. Peter sat up, his eyes still clouded with sleep.

"Who was it?" he asked.

Laura just stared at him for several seconds. It was over for them now. He would never leave his wife and children. His marriage might be ruined, but she would be the loser.

"Who the hell was it, Laura?" he asked. "What's wrong?"

"It's the center," she stammered. "There's some kind of trouble down there. They want you."

"The elevator center?" He came fully awake. "How the hell did they know where I was? Who was it on the phone?"

Laura started to get out of the bed, but Peter reached out, grabbed her arm, and pulled her back.

"Who the hell was on the phone?" he shouted.

"Your wife," she said, hanging her head, the tears coming to her eyes.

"Jesus," Rossiter swore, half under his breath. "Oh, Jesus Christ!" He let go of Laura, grabbed the telephone, and dialed, speaking to Laura over his shoulder. "Get dressed. You're going to have to drive me down there."

She padded across the bedroom and went into the bathroom, softly closing the door.

"Cargill," said the phone at Peter's ear.

"Stan? This is Pete."

"Am I glad to hear from you," the night manager said. "You'd better get down here right away."

"I'll be there in twenty minutes. What the hell is going on?"

"I tried to get you at home, but Liz said you were in Minneapolis. I called up there, and they told me you hadn't arrived, but to get ahold of you somehow and keep the cops out of it."

"Out of what?"

"We've got a guy here with a bomb. Carl found him down in L tunnel getting ready to set it."

"A bomb!" Rossiter shouted. "He hadn't set it yet?"

"No. Carl said he was just taping it up to one of the overhead conveyors."

"Was that the only one?"

The night manager sucked his breath, the sound clear over the phone. "Christ, Pete, we never even thought of that. We just assumed . . ."

Rossiter cut him off. "Get the night crew down there immediately. I want every tunnel searched, inch by inch."

"Yes, sir."

"And call the New Orleans P.D. bomb squad."

"But Minneapolis said no cops."

"I don't give a shit what they said! It's my elevator. Now get on it, Carl. I'll be down there within fifteen minutes."

As Rossiter hung up, Laura came out of the bathroom. She was wearing blue jeans and a T-shirt, and the tears were streaming down her cheeks.

He jumped up, grabbed his clothes, and started to get dressed. "Get your car out and bring it around to the front. I'll be taking it."

"I'm going with you," she said.

"No way. Some nut has planted at least one bomb down at the center. There may be more."

"I'm coming with you," Laura said defiantly, and before he could object again, she grabbed her purse and left the apartment.

Within a couple of minutes, Rossiter was at the front door of the building, where Laura waited for him in her Chevy Camaro, the engine running, the headlights on. The dense fog of the night had gotten worse, if anything, and as he jumped in the car he realized with a sinking feeling that it would take a hell of a lot longer than fifteen or twenty minutes to get across town.

"Let's go," he said, "but for God's sake, be careful in this shit. I don't want to be in an accident."

She pulled out of the driveway and headed at a crawl toward the freeway, the low beams barely illuminating the road one car length ahead of them. They didn't speak, both of them staring intently out the windshield, the wipers slapping back and forth, until they had made it to the freeway, and she was able to speed up to twenty miles per hour.

"What did my wife say to you?" Rossiter asked gently.

Laura glanced at him, her eyes red rimmed. "She knew you were there."

"What'd you tell her?"

Laura shook her head. "Nothing. I was frightened."

"Then she doesn't know for sure."

"She knows, Peter! Goddamn it, she called Minneapolis and they told her you weren't up there. If she didn't know about us, then why would she have called my number?''

One more piece of shit in an already overloaded pot. ''Laura . . .''

''Don't say it,'' she said. ''You've got your hands full now, so don't lie to me just to keep me quiet. When everything is settled at work, and you've had time to think this all out, then talk to me. But no lies, Peter. No false promises. I'm thirty years old, you're forty. We're old enough now for the truth.''

He reached out to touch her cheek, but she brushed his hand away. They continued in silence.

It was fifteen minutes before eight when they finally made it to the elevator complex, where they were stopped by the police.

Rossiter jumped out of the car. ''Get out of here now, Laura, or I'll have the cops take you away. I'll call you as soon as I can.''

She looked at him and smiled wanly. ''Good luck,'' she said. She turned around and headed back into the city.

Rossiter jumped into the back seat of one of the waiting cruisers, and they headed across the staging area toward the main office. There were fire engines, ambulances, police cars, and people everywhere.

''What's the status?'' he asked.

''They've found two other bombs, and they're looking for more.''

''When were they set to go off?''

''No way of telling for sure, Mr. Rossiter, but soon,'' one of the cops said.

''There's too many people here. If this thing blows, it'll go sky high. I want you to get everyone nonessential the hell out of here. Immediately.''

"Yes, sir," the cop said.

They pulled up at the main office, which faced the dock itself. The gigantic grain ship *Akai Maru* was lit up like a Christmas tree in the fog.

Rossiter jumped out of the cruiser and raced inside the building. It was jammed with policemen and elevator personnel. Everyone seemed to be talking at once. Telephones were ringing, and near the front window two police officers were tending portable radios, which hissed and blared with messages from the search teams below.

"Listen up, everyone!" Rossiter shouted. The noise did not diminish.

He jumped up on a desk. "Listen up!" he shouted at the top of his lungs.

Everyone turned his way now, and the noise began to subside.

"I want everyone not directly connected with the bomb search to get the hell out of here, and away from the elevator. Right now!"

"Pete! In here!" the night manager shouted from the doorway to Rossiter's office.

Rossiter jumped down from the desk, and hurried across to his office, where Carl, the chief engineer, and two plainclothes detectives stood around a small, seedy-looking old man seated on a chair in the middle of the room. He was smiling.

"Who the hell are you?" Rossiter demanded.

"He won't give us a thing . . ." one of the detectives started, but the little man smiled.

"Louie Benario," he said in a soft voice.

The detectives looked at him in amazement.

"Who sent you to sabotage my elevator, and why?"

Benario laughed out loud, and he pointed up to the clock, which showed one minute until eight. "It's too late!"

They all looked at the clock as the second hand swept up toward the hour, then at each other.

"Sound the siren!" Rossiter screamed. "Get everyone out of here!"

"Too late, too late," Benario sang. "My pretty, my pretty fire."

A dull explosion sounded from somewhere below them. Then something shook the building, and another, much larger explosion sent a part of the ceiling down.

"Jesus," someone swore as the lights went out, and then all hell broke loose as the entire elevator complex burst apart in a gigantic explosion that sent flames and debris nearly one thousand feet into the air, breaking windows over a two-mile radius and burrying the office area beneath thousands of tons of concrete, steel, and burning grain.

9

The hot North African sun hammered the open docks at the ferry terminal within the protected harbor of Tripoli. It was a few minutes after noon, and several last-minute passengers for the boat to Palermo shuffled across the quay and boarded. A thick miasma hung in the windless air over the minarets and domed mosques of the surprisingly oriental Libyan capital. Within the city, the noon traffic was heavy. Although much of the population slept during the hottest part of the day, business still had to continue; the country, despite its protestations to the contrary, had been irrevocably influenced by the West.

Among the final passengers was a tall, well-built Frenchman, with thick black hair, wide, dark eyes, and a handsome face that would have been more at home on the rocky beaches of Cap d'Antibes than here in this forsaken place of dust and poverty.

He was dressed plainly in a short-sleeved safari suit and soft desert boots. He carried two pieces of soft leather luggage.

At the head of the gangway, he was greeted by the ship's purser and deck officer, and a steward was assigned to show him to his first-class cabin for the thirty-hour trip.

"Have a pleasant voyage, Monsieur Riemé," the purser said, touching the bill of his cap.

"*Merci*, I will." He followed his steward forward to his cabin, where he ordered a bottle of good white wine and a light lunch of fish soup. He ate the soup and some bread, drank one small glass of the wine. He then poured the rest of it in his bathroom sink, careful to rinse all traces of the wine away.

He lay down and slept for one hour. When he got up, he rang his steward and ordered a bottle of bourbon and a bucket of ice. When it came he poured a small tot into a glass, sloshed a bit of it on his bed and on the carpeted deck, as if he had had an accident, and sent the remainder of the bottle after the wine down the sink.

Then he settled down to wait until nightfall, smoking Gauloise cigarettes one after another.

Henri Riemé, at twenty-nine, was young enough to have missed General de Gaulle's terrible betrayal of the French officer corps in Algeria during the fifties and sixties, but his father and three of his uncles had been left out in the cold and hung by fanatics.

For a time afterwards (his mother called those days the horrible years), the Riemé family had sunk into obscurity, the mother, Uncle Paul, and Henri living in a small flat on the Left Bank of Paris.

In the sixties, and into the seventies, when young Henri was attending school, it seemed as if the family would never make its mark on French history beyond the footnote in the texts listing the father and uncles among those purged.

It seemed that way until the Sorbonne, where young Henri, who was studying engineering, met Robert Sossoin, a radical from Marseille. They roomed together for two years. Then Henri had to drop out of school for lack of money. But meanwhile Sossoin had filled his head with Communist doctrine.

"The Communist Party is the future of France, Henri," Sossoin would argue endlessly.

"Look what it has done to the Soviet Union," Riemé would counter.

"Ah, the grand experiment you speak of now. You expect that in such a short time, with such a large nation, with so many different peoples, miracles can or should occur? It is only after time and effort, only after the sweat of the worker's brow runs hard and fast, that miracles will happen. There is no starvation in Russia. There are no homeless. They have brought themselves from a backward icebox of a nation to the most powerful country on this earth," Sossoin said fervently. "We must align ourselves with them. We must free France from the stagnating grip of capitalism."

Even those high-sounding words did not completely sway young Henri, however. His conversion did not come until nearly a year after he had dropped out of college, when he was working as a waiter at a touristy Left Bank café.

His uncle had died several months earlier, and his mother was ill, in need of hospital care. She was too proud to accept state care, and Henri was too poor to afford private doctors. At that propitious moment, Robert Sossoin showed up, offered money, and thus recruited Henri into the LPN—Le Poing Noir (The Black Fist). The LPN's avowed aim was redistribution of wealth by taking it forcibly out of the hands of the rich and placing it in the pockets of the deserving worker.

For the next few whirlwind years, Henri and his newfound group robbed department stores and banks, their targets becoming larger and larger, their methods more and more sophisticated, and the price on their heads ever greater.

In 1977, their activities came to the attention of the KGB resident in Paris, who contacted the LPN leadership and arranged for reorganization and training.

Riemé was one of the men selected to go to Libya and then Moscow for terrorist schooling: hand-to-hand combat, demolitions, and weapons, as well as secret codes, radio work, and languages, primarily Russian and English.

Eventually their control officer, whose real name they never knew, pronounced them ready to return to France to do some real work.

The officer was a little man, with intense eyes and a dark complexion. Sitting now aboard the ferryboat, Riemé remembered well that last meeting after they had graduated, when the little man clapped him proudly on the shoulder.

"You will become a first-class assassin to rival Carlos himself. An assassin for freedom."

Henri had been startled. He had thought of himself as an administrator, or perhaps a soldier, like his father and uncles. But an assassin? There was something faintly dirty about the notion.

Within two months of returning to France, however, he had been ordered to assassinate a minor political figure in Nancy, which he did with such sophistication and dispatch—and with such congratulations from his comrades afterward—that he was hooked. He had found his place. He was an assassin. An expert. His mother, who had died despite her operation, would have been proud of him, as would his father and uncles.

"For them," he had told himself. "For France, and for my family."

Those phrases had become his talisman, his prayer to the gods, before, during, and after each job.

And now there was a new assignment. It was the first to come directly from his little control officer. It would be a terrible blow against capitalism in France.

"The rich will tremble in fear," the little man had told him one week ago in Tripoli. The meeting had been arranged through a complicated line of intermediaries.

"But why this one?" Riemé had asked, studying a photograph. It showed a man in his early fifties, coming out of a modern glass-and-steel building, apparently in Paris.

"His name is Gérard Louis Dreyfus," the little man said. The name meant nothing to Riemé. "He is one of the most wealthy and most powerful of the international grain merchants. From France, he controls a huge portion of the world's food supply."

"I still do not see . . ." Riemé began, but the little man continued as if he had never been interrupted.

"I ask you, Henri, is there starvation in the world?"

Riemé nodded.

"Then it is the people who control the food to whom we must look. Men like Louis Dreyfus, who is known as the Octopus. He steals the grain of France and other nations, and then sells the food to the very rich for obscene profits. A man who does not deserve to live."

"The assassination of one man in such a large business would do nothing to stop it," Reimé argued.

"On the contrary, Henri. The Louis Dreyfus business is very special. It is entirely owned and operated by one family. By one man. Gérard. Eliminate him, and the business would take years to recover, if it ever would."

"Others would take its place."

The little man nodded sagely. "Not quickly. Not efficiently. And certainly not in France."

"For France," Riemé had said softly.

During the next five days, the plan, at once simple and yet stunning in its savagery, emerged. The LPN in Paris had made the arrangements, and Riemé was on his way.

It was just before midnight when Riemé rose from his chair and took off his shirt, laying it aside. Across the cabin, he opened one of his suitcases and extracted a thin, rubber life vest with a carbon-dioxide cartridge, which he donned. Then he put his shirt back on, making sure it totally hid the vest. If he was seen on deck, he wanted no one to notice it.

Next he unpacked a few of his clothes and scattered them around the room, leaving his wallet and passport lying conspicuously on the small writing table, as if he meant to return to his cabin. He would no longer need them, however.

At the door he listened, and when he heard nothing except the ever-present throb of the ship's diesels, he opened the door and slipped out.

He hurried down the corridor and out the hatch onto the main deck, where he waited for several moments.

There was no one about. Most of the passengers were already asleep in their cabins; only a few of them were in the bar forward.

Riemé moved aft, keeping in the shadows close to the bulkheads so that the officers on duty above on the bridge would have no chance of spotting him. The sound of the ship's engines was much louder at the stern, and he could hear the prop churning the water twenty feet below the rail.

Checking one last time to make sure no one was on deck to see him, he quickly climbed over the rail and jumped.

The boiling sea came up at him incredibly fast, and he hit badly, plunging fifteen feet beneath the water. He grappled with the carbon-dioxide cartridge beneath his shirt, finally found it, and gave a sharp tug on the lanyard. For a moment nothing seemed to happen, but then the vest tightened against his chest, ripping his shirt, and he shot up to the surface.

The ship was already a couple of hundred yards away. He cocked his head to listen for any sounds of an alarm, but there was nothing. It would be morning before it was discovered he was missing. They would find the empty wine and liquor bottles, and would come to the easy conclusion that poor Monsieur Riemé had gotten perhaps a bit too drunk, taken a stroll on the deck, and simply fallen overboard. An unfortunate but not uncommon occurrence.

Within twenty minutes, the ship was gone from sight, even its highest lights lost over the horizon. Riemé opened the large side pocket on his vest, removed the radio in its waterproof container, activated it, and held the antenna as high out of the water as he could.

For twenty minutes he bobbed up and down on the empty sea like that, utterly alone, even the stars overhead somewhat obscured by a thin haze. At last he heard the faint buzz-saw noise of an approaching boat.

He twisted around until he was able to pick out the lights, which flashed on and off at ten-second intervals, almost as if something were wrong with the electrical circuits. Then he took out his small but powerful strobe light, flipped it on, and held it out of the water.

Immediately the boat turned directly toward him, slowing down as it approached.

"Like clockwork," the little man had told him. "This job will go so smoothly that you will be in and out of France before the authorities have any idea what hit them."

The pickup had come at 12:43 A.M. Less than twenty-three hours later, at 22:28 P.M., Riemé was climbing into a legally registered, two-door Peugeot in Marseille, and heading north toward Paris five hundred miles away.

Near dawn he stopped at a small inn near the town of Briare on the Loire River, registering as Bennette Roget, a salesman from Le Havre. At this point he was less than one hundred miles from his target, on the Avenue de la Grande Armée, near the Arc de Triomphe.

He slept a few hours and had a moderately large breakfast. He took his time the rest of the way into Paris, arriving there shortly before noon. He went directly to an address on the Left Bank, which turned out to be a parking garage in a rundown section of similar structures.

With the car parked safely inside, next to a dark-blue, nondescript van he had been assured would be there,

Riemé laid his head back on the car seat, closed his eyes, and mentally readied himself for his task.

The weapon he would use was already in the van. After killing the afternoon at a movie, he would drive across the river to the office building, where he would park at exactly 6:00 P.M. Within five minutes, Gérard Louis Dreyfus would come out to his waiting limousine. Riemé would kill him and drive immediately back here. He'd take the car back to Marseille. A boat would be waiting there to take him to Barcelona and his plane to Moscow. There he would be given a new identity, and in due time another assignment.

André Blenault, chief comptroller for Louis Dreyfus operations in Paris, stepped out of his office on the third floor and hurried down to the receptionist near the elevator, hugging a fat briefcase to his chest. He was in a foul mood this afternoon, as he had been since one week ago last Sunday, when the cable from New York had arrived.

First there had been the trouble with the damned Vance-Ehrhardts, who had somehow managed to sign the France-Océanique shipping agreement. Next had come the Cargill coup, which gave the Minneapolis-based firm a solid foothold with the Canadian Wheat Board for the next five years. And finally, the cable: Newman, the filthy Marauder, was on the move again.

From what Blenault and others on the staff had pieced together, Newman had begun to set up a complex arrangement of subsidiaries within the world shipping community. Left to his own devices, he would, within a month, tie up damned near every scrap of tonnage currently available. And there was little or nothing they could do to block him.

The most damning aspect, the one that the New York cable had spelled out, or failed to spell out, depending upon the point of view, was that no one—simply no one —had an inkling of what the Marauder was up to. And that worried the staff, which in turn disturbed Blenault, which finally upset Gérard.

"Heads will roll. *Mon dieu*, heads will surely roll," Blenault muttered as he came to the reception area.

The young woman at the desk looked up, startled. "Monsieur Blenault?"

"His car, have you called it up yet?"

The woman looked up at the wall clock, which showed it was a couple of minutes before six, and without a word grabbed the telephone and dialed while the comptroller waited impatiently.

"Bring his car around now, please," the woman said. *"Merci."* And she hung up the telephone.

"If it's late . . . oh, heavens, if it's late. He simply does not need that kind of aggravation at this moment, don't you understand, you dolt?"

"Oui, monsieur," the poor woman said.

Blenault stared pointedly at her for another long moment as she fidgeted nervously, then turned as Gérard Louis Dreyfus approached.

He was a short man, with a thick, rich voice, and he was dressed, as usual, in a pin-striped suit. He smiled as he saw Blenault.

"Ah, André, are we ready for the weekend?"

"Oui, monsieur, I have the files you requested right here."

"Then let us be on our way."

As they rode down in the elevator, Gérard studied his

comptroller's face for a long moment. "Any further word from New York?"

"None as of the late-afternoon telexes."

"Then we will call them on the way home. I have told no one as yet, but I will be flying to New York tomorrow, and if need be to Moscow on Monday."

"Moscow?" Blenault asked, bewildered.

"*Oui*, André," Gérard said. "I have a feeling that our friends at Exportkhleb may be up to something."

They called it the "trader's nose," Blenault thought. It was absolutely amazing, but a good grainman, such as Gérard Louis Dreyfus, could smell out a large deal in the making, often even before the principals making the deal knew that they would make one.

"I have not heard of anything . . ." Blenault trailed off.

Louis Dreyfus smiled. "Marie Longchamps telephoned this afternoon, said she was certain she had seen Dybrovik in Geneva last week. Perhaps it was nothing. Perhaps it wasn't even him. But . . ." He shrugged.

"Where that man moves, there is trouble."

"And profit, my dear André."

They reached the ground floor and the doors slid open. The building's security guard jumped up from his position by the door, and Louis Dreyfus greeted him as he and Blenault stepped outside.

The company Rolls-Royce had just come around the corner, a plain van right behind it. The car pulled up to the curb as Louis Dreyfus and Blenault stepped across the sidewalk.

Later, from his hospital bed, Blenault would be unable to say clearly what had happened next, but he did remember the plain blue van with a French-looking driver pulling up beside the Rolls.

The driver's window was open, and as Louis Dreyfus turned to say something to Blenault, a dark, slender object was thrust out. There was suddenly a series of loud pops, as if a truck or some other vehicle were back-firing.

Louis Dreyfus was flung backward into the glass doors, a dozen holes erupting in his chest and face, blood splattering everywhere.

Someone screamed something. At the same moment a hard, very hot, compelling force slammed into Ble-nault's side and right buttock, driving him sideways, down on Gérard's already lifeless body.

"Mon dieu! Mon dieu!" some foolish woman kept screaming over and over, as Blenault tried to catch his breath.

10

The dusty white station wagon came up the deeply rutted road from the farmhouse in the hollow by the creek. As it topped the rise it stopped, and William Bormett got out.

He was a huge bear of a man. He was six foot four, and, last week on his fifty-first birthday, had tipped the scales at 275 pounds. In his younger days he had been the kid who could lift a young bull up on his shoulders; or lift the back end of a pickup truck; or toss seventy-five-pound bales of hay to the top of the hayrack all day long, then go out that night dancing and drinking.

Over the past years, however, Bormett had begun to slow down. His weight had redistributed itself, more going to his expanding paunch and less to his shoulders. But, like many succesful men, he had automatically compensated for his waning physical abilities by increasing his acumen.

He shaded his eyes now against the morning sun as he stared across his fields to the east, and he smiled with satisfaction.

Fifteen thousand acres of the finest land to corn anywhere in the world. It was an achievement rivaled by very few, and certainly equaled by no one.

It had begun with his grandfather, who had come to Iowa as a young man, where he planted two hundred acres to corn to feed his small dairy herd. Within a few years, however, the Bormett herd had died off from cow fever just at harvest time, and the corn had been sold as feed.

By the time William's father had taken over the farm, they were planting nearly a thousand acres to corn, which they sold to area dairy farmers. And the business prospered.

To the first crude drying bins that Grandfather Bormett had put up, William's father had added an extensive number of Butler corrugated-metal storage units, so that in time the farm began to take on the appearance of a major grain depot. As area farms came on the market, William's father bought them, tore down the fences, and planted more and more acres to corn, ever increasing his drying and storage capabilities.

Grandfather Bormett had died at the ripe age of 93, but his son died at the age of 56, leaving William in charge of eight thousand acres at the age of 24.

That was twenty-seven years ago. Since then, William had nearly doubled the farm's acres to corn, had purchased and maintained a fleet of twenty five semitractor trailers, and established what the *Des Moines Register* called the most modern corn-drying and -storage facility anywhere in the world, with a total investment in equipment, machinery, and land approaching the twenty-million-dollar mark.

The Bormett farm was definitely big business. A big business that William was justifiably proud of.

He was dressed, this morning, in a three-piece suit, with a subdued blue tie and an offwhite shirt. Looking at him, no one would have suspected he was a farmer, except that his large hands were roughly calloused.

Unlike many successful farmers who delegated all but the book work to hired hands, Bormett continued to put in his time on a tractor, on and in the silos, and in the machine sheds. He actively worked his fifteen thousand acres; he did not merely manage them, although he did have more than one hundred paid farmhands.

Pretty soon they'd be leaving for the airport, fifteen miles away in Des Moines, but before they left he had wanted to come out here and look at his fields. They were the reason he had been called to Moscow.

The invitation had come from the University of Moscow's Department of Agriculture, through the U.S. State Department, over to the U.S. Department of Agriculture, and then one week ago out here in the person of Stuart Finney, a tight-assed assistant of Curtis Lundgren, the Secretary of Agriculture.

Bormett had to chuckle now, thinking back on it. Finney had come to the farm with not so much as a phone call or a howdy-do, just marched up on the porch and banged on the door.

"Hello, I'm Stuart Finney, from the United States Department of Agriculture. I've come to tell you that you are going to Russia to speak to the Agriculture Department at Moscow University."

At first Catherine had just laughed at the man.

Laughed right in his face. But then he had looked so forlorn, she had invited him in for some coffee and sweet rolls.

Slowly, that afternoon, it came out that he was for real, that it wasn't some kind of a joke. Several telegrams and telephone calls to Washington, including a long conversation with Secretary Lundgren himself, finally convinced the Bormetts. The Russians did want him to come to Moscow to speak with their farm experts.

In the distance to the southeast, Bormett could see the little grain elevators at Adel. Nearly everything between where he stood now and those elevators was his land. All of it under cultivation. All of it corn, his cash crop. Except of course for the household vegetable garden.

Within a couple of years, if all went well (and everything had gone extremely well for the Bormetts for the last half-century), their holdings would be increased to more than twenty thousand acres.

If all that land were to be placed in one huge square, it would have been over five and a half miles on a side. Over thirty-one square miles of land to corn. An amazing amount of corn. A staggering pile of grain at harvest time.

As it was, his fleet of trucks had to run twenty-four hours a day during the harvest, back and forth to the railhead at Des Moines where there were large enough facilities to handle the shipment of their grain. With another five thousand acres, he'd have to think seriously about building his own rail spur to the farm. It'd be a hell of a lot more efficient and certainly a lot more profitable that way.

At his car door, he looked once again across the fields

he had worked since he was a boy. Already the corn was coming up in perfect green rows. A hybrid dent, the most common corn in the country, it would by harvest time have grown to twenty feet in height, with yields per acre that would have dazzled his father and totally stunned his grandfather.

The old saw "Knee high by the Fourth of July" was hopelessly out of date. July 4 was four days away, and it was already more than waist high.

He laughed again, and shook his head for the joy of it all, got in his car, swung it around, and headed back down the hill to collect his wife. She was going with him for the ten-day visit to Moscow.

Catherine was waiting for him out on the porch with their luggage when he pulled up in the driveway. She was a small woman, somewhat rotund, but with a pleasant, smiling face, rosy, dimpled cheeks, and beautiful, prematurely silver hair. Whereas William ran the farm operation, Catherine ruled the house with an iron will and a very firm hand. And although they were traveling to Russia (the first time anyone in the family had been outside the United States) so that William could tell the Russkies how to grow corn, Catherine felt it was her God-given duty to oversee the trip, since technically it did not involve the actual operation of the farm.

"William Owen Bormett," she scolded. "I've been waiting here on this porch for the past half-hour, wondering if somebody hadn't kidnapped you or something."

"Had to take a last look out at the east fields to see how they were coming along after the rain," he said, getting out of the car. He went around back and opened the tailgate, his wife right behind him.

"We've got barely an hour to catch our flight, and they wanted us there an hour early," she argued.

He smiled. "It's all right, Katy, we'll get there in plenty of time. They won't leave without us." He went up on the porch, got the luggage, and brought it back to the car. "Where are the kids? Are they ready to say goodbye yet?"

"They said their goodbyes last night at supper. Justin is in town, and Albert is out with Harold at the airstrip. Harold is giving him another flying lesson."

Bormett nodded, slightly disappointed that his sons would not be here to see them off. Yet at sixteen and nineteen, he himself had been much more interested in his own life than in that of his father or grandfather. They would come back into the fold in due time. It would be fifteen or twenty years yet, before they would have to take over the farm. There was plenty of time.

"You've got the tickets? Our travelers checks? The passports?" he asked his wife as he helped her into the car.

"Everything," she said.

Before he closed the door, he looked in at her. "Excited to be going?"

She grinned. "Plenty excited." She fingered her dress. "Do you suppose I'll be dressed okay for Washington?"

"You look fine, Katy, just fine."

They would be staying in Washington for two days, during which time they would be meeting with the Secretary of Agriculture and his people, as well as someone from the State Department who'd tell them what to say and how to act while they were in the Soviet Union.

It was a lot of nonsense, as far as he was concerned. Hell, he was just going over to talk farming with the Russkies. He wasn't going to give them any secrets, leastwise nothing they couldn't get themselves by studying American farm magazines.

"You are going over there representing the United States of America, Mr. Bormett," Finney had told him.

"I know that. I won't embarrass you."

Finney had smiled his tight-assed little smile and shook his head. "I'm sure you won't, sir," he said. "We—that is, Secretary Lundgren—mostly just wanted to meet with you in person and get to know you a little better before you leave."

"Wants to pump me full of propaganda. Shit, I fought the Commies in Korea. I know what the hell the score is. You don't have to tell me that."

"No, sir," Finney had said. "But before you leave, you will have to meet with Secretary Lundgren and someone from the State Department. It's required of all Americans before they go to the Soviet Union."

"Bullshit," Bormett had said. "But I won't fight you on it. Not at all. We'll meet with your boss and whoever else wants to meet with us. It's just fine with me."

"Oh, that's very good, Mr. Bormett," Finney had said, obviously relieved.

Their flight left at 8:30 A.M. They switched planes in Chicago, and arrived at Washington's National Airport a little after lunch, where Finney met them with a limousine and chattered incessantly all the way to their hotel.

"Secretary Lundgren is tied up today for lunch, but he wants to meet with you for breakfast about eight tomorrow morning," Finney said.

"I'm used to having my breakfast around five-thirty or six," Bormett said, poking fun at him.

"Oh, dear," Finney said. "I don't think Secretary Lundgren would be able to . . ."

"It's all right there, now," Bormett said. "I suppose I could hold until eight A.M. just this once."

In actuality Bormett had stopped eating big breakfasts years ago, preferring instead to work through until around 9:30 or 10:00, when he would stop for coffee and a doughnut. But he was a farmer, and in front of easterners, he wanted to behave like one.

It was like the old bib-overall joke. The city folks thought the bibs made a man look like an ignorant, sod-busting hick, down on his luck. The country folk knew the farmer wore the bibs cause they had large pockets to hold all his money.

"I'll drop you off at your hotel, where you can rest for an hour or so. You have a meeting at three with Leonard Ruskin, an Undersecretary with the Foreign Trade Mission Desk at State."

"An impressive title," Bormett said.

Finney smiled. "Then at five, the Vice-President and his wife would like to have cocktails with you and Mrs. Bormett at their home."

Catherine gasped, her eyes wide, and she began to blush.

"Now *that* is an impressive title, even though I didn't vote for the rascal," Bormett said.

"I didn't either," Finney said. "But don't tell anyone."

They all laughed at the little joke. Within ten minutes they were at their hotel, being shown their suite of rooms. Everything had been paid for by the Department of Agriculture, including, Finney informed them, their airfare to and from Moscow, their accommodations in the Soviet capital, and their meals and drinks.

"We have our own money," Bormett had protested, but Finney had shaken his head.

"Use it to buy souvenirs, if you'd like. Everything else has already been taken care of."

When Finney was gone, Bormett took a shower, and afterward, while his wife was in the bathroom, he ordered himself a bourbon and water from room service. He was sitting looking out the window at the capitol a few blocks away when she came out.

She was glowing. "Nothing like this has ever happened to us, Will," she said.

He looked up at her and smiled. She was a good woman, and although at times she was a bit shrill, he loved her.

"Are you glad you tagged along?"

"I wouldn't have missed it for the world," she said, but then her brows knitted. "It's just that I don't know what to wear to see a vice-president and his wife."

Bormett thought about that for a moment, then snapped his fingers. "When I'm meeting with the State Department people, why don't you go out on the town and buy yourself something?"

"I couldn't," she protested.

"Of course you can," Bormett said, crossing to the telephone. "I'll call Finney now and see if there isn't someone who could go along with you. Sort of show you around the town."

Later, Catherine described that first day in Washington as a "whirlwind," and even William had to admit to himself that it had been interesting. He and his wife had been treated with the utmost respect and interest.

At the State Department he was told nothing more than Finney had already told him: He was an American, and as such he would be representing all American farmers. The Russians had invited him because he was the best, and they hoped to learn as much from him as they possibly could.

Catherine, with the help of Finney's wife, had bought a lovely, offwhite cocktail dress, and they had gone on to meet the Vice-President and his wife.

Although Bormett had little or no regard for the present administration, he found the Vice-President a bright, amiable man who immediately impressed him with the statement that he, the Vice-President, was nothing more than a politician, whereas Bormett and men like him were much more important.

"The farmer has always been the backbone of this nation, Mr. Bormett," he said. "All the computer companies, steel mills, coal mines, and oil wells would be totally impossible without the basic human necessity: food. Food, which you provide us."

It didn't really matter that nowadays most of the Bormett corn was shipped to overseas markets; he was a supplier of food to a hungry world. His farm was a shining example of American knowhow and hard work.

Near the end of that pleasant meeting, Bormett had delighted everyone by admitting to the Vice-President that he had not voted for this administration, but if it was going to try for reelection, he'd be the first at the polls with his support.

Their flight was scheduled to leave the next afternoon

at 3:00, and the Bormetts went to bed early to get a good night's sleep. In the morning William was picked up by Finney, who took him over to a private dining room in the Department of Agriculture.

Bormett took an instant dislike to Secretary Lundgren.

"You're going to have to come to the understanding early on, Mr. Bormett, that the Russians are not, nor will they ever be, capable of farming the same way you do," Lundgren began.

"How so?" Bormett asked innocently.

Lundgren smiled superciliously. "They don't have air-conditioned tractors to ride around in, with stereo systems, two-way radios, refrigerators for cold beer."

Bormett could feel the color coming to his cheeks. "Tractors that pull twelve-bottom plows. Two-way radios in case of a breakdown so we can get a repair crew out there on the double. No beer boxes on my machinery."

Lundgren sniffed and dabbed his lips with his linen napkin. "They'll never have twelve-bottom plows, or fifteen-thousand-acre farms, either. Nor will they ever understand agribusiness and marketing, not in their society."

"I'm going over to speak with farmers . . ." Bormett began, but Lundgren cut him off.

"I beg your pardon. You are going to Moscow to speak with professors of agriculture. Book people who probably have never even seen a farm." He leaned forward, his elbows on the highly polished mahogany table. "You will be a cultural exchange program. We send orchestras, they send dancers. We send farmers, they send engineers. As long as we're talking, we're not shooting. Leastwise, that's the President's foreign policy in a nutshell."

Lundgren, as far as Bormett was concerned, was insufferable. "Tell me, Mr. Secretary, were you raised on a farm?"

Finney had been drinking coffee, and he choked, sputtering and coughing.

"As a matter of fact, no, Mr. Bormett," the Secretary said coldly. "I was born and raised in Chicago, and I attended Northwestern University. I am an attorney."

"I see," Bormett said, his voice equally cold. "I'll try not to embarrass this administration either in Moscow or back home."

"I'm happy to hear that. When you return, I'd like to meet with you again. We can talk at greater length about what you learned."

11

The large house high in the hills overlooked the magnificent harbor at the head of Lake Superior in Duluth. It had suited Kenneth Newman's needs as a grainman since the day he had moved here eight years ago. And in the weeks since he had brought his new bride here, it seemed to have suited her needs as well.

When he broke away from the Vance-Ehrhardt conglomerate, he had had his choice of any city in the world in which to work. New York would have been logical, as would Geneva or Paris or even Amsterdam. Those cities were financial centers.

Instead, Newman had chosen to live in a grain port where the commodities he dealt with would be ever present.

On the North American continent, he was left with three major grain ports: New Orleans at the mouth of the Mississippi; Minneapolis at the navigable head of the great shipping river; or Duluth-Superior, the westternmost port on the St. Lawrence Seaway.

Neither the climate nor the people of New Orleans suited Newman. Besides, Cargill had a very strong foothold in that city.

Minneapolis-St. Paul would have been fine, but Cargill all but owned that city as well.

Which left Duluth-Superior. The brisk climate suited Newman. The friendly, hard-working Scandinavian population suited him. And, best of all, the northern port city suited his willingness for a good, ongoing fight.

It had been touch and go, for as many years as anyone could remember, whether it was cheaper to ship grain to the river, load it on barges, haul it down to New Orleans, and then load it aboard grain ships, or cheaper to load the grain aboard trains at or near the farms, transport it to Duluth-Superior, and use the ultramodern handling facilities there to sort, grade, and load the grain directly aboard ocean-going ships.

For years the river-barge operators and railroad managements had been stimulating the agreement—and the business—with rate-schedule wars.

Competition like that was healthy for the grain business, he reflected this morning as he stepped out of the shower. But the explosion at Cargill's giant elevators in New Orleans, and Friday's gruesome murder of Gérard Louis Dreyfus by the French LPN, were the work of fanatics.

The world press had not yet made the connection between the two events, but Newman had. And the conclusions he drew worried him.

Without Gérard, the Louis Dreyfus clan's business would take years to recover. Already there had been a noticeable slump in the French and Mediterranean markets that would deepen as currently negotiated deals began to come to fruition.

Simply put, Gérard's assassination had placed a serious crimp on the European grain market. Georges André and the others would be hard pressed to remove it.

On this continent, Cargill's mammoth New Orleans elevator complex had been bigger in size and grain-handling capabilities than even the Duluth-Superior facilities. The destruction of that elevator would not ruin the gigantic Cargill Company, but it would seriously strain the firm's abilities to deliver grain that had been ordered and, in some cases, already paid for.

Which left South America, the third largest supplier of grain. Jorge Vance-Ehrhardt. If anything happened to Lydia's father, the results within the grain industry could be nearly catastrophic.

Back in his bedroom, as Newman began to dress, the worry that had been nagging him for the past day or two came again to the forefront of his mind: The fact was that the Newman Company stood to gain the most from it all.

With his secret Russian deal, he needed all the grain, and all the ships to transport it, that he could lay his hands on.

Louis Dreyfus was all but out of the picture, so he had almost the entire European grain market to himself, along with its shipping. With Cargill's New Orleans operation nearly shut down, grain that normally would have been shipped downriver would now be brought up to Duluth-Superior.

And, if something should happen to Vance-Ehrhardt the world would become Newman's alone . . . or rather, Newman's and Dybrovik's.

He knotted his tie, put on his jacket, and went downstairs.

Lydia was waiting for him with the morning newspapers in the breakfast nook overlooking Lake Superior, the Aerial Lift Bridge, and the harbor far below.

She was staring out the window at a Japanese cargo ship just coming under the bridge into the harbor, and when he entered the room, she looked up with a start.

"Good morning," he said. He went around the table, and they kissed.

"I was just going to send Marie to make sure you had gotten out of bed," she said, smiling. She seemed a little peaked this morning.

"Are you feeling well?" he asked, taking his seat.

Marie, their housekeeper, came in before she had a chance to answer, set a plate of toasted English muffins on the sideboard, and poured his coffee.

"Good morning, Mr. Newman," she said. "Will you be wanting breakfast this morning?"

"Just coffee, thanks," he said.

"Yes, sir."

Lydia was staring out the window again, and Kenneth reached across to touch her hand. She looked back at him.

"What is it?" he asked. "Are you bored here?"

She managed another smile. "No."

"I've been terribly busy these past weeks, and I can't say that it'll get much better until fall. But afterward we can go somewhere for a month or two. Perhaps back to Monaco to finish our honeymoon.''

She squeezed his hand. ''It's not that, Kenneth. When I married you, I knew that you were a busy man.'' She glanced again out the window. ''Besides, I can always take a plane to New York or Europe or someplace if I want to.''

''That's an excellent idea. Why don't you call up some of your friends and go on a little holiday? London would be nice. Or even Sardinia.'' Newman could hear how hollow his words were, yet he could not help himself. There were too many other things on his mind at the moment.

''I might go to Buenos Aires for a few days,'' she said.

''You miss your father?''

''I'm worried about him.''

Her answer startled him, because he had been worried about him, too. ''Isn't he feeling well? Have you spoken with him?''

''Come off it, Kenneth, for Christ's sake. You know goddamned well why I'm concerned,'' Lydia snapped, her voice rising. ''First it was Cargill, then Louis Dreyfus. My father may very well be next.''

''What about me?'' Newman said, instantly regretting the petty, selfish remark. ''I'm sorry, I didn't mean that.''

''I've hired a security service for you,'' Lydia said coldly. ''They're here now.''

''That's ridiculous.''

''No it's not. But my father will think so, and my mother is too weak to insist he take extra precautions when he travels. I'll have to go to him and make sure he'll be all right. Unless you don't want me to go," she said, looking pointedly into his eyes.

"Of course you should go if you want to, but I think you'd be going for all the wrong reasons. Call him first, then make your decision. See how he feels about Cargill and Louis Dreyfus."

"And report back to you?"

Newman said nothing.

"Who did you meet in Geneva . . ." she started, but then she clamped it off. "No. Don't answer that. I don't want to know." She shook her head. "He won't tell me anything over the phone, anyway."

"Then maybe there is nothing to it. Maybe the two incidents were just coincidence."

Lydia's eyes widened. "You've been thinking about it as well, haven't you?"

Newman nodded. "But the Cargill elevator was out there in the open for anyone to get to, and Gérard was never one for security precautions. On the other hand, your father lives and works on his estate. He's surrounded by staff and armed guards."

"In a country whose tradition is violence and revolution," Lydia countered.

"Speak with him first, before you go," Newman said. He had visions of his wife becoming caught in an assassination attempt, and it frightened him.

She lowered her head. "I'll call him later this morning," she said. She looked up. "Will you be late again tonight?"

"I'll try not to be. But call me at work as soon as you find out anything," Newman said. He finished his coffee, kissed Lydia, and left the room.

In his study he grabbed his briefcase, went into the

garage, and started his small Mercedes.

Out on the street, two men dressed in business suits were waiting in a gray Chevrolet sedan. When Newman passed, they pulled away from the curb and fell in behind him.

It gave him a curious sense of security, having them behind him, and yet he resented the invasion of his privacy that they represented, and at a deeper level he felt they were unnecessary. Cargill here, Louis Dreyfus in Europe. Vance-Ehrhardt in South America, if his fears were justified, would complete the triangle.

If his fears were justified, it would mean the Russians were behind it, in which case Dybrovik's mammoth grain deal was nothing more than a plot to hit at Western grain merchants—the Newman Company in particular.

But why? Dybrovik was a shrewd businessman, who had always played it straight. If he was playing some kind of game, and it got out, the Soviets would be hard-pressed in the future to secure any licenses to purchase Western grain. They would be cutting off their nose to spite their face.

Newman's office was a modern three-story building of glass and steel next to the Port Authority terminal on the waterfront. He had built it shortly after he selected Duluth-Superior as his base; his business had expanded so rapidly that the once too-large building was now bursting at the seams with employees.

The parking lot was nearly full when Newman pulled into his slot and got out of his car. The gray Chevy pulled up beside him, and the two men jumped out and hurried around to him.

"Good morning, sir," one of them said, while the

other scanned the lines of parked cars. "I'm Evans, from Tri-States Security. And this is Humphrey."

"I'll be in my office for the remainder of the day," Newman said, feeling a little foolish.

"Yes, sir. Mr. Coatsworth is there now. He'll explain the procedure to you."

Newman nodded and went into the building. The reception area had a grouping of plants and modern furniture to the right, and the receptionist and telephone operator to the left.

This morning a large man was seated on one of the couches, and when Newman came in he nodded.

"Good morning, Mr. Newman," the receptionist, a young, good-looking woman, chirped.

"Good morning. Is Paul here yet?"

"Yes, sir."

"Have him come up to my office immediately."

"Yes, sir. And there is a Mr. Coatsworth from Tri-States Security waiting to see you."

"Upstairs?"

"Yes, sir."

"Fine," Newman said. He went up to the third floor, where Paul Saratt was waiting for him with a huge man whose steel-gray hair was cropped military-fashion.

"Good morning, Paul," Newman said.

"Morning, Kenneth. This is Rupert Coatsworth, Tri-States Security."

Newman shook his hand. "Lydia told me this morning."

"There are a number of things I'll have to discuss with you this morning, Mr. Newman," Coatsworth said, his voice deep and booming. There was a bulge beneath his left armpit, and Newman realized with a start that the man was armed.

"Can't wait?"

"No, sir."

"You might just as well sit in on this, Paul," Newman said. He turned to his secretary. "Hold all my calls except for Geneva, Abex, and my wife."

"Of course, Mr. Newman," the woman said, and the three men went into Newman's office, which overlooked the terminal. A half-dozen foreign ships were tied up and loading.

"Evidently you do not feel our services are necessary, Mr. Newman," Coatsworth said perceptively.

"My wife does."

"And so do I," Saratt said. "Lydia and I discussed it yesterday."

"I'm busy this morning, so let's get immediately to the point," Newman said. He would go along with this, for a few weeks. At that time he'd make the decision whether or not to continue.

"First, my people will need your complete cooperation."

"As I said, I am a busy man, and I resent intrusions."

"My people are as unintrusive as humanly possible, given the circumstances. But if something should begin to develop, I ask that you do exactly as my people instruct you. Your life could very well depend upon that single act."

Newman nodded.

"Good. Secondly, we will need to be kept informed of your itinerary, as far in advance as possible."

"My secretary will be able to provide you with that."

"And last of all, I would like you, and perhaps your wife and Mr. Saratt, to come up with a list of people who would like to see you harmed, and their reasons."

"I know of no one like that."

"I'm sure you do, Mr. Newman," Coatsworth said with an air of authority. "All of us have enemies. No matter how farfetched you may think the idea, it would be of immense help to us. We do want to protect you."

"That would be a potentially dangerous list. Very sensitive."

Coatsworth smiled. "You may wish to check with the director of the Federal Bureau of Investigation in Washington and, internationally, with Interpol in Paris, Geneva, or London. We are a recognized and legitimate firm, I assure you."

"If I travel?"

"We will come with you. Are you planning on going somewhere soon?"

"Very likely. But I travel constantly, Mr. Coatsworth. All over the world."

"We will be at your side," Coatsworth said. He got to his feet. "I'll check with your secretary for your schedule. May we have the list by this afternoon?"

"I'll see what I can come up with," Newman said dryly.

At the door the security chief stopped and turned back. "My technicians will be here a little later this morning to sweep your telephones and electrical circuits. They are at your house now."

Newman nodded. When Coatsworth was gone, he sat back in his chair and shook his head ruefully.

"This time I agree with Lydia," Saratt said.

"Two weeks, Paul, then we review the situation."

"Fair enough," Saratt said. "But you told Coatsworth you would be going somewhere soon. Anything I should know about?"

"I'm going to Washington to speak with Lundgren."

"We have our licenses for stateside grain; or are you worried about the Justice Department finding out about our foreign activities?"

"I'm worried about the entire thing," Newman said, choosing his words with care. He still hadn't thought it out completely, but it seemed as if everything was somehow missing a beat. Off kilter. Out of sync. It felt wrong to him.

"All our subsidiaries are third- and fourth-party agreements, most of them on foreign holding companies. What can go wrong?"

"It's not that."

"What then? The Cargill and Louis Dreyfus business?"

"Partly. But it's this entire deal, Paul. I think we're being set up."

"So did I. But Dybrovik is taking the corn as and when we ship it, and the funds are being transferred without question into our TradeCon account in Zurich. So even if the bottom fell out tomorrow, we'd be safe."

"How close have the actual transactions been played?"

"To within a couple of hundred thousand tons on shipments, but we're going to have to start going after the futures market within the next week to ten days."

"Which has been made a damned sight easier for us because of Cargill's troubles."

Saratt started to say something, but then he held off, an odd look suddenly crossing his features. "You're not worried about a market manipulation. Not at all. It's something else."

"We're talking about as much as a hundred million tons of corn. Unprecedented. The largest deal in the history of grain trading.''

Saratt nodded.

"And no one seems to be overly excited. Least of all Dybrovik. And hardly anyone else, except for Louis Dreyfus, whose people were snooping around Abex, and Cargill, who cut their barge rates again last week. What the hell does that tell you?''

"There is interest in us. We expected that.''

"You're missing my point,'' Newman snapped.

"Evidently.''

"How much current corn will we be able to ship to the Russians before the supplies bottom out?''

Saratt shrugged. "Considering his seventy-five percent restriction, perhaps as much as seven or eight million tons.''

"The rest is in futures. As much as we can nail down.''

"On margin, with Exportkhleb's funds.''

"And our reputation.''

"I still don't see . . .'' Saratt started, but Newman cut him off.

"Suppose, for the sake of argument, that the Russians have a bumper year. Suppose they harvest all the corn they need—or nearly all the corn they need—with perhaps only a seven- or eight-million-ton shortfall.''

"Then the deal wouldn't make any sense. Why purchase futures? By the time they came out of the fields, we'd all know the state of the Soviet crop, and their game would be up. So why do such a thing?''

"I can think of two reasons right off the bat. The firs' would be for them not to honor their futures contracts They'd lose their ten percent, but the entire marke would go down the tubes . . . including our business.'

"That doesn't make any sense. What grudge do the Russians have against us?"

"The second would be that they'd go ahead and take delivery on the corn. All of it."

"To dump it back on the market?"

Newman shook his head. "To store it within the Soviet Union. A grain stockpile."

"To what end, for Christ's sake, Paul?"

"A siege?" Newman suggested, his stomach tight.

Saratt said nothing, although his mouth was open.

"We're stockpiling oil in old saltmines as a national crisis reserve. Why not stockpile food?"

"They wouldn't need it. Next spring they'd plant again, and in the fall they'd harvest."

"If they could. If their transportation network was still intact. If their population hadn't been decimated."

"Good Lord, you're talking war!"

"I don't know, Paul. I just don't know, but I think we should do what we can to find out."

"If you make waves, the entire structure could come down around our ears."

"I know it."

"It's crazy," Saratt said.

"Frightening, is more like it."

12

Newman was a pragmatist who made his decisions and accomplished his tasks a step at a time. That, despite the fact his agile mind could grasp dozens of seemingly disconnected events and unrelated details, and intuitively reduce them into recognizable patterns. His mother, who had died a few years after his father, had called this ability, evident since childhood, his "artistic talent." She had always maintained that her son would someday become a great painter, or perhaps even a poet, although she admitted he was nowhere nearly tragic enough for the latter.

His father agreed only insofar as his son's artistic temperament was concerned, but he maintained that such talent was best served in the business world.

"It's the creative ones who amass the fortunes, who build the bridges, or discover the oil, or make the deals," the old man said. "Not the plodders."

Newman stood at his window watching the crew clear the dunnage from the holds of a ship which had come in this morning for powdered milk, as he thought about himself and tried to justify what he was doing.

There had been nothing creative or artistic about his work this day. Through BanLine Shipping, Inc., his subsidiary in Savannah, he had secured three bulk-cargo vessels to carry paper to New York and then come empty down the St. Lawrence to Duluth for corn.

Through Abex in New York he had hired a fourth vessel, carrying flour to Buffalo, to take on corn for shipment to Gdynia in Poland.

From Masters & Kildare, Inc., a nationally recognized farm-survey firm (another of his subsidiaries), he had received the first reports on corn futures in this country; Blencoe, S.A., out of Brussels, had promised its international futures survey within a couple of days.

He had read a report from TradeCon, his financial holding company in Zurich, that another $11.5 million had been transferred from Eurobank in Geneva, bringing the total to well above $20 million.

He had perused masters' reports from eleven vessels now at sea carrying corn, heading toward seven different ports within the Warsaw Pact. He had studied the constantly fluctuating rate schedules of a dozen trucking firms, two river-barge companies, and the railroad.

The Teamsters here in Duluth-Superior were filing a series of grievances with the Port Authority that if left unchecked could blossom into a wildcat strike, so Newman had dictated a letter to Robert LaBatt, the Port Authority director, outlining his concerns and suggestions.

His secretary had secured an appointment for him with Secretary of Agriculture Lundgren at 2:00 P.M. tomorrow and had arranged for the company aircraft to be ready first thing in the morning.

One hour ago he and Saratt had put their heads together to come up with a list of people who would like to see the Newman Company harmed, and in particular Kenneth Newman himself put out of commission. It was a very short list. It did not include Dybrovik or the Russians.

And now it was the end of the day. Nothing essential had been accomplished that any one of his office people could not have managed nicely, and Newman felt a vague sense of dissatisfaction with himself and his work.

Such feelings were rare for him, and he had learned that they indicated he was on the wrong track; that he was ignoring some central problem. Yet he felt somewhat foolish that he had suggested to Saratt the possibility that the Russians were girding for a war.

Stop the deal, a voice at the back of his mind had nagged. Simply pull out. The easy part had been accomplished, or nearly accomplished. Within a month Exportkhleb would have its seven or eight million tons of corn. The big difficulties would come on the futures market, when other grain merchants began realizing that a significant portion of the available world crop had already been spoken for. The waves would begin then; the repercussions would spread like the shock from a nuclear blast. Prices would go wild. Shipping firms would revise their schedules sharply upward. But by then it would be too late. The damage would have been done. And if everything had been laid out correctly, it would be impossible to trace it back to the

Newman Company.

They would be safe. In fact, they would scream market manipulation as loudly as everyone else.

It did not bother Newman that he was violating U.S. antitrust and licensing laws. Food was food, and as long as it was being used ultimately to feed people, it didn't matter to him which people were fed. His job, as he saw it, was merely the redistribution of grain to wherever it was needed, and to make a profit as and where he could.

This deal with Dybrovik was profitable, there was no doubt about that, but the profits would not be excessive. Once the market went wild later this summer, corn prices would skyrocket, but by then he would have already sold his grain at the earlier, lower prices. The market profiteers would come later. They would be the ones to scream the very loudest.

Pull out? To what end, Newman asked himself as he stared blindly out the window. If his foolish fears were in fact groundless, he'd be the man who had backed out of the largest grain deal in history.

If he was right, however, and Exportkhleb was attempting to amass a crisis stockpile of food, then Dybrovik would not be deterred by Newman's refusal to do business. He would simply go to the other independents.

He shook himself out of his contemplations, straightened his tie, grabbed his briefcase, and went out the door.

His secretary was getting ready to leave as well, her typewriter covered. She smiled. "Have a good trip to Washington," she said.

"Thanks. Has Paul left for the evening?"

"I believe he's still in his office," she said, reaching for the telephone.

"Don't call, I'll stop down to see him on my way out."

"Yes, sir," the woman said.

Newman took the elevator to the ground floor, where his two bodyguards were waiting in the reception area. They jumped up when he appeared.

"I'll be just a minute," he said. He went into the trading room, where worldwide grain quantities and prices were constantly monitored, the figures flashed on overhead screens. The large room was mostly in darkness now. The basic work on the Russian purchase was being done by Newman Company subsidiaries around the world so that no suspicion would fall here.

Saratt was in his office at the rear of the room, talking on the telephone. He looked up as Newman came in, said something into the phone, then hung up and got to his feet.

"Ready to call it a day?"

"Just on my way out," Newman said. "I'll call you as soon as I finish with Lundgren tomorrow."

"You're not going to get much out of him."

"Probably not, Paul, but it's worth a try."

Saratt stared at him for a long moment, the expression in his eyes a mixture of concern and skepticism. "You're still worried about Dybrovik?"

Newman nodded. He found himself at this moment unable to share with his old friend the extent of his concern. "If we could get any kind of an indication of the expected Russian corn crop, it's help."

"The President has signed the grain extension with the Russians."

"That's small stuff, and it's in addition to what we're selling them," Newman said.

"Then I don't know what you expect to get from

Lundgren. If the President is convinced the Russians need only ten or fifteen million tons of grain—a big mix, including wheat—then they must believe the Russian shortfall will be normal.''

"Which would prove my point. If they only need ten or fifteen million tons, why order that as well as what Dybrovik wants us to supply?''

Saratt got up and came around his desk to where Newman stood just within the doorway. "We've been friends for a number of years, Kenneth. At the risk of straining that friendship, I have to tell you that you are running scared. I don't think it's just the grain deal with Dybrovik. There's something else eating at you.''

"Lydia hasn't been involved in this at all," Newman flared.

"I didn't mention her name, but since you did I must tell you that she—''

Newman cut him off. "Don't say it, Paul. I told you once before that I wanted you to do whatever you thought was necessary to protect our business, but if it involved Lydia, never to mention it to me.''

"Goddamn it, can't you see what's happening to you?''

"I can see what's happening to *us*, and I don't like it," Newman said harshly, and he could see that the comment had hurt his old friend.

"Talk to Lundgren then, and phone me when you're finished. But for Christ's sake be careful with him. He may be an ass, but he knows the business, and he knows us. If he gets wind of what's going on here, even a whiff of it, he'll scream Justice Department and they'll be on our backs.''

"I'm going for a chat, that's all. Newman Company

is interested in licenses for the new grain extension the President signed.''

Saratt nodded. It was clear from his expression that he wanted very much to say something else, but he was holding back. Newman knew that it concerned Lydia, but he could not bring himself to ask what it was, although he had a fair idea. When Coatsworth's security people had come back here to sweep the office telephones, they had said nothing about his home phones. It was either because they had found Saratt's tap, the one he was using to monitor Lydia's telephone calls (to Buenos Aires?), or it was because they had found nothing.

"Are you staying the night?"

"No. I'm going up to New York to check in with Abex. Roger is becoming concerned that we're not making any direct deals through him."

"You're not going to tell him, are you?"

"No," Newman said. "I'm just going to calm him down."

"Be careful."

"I will."

Back in the reception area, Evans and Humphrey rose to follow him out to the parking lot, and then across town to his home, where they took up position across the street.

He let himself in through the side door from the garage, and Marie met him in the vestibule.

"Good evening, Mr. Newman. Would you care for a drink before dinner?"

"That'd be fine. Where is Mrs. Newman?"

"She said that she would be traveling to Washington with you in the morning, and had some last-minute errands downtown." The woman obviously did not like Lydia.

"Did she say when she'd be home?"

"No, sir," Marie said.

Newman nodded. "I'll take my drink upstairs in my study."

"Very good, sir."

Newman showered and changed, then went into his adjoining study which looked down over the harbor and beyond to Lake Superior, stretching to the eastern horizon. Marie had brought up a snifter and a bottle of cognac. He poured himself a healthy measure, lit a cigarette, and sat down in an easy chair in front of the floor-to-ceiling windows.

"Keep booze out of your office," his father had told him years ago. "Otherwise you'll pour yourself a drink every time you make a deal, and every time a deal falls through. It's the habit that's been the death of more executives than any other cause."

Whenever he was troubled, he thought about his father. Not really a successful man, at least not by his son's present standards, but a man full of the elusive wisdom that could only be gained through hard living.

"The school of hard knocks," his father loved to say. "When the situation around you gets difficult, you have to roll with the punches, but never walk away from a fight. Follow your instincts, but never turn your back."

What about now? Newman wondered.

It was around one in the afternoon, when the Newman Company jet, its twin-eagle logo gleaming on the vertical stabilizer, touched down at Washington's National Airport and taxied to the private aviation terminal.

Two burly men wearing business suits stepped out of the aircraft and sharply scanned the area. Inside, Newman was putting on his jacket.

"You don't have to do this," he said to Lydia, who stood facing him. He had a heavy feeling that he had done the wrong thing.

She smiled sadly. "You're my husband. Naturally I'll help."

Newman had debated with himself last night, as he waited for her to come home, whether or not he should tell her about his deal with Dybrovik. In the end he had decided she would *have* to know something if he was to put an end to an impossible situation: his business partner spying on his wife for the good of their business.

He hadn't told her about that, of course, nor had he told her the extent of the Exportkhleb deal. But he had told her that he was dealing with Dybrovik, and he spoke a little about his fears that the Russians were up to something.

"So what do you expect to find out from the Agriculture Department?"

"Dybrovik wants to purchase a lot of corn from us, in addition to the deal the President has already agreed to. I want to know what the Russians' actual corn shortfall is projected to be. Lundgren should have that information."

"Won't that tip him off that you're up to something?"

"I don't think so. Officially I'm coming to him to inquire about grain licenses with the Soviets. It's information I'd have to know in order to do business with them."

After a moment's hesitation, Lydia had said, "I could probably get that information from Grainex for you."

Grainex was the Vance-Ehrhardt subsidiary in New York City. Like all the larger grain firms, Vance-Ehrhardt, Ltd., had its network of friendly informants within the world's grain-trading bureaus. It was one of the methods of doing business. But among the top half-dozen top companies, Vance-Ehrhardt's information-gathering capabilities were second to none.

"I couldn't ask you to do this," Newman had said, although it was exactly what he had wanted. His deceit, even now, gave him a deep pang of guilt.

"I'll take the plane to New York while you're meeting with Lundgren."

"I'll come up on one of the commuter flights," Newman said.

"Between us we'll find out what's happening."

"Are you sure you want to do this, Lydia?" he had asked a dozen times, and each time she assured him she did.

But now in the airplane, facing her, he could see that she was deeply troubled, and he was sorry that he had involved her. Their relationship was a fragile one at best, and he feared now that he had probably strained it badly.

"I should be up in New York by eight at the latest," he said.

"I'll stay at the Plaza. We can have dinner in our room. We'll have a lot to talk about," Lydia said with a tiny sigh.

Newman took her into his arms, and held her close for a few moments. "I'm sorry, Lydia," he said softly.

"Don't be. You're a grain trader. I knew that when I married you. We practically grew up together. And I love you *for* it, not *despite* it."

13

It was night again, cold and very damp, deep in the forests along the Paraná River. Far to the southeast was Buenos Aires, to the northeast the border with Uruguay, and ten miles to the northwest the Vance-Ehrhardt estate.

Juan Carlos crawled wearily out of his sleeping bag and pulled on his boots before he unzipped the tent flap and crawled outside.

They had been expecting to remain in position for two days. But that had stretched to eight, and it was already July 6. Unless they received their signal to begin this night, it would go into the ninth day. Juan Carlos did not know if he or any of them could stand that.

In the dim light he could see Teva and Eugenio seated around the small kerosene heater, smoking and talking. Although he could not quite hear what they were saying, he could tell by Teva's gestures that she was excited. But then, she was always excited about something.

He relieved himself behind the tent, and he went over to them. They looked up as he approached. Teva's face was bright, and Eugenio's eyes were wide. They were smiling.

"What is it?" Juan Carlos asked.

"It came," Teva bubbled. "We have our signal. We got it tonight."

"The message came? You're sure?" Juan Carlos asked. His bowels suddenly felt loose.

"Just half an hour ago," Eugenio said. "We leave tonight at ten, and strike at one."

"Why didn't you wake me up?" Juan Carlos demanded. It was he who should have taken the message. He was the field commander here.

"Take it easy, Juan," Teva said, reaching up for his hand and pulling him down. She gave him her half-smoked cigarette, and Eugenio poured him a cup of very black, very bitter coffee.

"We wanted to let you sleep as long as you needed to. All of us will need our strength, but especially you," Eugenio said. He was smiling, and for just a moment Juan Carlos wondered if his old friend wasn't being sarcastic. But then the moment passed.

"It is only eight-thirty," Teva said. "We still have an hour and a half before we have to move out. There is plenty of time."

"The others are still asleep?" Juan Carlos asked, looking over his shoulder.

Teva nodded.

"Good. We will let them sleep for another half-hour," Juan Carlos said, somewhat mollified. At least he hadn't been the last to find out that this would be the night of action. He took a deep drag on the cigarette, then sipped at the coffee.

There were seven of them here, including Juan Carlos, Teva, and Eugenio, and seven aboard the river boat that would at this moment be heading up the Paraná toward the Vance-Ehrhardt estate. Two complete cells. Two fighting units, dedicated selflessly to one goal: liberty for Argentines.

Juan Carlos smiled to himself as he thought about the political lectures and jargon. Classrooms and books were one thing, but this now—action in the field—was what it was really all about.

Teva and Eugenio were both looking at him when he glanced up out of his thoughts. He grinned. "It is a good thing we are doing tonight . . . striking a blow for liberty."

"The fucking pigs will run in fear when we are done." Teva spat out the words, her eyes locked suddenly into Juan Carlos'.

He knew the look, and he nodded as he stubbed out the cigarette and put his coffee down.

Without a word he and Teva got to their feet and went back to his tent, where they crawled inside. Juan Carlos zipped the flap.

Teva was breathing hard. Her nostrils flared as she pulled off her fatigue jacket and then her olive-drab T-shirt, exposing her small, firm breasts.

"Hurry, Juan," she said urgently as he began tearing off his clothing. "Jesus and Mary, I need you. Now!"

When they were both nude, they fell into each other's arms on the sleeping bag, and she went crazy, kissing him all over his body, taking him in her mouth, running her tongue around his testicles until he was almost ready to come.

He pushed her over on her back, and bit hard on her breasts as she held his head between her hands, and then he was inside her, penetrating deeper than ever before, her legs up very high, her knees up under his armpits.

He reached under her and grabbed her buttocks, pulling them up to meet his thrusts; faster and harder until her body went rigid, and she let out a stifled scream at the same moment he came, the pleasure coursing through him in waves that seemed as if they'd never end.

When they were finished, they lay in each other's arms, sharing a cigarette. Their coupling had always been harsh and very quick, but afterward they would be tender with each other.

"Juan," she said, "do you ever think about dying?"

He looked at her. "All the time," he said softly. "I know that I won't live to be an old man and have grandchildren and sit in the sun at the park."

"That doesn't really bother me," she said after a moment or two of reflection, "even though I know it is probably true." She raised herself on one elbow, her breasts rising and falling as she breathed. "But if something should happen to either or both of us tonight, I want you to know that I love you."

Juan Carlos smiled. "Nothing will happen to us, Teva, not tonight. But when it does, I want you to know that I love you, too."

"Thank you," she said, lying back.

They headed out at 10:00 P.M. sharp, after dismantling the tents and heaters, and burying them away from the camp in the forest. They would no longer be needing them.

Each of them carried an Israeli Uzi submachine gun with its folding stock and several extra forty-round clips of ammunition, plus four F31 American fragmentation grenades. They were dressed in British commando camouflage fatigues and wore American jungle-combat boots.

Juan Carlos, carrying the two-channel radio the little man had supplied them, took the lead. Within fifteen minutes they had settled into a quiet, distance-consuming pace, roughly parallel to and a mile up from the river.

As they marched, he reviewed each step of their penetration of the Vance-Ehrhardt estate. At their second meeting, the little man had produced a scale model of the estate, pointing out the routes in and out, Jorge Vance-Ehrhardt's private quarters, and the relationship of the main house to the other buildings, the river, and the airstrip to the north.

There were armed guards on the grounds and within the main house itself, he had told them, but fourteen trained soldiers, armed with grenades and automatic weapons, would cut through them with little or no trouble.

"The difficulty in this assignment is getting to Vance-Ehrhardt without harming him," the little man had said. "If he is killed, his value to you as a hostage will of course be ruined."

"We're not going to let him live," Juan Carlos had protested.

"Of course not," the little man had replied. "But we must get him out alive in order to make the recordings of his pleas for mercy. Afterward, when he has served his purpose, he will be disposed of.''

They had all smiled at such brilliant logic and looked forward to setting their plans into motion. That time had come at last, and Juan Carlos could feel the old combination of fear and pride marching with him.

Around 11:00 P.M., they stopped for their last cigarette and something to eat, as an airliner from Buenos Aires roared far overhead on its way north, probably to Miami.

Before too long now, Juan Carlos thought, he and Teva would be on such an airplane. Only they would be traveling to Libya, to safety, to a heroes' welcome.

He could almost taste that welcome now, the anticipation was so intense within him. Afterward, after a long vacation, they would receive more training, and they would be given another assignment. Possibly back in Argentina, but possibly in another part of the world.

"You must always remember, Juan Carlos," his Libyan instructor had told him, "that liberty is not exclusively an Argentine word. It is the international battle cry."

After this evening, then, he and Teva and possibly Eugenio would be joining the international fraternity of terrorists. The prospect filled Juan Carlos with a huge sense of importance.

"Are we ready?" Eugenio asked at his shoulder, and he looked up, then nodded and got to his feet.

"From this point on there will be absolutely no noise, he said to the group. "No talking, no noise whatsoever. Each of you knows his or her job. The strike begins at one o'clock A.M. By one-thirty, we should be well away, and by three-thirty back to our camp for the rendezvous with the helicopter."

"Libertad," Teva said softly after a moment of silence.

"Libertad," they all repeated, and Juan Carlos headed out, Teva directly behind him, Eugenio bringing up the rear.

It was nearly one in the morning, and although Jorgé Vance-Ehrhardt was tired, he had not been able to sleep all night. For the past hour or so, he had been sitting out on the south veranda, smoking and sipping a light red Portuguese wine.

From behind the house, away from the river, he could hear the horses in the stables snorting from time to time, and in the opposite direction, toward the forest, the occasional night hunting cry of a jungle bird.

Vance-Ehrhardt had many things on his mind this night, chief among them his daughter and her husband. His people at Grainex in New York City had telephoned this afternoon with the disturbing news that Lydia had visited their statistical crop-survey department. They had, of course, told her she would have to get authorization for any inquiries directly from her father, and all evening he had expected her to telephone. But she hadn't.

The most disturbing aspect of the entire situation was not Lydia's obvious wish to help her husband in his business by making use of her Vance-Ehrhardt birthright; it was the nature of the information she was seeking. She had asked for Soviet crop projections, especially corn.

Rumors had been flying of a large Soviet grain buy. No one, not even Grainex, had been able to verify the rumors, nor were they able to pinpoint who was doing the buying.

But someone was active—overly active. And Lydia's visit suggested that it was Newman.

Even thinking about the ingrate raised Vance-Ehrhardt's blood pressure. Newman had stolen the Vance-Ehrhardt respect, some of its business, and finally Lydia.

He shook his head sadly. The fact of the matter was, he still liked and respected Newman. It was a terrible burden he carried.

He got tiredly to his feet. At the edge of the veranda, he leaned his weight against the marble balustrade and stared out toward the jungle, although he wasn't really looking at anything in particular. Instead, his mind had turned to another worrisome topic—violence. The explosion at Cargill's New Orleans facility and the brutal murder of Gérard Louis Dreyfus.

Both the elevator and the man had been vulnerable; both had been needlessly exposed to just that kind of risk. And yet, what kind of sick world was this in which a man and his achievements could not be safe?

Here in Argentina, everyone understood violence. It was a nation of violence, on a continent of violence. But Europe and North America were different. Supposedly more civilized.

Vance-Ehrhardt sighed deeply, then turned back into the house, passing Alberto, one of the outside guards he had put on two days ago.

"Good evening, sir," the man said, but Vance-Ehrhardt was lost in thought and did not hear him.

Inside, he trudged upstairs to his second-floor bedroom, where he crawled into bed next to his wife, Margarita, who was sound asleep.

The Cargill elevator, the murder of Louis Dreyfus, and now Lydia's strange inquiries; all those troublesome thoughts intertwined in his mind as he tried for sleep.

Moments later, an explosion shattered the still night air, followed closely by the sound of gunfire. Vance-Ehrhardt, his heart racing, jumped up from the bed, threw on his robe, and got his loaded automatic from the nightstand.

"Jorge?" his wife cried out. "What is it?"

"Stay there," Vance-Ehrhardt snapped, heading out the door. "No matter what happens, don't come out of this room."

Juan Carlos had waited with his people at the edge of the forest until the explosion on the river had come, and seconds later he led them directly across the wide lawn.

They had expected little or no resistance from outside the house, but within the first thirty seconds Eugenio and one of the others had gone down, and the rest of them had taken refuge behind the statues that dotted the lawn.

Without hesitation, the others laid down a heavy line of fire along the front of the house, tossing the fragmentation grenades, which sprayed a huge area with deadly shrapnel. Juan Carlos switched the radio first to Channel A, which was monitored by the waiting helicopter crew, and then to B, which was being monitored by the cell on the river, and shouted the contingency code: "Helpmate one! Helpmate one!"

Within moments the gunfire from the river area intensified. He patiently counted to sixty, then gave the order to move forward.

It was too bad about Eugenio, he thought as he ran.

He fired, then ducked behind another marble statue.
Run, fire, cover. But they had all understood the risk.
Eugenio had taken two hits, one in his chest and one in
his face, either of them certainly fatal. But their instructions had been precise: If a comrade goes down, he will
be left mercifully dead for the protection of all of us. If
he is not dead by enemy gunfire, the unit commander
will make sure he is dead. He was glad it had not been
necessary to finish the job with Eugenio.

Within three minutes the firing from the river ceased,
and as Juan Carlos, his remaining three soldiers, and
Teva reached the veranda, the river cell was coming up
the path on the run.

"Keep the alternate path open," Juan Carlos radioed
on B. "We're going in."

"Roger," the hand-held radio blared.

They scrambled over the balustrade, crossed the
veranda where four of Vance-Ehrhardt's bodyguards
lay dead, and crashed through the French doors.

Two men on the stairs leading to the second floor
opened fire; Juan Carlos and Teva returned it. The two
men slammed up against the banister, one of them going
over it and hitting the parquet floor with a dull thud, the
other slumping down, then tumbling down the stairs.

One of Juan Carlos' men had gone down, and
without hesitation he turned and fired a short burst into
his head.

"Teva and I will go up for Vance-Ehrhardt," he said
to his remaining two soldiers. "Keep this exit open, no
matter what!"

Teva started up the stairs. Vance-Ehrhardt appeared
in the upper corridor, and he raised his automatic and
fired two shots. The first went wide, but the second hit

her in the right shoulder, just below her collarbone.

She let out a small cry and fell back against the banister. Juan Carlos, halfway up the stairs, raised his submachine gun to fire. But he hesitated as Vance-Ehrhardt stepped back, seemingly having trouble with his gun.

Juan Carlos leaped the rest of the way up the stairs and was on the older man before he could fire his automatic, knocking the gun from his hand.

"Jorge?" a woman's voice called from farther down the corridor.

There was gunfire from below.

"Run, Margarita," Vance-Ehrhardt shouted, but Juan Carlos shoved him aside.

"Out here, woman, or this man dies!"

"Jorge," the woman screamed.

"Move it! Now!" Juan Carlos shouted, and Vance-Ehrhardt's wife, in her nightdress, no slippers on her feet, came out into the corridor and into her husband's arms.

"Downstairs! Now!" Juan Carlos snapped. He was sweating and his heart was hammering out of his chest. He was riding high.

As they started down the steps, Teva was getting to her feet and raising her weapon.

"Are you all right?" Juan Carlos asked.

"I'll live," she said weakly.

"Kill her!" one of the men below shouted.

Teva swiveled around and fired two short bursts from her hip, slamming both men backward out the remains of the French doors.

"Bastards," she spat.

Juan Carlos laughed out loud as they herded Vance-

Ehrhardt and his wife the rest of the way downstairs. At the door he stopped and brought out his radio.

"We have our objective. Can we come?"

"We have the path," the radio blared.

Juan Carlos shoved Vance-Ehrhardt and his wife outside and helped Teva as they went across the veranda, down the steps, and around to the path that led to the airstrip. They were met fifty yards from the house by four men from the other cell, who without a word grabbed Vance-Ehrhardt and his wife, and the eight of them hurried down the path as their helicopter, running without lights, touched down.

They had done it! They had actually done it, despite the heavy resistance. They were home free!

14

It was late, nearly four in the afternoon, when William Bormett left the podium and went back to his seat at the speakers' table. His audience in the big hall, mostly young agriculture students, was standing and applauding him. Each of the four previous days had seen the same conclusion. The same beginning, for that matter. In the morning he was introduced, and immediately he launched into the story of the Bormett farms, beginning with his grandfather's immigration to Iowa. By late afternoon he had brought his audience up to date, including his plans to increase his land to corn to twenty thousand acres.

Dr. Nikolai Lubiako, dean of the School of Agricultural Engineering here at the University of Moscow, had gotten up from his seat. As Bormett sat down, he raised his arms for the applause to end.

"An amazing achievement," his unamplified voice thundered throughout the great hall. "A tribute to the ongoing dedication of a family to agriculture."

Catherine was seated in the front row, off to one side, and Bormett winked at her. She winked back, although it was obvious that she was very tired.

This trip had been hard on her. The food had not agreed with her system, and their room at the Metropole Hotel downtown, although nice by Soviet standards, was not up to hers when it came to cleanliness, so she really had not been able to relax.

For the first couple of days she had faithfully attended his morning and afternoon lectures, but then, since each day's talks would be the same, she had gone sightseeing and shopping with their Intourist guide in the mornings. Now, at the end of the fifth day, with several more days stretching ahead of them, it looked as if she wanted to do nothing more than go back to their room, take a nice hot bath (if the water pressure was up tonight), and crawl into bed.

Bormett couldn't have agreed more. Although his reception here had surprised—and in some ways exhilarated—him, he too was tired.

"This afternoon we have a special surprise for you," Dr. Lubiako was saying, and Bormett looked up as a tall, blond young man left the audience and joined the dean at the podium.

"Here with us today we have Arkadi Fedorovich Kedrov, a distinguished man whom many of you know as the special agriculture correspondent for *Izvestia*. Some of you, perhaps, do not know that he is a graduate of our school and has traveled extensively through the American farmbelt states of Iowa, Kansas,

Nebraska, Wisconsin, and Minnesota.''

The applause was thunderous, and Bormett was confused. He hadn't been expecting this. At this point Dr. Lubiako usually made a number of nice remarks about him, and then dismissed the session. Afterward, there was half an hour or so of individual questions from students who had remained behind, and then he and Katy returned to their hotel for dinner or attended a reception the university arranged for them.

Two students brought in another podium, which they set up a few feet from the one in front of Dr. Lubiako and Kedrov. Lubiako gestured for Bormett to come up.

Bewildered, he got to his feet amidst more applause, and approached them.

"I am very pleased to meet you, Mr. Bormett," Kedrov said, smiling.

"I am sorry, Mr. Bormett, for this last-minute surprise, but Arkadi Fedorovich was kind enough to break away from his very busy day to join us," Dr. Lubiako said.

"We will keep it very short," Kedrov said. "No longer than a half-hour. You must be very tired."

"I am," Bormett mumbled, still mystified at exactly what was going on. "But we're keeping what to a half-hour?"

"Oh, please forgive me," Dr. Lubiako said. "I am sorry. Arkadi Fedorovich here has agreed to an informal debate with you on the hybrid issue."

"What?" Bormett asked, stepping back.

Kedrov reached out and drew him back. "Dr. Lubiako is a very old friend, but like many academicians he tends to make everything seem more formal than it is. I had hoped that you and I could speak to the young people here about hybrids. Corn, if you'd like. I'm sure that you could say much about the subject."

"I'm very tired," Bormett said. There was no way he wanted to get into any kind of debate with these people.

"I understand, sir," Kedrov said smoothingly. His breath smelled of cloves. "And I promise you I will hold it to no more than thirty minutes."

"I still don't see what you want from me."

Kedrov glanced at Dr. Lubiako. "I'll just ask you a few questions, and we can discuss the answers."

"What kind of questions?" Bormett asked.

The audience had sat perfectly quiet throughout all of this, and Bormett felt ill at ease standing here like this.

"Well, I, for one, am worried about hybrids. I think we should move away from them."

"Impossible," Bormett said. He was on very familiar territory now. "Without hybrids—at least in corn—our output would drop by seventy percent, and the chance for corn blight and other diseases would be raised dramatically. All modern farming would come to an end."

Kedrov laughed and slapped Bormett on the shoulder as he turned to face the audience. Dr. Lubiako backed off and took his seat.

"Mr. Bormett has kindly consented to discuss the question of hybrids with us this afternoon," Kedrov said, and there was more applause. "When I told him I thought we should move away from the trend toward hybrid planting, he disagreed wholeheartedly."

There was a smattering of applause, and Kedrov turned back to Bormett. "Won't you share your views with us?"

For just a moment Bormett felt very uncomfortable.

But then he looked down at Catherine, who was smiling, and she nodded for him to go ahead. It *was* a subject that he was familiar with.

"Without hybrid seeds," he began, "farming would be pushed back fifty years."

"Could you be more specific, Mr. Bormett?" Kedrov asked.

"As I told you just a moment ago, without hybrids the output of my farm would drop by as much as seventy percent. And unless the weather remained nearly perfect for the entire growing season, which it never does in Iowa, then there would be a very good chance for disaster."

"But aren't we inviting disaster by the very use of hybrids?" Kedrov asked.

"I don't understand."

"The genetic base of our major food crops the world over is narrowing, Mr. Bormett. Narrowing at a frightening rate. Most Western agriculture—and I'm talking now about the major crops: corn, wheat, and soybeans —is based on less than thirty species."

"If that is the correct number, those hybrids have been engineered for exactly the soil and climate in which they will be grown. Hybridization is why, in the United States, we will produce four hundred million tons of corn this year."

"If all goes well, Mr. Bormett," Kedrov rejoined. "If all goes well. Diversity is the first line of defense, however, against diseases and pests. Look at the outbreak of wheat stem rust in 1954, or the southern leaf blight in 1970 in which tens of thousands of acres of corn were destroyed. All because the acres were planted with a single hybrid that happened to be susceptible."

Bormett had to smile at the simplistic view. "Surely, as an agriculture expert, you understand that there is no such thing as a guaranteed crop. Even the best of hybrids can be attacked. But no more so than a natural variety."

"And your solution to that problem is . . .?"

"New and more hardy hybrids."

"Hybrids, which cannot reproduce themselves, cannot be saved for seed? Hybrids that are totally dependent upon fertilizers and pesticides?"

"Chemically aided farming is a fact of life," Bormett argued, "hand in hand with genetic engineering. Using these advances, the United States has become the breadbasket of the world."

The audience was utterly silent.

"Your operation, Mr. Bormett, is dependent totally upon Exxon and Standard Oil and other gigantic conglomerates. Your chemicals are petrochemicals. Your farming is based on oil, our dwindling resource. When the oil runs out, and your hybrids can no longer survive, then what will happen to us all, Mr. Bormett?"

The applause was thunderous once again, and for the next twenty minutes Kedrov delivered a diatribe on the foolishness of Western farmers, calling for the Soviet farmer to lead the way back to diverse, organic farming, ending at last with the remark: "Our only salvation against certain worldwide famine is varietal planting."

Bormett was given his chance for a final statement, but he was able to do little more than repeat what he had already said about output per acre, and the old saw about corn being knee high by the Fourth of July.

The applause came again, and Dr. Lubiako and Kedrov shook his hand and congratulated him as the students began filing out of the hall.

"You had me nearly speechless when you told us that the United States was the breadbasket of the world, because it's so true, and I really had no defense," Kedrov gushed.

"Brilliant, Mr. Bormett, simply brilliant," Lubiako said, beaming. "One of the very reasons our selection committee chose you for this program."

"There will be a little gathering at my home outside the city this evening," Kedrov said. "I would be very pleased if you would be able to join us."

"I don't think so," Bormett said. Catherine had joined them on the platform, and he looked at her.

"Please do, it would be a great honor for us all," Lubiako said.

"Go ahead, William," Catherine said.

"I thought you were tired."

"I am. I'll stay at the hotel and go to bed early."

"I'm not going to leave you alone."

"Nonsense," she insisted. "I need the rest without you prowling around the room all night."

"Then it's settled," Kedrov said smoothly. "I will send a car for you at seven. See you then." He turned and left the platform.

"A brilliant man," Dr. Lubiako said. "You'll enjoy his little gathering tonight. Always very interesting people."

Bormett insisted on having dinner with his wife before he left, and when he was ready to leave she had already taken her bath, and had gotten into bed.

"Have a good time, William, but don't be too late."

"I'll be back as soon as I can get away," Bormett

said, kissing his wife on the forehead. He took the elevator down to the lobby, where a chauffeur and his Intourist guide were waiting for him.

The evening was warm, and the drive north out of the city pleasant. The Intourist guide pointed out various buildings and institutions, including the All-Union Agricultural Exhibition which Dr. Lubiako had promised to show him over the weekend.

Beyond that, the road changed to a narrow black-topped highway that ran through birch forests in full bloom now, the moonlight shimmering on the white bark, making it seem like an enchanted tunnel.

"Mr. Kedrov is a very influential man," the Intourist guide, a young, good-looking woman, said to him. From her briefcase she pulled out a bottle of bourbon and two small glasses. She poured him a drink. "The past few days have been a strain on you, I can tell," she said gently.

Bormett took his drink as she poured herself one, then raised her glass in a toast. "To friendship," she said.

They clicked glasses, and drank. "I don't think I can remember your name . . . I've been so busy."

"I am Raya, and I'm an agriculture student at the university."

"You are?"

"Yes," she said earnestly. "I have listened to each of your talks. It must be fascinating, operating such a huge farm back in Iowa." She laid a hand on his knee.

Bormett looked a little more closely at her, and she smiled, showing perfectly white teeth.

"Forgive me if I seem a bit forward, but I've always been attracted to big men like you," she said.

Bormett didn't know what the hell to say or do. And yet he found himself enjoying her attention for now. As long as it didn't get out of hand, he'd go along with her.

He drank the rest of his bourbon and held out his glass for more.

"Now tell me something about yourself," she said as she poured him another drink.

They drank and chatted for the rest of the hour-long trip out to Kedrov's country home. By the time they arrived, Raya seemed quite tipsy and Bormett felt light-headed himself.

Inside, soft music was playing, there was food and drink laid out on tables, and a dozen men and women were dancing or sitting around talking.

Kedrov and Lubiako met them at the door, introduced Bormett around to the other guests, whose names and positions he would never remember, and within a half an hour he found himself dancing closely with Raya. She reminded him in many ways of what Catherine had been like as a young woman.

In between dances, Raya would pour Bormett another drink, and quite soon he relaxed, no longer giving a "good goddamn," as he told her, "how drunk he was, how late it was, or where he was."

The rest of the evening was sketchy in Bormett's mind, except that some time after midnight he followed Raya up to one of the bedrooms because she said she needed help with something. Once there, she closed and locked the door, then took off her clothes and lay down on the bed, her legs spread.

"Please, William," her sensuous voice penetrated the mist in his brain. "Please."

He undressed, except for his socks, and got into bed

with her. She pushed him over on his back and took him in her mouth, and for the next hour they did things together that he had never even thought of doing with Catherine. All of it excellent, all of it extremely pleasurable, and all of it without a thought of his wife.

Bormett woke at eight on Saturday morning back in his own bed at the hotel, with a splitting headache and a very foul taste in his mouth.

Catherine stood over the bed, a steaming cup of coffee in her hand and a rueful smile on her lips. "That must have been quite a party," she said.

He sat up, his head nearly splitting apart. "Oh, God," he moaned.

She laughed. "Dr. Lubiako wasn't in much better condition that you, but he spent at least ten minutes apologizing for bringing you home so late."

Bormett looked up at her, about to ask what time Dr. Lubiako had brought him back, when he suddenly remembered just what it was he had done, and his heart skipped a beat.

"Well, it serves you right to suffer like this," Catherine said. She handed him his coffee. "Dr. Lubiako called ten minutes ago and said that, even though there's no lecture this morning, you're to come over to the university as soon as you're ready—and I'd add, able. Someone there would like to meet with you. A farm region commander, or something like that."

"I don't think so," Bormett said.

"Raya is picking me up in the lobby in a couple of minutes. We're going shopping. We'll meet you for late lunch back here."

Bormett's stomach flipped over at Raya's name, and

he could feel the blood rushing to his ears. Christ, what had he done? What was Lubiako thinking about him now? How could he face Raya, let alone Katy?

Catherine pecked her husband on the cheek and went to the door. "A university car and driver are waiting for you downstairs. Don't keep them waiting, William," she said brightly.

For several long minutes, Bormett sat in bed, sipping his coffee and thinking with great shame of what he had done last night. In all his years with Katy he had never been unfaithful. Not once. Until now.

He dragged himself out of bed, showered and dressed, and went downstairs.

At the university, Dr. Lubiako was in his office waiting for him, a bright smile on his face.

"Good morning, my old friend," he boomed jovially. "How do you feel?"

"Not well," Bormett said, sitting down. "I would like to talk with you."

"Of course, and I with you, but at this moment there is someone else here who would very much like to speak with you."

Bormett started to rise.

"No, no," Lubiako said, getting to his feet. "You stay here and use my office. I will go fetch our visitor, and you two can have a nice long talk. Afterwards, I believe you will be meeting your wife for lunch."

Lubiako went out, and a few seconds later a little man with large dark eyes and a swarthy complexion came in, a smile on his face. He was dressed in some kind of uniform, and he carried a manila envelope.

"Good morning, Mr. Bormett," he said.

"Good morning, Mr. . . ." Bormett trailed off.

"My name is of no importance." The little man perched on the edge of the desk just a foot away from Bormett. "I think I will be able to offer some assistance to you."

Bormett had a funny feeling in the pit of his stomach. Whatever it was the little man was going to tell him wasn't going to be pleasant.

"I've come to see you this morning because I would like to do a little horse trading with you. I think that is the proper term." The little man opened the manila envelope and extracted a dozen large glossy photos. He handed them to Bormett, whose heart nearly stopped.

They were pictures of him and Raya in bed. He looked ridiculous in one of the shots; he looked disgusting in some of the others.

Katy could never be allowed to see these. Never in a million years. It would be the end of their marriage. The end of everything. He glanced up. "What do you want?"

"I need a favor, Mr. Bormett. Not a very large favor, and certainly nothing illegal by your own country's laws. I'm not, as you may fear, trying to recruit you to spy for the Soviet Union. But you can be of some small help to me."

NIGHTMARE

Whether at Naishápúr or Babylon,
Whether the Cup with sweet or bitter run,
  The Wine of Life keeps oozing drop by drop,
The Leaves of Life keep falling one by one.

—Rubáiyát of Omar Khayyám

"Something damned funny is going on," Curtis Lundgren said. He and Michael McCandless were having drinks in a dark corner of one of the Watergate lounges.

"Why would I lie to you, Curt?"

Lundgren waved his cigarette vaguely. "Oh, I believe you, all right. You'd have no reason to make up a bull-shit story like that. But among other things, it's damned funny the President never passed your report on to me. Damned funny."

"It may just have slipped his mind."

"I doubt it. But that's not all," Lundgren said. He leaned forward, and his voice took on a conspiratorial tone. "I know it won't come as any great revelation to you, Michael, but the fact of the matter is, neither of us is very well liked at the White House."

McCandless started to object, but Lundgren held him off.

"The only reason I've still got my job is that the old man doesn't want to rock the boat at just this moment. He and Wellerman have got something cooking, and they're too busy right now to bother with people like us."

McCandless just looked at Lundgren. He had gotten the same impression himself, except that he included his own boss, the DCI, in the presidential circle. Something

193

definitely was up, but no one was talking about it.

"This is going to become a political bombshell in the fall. I tried to tell that to the President."

"Don't I know it," Lundgren said. "If the Russians harvest all the grain you say they've planted, our farmers will go down the tubes . . . literally down the tubes."

"The latest SPEC-IV *satellite data show the crops are coming up. The weather over there has been holding so far, despite predictions to the contrary. Another couple of months or so, and even a hard, early winter won't put too big a dent in their harvests."*

"But the Russians are buying more grain, you do know that."

McCandless nodded. "I read the President's announcement. But it's only in small amounts. Probably just to cover themselves in case they do have trouble getting the grain out of the fields."

"That's just it. I think they may be up to something else. Do you know what Exportkhleb is?"

McCandless shook his head.

"It's the Soviet grain-trading bureau. Any grain bought or sold by the Russians goes through Export-khleb. If it's a big deal, it goes through one Delos Fedor Dybrovik."

McCandless nodded. What was the man getting at?

"Dybrovik has been seen in and out of Geneva. And whenever that man is on the move, it usually means something very big is in the wind. But so far there's been nothing—and I mean absolutely nothing. Except for Kenneth Newman."

It was another unfamiliar name to McCandless, and he said so.

"They call him the Marauder. A silly title actually, but from what I know of him he's definitely earned it. He's an independent grain dealer. Works mostly out of Duluth, Minnesota, but he has offices in New York and, it's rumored, blind subsidiaries in damned near every major city in the world."

"He's big."

"Not as big as a McMillan of Cargill, let's say, or a Louis Dreyfus."

McCandless sat forward at those names. "Wait a minute," he said.

Lundgren smiled, the grin feral. "I've struck a nerve, perhaps?"

"Cargill's New Orleans elevator center exploded. Arson. A hundred forty people killed."

Lundgren nodded, still grinning.

"And Louis Dreyfus—one of their chief executives was assassinated in France."

Again Lundgren nodded. "Then there's Vance-Ehrhardt in Buenos Aires."

"Jorge Vance-Ehrhardt and his wife were just kidnapped! It was on the wire Friday," McCandless said, stunned. He looked up. "But what about Newman? Has something happened to him as well?"

"He's dealt with Dybrovik before. And Thursday—just hours before Vance-Ehrhardt was snatched—Newman came to see me, asking about Soviet crop projections."

"What'd you tell him?"

"Not a thing. He wouldn't play ball with me. I was willing to trade him information, but he was Mr. Innocence."

"You think he has something to do with Cargill,

Louis Dreyfus, and Vance-Ehrhardt?''

''Who knows, Michael, who knows? The man is certainly capable of it,'' Lundgren said. Again he sat forward. He lowered his voice. ''What I need is a big favor from you. I think, between the two of us, we can give the President something he cannot ignore.''

''Go ahead,'' McCandless said cautiously.

''I want Newman. I want to know what he's up to. I want to know if there is any connection at the moment between him and Dybrovik.''

McCandless nodded. ''It shouldn't be too difficult.''

''Another interesting little tidbit. You'll never guess who Newman is married to.''

McCandless couldn't.

''Lydia Vance-Ehrhardt.''

''The same family?''

Lundgren nodded, and then laughed out loud. ''The same.''

15

Throughout this period Kenneth Newman would remember the feeling of fatalism that had come to him with the kidnapping of Jorge and Margarita Vance-Ehrhardt. It was a time of high drama and great emotion which was made somehow unreal by the curious sensation that he was an observer at a particularly bad play.

The actors were there in front of him, moving through their carefully prepared stage directions, voicing their patiently written lines. And no matter what he did or didn't do, he would not affect the certain outcome by one whit.

The sensation was doubly curious because it was complete. Not only was he an observer, but he as an observer was acutely conscious that he had his own life as well; that at any moment he could simply get up from his seat and walk out into the real world. His own real world.

A strong sense of interest (there were those who called it perversity) made him want to stay to the end. The actors, after all, had their own lives beyond the drama of the stage, and he wanted to stick around long enough to discover what they were, and perhaps help the performers through their post-production blues.

It was a few minutes before eleven on the morning of July 12 when the car carrying Newman from the Vance-Ehrhardt estate raced through Buenos Aires and came to a halt in front of the Federal District Police Headquarters.

Humphrey, one of Newman's bodyguards, leaped out of the car as Evans got out on the other side. Both of them scanned the street before Humphrey opened the door for Newman, who got out and strode across the wide sidewalk and into the building.

Two armed guards flanked a young, uniformed man seated at a reception desk. He looked up as Newman's heels echoed loudly on the marble floor of the very busy ground floor.

"Señor?" the young man asked pleasantly. The guards had stiffened to attention when they realized Newman, an obvious foreigner, had brought two armed men into the building with him.

"I have an appointment with Capitán Perés," Newman said.

"Your name, señor, *por favor*."

"Kenneth Newman."

The young man picked up the telephone, spoke in rapid Spanish, and then nodded up at one of the policemen. "Escort Señor Newman upstairs."

Telling his men to wait in the lobby, Newman followed the policeman to a private elevator around the corner. On the fifth floor another burly, dark-skinned armed guard took over, escorting him down a wide corridor to an office that looked out toward the Plaza del Congreso, behind which the Argentine government met.

It was a large room dominated by an immense leather-topped desk, behind which sat one of the most obese men Newman had ever seen. The fat hung on him in huge folds, and his face was so grossly bloated that his eyes and mouth were little more than indentations. He got ponderously to his feet and moved like a battleship around the desk, extending his massive paw.

"Señor Newman, I am so very pleased to meet you at last. I am Reynaldo Perés, captain of police." The man's voice was gentle, belying his great size.

Newman shook his hand. "Thanks for seeing me on such short notice. I know how busy you must be."

"Yes, it is a horrible tragedy, for which I feel personally responsible." He motioned for Newman to have a seat, then went back behind his desk and sank into his chair.

"How so?"

"I had spoken at great length with Señor Vance-Ehrhardt, begging him to increase his security measures. A perimeter fence with infrared monitoring devices could have saved him."

"Then you should hold yourself blameless."

Captain Perés smiled. "Very generous of you, sir, and yet I cannot help but feel responsible. It was up to me to make certain that the Montoneros were kept under control. Even now we are rounding up known members." The big man sighed deeply. "But, alas, it is like closing the barn door after the horses have fled, as you say."

"Has any contact been made? Or any ransom demands?" Newman asked.

"None, but contact will come. And let me assure you, we will find and punish them. But before they are put on trial, we will find out who ordered and engineered this cowardly attack."

Newman felt a cold wind. "You don't believe it was simply an act of terrorism, then?"

Perés held his silence for a moment. His eyes narrowed. "We will know better when a ransom demand is finally made. But certain factors have been brought to my attention."

"Anything I can help with?" Newman asked. "I was a friend of the Vance-Ehrhardt family."

"*Was*, Señor Newman?"

Newman had the distinct impression Perés was playing some kind of game with him. "As you probably know, I am married to Jorge's daughter, Lydia. As you also probably know, the family did not exactly approve of the marriage."

Perés nodded sagely, as if Newman had just given him the theory of the world in twenty-five words or less. "Isn't it also true, Señor Newman, that you worked for the Vance-Ehrhardts for some years? Were in fact a student and then a close personal friend of Jorge himself?"

"Yes, that is true."

"Is it also not true that when you opened your own business, you . . . shall we say . . . persuaded a number of Vance-Ehrhardt's business associates to come along with you?"

Newman smiled. "It is a fact of doing business, captain. I did not steal them away, I merely offered them better deals. The decision was theirs."

"Is kidnapping also a way of doing business?"

Newman wasn't really surprised at the question. He had felt it coming from the moment he walked into the room. "It was I who requested this meeting, Captain Perés."

"Clever, perhaps?"

"Concerned that I might be able to offer some help."

Perés sat forward in his chair, his hands folded together on the desk. "I would be most interested to hear what you might have to say."

"In the United States last week, an arsonist destroyed a major grain-elevator complex owned by the Cargill Company. In France a couple of days later, Gérard Louis Dreyfus, the head of a very large grain-trading house, was assassinated."

"Interesting," Perés said. "And you are suggesting now that Vance-Ehrhardt's kidnapping is part of some worldwide plot?"

"It is possible."

"Who has the most to gain from all this activity?"

"I do," Newman said. "That is to say, my company does."

Perés seemed to contemplate that for a few seconds. "It is why you have brought bodyguards with you?"

"They were my wife's idea," Newman said. "And now, on reflection, I expect she was prudent in hiring them."

"I see," Perés drew the words out, studying his hands. He looked up, a hard glint in his eyes. "Why is it you truly requested this interview with me, Señor Newman? As I have said, I am a busy man."

"I sincerely would like to help my wife's family."

"Then return to the United States. Take your wife with you, if she will go, and leave us to our troubles. We neither need nor want you here."

Perés got to his feet and came around his desk as Newman got up. "I would like you gone by this time tomorrow. I am sure the family will understand—those of them who care, that is."

"What . . .?" Newman began.

"Goodbye, Señor Newman," Perés said firmly.

Taking the elevator back down to the first floor, Newman was wondering what Perés had meant. *If she will go?* And he wondered why the man hadn't pressed him about the Cargill and Louis Dreyfus business. Lost in thought, he did not notice the frank looks of animosity he elicited as he crossed the lobby and headed out the door, but he noticed his bodyguards falling in behind him and wished the hell they were someplace else right now. Even Duluth.

"Where to now, Mr. Newman?" Humphrey asked.

Newman looked up. "Home," he said. "I mean, the Vance-Ehrhardt estate."

It took an hour to drive back out to the estate, and Newman was lost in thought for the entire trip.

Perés was one of the most powerful men in the city of Buenos Aires, and among the most influential men in the federal government. "Buenos Aires and its surroundings belong to Reynaldo Perés," he had heard one of Lydia's uncles say. The Vance-Ehrhardt family was well known here. So what did Perés know about Lydia that Newman didn't?

At the Vance-Ehrhardt access road, the car was met by half a dozen armed men, standing around two cars and a jeep.

"Do you know any of these people, Mr. Newman?" Evans asked as they approached.

Newman sat forward, looking out as they pulled up. One of them was Simon Vance-Ehrhardt, Lydia's uncle. He had never seen the others.

"I know the one in the safari jacket. He's a Vance-Ehrhardt."

"I don't like this, sir."

"We'll just see what they want," Newman said. As he started to get out, Simon and two of the others, their rifles raised, came toward the car.

Newman's bodyguards reached for their guns, but Newman held them back.

"Turn around and get the hell out of here," Simon Vance-Ehrhardt snarled, stopping a few feet away.

"I've come for Lydia," Newman said. He didn't like the looks of this at all. Simon's jaw was tight, and the cords stood out on his neck.

"Leave while you are still able!"

"Not without my wife, Simon."

The man raised his rifle higher and flipped the safety off. Instantly, Evans and Humphrey had their weapons out, safeties off.

Simon laughed. "Two against six. Not very good odds."

"No. So you will either kill me now, or let me see Lydia."

"Bastard," Simon hissed. "She is not here."

"Where is she?" Newman demanded.

"Gone."

"Where?"

"Into the city."

"The office?"

Simon nodded.

Newman stared at him for several long seconds. "Whatever you think about me, Simon, you're wrong. You are all dreadfully wrong. I wanted to beat Jorge at business, but not like this. I've come here to help."

"I am rapidly losing what little control I possess, you gringo son of a whore. Leave now while you are still able."

Newman shook his head in sadness. Ten years ago Simon had been one of his favorites.

"Where are my things?"

"Lydia had them sent to the Royale. You have a room there, for tonight."

"Simon . . ."

"Go, Newman. Never come back. It is my last warning."

Newman closed the car door, and his driver spun around on the road and headed back to the highway.

"If you don't mind me saying so, sir, I think you should go home. They don't like Americans here as it is, and you especially."

"I'll release you from your contract and put you on a plane this evening."

"No, sir, we couldn't do that. But I'm telling you that we cannot guarantee your safety against these people. It's their country. They'd have the protection of the police if it came to a shootout."

"We'll leave in the morning," Newman said. "For now, take me to the Vance-Ehrhardt Building downtown."

The Vance-Ehrhardt Building was just off the Plaza San Martín, the upper floors enjoying a panoramic view of the city to the south and west, and to the north and east the vast harbor and the Río de la Plata.

No one stopped them as they took the elevator to the tenth floor. There, at the open door to her father's office, Lydia was waiting, wearing a severely cut business suit. Half a dozen Vance-Ehrhardt executives were waiting in the reception area, and they all looked up, hard expressions in their eyes.

"In here Kenneth," she said. "Your muscle can wait for you. We'll just be a minute or two. I'm very busy at the moment."

Newman's heart flipped over. There was no warmth at all in the way she looked at him. He could have been a perfect stranger. He knew she was affected by the kidnapping of her parents, but he hadn't expected this. Christ, everyone was blaming him.

"We're leaving in the morning," he said, entering the office with her.

Lydia closed the door, and Newman tried to draw her to him, but she brushed his hands away and sat down behind her father's desk.

"That is a good idea, Kenneth," she said. "I think Buenos Aires might be dangerous for you at this moment."

"And for you," Newman said, approaching the desk.

She looked up at him, her face devoid of any expression, and she shook her head. "I cannot leave," she said. "I have a business to run here."

"You're my wife."

"You are my competitor! Cargill, Louis Dreyfus, and now my parents. You have the most to gain in all this, Kenneth. You!"

"That doesn't mean I engineered this, for Christ's sake!"

"No, it doesn't, but I'm sure if we talked to your pal Dybrovik, we might come a little closer to who did."

Newman took a deep breath, letting it out slowly as he tried to block the heavy sadness that threatened to well up.

"The Russians would have no reason to do all this. They'd never get another grain contract."

"Perhaps not, but perhaps Dybrovik is not working independently. Perhaps he's being directed."

"By whom? And to what end?"

"I honestly don't know yet, Kenneth, but I intend finding out."

"And then what?"

"And then I will stop whatever it is you and they are doing."

"You can't do this, Lydia. If you want, I'll stay here and help."

"You have your own business to run."

"Together we can operate both."

"A merger?"

Newman shook his head. "No. Paul can run my operation, and I can help you here until your parents are released."

"Do you expect they will be released?"

"Yes. As soon as whatever ransom demand they make is met."

"You still don't understand, do you?" There was a glint of tears in her eyes. "You stupid, naive fool."

"Understand what, Lydia?" Newman asked.

"Even if there is no connection between the kidnapping of my parents and the Cargill and Louis Dreyfus things, the Montoneros never return hostages. Never!"

"Then let me help find them quickly."

"Get out of here. Go back to the States and take care of your own business. Leave me here. Don't you see? I no longer want you."

"I don't believe that."

"Get out of here!" Lydia screamed, jumping up. "Get out of here, you bastard! Get out!"

Newman stepped back, staggered by her intensity. The door behind him crashed open. Several of the Vance-Ehrhardt executives burst into the office, along with Newman's two bodyguards.

"Get him out of here," Lydia yelled. "And don't let him back in the building. If he tries, I want him shot."

Newman sidestepped the others, and his bodyguards moved between them.

"I'm not giving up on you, Lydia," he said. "If I can't help here, I will do what I can outside the office. You are my wife."

One of the executives, an older man, spoke with passion: "Leave, Mr. Newman, or I will personally see to it that you are shot."

Lydia had come around the desk, a sneer on her lips. "If I were you, I'd run back to Duluth as fast as I could, in order to save my business. As of this moment, Vance-Ehrhardt is coming after you."

16

The Royale was a brand-new, twenty-story hotel downtown on the Avenida Córdoba, and Newman's reception was obsequious. The reservation had been made by a Vance-Ehrhardt, which made Newman a VIP, so there was absolutely no trouble coming up with an adjoining room for his two "business associates."

His clothing, which had been sent over from the estate, had been carefully hung in his suite, and the hotel had provided chilled champagne, fresh flowers, and a basket of fruit.

It was all very unreal without Lydia.

The bodyguards made a quick inspection before they would allow Newman to come in; when they were satisfied, they went into the next room, leaving the connecting door open.

"If there is anything at all we can do for you, Mr.

Newman, please do not hesitate to ask," the assistant manager said.

"I may not be leaving tomorrow, so hold this suite open for me." A moment later the door closed and he was alone.

From the window he could see the Vance-Ehrhardt Building rising above the park, and he could envision Lydia there, her sleeves rolled up, a wisp of her blonde hair hanging over her forehead as she worked to keep the Vance-Ehrhardt conglomerate afloat.

Somewhere within the city, her father was being held hostage—that is, if he was still alive. The police had been told by informers that a helicopter had brought the Vance-Ehrhardts and their captors inland, where they were seen entering a van. The van had been found on a narrow street in the *villa miseria*, and now the police, aided by federal troops, were searching the area, shack by shack in hopes of flushing the kidnappers out.

His relationship with Lydia depended in large measure on how successful they would be, how quickly her parents could be returned. Once her father was back at the helm, Newman had little doubt that Lydia would return to him.

Despite the fact that his love for her tended to hamper his clear thinking, he could understand her loyalty. For more than a hundred years the family and the business had grown and prospered together. The business *was* the family. Now, in this crisis, Lydia could not turn her back on her upbringing. Her husband, and even mourning for her parents, came second to protecting the business.

Newman regretted Lydia's knowledge of his business arrangement with Dybrovik. But when he had told her about it, he had never dreamed that a situation like this would occur. But what she did with the information was another matter entirely. A worrisome matter.

The telephone rang, and Newman turned away from his musings at the window to answer it.

"Mr. Newman, this is the hotel operator. I have a Mr. Saratt from the United States who wishes to speak with you. Will you accept the call?"

"Yes, put him on," Newman said.

"Kenneth, is that you?" Saratt's voice sounded hollow and very distant.

"Yes, it is, Paul, and I'm glad you called."

"How is everything down there? I thought you were staying at the Vance-Ehrhardt estate."

"They kicked me out, but it's a long story."

"You'll have plenty of time to tell me all about it; you're going to have to come back here immediately."

Alarms began jangling along Newman's nerves. "What is it, Paul?"

"TradeCon has just shown an incoming transfer of a very substantial amount. And I mean substantial."

"Is he intending to go after the futures market already?"

"I would assume so, but it came out of the clear blue sky, without a word from him."

What the hell was Dybrovik doing now? If it was merely a routine transfer of funds for grain already shipped, it would be one thing. But Saratt did not use "substantial" lightly.

"How much, Paul?"

"You sitting down?"

"Close to it."

"Five hundred million."

"Swiss francs?"

"Dollars."

"Jesus." Newman sank down on the edge of the chair. "He's serious."

"Very," Saratt said dryly. "So what do we do now?"

The big question. With that kind of money, Dybrovik apparently wanted all the futures bought on a cash basis, not on margin. Nearly unheard of. But complicating the affair was Lydia. She would be moving very soon either to establish a link with the Russians or to snap up all the corn futures as she could get her hands on. Fortunately, he had not told her the extent of the deal; otherwise she would have completely swallowed them up.

"Buy," Newman said. It was the only answer.

"How much?" Saratt asked, excitement in his voice.

"Every bushel you can get your hands on."

"Cash?"

"Cash, if need be, but take everything on margin you can get your hands on. We'll save the cash reserves."

"In case he tries something funny?"

"Exactly." The biggest complication of all was the likelihood that someone else would find out. A half-billion dollars was not moved about without attracting a lot of attention. Someone would be watching them now, and watching them very closely.

"When are you and Lydia coming home?"

"Lydia's staying here. She's taken over the business until her father is returned."

"I'm sorry," Saratt said after a slight pause. "Has there been any word yet?"

"None. But they want me out of Buenos Aires."

"Maybe it'd be for the best, Kenneth. I don't think

Argentina is a particularly safe place for you to be at the moment."

"I agree. But I want you to stay there and do what you can with the Chicago market."

. "How about you?"

"I'm going to Geneva to find out what the hell is going on."

"When?"

"Probably first thing in the morning, depending upon what happens or doesn't happen down here."

Again Saratt hesitated a moment. "Be careful, Kenneth."

"I will," Newman said. "I'll call from Geneva."

"Be careful," Saratt said one last time, and he hung up.

Newman was about to go back to the window when Evans came in from the adjoining room, a concerned look on his face. He went directly to the television set and switched it on.

"You'd better see this, sir," he said. "It just started a minute or so ago."

"Vance-Ehrhardt?" Newman asked.

Evans nodded. "It was a recording of the old man's voice, from what I understood, along with a ransom demand."

A picture came on, and the sound came up. A serious-faced announcer seated behind a desk was saying something in Spanish about the continuing police efforts, under the capable leadership of Reynaldo Perés. Then the photograph of Jorge Vance-Ehrhardt filled the screen, and his familiar voice began speaking. It sounded raspy, as if he was very tired, or perhaps on some sort of drug.

"Peoples of Argentina, I have done you wrong. My company has done you a terrible injustice. It is a thing that can never be completely forgiven. But my generous captors have shown me a way to make up for my crimes. This act will, of course, in no way expunge my evil, nor do I beg now for forgiveness, or even mercy."

It wasn't Jorge speaking, or at least it wasn't the man Newman had known for years. Whatever they had done to him made him sound lifeless, wooden. And he was obviously reading from a prepared script, because he never talked that way.

"I instruct my directors to use one hundred million dollars of company funds, in U.S. currency, to purchase gold on the open market. Half of that gold shall be spent to purchase food, medical supplies, and farm equipment for our peasants on the pampas. Those glorious, toiling workers, from whom I have profited by grinding their bodies into the dust of the earth, shall be rewarded.

"The second half of the gold must be deposited in the account of the Argentine Liberation Army at the National Bank of Libya in Tripoli. The money will be used to finance Argentine freedom fighters, who will very soon be coming to liberate our homeland from the oppressive yoke of imperialism."

Newman grabbed the phone. When the operator came on the line, he had her place a call to Duluth. While he was waiting for it to go through, he watched the television.

"I am sorry for my sins," Vance-Ehrhardt was saying. "And even though I am a criminal in the eyes of my people, I will be allowed to return to my home and my loved ones if the simple demands I have stated are met within seventy-two hours."

Vance-Ehrhardt's photograph was replaced on the screen by Captain Perés standing outside the police building. He was surrounded by reporters.

"What is being done at this moment, sir?" one of the newsmen asked.

"We are doing everything within our power to track down and apprehend these reprehensible criminals," Perés said with a flourish. "Although I cannot, for matters of security, disclose the exact progress of our case, I can assure you that we are close, very close indeed, to making an arrest. . . ."

"I have your party on the line, Mr. Newman," the hotel operator said.

Newman turned away from the television. "Paul?"

"It's me," Saratt said. "The Vance-Ehrhardt thing is on the TV. CBS has picked it up."

"I want you to be on the lookout for a Vance-Ehrhardt mass purchase," Newman said, and he could hear Saratt catching his breath.

"That's shitty business, Kenneth, if you're planning what I think you are."

"I want them blocked, Paul. At every avenue, I want them outbid."

"Kicking them when they're down? What the hell is happening to you down there?"

On the television Perés was still talking with the news-people. "Listen to what I have to tell you, without comment. And when I'm finished, I want you to get to work immediately."

"I understand."

"In Washington, Lundgren wouldn't give me a thing."

"I figured as much."

"However, Lydia also went to Grainex for the information."

"I hope you're not going to tell me what I think you're going to tell me."

"I told her, Paul. Not everything. Not the extent of the deal, but I told her."

"Jesus, hell, and Christ!" Saratt shouted in frustration.

"She's calling the shots now. I want her blocked."

"It may be too late."

"I don't think so. We have the available funds now, and Vance-Ehrhardt is going to be cash poor if they meet the ransom demands."

"And if we get caught short?"

"Buy it all on margin. They don't care as long as we can deliver."

"You're putting us way the hell out on a limb, Kenneth!"

Newman laughed. "Haven't we always lived dangerously?"

"I'll do what I can from this end," Saratt said.

Newman hung up. Perés seemed to look directly at him from the television screen, a feral grin on his lips.

"There are a number of curious elements to this business—international elements—that we are vigorously working on. And I promise you that we will leave no stone unturned in our efforts to return the Vance-Ehrhardts to their loved ones, and to the nation."

The newscaster was back, and behind him was an aerial photograph of the Vance-Ehrhardt estate, with arrows pointing to the routes the terrorists had apparently used to gain entry and return to the airstrip.

"Mr. Newman," Evans said, and Newman looked away from the television. "We're leaving in the morning?"

"Yes."

"Very good, sir. I spoke with Mr. Coatsworth, and he suggested in the strongest of terms that, until you leave the country, you not move from the hotel nor allow any visitors up here."

"I can't guarantee any of that, but we will be leaving."

"Back to the States?"

"Geneva, Switzerland."

"Very good, sir," the man said, and the doorbell chimed. He immediately pulled out his automatic, flipping the safety off and levering a round in the chamber.

Humphrey stuck his head in the doorway, his gun in hand. "Are you expecting anyone, sir?"

Newman shook his head.

"Then please stand back," he said, and he motioned for his partner to go to the door.

The doorbell rang again. "Kenneth?" a woman's voice said from out in the corridor. It was Lydia.

"It's my wife," Newman said, starting forward. "Let her in."

Evans motioned him back. "Just a moment, sir." He went to the door and opened it slightly.

"Is my husband here?" Lydia demanded.

"Are you alone, ma'am?"

"Open this goddamned door, I have to see him!" Lydia shouted.

The bodyguard glanced back at Newman, who nodded, and he opened the door. She stormed in.

"Get out. I want to be alone with my husband."

Newman nodded. His bodyguards went back into

their own room and reluctantly shut the door.

"You have to get out of Buenos Aires immediately, Kenneth," she said.

"I'm leaving in the morning," he said, staring at her. She was beautiful, and he ached at the thought of her, and what they were doing to each other.

"No, you must leave now. I've telephoned Jacob to have your plane ready for you. By the time you get out to the airport, the crew will be waiting."

"I'm sorry about your father . . ." Newman began.

"Goddamn it, Kenneth, listen to me! You have to leave."

"Why?"

Lydia glanced toward the door to the other room and lowered her voice. "Perés doesn't have a clue as to what's going on, but he thinks that you're behind it somehow."

"Do you believe that?"

"Of course not," she said. "But Perés does, and he's going to make you his scapegoat."

"I don't understand."

"Ever since the Malvinas fight, the government has been insane to find some way in which to strike back at Americans. You're here now, and a perfect target."

"I'm going to be arrested?"

"He's going to have you assassinated."

"He'd never get away with it."

"He'll get away with anything he wants right now. The mood of my people is very bad."

"I'm not leaving without you."

"Don't be a fool. I have to stay here until my parents are released. Until this entire mess is cleaned up."

Newman, at that moment, saw a side to Lydia he

didn't particularly care for. It didn't seem to matter to her if her parents were released alive or killed; all that mattered was clearing up the mess so that business could be brought back to normal.

"Simon can take over," Newman said.

"Simon is an old fool," Lydia snapped. "I want you out of here this evening."

"And if I don't go? If I remain here to help? Or wait for you?"

Her left eyebrow rose. "Then Vance-Ehrhardt will crush the Newman Company, and there will be little if anything for you to return to, if you survive."

"Lydia . . ." Newman started toward her, but she cut him off with an imperious toss of her head.

"Stay or go, Kenneth, I don't really give a damn. Stay, and you probably will be assassinated. Go, and at least you will have a fighting chance to save your business."

She turned on her heel and left the room before Newman could stop her, leaving him with the feeling that he hadn't really tried with her. The Lydia Vance-Ehrhardt who had just left wasn't the woman he had married. Or was she?

It was dark when Newman and his bodyguards went down to the basement garage where they met Jacob, the steward from Newman's aircraft, standing by a blue Ford LTD. The man was obviously frightened.

"There have been police around the airport all afternoon," he said.

"Did they say anything to you?"

"No, sir, they just sit there and watch. We're cleared to leave as soon as you're on board."

"If it's true that Perés is going to try for you, it may happen out at the airport," Evans said.

"I don't think so," Newman said. "His uniformed officers won't do it. He'll have someone else pull the trigger, so that he can make a big show of going after the killer. If I can get out to the airport, in plain sight of his men, they'll have to let me go."

"We can't take this car, then," Jacob said, gesturing toward the LTD. "They know that I've come to pick you up. And they'll recognize the car you've been using."

"We'll have to borrow another one," Newman said, looking around the nearly full garage. "How are you gentlemen at hot wiring?"

The bodyguards smiled. Within five minutes they had found an unlocked Mercedes sedan and started the engine.

Newman and Jacob climbed in the back and ducked down so that they would not be visible from outside. They got away from the hotel without incident.

"Anyone following us yet?" Newman asked.

"No, sir," Humphrey said, and Newman and Jacob sat up.

"We'll be all right until this car is discovered missing," Newman said, looking out the rear window. "As soon as it's called to the police, Perés will know what happened."

"That'll take time. We'll be at the airport within a half-hour," Humphrey said.

They passed the Vance-Ehrhardt Building in the heavy evening traffic, and Newman looked up at it. Lydia was up there working. He had the gut feeling that he would never see her again. Once this was over, their marriage would be finished. And behind it all was Dybrovik.

No one stopped them or followed them, and within half an hour they were beside the Newman Company aircraft parked at the business aviation terminal.

There were several police cars parked alongside the building, with half a dozen officers on the rooftop observation platform.

Newman hurried up the boarding stairs, the engines coming to life even before he was strapped down. Jacob closed and dogged the hatch, and they headed out the taxiway. Within five minutes they were airborne, the city lights of Buenos Aires falling behind them. Lydia was down there girding the Vance-Ehrhardt empire for battle, while her parents were held captive and other desperate men spun out their own plans.

17

Newman arrived at the Banque de Genève a few minutes after two on Thursday, without an appointment.

It had rained all week in Geneva, and the mood of the city was dark, almost as if the Swiss somehow understood that they were a party to a world food war, much as they were a party to the oil war with their management of Arab petrodollars. The dollar figures in the grain trade were not as large as in the oil market. Oil money regularly came in denominations in the billions, but the overall effect (although there were very few who understood it) was greater. A bushel of wheat or corn, in the last analysis, had a greater bearing on the well-being of the human race than a barrel of oil.

The mood of the city suited Newman so well, however, that he hadn't even noticed the offhand surliness of the airport attendants, or the unusual reserve of the desk manager at the Hôtel Beau Rivage.

The bank was housed in a nondescript, four-story yellow-brick building, with barred windows and a small brass plaque at the front door the only signs that it was not merely an apartment house. Just within the door was a small vestibule that smelled of varnish and fresh paste wax, its polished brass coathooks gleaming in the gray light from a line of frosted-glass windows above.

Straight ahead, down a short, high-ceilinged hallway, was a wooden door with a brass plaque marked PRIVATE; to the left an open doorway led into a very small reception room, which was equipped with a tiny desk and a staid-looking man in morning clothes and gold pince-nez. He looked up as Newman came in.

"I would like a word with Monsieur Montillier," Newman said.

The receptionist sniffed disapprovingly. "I am dreadfully afraid that would be impossible, unless, of course, you have an appointment, Mr. . . . ."

"Tell him it is Mr. Kenneth Newman. I am a principal officer of TradeCon, Limited."

He stared down at the receptionist until the man got slowly to his feet.

"If you will be so kind as to wait for just a moment, I will see if Monsieur Montillier is available," the receptionist said ponderously as he left through the door behind his desk.

Within less than a minute the man was back. He ushered Newman through the door, down a very narrow corridor, and up a half-flight of stairs to a large office at the rear of the building. It was furnished with a Louis XIV desk, ornately carved and gilded, a matching armoire, and several glass-fronted bookcases. A massive globe of the world on heavy wooden gimbals was set in front of a tall leaded-glass window.

Armand Montillier, the managing director of the bank, was a small, dapper man, dressed like the receptionist in a dark coat, pin-striped trousers, wing-collared shirt, and black French cravat. His hair was totally white, as was his narrow goatee, which made him look for all the world like a Swiss version of Kentucky Fried Chicken's Colonel Sanders.

A dangerous illusion, Newman thought as Montillier rose, extending his hand across the desk. The man controlled billions of dollars in deposits.

"Mr. Newman, so good of you to stop by to see us," he said, his voice soft, his English Oxford.

Newman shook his hand. "Thank you for seeing me on such short notice." There were a couple of Renoirs on the walls, each with its own ceiling-mounted spotlight. The books within the ornate cases were all leather bound, stamped in gold, and probably rare editions. A Persian carpet covered a large portion of the highly polished wood floor.

Montillier smiled. "For a valued client my door is always open. May I offer you some coffee, perhaps a little wine or cognac?"

"Cognac would be nice, if it's not too much trouble."

"No trouble at all, I assure you," Montillier said, and he poured them both a drink. "And now, if you would like to have a seat, we may commence whatever business has brought you here," the banker said, again smiling. "Although I suspect it may have something to do with the Eurobank transfer of funds to your TradeCon account."

Newman sat down and took a delicate sip of the fine brandy.

"I would like to see the status of my account, with daily balance tabulations for the past thirty days."

"Of course," Montillier said. He picked up his telephone and said something into it so softly that Newman could not hear him. "Those figures will be here momentarily. Is there something amiss, perhaps, something you would wish to change?"

"No," Newman said. "On the contrary, I continue to be pleased with the services of your fine institution."

Montillier nodded. "Then you wish, perhaps, investment advice?"

Newman sat forward. "What I wish most for is discretion, monsieur. Absolute discretion."

Montillier reacted as if Newman had slapped him in the face. The color left his cheeks, and it seemed for a moment as if he was having difficulty catching his breath.

The door opened, and the receptionist entered and laid a buff-colored folder on the desk, then turned and left, giving no indication that he had noticed anything wrong with Montillier.

"I am wounded, monsieur . . ." Montillier began, but Newman interrupted him.

"If I may see my daily balances?"

The banker held Newman's gaze a moment or two longer, then picked up the file, opened it, scanned the figures, and passed it across.

"If, in any way, you have been dissatisfied with our services, I would be more than happy to look into your specific complaints."

"On the contrary," Newman said, looking over the

tabulations. "I am, and I continue to be, very happy with our arrangement here, as I have already said." The daily balances in the TradeCon account had risen from a start of slightly more than $350,000 to an average high of around $20 million, until two days ago. Then a Eurobank transfer of funds totaling $507 million had come in from a numbered account.

Newman closed the file and laid it back on the desk, then took a drink of his cognac. There had been no mistake. The money was there. The numbered account was Dybrovik's, or rather a blind account of Exportkhleb's; Newman had recognized the number.

"You are familiar with my business dealings, monsieur," Newman began. "And I trust that you are satisfied that I am indeed a legitimate businessman."

"Again I am wounded, Newman. There has never been the slightest question as to your integrity where it concerns Swiss law—for that is what we are talking about here—and I shall confine myself to that issue and no other."

Swiss laws were very harsh; their most stringent federal statutes dealt with the area of secrecy. For any bank employee or officer to divulge the status of even the smallest account to anyone—absolutely anyone, including government representatives—was punishable not only by instant dismissal, but by fines of $10,000 and more, and imprisonment for as long as twenty years.

"That is comforting, monsieur, but no less than I expected," Newman said. "There could be a problem in the future. I want to make you aware of it."

"I am at your complete disposal."

"Very soon there will be a great deal of activity within

the TradeCon account. The Eurobank transfer is only the beginning.''

"I see," Montillier said, clasping his hands in front of him on the desk. "Please continue."

"This activity will take the form of numerous and often quite large transfers of funds, many of which will be from outside Switzerland. Your discretion, monsieur, has never been in question in my mind. However, there are those who pride themselves on a certain ability to deduce active business arrangements merely from the frequency of fund transfers.''

Montillier smiled thinly. "I understand perfectly, Mr. Newman. Let me assure you that each and every payment to, or debit from, your account will be handled on a highly personal basis. No matter the number or the frequency. The sheer act of transfer shall be kept as confidential as the actual status of your account, or indeed its very existence.''

Newman finished his cognac and set the glass down. "Then my business here today is concluded." He got to his feet, and the banker followed suit.

Newman had no illusions about Swiss law, or any other law for that matter. When the stakes became high enough, some would be willing to bend or break the rules. Swiss law was inviolate only in Switzerland. If a man—Montillier, perhaps—was willing to abandon his position here in Switzerland, say for something in Buenos Aires, he could do it, providing he was not intercepted before leaving this country.

All Newman had done today—the only thing he had hoped to do, besides making absolutely sure the Eurobank transfer had actually occurred—was to put Montillier on notice that TradeCon would be watched, and watched very closely, for any irregularities. If anything should come up, Newman had told Montillier in effect that he would go straight to the Swiss authorities.

"I am so happy that you spoke with me about a matter of such concern to you. Again let me assure you that you may have the utmost confidence with us."

"I do," Newman said. They shook hands.

Back downstairs, the receptionist showed him out the door. It was still raining.

It was late, nearly ten o'clock in the evening, and still misty, when Newman drove his rented car off the lakeshore highway just past Coppet and stopped at the beginning of the narrow gravel driveway. Behind him, the headlights of the second car bounced up the road and swung directly on him as he got out and walked back.

Evans cranked down his window. "What is this place, Mr. Newman?"

"This is as far as you go. About a hundred yards farther up is the house."

"We'll follow you."

"No, you won't," Newman said. "I won't be long. A half-hour at the most. Probably less. The place is crawling with security people."

The two bodyguards looked at each other. "You're making it very difficult for us to do our job, sir."

"Can't be helped," Newman said. "Turn your car around and wait here."

"What if someone comes?"

"Stop them, find out who they are, and let them pass."

"A half-hour?"

"Probably less," Newman said. He went back to his car, continued down the driveway, and stopped in front of the house Dybrovik was using as his headquarters.

There were several Mercedes, a Citroën, and a couple of small Ford Cortinas parked out front and around the side. The house was lit up like a Christmas tree.

As Newman pulled up, a heavily built man in a dark suit came down from the porch. He frisked Newman the moment he stepped out of the car.

Newman wondered how the Russians were getting away with something like this. It would not be possible in the States, but then the Swiss had a habit of turning a blind eye to anything that was financial in nature.

"He is waiting inside for you," the man said, his English guttural.

Dybrovik, his shirt sleeves rolled up, came into the main hallway, clutching a thick sheaf of papers. He was not smiling.

"What brings you out here tonight?" he asked.

Newman had called earlier to make the appointment. Dybrovik had hesitated before agreeing.

"We have to talk."

"Is something wrong? There is not enough money? You are having trouble with purchases or shipping?"

"We have to talk. In private, Dybrovik. No microphones, no listeners."

Dybrovik looked at him as if he were speaking nonsense. "Don't cause me such worry, Kenneth. If there is a problem, tell it to me straight out, and let's see if we cannot come up with a solution."

Newman said nothing.

Dybrovik began to squirm. "Everything we do here, Kenneth, is being recorded. Even now our conversation is on tape. Please, you cannot do this to me . . . to our arrangement. Is it not profitable, as I promised?''

Newman jerked his head toward the front door. Dybrovik's gaze flickered that way, and he nodded.

"I wanted to make sure that you will continue transferring funds into my TradeCon account."

"We have passed more than five hundred million dollars over."

"The amount of grain we are purchasing will amount to four times that, probably more by the time we are finished."

"And you have come here seeking assurances?" Dybrovik asked. He laughed. "Is that all?"

"Basically."

"You have them. You have my personal word."

Newman again nodded toward the front door.

"And now I must return to my work. As you know, Soviet ports alone can handle less than fifty million tons of grain per year. We are working very hard at this moment to set up alternate receiving centers and storage areas. It is not easy. But let me walk you to your car."

"I was getting nervous," Newman said.

"Very uncharacteristic of you."

"The numbers are much bigger than anything we've handled before."

They stepped out onto the porch. The burly character who had frisked Newman emerged from the shadows and said something to Dybrovik in rapid Russian.

Dybrovik shook his head and said something in return. The guard glowered at Newman, then disappeared in the shadows again.

"You have a car waiting for you out by the highway?"

"Bodyguards," Newman said. They stepped down off the porch and walked around the front of his car. "Can we be heard out here?" he whispered.

"No," Dybrovik said, "but we are being watched."

Newman glanced back up at the house. He was certain he saw a movement, in one of the upper windows, but then it was gone.

"What is so mysterious that we have to take this risk?" Dybrovik was smiling and nodding his head, as if Newman was telling him a joke.

"I want to know what the hell is going on," Newman hissed.

"I have no idea what you are talking about," Dybrovik said, smiling but sounding alarmed.

"First Cargill in New Orleans, then Louis Dreyfus in Paris, and now Vance-Ehrhardt in Buenos Aires."

Dybrovik looked sharply at him. "You think that my government has had something to do with those things?"

"It's goddamned suspicious. You and I are doing business, the biggest business in the history of grain trading, and my company benefits the most from those disasters."

"Newman, my old friend, I assure you we had nothing to do with those heinous acts. I was going to convey my sympathies to your wife." Dybrovik looked back at the house.

"I wonder what would happen to you if I kept the money you have already transferred into the TradeCon account and didn't ship the grain."

Dybrovik stepped back a pace, as if Newman were a demented, dangerous animal. "You would never again receive a grain commission from anyone. Your name and your business would be ruined. And we would recover our money through the International Court at the Hague.''

"No, you wouldn't. But that is exactly what I intend doing if it comes out that your government was in any way responsible for Cargill, Louis Dreyfus, or Vance-Ehrhardt.''

"I have already told you . . .''

"I know what you told me,'' Newman said sharply. "What I'm telling you is that you had better make damned sure that some overzealous KGB colonel or general hasn't decided to help things along by eliminating my competition. My own government would support me in this. I think you know that.''

Dybrovik seemed genuinely pained. "Are you sorry now that you have become involved with this deal?''

"Not yet,'' Newman said. "But I am concerned.''

Someone came out of the house. "Delos Fedor?'' he called from the porch.

"My assistant.'' Dybrovik turned around. "What is it?''

"There is a telephone call for you. Urgent.''

"I am coming,'' Dybrovik called, then turned back. "What can I say that will assure you, Kenneth?''

"Give me your word that, to your knowledge, there is no plot.''

Dybrovik nodded.

"Delos Fedor, the telephone,'' his assistant shouted.

"And give me your word that if you should find out something, you will let me know.''

Dybrovik smiled. "I could never give you my assurances on that, Kenneth. We are partners in a grain-trading deal. Business associates, not countrymen.''

It was the answer Newman had hoped for, because it was truthful. He patted Dybrovik on the arm. "For now, nothing will be changed, then. We are purchasing corn futures."

"On margin," Dybrovik said. "I was led to understand that the purchases would be made on a cash basis."

"How I run my business is my concern," Newman said harshly. "You keep the money coming, and I'll continue purchasing corn."

"And yet you question me?"

"When it comes to assassination and kidnapping, yes," Newman said. He climbed into his car, and when he had the engine started, he and Dybrovik looked into each other's eyes for several long seconds.

"My wife has taken over the Vance-Ehrhardt conglomerate until her father is returned."

"I am very sorry for you, my old friend."

"She has gotten wind of the fact that you are up to something. Someone apparently spotted you here in Geneva."

"Will she come here to try and deal with me?"

"Perhaps not she herself, but I expect she will be sending someone."

"I shall tell them nothing."

"Thank you," Newman said. "Say hello to your wife for me."

Dybrovik flinched, but he nodded, and Newman left.

18

Delos Fedor Dybrovik was what his wife used to call a deep thinker. And lately, over the past few weeks, he had been doing a lot of that. As long as he was able to keep a distance between himself and the little man, he could manage his perspective, to a degree. He could think of the little man in more realistic, less frightening terms. A bureaucrat. Someone who had the ear of the Party. Probably held a rank, almost certainly KGB. Someone who could wipe out all record of Dybrovik's past transgressions.

In Geneva, at arm's length from the little man, he had toyed with the idea of running to the United States. But he knew that, once he was there, he would not be happy. He'd miss his life at home. Besides, he still wanted to continue with the largest grain deal in the history of the trade. Even though it was becoming tainted in his mind.

Even though he was filled with doubts about exactly what the little man was up to. A Great Grain Robbery was one thing, but Newman's questions last week about Cargill, Louis Dreyfus, and Vance-Ehrhardt had brought other, darker fears to mind. Assassination and violence. But to what end?

Entering the Ministry of Transportation Building in Moscow this warm Friday afternoon, with more fear in his heart than he had ever imagined he could bear, and with the intention of finding out what was going on, Dybrovik had to wonder if he wasn't experiencing the very last days of his life. He had almost convinced himself that the little man had killed Larissa, for no other reason than to insure cooperation. If he felt he was being betrayed, wouldn't he kill again?

He had been back from Geneva twice since the grain purchase had begun, and that was to raid the home staff for additional help. The little man had come up after office hours, each time, for a status report, had praised Dybrovik, then had left as quietly as he had come. Dybrovik was certain that the little man would be back again this time for an update, and he was going to have to keep his head while he lied to him. Given enough time, he'd be able to pave the way to make his lies more creditable. At least long enough for him to find out what was going on—and then get out, if need be.

It had taken a week after the meeting with Newman for him to get up the courage to return to Moscow and do what he knew he had to do. During that time he had set up some insurance for himself, as well as devised the ostensible reasons for his return: the necessity of coming up with sufficient grain-handling capacity to manage the amount of corn that would begin arriving in October aboard Newman subsidiary ships. Storage facilities would have to be secured or built, and a distribution network arranged to handle the massive influx.

All in all, it was a gargantuan problem that Exportkhleb could no longer ignore, although it was not within the bureau's actual purview. The State Ministry of Transportation handled that aspect, but Dybrovik felt that a case could be made for his putting out feelers.

But he was skating on thin ice. The little man had told him point blank that there would be no deviation from the buy order. One hundred million tons of corn. Bought in total secrecy. "Merely buy it, Delos Fedor. The rest will be up to me."

Newman feared that Exportkhleb would end up holding massive amounts of grain, while much of the world suffered shortages that the United States could not fill. Exportkhleb would then step in with its grain, selling it at a premium. Newman would be caught in the middle then, as a traitor to his own country, with nowhere to turn.

Dybrovik's fear, on the other hand, was that something much more sinister was under way. If the major corn merchants, such as Cargill and Louis Dreyfus and Vance-Ehrhardt—and, in the end, Newman—were ruined, were put out of business, and if the Soviet Union owned major stockpiles of corn, there would be serious trouble for the U.S. if something happened to its own supplies. He had to find out.

He had spent most of the morning alone in his Prospekt apartment, finishing paperwork and thinking about his wife. From time to time his eyes strayed to the bathroom door. Although he felt remorse, it was not an all-consuming passion, because her death—the way he had seen her hanging there—was not fully real to him. He could not allow it to be. Surely Larissa would be back soon.

Just before noon he had gone directly to his office, where he had been stopped five times by various staffers who renewed their condolences on the death of his wife, told him he was doing a tremendous job, and asked if he had brought back any American cigarettes or Swiss beer.

The buy from Newman had been compartmentalized. The staff in Geneva knew that they were purchasing huge amounts of grain from a seemingly endless list of minor brokers. But the Moscow staff had no knowledge of the extent of the deal. The regular staff, that is.

At 1:30, Mikhail Andreyev, the bureau's market analyst, had come in with the latest world grain price projections, which showed rice steady, wheat and soybeans up eight and nine cents a bushel, and corn up to $6.05 American, nearly fifty cents above normal.

"Maybe our latest small corn buys are having an effect on the market, but we can't attribute much more than a few pennies to our movements," Andreyev, a shuffling old man, said. There was an odd expression in his eyes.

Dybrovik tried to concentrate on what the old man was saying, but it was difficult.

"Cargill and Louis Dreyfus certainly are having a more significant effect on the market, but it is still too early to tell what the Vance-Ehrhardt kidnapping has done."

"You think it will affect the market as well?"

"Certainly the spot market, depending upon what the

kidnappers' demands are, and how fast Vance-Ehrhardt is returned. If he is returned at all."

Half an hour later, Boris Stepanovich Gordik, Exportkhleb's assistant director, popped in with the proud announcement that the Thai rice market had been cornered and that U.S. rice would be shunted through their agents in Hong Kong in sufficient quantities for Exportkhleb to pick up at least a few thousand tons.

"Bits and pieces, Delos Fedor, but we should be able to cover our needs now without undue strain."

"You have done a really excellent job in my absence. You should go to Hong Kong to supervise the buy. Don't you think so?" Dybrovik asked.

Gordik puffed up, his face lit with a huge grin. "I believe the buy would certainly go much more smoothly if I were there to oversee it."

"Then you may leave early next week."

"Will you be remaining here, or are you going to return to Geneva?"

"Unfortunately, I'll be returning within the week, but the staff will be able to handle anything that comes up. Comrade Shalnev will be here as well."

Gordik looked over his shoulder, then came a little closer and started to speak, but Dybrovik cut him off.

"Enjoy Hong Kong, and give my regards to your wife."

Gordik stepped back. Everyone in the bureau hated and feared Shalnev, who had instituted a new Office of Doctrinal Compliance. Three people had already lost their jobs because of his meddling. He was a ruthless, tight-lipped bastard whom you couldn't talk to. Only Dybrovik knew that Shalnev was in the bureau at the little man's behest. It was Shalnev who was handling the

large Western currency transfers to Exportkhleb's Eurobank account, without a single person knowing about it,
bypassing the bureau's own banking section completely.

Gordik was an ass, but Dybrovik liked and trusted
him. He was honest and steady, and had an excellent
grasp of the international grain market. Dybrovik did
not want the man getting himself in trouble now because
of his loose tongue.

"Thanks," Gordik said, understanding what
Dybrovik had done for him.

Dybrovik went down the hall to Shalnev's domain
next to the computer center. The man was a short,
stocky bulldog, with thick, greasy hair and bulbous
Ukrainian lips. He always seemed to be drooling.

"Delos Fedor, welcome back," the man boomed. He
grabbed Dybrovik in a bear hug, kissed him on the lips,
and then released him. "Things are going well, from
what I hear," he said softly.

"Very well, Comrade Shalnev."

Shalnev laughed. "You have forgotten what I told
you. We are friends here. Good friends, you and I."

Dybrovik said, "Newman came to me for
assurances."

"I listened to the tape. He is no fool, but he is acting
like one. He is up to something."

"I gave him my assurances."

"He has five hundred million dollars of our money.
We in return have less than one-tenth that in grain."

"The remainder is in futures. Corn that has not been
harvested yet."

"Which he is buying on margin," Shalnev rumbled,
his earlier open good humor gone.

"It is a routine way of doing business, Yuri Pavlovich, but he has become suspicious because of recent happenings.''

"So have I," Shalnev said ominously. "It is your task to see that this goes smoothly.''

"It has so far, although corn is up.''

Shalnev licked his lips, a chilly expression in his eyes. "Why have you returned? Your work is not finished there.''

"No, it isn't. But Newman has returned to the United States, and I have a bureau to run. The Americans will be expecting a trade delegation within the month to work out details now that their stupid grain embargo has been lifted. We must be ready for it, lest suspicion fall our way.''

Shalnev was not a grainman, so he had to take Dybrovik at face value. "When will you go back?"

"Soon," Dybrovik said. "Within a week.''

"Before you leave, I will need your fund-transfer expectations.''

"You'll have them, along with the shipping schedules through the fall and again for the spring. I don't know about the winter . . .'' Dybrovik let it trail off, as if he were thinking to himself.

Shalnev picked up on it. "I will need the tonnage projections as soon as you have them.''

Back in his own office Dybrovik closed his door, lit a Marlboro, and poured himself a stiff shot of Scotch with shaking hands. Shalnev needed the *tonnage projections?* It meant he was involved not only with banking, but with shipping as well. To what extent was the little man controlling transportation? If the corn was being bought for Russian use—which meant that the surpluses would be nonexistent, that there would be a corn shortfall—then a distribution network of huge proportions would be abuilding. If the promised surpluses materialized, then this was another Great Grain Robbery, and no special distribution network would be needed, for the corn would not actually be shipped into Russia. Finally, suppose the surpluses materialized, but the little man planned to stockpile the American grain for some reason. In that case, the Newman subsidiary ships would bring their loads to a few ports where massive storage facilities would be ready.

Dybrovik wanted to know. He had to know.

He telephoned Vladimir Valentin Vostrikov, who was head of interbureau liaison for the Ministry of Transportation.

"Good afternoon, Vladi."

"Delos, my old friend, how are you? I didn't know that you were back in town."

They had often worked together.

"I just returned last night."

"Listen, we were sorry about Larissa. It came as a big shock. I didn't hear until last week."

"Thank you, Vladi. Work is helping, believe me. Which is why I telephoned. I would like to talk with you this afternoon. We may be facing some problems soon."

"Yes, big things are on the wind, Delos, but not to talk about, if you know what I mean."

Why not, Dybrovik wondered. Had the little man gotten to him as well? He took his shot. "I have spoken with Shalnev about this."

"I see," Vostrikov said, his tone suddenly guarded. "Three o'clock, then."

Before he left Exportkhleb, Dybrovik gathered up

tonnage projections by dates and amounts for all the grain that would—or would not—be coming into Soviet ports over the next twelve months. The corn buy had been spread over dozens of shipping companies, arriving throughout the year. Vostrikov would of course see right through the scheme, understanding that Exportkhleb was purchasing a mammoth amount of corn, and probably from the United States. But Dybrovik had his argument ready: Since the grain was to be shipped to the Soviet Union, then he had to make sure they would be able to handle it as and when it came.

But, as he entered the Ministry of Transportation Building a few minutes before three, he knew he was taking a great risk by snooping around. If the little man found out about this meeting, he might not accept Dybrovik's explanation. *Merely buy it, Delos Fedor. The rest will be up to me.*

The security guard called Vostrikov to come down, and a couple of minutes later he showed up with a visitor's pass which he clipped on Dybrovik's lapel. He said nothing until they were riding up to the fourth floor in the ancient elevator.

"I don't mind telling you, I don't like this. Not any of it. And now you show up, wanting to talk. What is happening, Delos?"

"I was hoping you would tell me. You said big things were happening. What did you mean?"

"I was shooting off my mouth to an old friend," Vostrikov said sadly.

Vostrikov's office was a tiny room with a large map of European Russia tacked on the wall. Vostrikov took off his jacket and tossed it aside. He poured them both a vodka, then waved vaguely toward a chair as he went to the window and looked outside. It was a lovely, sunny day.

"What can happen on such a day as this?" he asked rhetorically. He tossed back his drink, then turned and poured himself another, offering more to Dybrovik, who shook his head.

"What's wrong, Vladi? Why the long face?"

Vostrikov looked at him, drank his second vodka, and poured another.

"I got to thinking after you called me, you know. About Shalnev. And I asked myself, how does my old friend from Exportkhleb know the name Yuri Pavlovich Shalnev? So I called Comrade Shalnev downstairs in his office, just to ask him. He was not there, in banking. So then you know what cute thing I did?"

Dybrovik had been quite sure that Shalnev was the little man's watchdog over this entire operation, but hearing that he had an office here was startling. It *proved* the connection. Vostrikov was involved as well. He wondered what hold the little man had on him.

"I called Exportkhleb on a whim. Not to talk to you. No, I asked to speak with Comrade Shalnev. And of course you know he was there. I tell you, Delos, I was so frightened that I hung up the telephone without giving my name. I just hope to hell my telephone has not been monitored. I have been sitting here in fear and shame."

Fear and shame? The little man's hold was evidently powerful. And his orders explicit: secrecy would be maintained at all costs. He had an excuse for being here, but poor Vostrikov had none for calling Shalnev at Exportkhleb.

"Please leave, Delos. Go now, before more damage is done."

Dybrovik forced a smile. "What damage, Vladi? You speak as if there is some dark, nefarious plot underfoot here. I have come merely to discuss the transportation of the year's grain with you. There will be more than usual. Much more."

Vostrikov nodded. "I know it all too well. We have been getting ready for months. Quietly. No one around here really knows what's happening. Except for me." He tossed back his drink and immediately poured himself another, this time not bothering to offer Dybrovik more.

"It'll be the largest gathering of railroad cars in our history, Delos. By September all the grain will be moving. But you know all that. You know Shalnev. You must know the rest. Right, Delos?"

Dybrovik was about to correct him, to tell him that Newman's grain wouldn't begin coming until October, and it would be shipped throughout the year, not finishing until late spring or early next summer. But again something held him back.

"Where the ships will be found to get rid of it all, I couldn't begin to tell you. But the grain will be there, ready to ship."

The grain will be there, ready to ship. What the hell did that mean?

Vostrikov had turned away with his vodka and was once again staring out the window across at Lennin's mausoleum as Dybrovik got to his feet.

He had come here seeking answers, and he had found them. Only they were answers of a far different sort than he had expected. A far different sort.

19

The United States Department of Agriculture was housed in a large, traditional building between Jefferson Drive and C Street. Its columns and windows faced the Mall, southeast of the White House. Newman and Paul Saratt had arrived in Washington just an hour ago and had taken a cab over, sending Jacob along to the Newman Company apartment in the Watergate with their bags. At the north portico of the great building, they paid the cabby and mounted the stairs to the main floor, then took an elevator upstairs. On the way up Newman reflected on all that had happened since Dybrovik's call had been routed to him through Abex, and tried to put it into some understandable order. Cargill, Louis Dreyfus, and Vance-Ehrhardt. All direct strikes against the grain industry. He wondered if he shouldn't include his wife's defection as a blow against himself. But if the other events had indeed been engineered by one hand (as he suspected), then Lydia's refusal to return home came only as a serendipitous benefit to the plotter. Lydia's people were hitting some of the spot markets, and there had been a minor drive for corn out of Milwaukee, but the Newman Company had been there first, and Vance-Ehrhardt's efforts were mostly ineffective for the moment. He was certain that Lydia had sent someone to speak with Dybrovik, but her mission had evidently failed, because the Russians continued to play ball.

"Upstairs, the reception area was very large, and tastelessly decorated with a lot of chrome-and-glass furniture. The receptionist was a youngish woman who seemed to match the place. Even her green eyeshadow was the same shade as the cushions on the furniture.

"Mr. Newman and Mr. Saratt to see Secretary Lundgren," Saratt said.

"We have been expecting you," the receptionist said in a syrupy voice. She picked up the telephone and pushed one of the buttons. "Mr. Stansfield, they've just arrived, sir," she said. "Certainly." She hung up and smiled. "Mr. Stansfield will be right with you gentlemen."

It was a new name to Newman. He gave Saratt a questioning look, but Saratt shook his head.

A moment later, a thin, mawkish-looking man appeared and bustled directly up to them, holding his hand out as he came.

"Aubert Stansfield, Undersecretary for Foreign Agricultural Trade," he said in a reedy voice.

"Secretary Lundgren phoned last night. Here we are," Newman said tersely.

Stansfield was taken back by Newman's obvious coldness, but he recovered smoothly. "If you will just come with me, the Secretary is waiting for you."

Curtis Lundgren was a small man, a full head shorter than Newman. Everything about his face suggested a supercilious attitude, from his round nose to eyes made owlish by thick glasses, to the seemingly permanent sneer on his lips. His hair was thinning although there was no gray in it, and Newman strongly suspected he used hair tint. He was dressed, as usual, in a plain blue suit, with a white shirt and conservative tie. He got to his feet and came around his mammoth desk when they walked in.

"Kenneth," he said with a soft politician's voice, "I'm glad you could come on such short notice. I've been worried for both of us for the past few days. We just had to talk."

"You know my vice-president in charge of operations, Paul Saratt?"

The two men shook hands. "I've heard your name. Weren't you with Cargill at one time?"

"Continental," Saratt said. "Years ago."

"Good company."

"Among the better."

Newman and Saratt followed Lundgren over to the grouping of chairs.

"Would you like me to sit in on this, Mr. Secretary?" Stansfield asked.

"By all means, Aubert," Lundgren said expansively. "We'll be dealing on your turf, so to speak."

They all sat down, and there was an awkward silence. Newman was damned if he was going to help them out of it. He and Paul had discussed the meaning behind

Lundgren's summons to Washington, and they had both reached the same conclusions. The man had somehow gotten wind of the fact that the Newman Company was dealing with the Russians. How much he knew about the deal, however, was going to be the crucial factor, along with where and how he had gotten his information.

Two walls held bookcases filled mostly with lawbooks, but on the other walls were enlarged photographs of various military aircraft, including a squadron of B-52's in formation flight. A curious choice for the Secretary of Agriculture, Newman thought. In fact, they could almost be in the office of the Secretary of Defense, except for the Farm Bureau magazines stacked in three neat piles on the coffee table in front of them.

"A hobby of mine," Lundgren said, seeing Newman look at the photographs.

"I am a very busy man, Mr. Secretary, if you could get to the point," Newman said.

The remark stung, and Lundgren bridled. "You've jumped the gun, and it has us worried here."

"I don't know what you're talking about."

"The Soviet grain-trade agreement, what else?"

Newman sat forward. "You're going to have to be more specific than that."

Lundgren smiled. "Come on now, Kenneth. You were seen by two different reliable people in Geneva on two different occasions."

"The department is spying on me? Is that what you've called me in to tell me?"

"Get off your high horse, Newman," Lundgren snapped. "You're well known within the trade. You were spotted in Geneva, that's all."

"So what?"

"Dybrovik has set up some kind of operation near Coppet. The Swiss won't tell us a thing, and we can't get close enough to it to find out much."

"Newman and Dybrovik in the same city—therefore they are dealing?"

"Are you denying it?"

"I'm just trying to figure out how you think," Newman said. "Have my licenses been approved?"

"Coincidentally, they have," Lundgren said, and Stansfield opened a file folder and passed the documents across to the Secretary. "Now that the embargo has been lifted, the Newman company is authorized to ship seven hundred fifty thousand tons of grain to the Soviet Union." He handed the documents across to Saratt.

Newman laughed. "We've already shipped a bit more than one million tons, including soybeans, barley, rice, and wheat."

"I see," Lundgren said, sitting back. "Without licenses."

"That's right. The embargo has been lifted, and you're not going to set yourself up here in Washington as the paymaster, telling each company how much grain it can or can't ship, doling out the tonnage to those who please you. We don't do business that way."

"We do now."

"No."

"Are you threatening me?" Lundgren asked. "I could have all your licenses."

"The Mexican government has already asked that I set up my business in Mexico City. I'm giving it serious thought."

"If you will permit me to interrupt, gentlemen?"

Stansfield asked. Lundgren glared at him, but said nothing. "There have been . . . how shall I put it . . . some very strange indications on the foreign market over the past few weeks."

Now it comes, Newman thought.

"Secretary Lundgren brought it to my attention the day after the Cargill elevator explosion. He wondered what effect the disaster might have on our European trade. I expected there might be some slight agitation— at least a slight bit—that Cargill might not be able to fulfill its obligations. So I went looking."

"What did you find?" Newman asked.

"Not a thing. That is to say, none of my foreign contacts seemed the least bit worried at first. Your company picked up some of the slack from Duluth-Superior, and Louis Dreyfus managed the rest."

"We certainly didn't pick up any slack after Gérard was assassinated," Saratt said.

"We found no indications of it," Stansfield said. "But what we found curious were the bodyguards you hired. Can you explain that?"

"It was my wife's idea. She felt I might need the protection. I no longer have them."

"Then came the Vance-Ehrhardt kidnapping," Stansfield continued. "And Mr. Newman, please, pass my condolences on to your wife. I hope that everything works out well."

Newman nodded. The bastards had been spying on him, or at least around him. "What has all this to do with the Newman Company? If you could just come to the point."

"I'm coming to it, sir," Stansfield said, but Lundgren cut in.

"Coincidental to those happenings, Dybrovik shows up in Geneva, you do too, and within weeks the corn market begins to show signs of meddling."

"Are you accusing me of market manipulation?"

"I'm accusing you of nothing," Lundgren snapped. "I wanted to talk to you to clear the air."

"Of what? Clear the air of what?"

"Misunderstanding. Your license to deal with the Soviet government will be extended to one million tons, no more. So you are finished trading with them. I'm doing that much for you in return for your providing me with information about Dybrovik, and what the man is up to."

"I don't know what you're talking about," Newman said. "And even if I did, it would be none of your business."

"Foreign relations are this administration's business!" Lundgren exploded.

"I think this meeting is concluded." Newman and Saratt got to their feet.

"Not so fast," Lundgren said, jumping up. "You were here before asking about Soviet crop projections. Can you explain that?"

"It was common knowledge that the President was lifting the grain embargo. I wanted some indication of the depth of trade."

Lundgren was obviously unconvinced, and it was clear that he was controlling his anger only through great effort. "The Newman Company has shipped all the grain it is going to ship to the Soviet Union. Should we find out that you have violated this order, you will be prosecuted. Have I made myself clear?"

Newman looked at the man in disgust. "The day that

this government, or any other government, regulates the grain trade to the extent it regulates nearly everything else will be the day the world's food chain will snap. And that's not merely my opinion, Lundgren. Ask Bunge or Cargill or Continental or any of the others; they'll tell you the same.''

"When it comes to dealing with a foreign power inimical to the United States, every aspect of trade becomes this administration's business. Every aspect, Mr. Newman.''

"God help us if Congress ever gives you the power to make it so,'' Newman said.

"And God save us from profiteers like you,'' Lundgren said furiously.

Newman wanted to punch the bastard in the face, but he held himself in check. Instead, he and Saratt turned and left the office.

"What the hell is the matter with you, Kenneth?'' Saratt asked as the elevator doors slid closed.

"The son of a bitch has been spying on us.''

"So what? If he could have proved anything, he wouldn't have called us in; he would have done whatever he wanted to do. We're just going to have to be careful with Dybrovik, that's all.''

"What do you think Lundgren and his crowd are going to do when it gets out?''

"It's not going to get out,'' Saratt said. "At least not our part in it. Are you having second thoughts?''

"I've been having second thoughts since day one, Paul. But it was either us or someone else. And so far Dybrovik has been true to his word. We'll just have to wait and see.''

They stepped off the elevator and headed toward the main doors, only to see Stansfield rush around a corner and cross the lobby to them. He had apparently taken the stairs down; he was out of breath.

"If I could have a word with you, Mr. Newman," he said.

"Did Lundgren send you down?" Newman asked.

"No, sir. I'd be fired if he knew I was here."

Newman believed him. "What is it?"

"You *are* dealing with the Soviets," Stansfield said, and when Saratt started to object, he held him off. "Hear me out, please. We know that you are dealing with the Soviets, we just don't know exactly how, although I can guess. And if I'm right, then you must know that the Soviets are planning on a massive corn crop. I mean really massive. The biggest in their history. It's no less than a major agrarian reform."

"How do you know that?" Newman asked. He had been afraid of just that; he was afraid again.

"Satellite data. Which is one more thing I should not be telling you."

"Why do you come to me?"

"Because I think you believe in what you're doing, and I think you're an honorable man. If the Russians are up to something, which we believe they are, I wouldn't want your company to be their tool."

Newman and Saratt looked at each other. "Why didn't Lundgren tell us this?" Newman asked.

"I don't know, sir. I truly do not know," Stansfield said, and he looked over his shoulder. "I have to get back. I just wanted to make sure I caught you before you left the city."

"Thank you," Newman said.

"*Are* you dealing with the Russians, sir?" the man asked.

Newman just smiled at him.

In their taxi, heading across town to the Watergate, neither man trusted himself to speak, each lost in his own dour thoughts.

Saratt finally broke the silence. "If Stansfield is telling the truth . . ."

Newman nodded. "We'll have to find out, but I have a feeling he is."

"So what's next?"

"We're going to have to put it to Dybrovik."

Saratt looked at him in disbelief. "You don't mean to tell me that we're going to go through with this. That you're even considering continuing?"

"You're damned right I am, Paul. We're going to keep on buying futures with Soviet money. We're not shipping much corn now; the big shipments won't start until October."

"And if it is a market manipulation?"

"*We*'ll have the futures, not the Russians. At low prices. We'll sell on the open market."

"The Russians would howl."

"I don't think so. They'd have too much explaining to do. They'd be happy to get their money back."

Saratt fell silent again. He was still bothered.

"What's eating you, Paul?" Newman asked.

"There's more to this than Stansfield has told us. I'm convinced of it. Dybrovik is just too smart to try and pull another Grain Robbery. He'd have to know we'd find out sooner or later."

Newman shrugged. He was remembering the look on Dybrovik's face the last time they had met. The man had been holding something back. He had been frightened.

"Let's get a telex off to him in Geneva. I want a

meeting on neutral ground."

"Athens?"

"Anywhere, it doesn't matter. I'm going to lay it all out for him and see what he does."

"I think we should just back out of it, Kenneth, and leave well enough alone."

"I won't quit. We'll hang on a bit longer, at least until I meet with him. Maybe we can come up with some kind of a holding agreement. If worse comes to worst, we'll sell him the futures but ship the grain to an intermediate, neutral port until we find out what the hell is really going on."

The telephone was ringing when they got to the apartment, and Newman answered it as Saratt poured them each a drink.

It was a person-to-person call to Kenneth Newman from Lydia Newman. He took it in the bedroom.

"Lydia! God, it's good to hear from you," Newman said, when the connection was made.

"I talked with Coatsworth from Tri-States Security, and he told me that you had canceled your security contract," Lydia said in a rush. There was something wrong. "He's sending someone down from New York. They'll be there sometime this afternoon. Stay where you are until then. Someone is trying to kill you, do you understand?"

"No, I don't, Lydia. What the hell are you saying? Who's going to try to kill me, and why?"

The doorbell rang again. "Hold on," Saratt shouted.

"You're in danger, Kenneth, please believe me. It's Perés, he's been crazy ever since you managed to get away."

"You say Perés is going to have me killed?"

"No, not him—*because of him!*"

"I don't understand . . ."

"I can't talk any longer. I must go. Please be careful, darling. Please!"

"Lydia?" Newman shouted, but the connection was broken.

From the living room came a tremendous explosion. Glass flew everywhere and the lights went out.

"Paul?" Newman shouted, tearing open the bedroom door and leaping into the living room.

Flames were eating at a huge hole in the wall where the door used to be. Bits and pieces of tattered flesh and clothing were spread all over the floor.

20

Lying back on the dilapidated davenport in his apartment, Dybrovik could, without moving his head more than an inch or two, see the kitchen to the right, the front door in the vestibule to the left, and straight ahead, the window overlooking the darkness that was coming to the city.

Yesterday, after speaking with Vostrikov at the Ministry of Transportation, he had come home, fixed himself a supper of boiled potatoes, onions, and fish, and then drunk himself into a stupor.

This morning he had awakened late and tried to telephone Gordik at the bureau to tell him that he had work to do at home, and would not be in until much later. But there had been no answer. Only belatedly, after he had hung up the phone, did he realize it was Saturday and no one would be at the office unless there was a special assignment.

He had taken a shower and begun to get dressed when it dawned on him that there was nowhere for him to go. Ordinarily he would have gone to his office anyway, but now he felt there was no need for it. He was burned up. Expended. His talk with Vostrikov had done all that. In one fell swoop he had used up his one and only chance —the little man—and now he was done.

Vostrikov had a big mouth, and he was running scared. He had already tried to contact Shalnev at the bureau, and that would surely have tipped off the little man that something was going on. Someone was meddling.

"It's the end," he told himself at one point, holding the vodka bottle straight out away from him and addressing it as if it were a mirror and he could see his image in it.

He drank most of the morning, falling asleep again for a few hours. At about two o'clock he roused himself enough to get dressed and walked the few blocks to the government liquor store, where he purchased more vodka. The Foreign Exchange Store was closed on Saturdays, so he could not get Scotch or more American cigarettes, but that didn't matter either, he kept telling himself. He had been born a Russian, he would die a Russian.

It was market day, and the Prospekt was busy with traffic as well as pedestrians of all sizes, shapes, colors, and ages. But he had been on his guard ever since meeting the little man, so he spotted the two men behind him. He took them to be either civil police or KGB officers. They were following him. Just as they had been following him for the past five weeks. They'd never let him go. They'd hound him to the ends of the earth.

Only he was going to fool them all, including the little man. He wasn't going to run. He was going to return to his own little private hole and wait for them to show up.

Back in the apartment, he took off his coat and tossed it aside, then opened a fresh bottle of vodka and poured himself a stiff drink. He went to the window and looked down at the street. The two men who had followed him were climbing into a black Zil, which pulled out into the street and took off.

Was he imagining it all? He continued to stare down at the street where the car had been. Hadn't he seen the men around the building before? Wasn't it possible that they were tenants in this very building, and so had a legitimate right to be hanging around?

He drank his vodka, poured himself another, and then laid his head back on the couch.

He was in Montreal again, with Susanne. They were climbing the stairs to her flat in Outremont. They had been out dining and dancing. It was dark then. She switched on the lights when they came in; he went around turning them all off. She came out of the bathroom wearing only a towel, and he gently slipped it off, releasing her lovely breasts and exposing the delicate tuft of pubic hair. "Delos," she breathed into his ear. "Take me right here. On the floor." And he did.

Thinking of it now made him ache for her.

He turned and looked at the bathroom door. It was tightly closed. Not like the evening he had come home to find the little man waiting for him. The door had been ajar that time.

He set his glass down and walked unsteadily to the door. For several seconds he could not bring himself to touch the doorknob, let alone open the door. But finally he mustered the courage and did it.

The bathroom was empty, of course; he released a sigh of relief and laughed. What had he expected? Larissa had died weeks ago. Her body had been cut down by the ambulance attendants, he had received a document—death by suicide—and her body had been cremated. Her clothes and pitifully few belongings he had given to the woman downstairs, and there was nothing, absolutely nothing left in the apartment to remind him of her. Except her aura. Her spirit. Whatever.

He could sense her presence here in the bathroom. He could almost see her hanging from the light fixture. He could almost smell her musky odor and feel her body next to his in the bed. He could almost hear her speaking to him. Calling from some unutterably vast distance. "Delos," she was calling. "Delos. It was he who killed me."

Insanity, he told himself, firmly closing the bathroom door. It was pressure that had created such feelings. Pressure and too much drink.

He poured another drink and threw himself down on the couch.

Newman was worried about Cargill and Louis Dreyfus and Vance-Ehrhardt; on the other hand, the little man was worried about secrecy. Newman was direct and straightforward. The little man was devious and insinuating. Newman was harsh, however, the little man gentle. Newman was a businessman, the little man a KGB officer.

He turned that thought over in his mind as he absently reached out for his glass, drained it, and poured still another drink.

Newman had warned him against an overzealous KGB officer. But the Americans were always warning against dark plots of one sort or another.

In the beginning the project had been exciting; the only worry was that it wasn't really true. That there would not be the funds the little man had promised to do the sweeping things he wanted done.

But the money was there. Shalnev was making sure of that.

He held his vodka glass up and looked at the bathroom door through the clear liquor. Larissa. What would you have advised?

Dybrovik felt totally alone. Not only was there no one here to comfort him, there was no one to talk to. No one to turn to. No one in this city whom he could trust.

It would be so easy, he thought lying back on the davenport, to let go and trust his fate to the little man. Even now. But he just could not. There would be no grain shortfall this year, there would be a surplus. So why one hundred million tons of corn? What were they going to do with it? And where had the money come from? The Central Committee? Did the Party know of this? Did it approve?

"You think too much," Larissa would have said. But now she was dead. He finally understood it in his bones. Ashes to ashes, dust to dust. She was dead. Murdered. He had always known it, ever since his first conversation with the little man; he had simply not allowed himself to think about it.

He got up from the couch and staggered into the kitchen. Larissa had died. Here. Would he be next? From a drawer he pulled out a large butcher knife and held it up in front of his face.

He had never killed a man before. The thought had never even crossed his mind. But he could hear Larissa now, calling to him for help. And he could see Newman standing by is car in front of the house at Coppet, warning him. And he could see the fright on Vostrikov's face.

Someone knocked at the door, and Dybrovik spun around, almost losing his balance. The little man had come for him! It was no longer a matter of speculation. The end was now!

He moved out of the kitchen and into the living room where he paused in front of the couch, his eyes never straying from the door.

The knock came again, much louder now, more insistent. "Dybrovik? Are you in there?"

Through his vodka-numbed brain, he could not identify the voice, although it sounded familiar. In his mind he could see the little man sitting across the room in the corner. His voice had been soft. Scolding. Like a mother speaking to her naughty child.

He stepped closer to the door, unconsciously bringing the butcher knife higher.

The little man had killed Larissa. The thought consumed his brain, and with it came the consuming resolve to avenge her death and so put an end to the terrible things that were happening. Cargill. Louis Dreyfus. Vance-Ehrhardt. And now him?

"I know you're in there," the voice called again, and Dybrovik stiffened, tightening his grip on the knife.

Of course he knows I am in here. His people watched me go out and then come back. They knew I was here, and they reported to him.

Dybrovik slipped the lock with his left hand while

holding the butcher knife over his head with his right, and then stepped back.

"Come on," he said, the words slurred.

The door opened. "That's better," Shalnev said, stepping across the threshold at the same moment Dybrovik brought the butcher knife down with every ounce of his strength.

The blade deflected off Shalnev's collarbone, then buried itself deeply in the man's neck, severing the carotid artery.

Shalnev lurched powerfully backward. Dybrovik lost his grip on the handle.

"Shalnev," Dybrovik whispered in abject horror.

Shalnev's eyes were rolling as he stumbled farther out into the hall, clawing at the knife jutting obscenely from his jacket collar.

A slight bubbling sound emerged from Shalnev's mouth, and then his knees buckled. His eyes rolled up into his skull, and he fell on the floor dead, a look of surprise on his face.

It was still early, only a few minutes after ten in the evening, when Vladimer Valentin Vostrikov answered the telephone in his apartment.

"There has been an accident, Comrade Vostrikov," a voice at the other end said.

"Who is this? What accident?"

Vostrikov's wife and daughter looked up, concern in their eyes.

"You are needed at the ministry, comrade. It is an emergency. Please hurry."

"Who is this calling?"

"Everyone is being telephoned, comrade. I am only

following orders. It is terrible. We are all needed. Please hurry.''

''I don't know who this is, but I certainly will report this to the authorities,'' Vostrikov said with more courage than he felt. His wife had gotten up and she stood by his side, her hands to her mouth. He had not told her about what had happened with that bastard Dybrovik, but she had guessed something was wrong.

''It is assassination. Director Lysenko. There can be no civil police. You must understand, I am under orders. We all are under orders. You must come at once.'' The caller hung up.

''Assassination? What are you talking about? Who has been assassinated . . .?'' Vostrikov sputtered, but then he realized he was speaking to a dead phone.

''What is it, Vladi?'' his wife asked, her eyes wide.

''I don't know. They want me at the ministry.''

''Who has been assassinated?''

''I don't know.''

''It is trouble for us. I can feel it. I knew something would happen by the way you came home. You have drunk entirely too much tonight. You can't go to your office this way. The others—Comrade Lysenko—will see you this way and know what you have been doing.''

''Keep your peace, woman,'' Vostrikov roared. He pushed past her, went into the bedroom, and grabbed his jacket from the closet. If there was trouble at the ministry, and they wanted him—Vladimir Valentin— then he would comply. Who was he to question such a telephone call in the night?''

His wife had followed him into the bedroom, and she was wailing and screeching that their lives were ended, that he was a foolish, foolish man who had surely done something to bring shame and exile down on their heads.

He brushed her aside and without a backward glance left his apartment, hurrying downstairs and out into the mild evening.

By God, it was easy to put two and two together. Some insane person had assassinated Director Lysenko, and now they needed the staff gathered to find out who had done it, and further, to plan for Monday. After all, even without a director, the ministry would have to continue. There was so much to be done.

Thank heavens the subways were still running. Otherwise he'd have to walk, and it was more than two miles.

At the end of the block, as he started across the dark street, an automobile turned the corner a block away and headed toward him. He was halfway across the street when he decided that he could not make it ahead of the oncoming car, so he stopped to wait for it to pass.

He could not see much of the car, just the headlights bearing down on him, so he turned his eyes away from the glare.

He was still worrying about the work of the ministry when the car struck him, hurling his body upward to crash through a second-story window.

Dybrovik paused about two blocks from the bureau and lit a cigarette, turning sideways as if to block the wind. He studied the street and sidewalk behind him, but there was no one. He had not been followed. They didn't know. Yet.

His passport and travel documents, along with a small amount of German marks and British pounds—general disbursement funds under his direct control—were back in his office. The timing would be tight, but if he could get out of the city tonight by train to Leningrad, and from there to Vyborg and into Finland, he would be free. They would not think to look for him in that direction. They'd expect him to try to hide in Moscow or foolishly attempt to get on a flight to Geneva.

He inhaled the smoke deeply into his lungs, then started walking again as he exhaled through his nostrils.

But what the hell had Shalnev wanted? Somehow Shalnev must have connected him with Vostrikov's telephone call.

Had it gotten back to the little man? Had Shalnev like a dutiful little puppy immediately reported his concerns? Had he recorded in a log somewhere that he was going to Dybrovik's apartment? Was there a record? Or did Shalnev enjoy a certain autonomy of movement? Maybe he had merely come to pay a social visit.

The building that housed Exportkhleb was dark. Dybrovik went around the block to a side entrance, where he unlocked the door with his own key. Inside, he leaned against the door and tried to catch his breath. Shalnev's body had been so damned heavy, and it had leaked blood all the way into his bathroom. It had taken more than an hour to clean the hallway, and then the living room, so that someone would have to come all the way into his bathroom, and then pull back the shower curtain, to find the body.

He shuddered as he went down the wide corridor and hurried up to the third floor.

At the door to his office he paused again, Shalnev's image in his mind's eye. Whatever the man had expected, he definitely had not expected to die this night. There had been a look not of terror or pain on his face, rather a look of complete surprise.

Inside, Dybrovik crossed the trading floor and went into his office. He flipped on the light.

"Good evening, Delos Fedor," the little man said from his seat in the corner.

21

William Bormett left the house a few minutes before 7:00 A.M., went across to the barn for his old, battered pickup truck, and headed out to the east five thousand.

He was frightened. Catherine had seen it in his eyes. Ever since Moscow, his days had been dark and his nights ominous, but the worst part of all had been facing his wife. Every time he looked into her eyes, he had the urge to tell her what had happened, tell her what they were making him do. But he could not. Courage, he tried to tell himself over and over again, would see him through the mess. But each time he tried to tell her, his insides would quiver and his knees get weak.

Overwork, he had told her instead; that, and concern now that the harvest wasn't too far off. Storage bins had to be completely emptied, the last remnants of the grain sold on the spot market to the local elevators. The dryers on the old Emporium farms had to be overhauled now that they were switching to natural gas. And he'd have to get down to Des Moines to speak with Lon Harvey at the employment office about his seasonal help.

"You'll manage, Will, you always do," Catherine had said this morning, her voice soft, her eyes innocent.

She knew that something was wrong. She knew! Christ, maybe he talked in his sleep.

Above the farmyard the road turned into nothing more than a heavily rutted track through a narrow stand of oak and box elder, where they went squirrel hunting, before merging, on the far side of the hill, with the access road from the highway.

He stopped at the crest and looked out across the largest of his fields. The corn was already topping twelve feet, the tassels waving in the breeze another eighteen inches above that. The ear size and moisture content were definitely up to standard, and there had been very little damage from corn borers or other pests this season. The county extension agency forecast a bumper crop. And Bormett was frightened.

In the distance, beyond his fields, he could see the highway that came up from Des Moines, the link with the outside world over which his entire crop would flow to the railhead.

"A small favor, that is all," the little man had said, perched on the edge of the desk in Moscow, holding out the photographs. What in God's name had he gotten himself into? "Go home. Go back to work. You will be contacted with instructions."

The trip home had gone by in a blur, and so had his little chat with Secretary Lundgren, who was pleased at how much Bormett had evidently learned on the trip. "Go home and get back to work, Mr. Bormett," Lundgren had said at the end, and it had severely startled Bormett that his words had so nearly echoed those of the little man in Moscow.

A white truck came into view out on the highway, slowing for the access road. Bormett stiffened.

The contact had come ten days after he and Catherine returned home. His nerves had finally begun to settle down, and way at the back of his mind he had begun to entertain the slight hope that everything that had happened to him in Moscow was nothing more than a bad dream. He was home now; they wouldn't dare try anything here in Iowa.

Several times each week, year round, farm-equipment and chemical salesmen would show up with their catalogs and their pitches, and Bormett never refused to see them. Many of his farm innovations had come from such salesmen; they represented companies that were deep into agricultural research.

"Allied Farm Chemicals, Inc., New Orleans, Louisiana," the man's card read. It was a company new to Bormett, and he said so to the tall, husky salesman.

"Yes, sir, we're brand new in the agricultural business. Started out as a chemical research company and we just began hitting on some new pesticides and blight inhibitors that seemed to be so much better than the competition we just had to market them." The salesman had a southern accent, and he was very jolly. He had the look of success about him. Bormett liked that. Too many of the drummers who called on him were on their last legs, fighting for anything they could get, and they'd tell any lie for just one sale.

"I took the liberty of looking over your fields, sir," the salesman began as they went into Bormett's study.

"What'd you say your name was?" Bormett asked. It wasn't on the card.

"Bud's the name. I want to tell you that you've got some of the finest acres to corn out there that I've seen in my born days. Lovely. Really good, and I want to help you keep them that way." He pulled out a thick looseleaf notebook from his briefcase and laid it down on the desk in front of Bormett.

"CeptCat 1-3-4 is what you'll be needing, sir. A combination blight inhibitor and pesticide." The salesman flipped the notebook open to a full-color photograph of Raya lying on the bed nude, her legs spread, while he stood over her, his trousers and underwear off, taking off his shirt.

Bormett gasped, and looked over his shoulder toward the study door. It was open. Catherine was just down the hall in the kitchen.

"For an operation this size, I'd say you'll be needing fifteen thousand gallons," the salesman continued as if nothing out of the ordinary were happening.

He flipped the page to a photograph of Bormett lying on his back, his eyes half closed. Raya, curled up between his legs, had him in her mouth. There was a half-smile on his lips.

"Oh, God," he said under his breath.

"If you order today, you will get a generous discount, Mr. Bormett, and we can have your chemical out here first thing in the morning." The salesman flipped the notebook closed.

"Seven o'clock," Bormett said. "The tank farm on the east five thousand. The access road is just off Highway 6."

"I know the road, sir," Bud said. "It works best as an evening spray, with a sixty-to-one mixture, a gallon of concentrate per acre, as I said." He got to his feet and smiled. "Thanks, Mr. Bormett. Thanks very much."

And now the truck was here. Bormett drove down to where the tanks clustered at the edge of the fields. Some of the tanks were marked anhydrous ammonia, a common fertilizer, while others had no labels other than numbers, and were used to mix whatever pesticide needed spraying.

Bud was driving the truck, and he had a huge grin on his face as he stepped down from the cab. "Which tank do you want this in, sir?" he asked.

"I can't do this," Bormett said, looking the man in the eye.

The salesman's expression didn't change. "Sure enough," he said, and he turned to climb back into his truck. "The package to your wife will be delivered at the same time it'll be sent to the *Des Moines Register* and to Secretary of Agriculture Lundgren. I'm sure they'll understand when you explain to them what happened."

"Wait," Bormett shouted. He wanted to grab the man and throttle him. He wanted to pound his head into the ground.

The salesman turned back. "Yes, sir?"

"You son of a bitch," Bormett said.

The salesman stepped forward, his grin fading. "You will be watched. Every moment of the day and night. We will expect you to do what you are told. Immediately. Beginning this evening."

Bormett stepped back.

"What tank shall I fill?"

Bormett motioned toward the largest of his mixing tanks, then turned and went back to his pickup truck and climbed in behind the wheel.

The salesman was pulling a hose from the truck over to the mixing tank as Bormett started his pickup, turned around, and headed back the way he had come.

At the top of the hill, he stopped again and looked down toward the tank farm. The truck was still there, its hose snaked over to the tank.

He put the truck in gear, went over the crest of the hill, and desperately tried to think of some way out of his dilemma. But there was no way. No way at all, for him.

There was little doubt in Bormett's mind about the chemical they had sent. It wasn't a simple pesticide. He knew that. It contained something that would most likely attack his corn, either killing it outright or seriously stunting it. The question was, why had they picked on his farm? Why did they want to ruin his crop?

He could see the stage at the university in Moscow, with the students arranged out in front of him and the newspaper correspondent Kedrov next to him. They were arguing hybrids.

Our only salvation against certain worldwide famine is varietal planting, Kedrov had said.

But surely the ruin of one farm, even a farm so large as this one, would not prove Kedrov's position that the use of hybrids was inviting disaster. Surely such an act would be little more than an embarrassment.

So what then? What else were Kedrov and the little man trying to prove? Whatever it was had evidently been planned for some time. They had selected him as their guest, and had set up his talks with the State Department and the Department of Agriculture. Oh, they had set him up all the way, making sure that he would be receptive to Raya, making sure that Catherine would be too tired to go to the party that night. God in heaven, they had set him up, and like a randy old fool he had fallen hook, line, and sinker for the oldest gambit in the world.

He parked his truck in front of the barn and sat there a moment, his large hands tightly gripping the wheel.

Yesterday, after the salesman had left, Bormett had telephoned Bob Hodges over at the county extension office and asked him if he had heard of the chemical CeptCat 1-3-4. Hodges had been enthusiastic.

"Sure thing, Mr. Bormett. It's one hell of a fine pesticide. Has a built-in blight inhibitor, and best of all it's moisture resistant for those first critical eight or ten hours. Are you thinking of using it?"

"I heard something about it, thought I might give it a try."

"It's on the expensive side, from what I understand, but the FDA and USDA both give it a fine recommendation. I've got the circulars on it. Want to see them?"

"You might as well mail them out," Bormett had said, but of course it didn't make any difference what the circulars said. The chemical that he'd have to spray on his fields tonight might or might not be CeptCat 1-3-4, and, if it was, almost anything could have been added to it.

But why? He kept coming back to the same question. Why had they selected him?

He finally got out of the truck and went over to the operations office attached to the big machine building. Inside, Cindy Horton, the farm secretary and girl Friday, had just poured herself a cup of coffee and was sitting down at her littered desk. She was in her early fifties and grossly overweight. But she had a lovely face. She looked up and smiled.

"Good morning, Will . . ." she started, but she let it trail off, a look of concern coming over her features.

"What's wrong, Cindy? Cat got your tongue this morning?" he asked.

"I was just going to ask you the same thing. You look as if you've seen a ghost."

He forced a smile. "You tell me the same thing every year about this time, and every year I tell you that I always worry around harvest time."

She nodded, but said nothing. She and her husband Joseph, who was the general field foreman, had worked for the farm for nearly twenty years, she running the scheduling, payroll, and maintenance programs, and Joseph handling the machinery and every aspect of the field work. Between the two of them, they knew the farm as well as, if not better than, anyone, Bormett included.

"Where's Joseph?" Bormett asked. He was going to have to be more careful in the future; Catherine used to tell him that he wore his heart on his sleeve.

"In the combine shed. There's some trouble with the impellers on number seven."

"I've got to talk to him. We have some pesticide to lay down."

"Do you want to schedule it?"

Bormett nodded. "Let's do the east field tonight, if Smitty can get free. We can do the north tomorrow, the south on Friday, and the west in a couple of hours Saturday."

"Albert's crew is free as well," Cindy said, looking at the scheduling board. "He could work on the west and south fields all day tomorrow.''

"Has to be evening. We're spraying CeptCat. Start about four I'd say. But don't go beyond ten.''

She nodded. "Have we got it in stock?''

"In the main mixing tank on the east field. Sixty to one. But I'll set that up with Joseph.''

"Are you sure everything is okay, Will?'' she asked.

He forced another smile. "You're getting to be quite a nag. Think I'll have to talk to Joseph about you one of these days.

"Get out of here, William Bormett, or I'll tell Catherine you've been flirting with me again.''

He left the office and went around the building over to the combine shed where they kept their ten corn harvesters. His knees felt a little shaky, and his mouth was sour.

Joseph Horton stood atop one of the combines, wiping his hands with a greasy rag.

"You have it fixed yet?'' Bormett called up to him.

"I'm going to have to run in to John Deere this afternoon. We've got a gear-box problem.'' Horton stuffed the rag in the back pocket of his coveralls and climbed down.

"How about the others?'' Bormett asked.

"They're looking pretty good. Four is going to have to be scrapped at the end of this season. We've just had a hell of a time with it, and I sure don't want a repeat of last year.''

Bormett was only half-listening to him now. Another thought had suddenly come to him. It wouldn't really do much good, but at least he'd know what was in the mixing tank.

"I'm going into town this afternoon,'' he said. "I'll

order the parts. I have another job for you."

Albert Straub, one of the shift foremen, came in. "Cindy says we've got some spraying to do," he said as he joined Bormett and Horton.

"That's right," Bormett said. "Starting this afternoon." He turned back to Horton. "We just got the chemical this morning. I'll want it in the fields no later than Saturday evening. It's a late-afternoon blight inhibitor and pesticide. CeptCat 1-3-4."

Horton's face lit up. "Charlie Parker was talking about it last week. I didn't think you'd be ordering it, though."

"Well, it's here, and I want it out, starting with the east field this afternoon. Cindy is scheduling the crew right now."

"What brought all this up, Will?" Horton asked reasonably.

Bormett started to flare up. His nerves were on the raw edge, but he held himself in check. "It's a little experiment. I think we might be able to coax out another two, maybe two and a half percent in our yield."

Horton had a strange look on his face, but he nodded. "Sure thing, Will," he said. "I'll get the gearbox number for you. I already called Stew. Said he had it in stock."

For most of the morning Bormett lost himself in work, overhauling the dryers on the old Emporium farm across the highway. It wasn't until a few minutes before eleven that he came back to the farmyard. He parked behind the main chemical-storage shed, away from the house.

Inside the shed, his heart pounding, he quickly gathered up half a dozen nearly empty pesticide and fertilizer containers, and took them out to his pickup truck. He then rinsed out an old plastic gallon milk container and put it on the truck as well. Driving around to the other side of the farmyard, he stopped at the combine shed for the old gear box, then went on to the office. Cindy was eating her lunch alone.

"I'm going into Des Moines with the gear box from number seven. Tell Joseph that I'll be back around suppertime. I'll come out to see how the spraying is going. Oh, and tell Katy that I went into town."

"I've got the crew scheduled. We can double up tomorrow after all, if you want, and finish before Saturday."

"Sounds okay to me," Bormett said.

Instead of heading over to the highway, he drove down to the tank farm and pulled up by the main mixing tank. He took the empty gallon jug and went around to the tank's inspection valve, where he carefully filled it and replaced the cap.

The chemical smelled like rotten eggs and made Bormett's eyes water. Whatever it was, he would know within a few days. The university agricultural laboratories in Des Moines would analyze it. The chemical would already have been sprayed on the fields. And it would be too late to do anything about it. But at least he would know.

22

The apartment was small and very dirty, and nothing like what Juan Carlos had expected. For nearly three stinking weeks they had remained here alone, out of contact except for María Soleres, the old landlady downstairs, and therefore totally out of touch with what was happening just outside their doorway.

He sat by the window looking down at the tiny rear courtyard filled with trash, holding his knees up to his chest and slowly rocking back and forth.

There had been food and some wine here when he and the others had first arrived with Vance-Ehrhardt and his wife, but within a couple of days it was gone, and the landlady began bringing their meals twice a day. But no wine.

By the sixth day there was no one left except Juan Carlos, Teva, and of course the prisoners. "You will hold them here until your instructions come," María Soleres had told them that day. "They won't give you any trouble. Just keep them tied up."

"We are supposed to be on our way to Tripoli," Juan Carlos had protested.

"I don't know about that," the snaggletoothed woman had creaked. "I only know that you are to remain here. You cannot leave them alone. You must remain here. Those are your instructions."

"Then bring us wine."

The old woman had laughed. "No wine. You will get drunk and make a mistake. Perhaps you will shoot your guns, and Perés will be here." She had laughed again, turned, and left.

In the second week it had seemed as if Teva were recovering from her wounds, but then in the tenth night she had had a relapse, and Juan Carlos had begun to fear that she would die.

There will come a time when you are alone, and are expected to hold a position. The words of his instructor had come back to him.

"Then you must be strong," Juan Carlos had mumbled out loud. "Then you must think of your brothers and sisters in the revolution, and you must be strong for them."

That night, when the landlady had come with their supper, Juan Carlos had made her promise she would bring some medicine for Teva. "She will die without medicine," he said. "And if that happens, I will kill the other two, and then come down and kill you."

Within two hours, she had returned with bandages, antiseptic ointment, and penicillin tablets.

At first, Teva's condition had remained unchanged, but then on the thirteenth day her fever had broken, and she had woken up, demanding food, although she was still disoriented and somewhat delirious.

"Juan," she called his name weakly now. He looked away from the window, but he did not get up.

On the very first day, they had made the long tape recording. The little man had written the speech, and Vance-Ehrhardt had dutifully recited it as soon as Juan Carlos had placed a gun to his wife's head.

In a way it had been a bitter disappointment that he and Teva were not immediately going to Tripoli, yet in another way it was exciting that they were to remain to see the entire thing through.

At least it had seemed that way at first. But now, he shook his head in despair. But now, each day was nothing. Each day his anger rose, his frustration deepened, and his fear solidified that they would never leave this apartment alive.

"Juan," Teva cried again. Her voice was weak and hoarse. Although her fever had left her, she didn't seem to regain her strength, nor did the wound in her shoulder want to heal. It was still very tender to the touch, inflamed and draining. He had to pick her up and take her in to the toilet several times a day, and he supposed that was what she was calling him for now. But she would just have to wait this time.

Then there were Vance-Ehrhardt and his whore of a wife. They had both been subdued at first, especially whenever a gun was held to the woman's head.

But they too had been losing strength. It was the food, Juan Carlos figured; even he no longer felt strong. Now they merely lay in their bed all day and all night, barely moving, even when food was brought to them.

Juan Carlos had kept them tied up until three days

ago, when the woman had gotten sick and puked all over herself. Then he had untied them both and ordered Vance-Ehrhardt to clean up his wife's mess. Since then he had let them remain untied. They were too weak to give trouble.

"Juan, please help me," Teva cried pitifully, and Juan Carlos finally got up and went into her room.

A stench assailed his nostrils the moment he entered, and he realized with a sinking stomach that she had soiled the bed.

"I am sorry," she cried, the tears coming to her eyes. "Oh, God, Juan, I am sorry, but I could not help it. I am so weak."

Juan Carlos could feel tears coming to his eyes too, as he looked down at the pathetic creature on the bare mattress. She was dressed only in a bra and panties, despite the cold; her other clothing was too filthy to wear. And now the mattress was soiled, and he could see where her wound had leaked again, leaving a large, dark stain on the bandages.

In Libya, out on the hot, clean desert, their instructor had taught them to lie for hours without moving, no matter the conditions.

If a snake comes to lie down beside you, then you know you have blended with nature, and your enemies will not see you. Remember that.

But this was not Libya, nor was it the hot desert.

"Please help me, Juan," Teva cried.

"Uno momento, querida," he said tenderly, and he turned and went into the bathroom, where he ran rusty brown water into the dirty clawfoot tub. He skipped off his clothes and quickly washed them in the tub, wrung them out, and hung them over the windowsill.

Nude, he went back into the odoriferous bedroom where Teva was babbling deliriously, took a deep breath, and reached over and picked her up. He carried her into the bathroom and laid her gently in the tub.

"Mi querido, Juan," she said hoarsely, opening her eyes.

Juan Carlos took off her bra and panties, and threw them in the already clogged toilet. There was no soap, but he managed to rinse her off, nevertheless, and then pulled the plug. When the filthy water had all drained, he rinsed the tub and began filling it again with luke-warm water, the hottest it would come.

"We have them," she said loudly at one point. "They will not get away. The ransom will come."

'The ransom will come." He crawled into the bathtub with her and cradled her in his arms as they sat in tandem.

"My shoulder," she whimpered.

He shifted to the left so that he would not be touching her shoulder. She had lost a lot of weight; her tiny breasts sagged limply and her ribs stood out. She was no longer desirable, although Juan Carlos could remember in vivid detail their lovemaking over the past months. It had been wonderful.

"When we get to Tripoli," she mumbled, lying back against him, "we'll go swimming on the beach. You will take me to the beach?"

"We'll go swimming on the beach," Juan Carlos echoed, his heart aching.

"We're going to get out of here," she said, stiffening in his arms. "Has he called yet?"

"He has called," Juan Carlos lied. "We are leaving as soon as we get cleaned up and dressed."

"We are leaving?"

"Very soon, Teva."

Somehow she managed to turn far enough around so that she could look into his eyes. Her breath was very bad. Her eyes widened and her nostrils flared. "Let's do some fucking, Juan. Before we go. Make love to me."

The tears were streaming from Juan Carlos' eyes now. "Turn around," he said gently. "I will begin."

"From behind?" she said. "I like that."

He put his hands on her breasts and kneaded the nipples. She arched her back slightly.

"Juan, I love you," she said weakly. The dressing on her wound had gotten wet, and she was bleeding very hard now.

"I love you too," he said, running his hands up from her breasts to her neck.

She bent forward and just managed to kiss his right wrist as he brought his legs up around her waist. He locked his ankles together so that she would not be able to move away from him.

"Juan," she said.

He closed his eyes and let his fingers find her throat. He began to squeeze, gently at first because he was finding it difficult to muster the courage, but then harder.

Her body began to squirm, and then thrash, her movements very weak as he continued to squeeze harder and harder, the tears coming from his closed eyes. "Teva," he cried. "Teva. Teva. Teva." He chanted her name until her pitiful struggles finally ceased.

He kept squeezing for a long time, until his fingers cramped. He unlocked his legs from around her waist, and carefully eased himself up and out of the tub, gently laying her back.

Her eyes were open, bulging out of their sockets, and blood ran from her mouth where she had bitten through her tongue. The sight was not pretty, but it didn't really matter. She was no longer Teva. Teva had died weeks ago.

He turned away from her and dried himself off, then padded into the other room, where he stood in a daze for a long time, looking at the machine guns on the floor by the couch; at the radio over which nothing came any longer; and at the remains of this morning's meal.

Nothing had come from Vance-Ehrhardt's message on the radio. No one had come here rejoicing with a message that they had won. The little man had sent no one. No one except María Soleres with food and medicine, but no wine.

So it was finished. Or at least in Juan Carlos' mind it was finished. He no longer cared what happened. The little man had brought this down on them. The plan had been an excellent one, the kind that always attracted world attention for the cause. But with this operation there had been only slow death. The little man had not come back. He had lied to them, had left them here. It simply was not fair.

He went into the other bedroom. Vance-Ehrhardt and his wife were lying in each other's arms. They were both awake, looking at him, Margarita's eyes wide at the sight of his nude body.

"What is happening?" Vance-Ehrhardt asked. Although his voice was weak and ragged, there was a certain dignity in it that infuriated Juan Carlos.

Juan Carlos walked around to Vance-Ehrhardt's side, doubled up his fist and struck the woman in the face with all of his might, knocking her unconscious. In the next instant, he clamped his fingers around Vance-Ehrhardt's neck and squeezed.

The old man was not much stronger than Teva, and he battered Juan Carlos with his hands and feet, his struggles nearly overpowering. But he weakened rapidly, and after he lay still, Juan Carlos continued to squeeze.

When he was sure the old man was dead, he rolled him away from Margarita, who was just beginning to regain consciousness, and seized her neck, crushing her windpipe with the last of his waning strength. Then he crawled back into the living room and collapsed on the floor.

A large black spider had constructed an elaborate web between the rungs of a chair, and it waited in the corner for its unwary prey to come along. A scorpion, its deadly tail curved up over its head, started up the leg of the chair. The spider was unaware of the intruder. The scorpion was hunting.

Henri Riemé lay in his bed, bathed in sweat, watching the life-and-death drama unfolding across the room from him. It was 1:00 P.M., the height of the Libyan afternoon, and the temperature in Tripoli was 110 degrees Fahrenheit and climbing.

There had been a change of plan. Instead of flying on to Moscow from Barcelona, to where he had made his way three weeks ago, he had been instructed to return to Tripoli and await further communiqués. Which he had done, with inhuman patience. But Riemé was not human, he reminded himself. He had not been human for years. He was nothing more than a killing machine.

Neither content with his lot nor dissatisfied with it. Merely accepting the fact that he functioned.

Someone knocked on his door. Moving incredibly fast, he rolled off the bed, snatched his silenced automatic from beneath his pillow, levered a round into the chamber, and flipped the safety off as he knelt to the right of the door.

"Oui?" he called.

"It is the concierge, monsieur. Your message has arrived."

Riemé recognized the voice. He rose, shifting the automatic to his left hand and unlatching the door with his right.

"Oui?" He looked into the frightened eyes of the old man.

"There are two men waiting for you downstairs. They have a car. It is time to go."

Riemé remained motionless.

The concierge fumbled with his words for a moment, then said, "It is time by the clocktower to go, monsieur."

Riemé nodded. The code words were correct. *"Merci.* Please have my bill ready, I will leave momentarily."

"Your bill has been paid, monsieur. Shall I tell your friends you will be down soon?"

"Tell them nothing," Riemé said, and he closed the door. He remained standing there for a long moment, until he heard the concierge leave. Then he turned and threw his few things in his suitcase, draped his jacket over his gun hand, and left the room.

He took the back stairs down, emerged into the alley, and hurried around to the street. There he saw a Citroën sedan parked at the curb, the driver behind the wheel, another man standing in the hotel doorway.

Riemé crossed the street at the corner, walked down the block until he was even with the car, then crossed directly to the driver and placed the barrel of his gun against the man's temple.

"Who has sent you?"

The driver looked up, his eyes bulging. "It is time by the clocktower," he squeaked.

"Where am I to go?"

"Not Moscow," the driver said. "Your plans have been changed since Paris."

The man by the hotel door glanced over. Seeing that something was wrong, he stepped aside and reached in his jacket.

"Tell your partner you are both dead if he pulls out his gun."

"No, Claude! It is all right! It is he," the driver called over. There was a lot of traffic, but no one else was paying them any attention.

Riemé nodded, and slowly the other man relaxed and took his hand away from his coat. He came over to the car.

"You gave me a fucking scare, you son of a bitch," Claude said.

Riemé cocked the hammer of his automatic and pointed it at the man. "Monsieur?"

The man's eyes widened, and he stepped back. "Oh, Christ, pardon me. Didn't mean a thing, *mon brave*."

Riemé said nothing.

"We have a new assignment for you. Sealed instructions. We're to get you to the airport. You are going to Buenos Aires. There is something to be cleaned up there."

María Soleres had not come at eight with their supper, and by ten-thirty Juan Carlos was very hungry. He had put Teva out of her misery, and they had planned on killing the Vance-Ehrhardts in any event, so the operation was still functional as far as he was concerned. But he could not remain here. Not like this, without food. Even the little man could not expect that from him.

Wearily Juan Carlos dragged himself over to the pile of weapons in front of the couch, picking up one of the Uzi submachine guns and two spare clips of ammunition, which he stuffed in his pockets.

If need be, he told himself, he would hijack an airplane and force the crew to take him to Libya. Colonel Qaddafi would receive him. He would be a hero of the people.

At the door he stopped to listen, but there was no sound from outside, and after a minute he opened the door.

The apartment was on the fourth floor, the landlady's apartment on the first. There was a stairwell in the middle of the building.

He moved silently to the railing and looked over, pulling back immediately. There was someone below. On the first floor.

Again he looked over the railing, and this time he waited long enough to see that it was María Soleres and a dark-haired man. Talking.

Quickly, his heart hammering, Juan Carlos started down the stairs, moving on the balls of his feet so that he would make absolutely no noise.

She had not come with their dinner. Was she now speaking to the police? Telling them about the people in the apartment on the fourth floor?

At the second-floor landing, Juan Carlos moved a little closer to the rail. He could hear the words now.

". . . come to help them," the man was saying. He spoke with a French accent.

"They are all dead up there, I think," María Soleres said. "I saw through the skylight. The woman is dead in the tub, and the other two are dead in the bed."

"What about Juan Carlos? Is he dead as well?"

"He was lying on the floor in the living room without clothes. He was dead, I think."

"Why didn't you go in?"

"I want no further part in this. You may go up and take them away. I want no further part in it."

"I will need your help."

"No," María Soleres said sharply. "I will call the police, if need be."

Juan Carlos crept farther down the stairs, until he was at a spot where the stairs turned a corner, around which he would be in their view.

"No . . ." María Soleres started to say, but her voice was choked off, and sounds of struggle came up the stairs.

It served her right, Juan Carlos thought as he stepped around the corner.

The dark-haired man with the French accent looked up from the inert form of María Soleres, raised his gun, and fired, hitting Juan Carlos in the throat and driving him back against the wall.

Juan Carlos raised his Uzi as the Frenchman fired again, and his finger jerked on the trigger. Just before everything went dark, he saw that the Frenchman was falling backward, several red holes in his chest and stomach.

23

It was hot in Atlanta when Newman stepped off the plane and crossed the tarmac to the Ford LTD waiting in front of the terminal. Janice Wilcox, Paul's widowed daughter, was waiting by the car.

She was a tall woman, with a pleasant face that was somewhat reminiscent of her father's, and a trim, almost athletic body. Paul had recently bragged that his daughter, at thirty, looked more like a girl of eighteen. She wore a black dress, a small black hat, and a dark veil across her face.

"I'm sorry, Janice," Newman said as he reached her.

She lifted her veil, and he kissed her on the cheek. "I'm glad you could come, Kenneth. I wanted to talk with you before we met the others."

"Has there been any trouble with the arrangements, anything I can help with?"

She shook her head. "I want to know what happened there, Kenneth," Janice said without preamble as they drove off. She was a very strong woman. A junior executive with one of the insurance companies here in Atlanta. She wasn't giving way to hysterics now.

"There was an explosion, which was probably meant for me. Paul just happened to be there," Newman said.

"What were you two working on?"

"I can't say, Janice."

She turned toward him and lifted her veil. "Is that what you told the police?"

"Yes. But I also told them that I think I know who killed him, and why."

Janice's complexion was pale and her eyes moist. Her lower lip was quivering at last. "I'm listening," she said after a slight hesitation.

"It has to do with Lydia, my wife."

"The Vance-Ehrhardt Company had him killed?"

"No," Newman said. "While I was down there I had a run-in with the chief of the Buenos Aires police, Reynaldo Perés. Lydia warned me twice that he wanted to see me dead. Wanted to put some of the blame for her parents' kidnapping on me."

"That's insanity. Isn't it?"

Newman nodded. "I had just hung up from talking with her—she called to warn me that I would be assassinated—when the bomb went off."

"My father was devoted to you. He spoke often of his work. How much he admired you. Said you were a man of principles. He told me once that you were the most honest man he had ever met. I told him to go out on his own. Start his own business. He had plenty of money. He had the knowledge, and certainly the talent. He could have made it. But he told me that he'd never leave you so long as you wanted him as a business associate.''

Newman was touched. He and Paul had become close friends over the years. Yet he had never known just how devoted Saratt had been. His death had been a terrible blow, made even worse by what Janice was telling him.

He reached out and touched her hand, but she jerked away as if she had been burned.

''The service is at two,'' she said. ''Afterward some friends and relatives will be coming to my house. But your presence isn't necessary. I'm sure you have a lot of work to attend to. We don't want to take up much of your time.'' She didn't have much control left.

''Stop it, Janice,'' Newman said gently.

She was finally crying.

''I loved him too. He was a friend.''

''Catch his murderers, Kenneth. Catch the bastards and string them up,'' she said through clenched teeth.

''Yes,'' Newman said. But it would not be that easy. They'd probably never catch the real murderer, Perés, and it wasn't likely they'd catch his henchmen who had actually placed the bomb. He, or they, were probably already back in Buenos Aires.

Paul's remains—what the coroner had been able to reassemble—had been sent back to Atlanta for cremation. The minister who gave the sermon was evidently an old friend of the family, because he spoke in a choked voice of Paul's childhood. There were a lot of people at the service, only a few of whom Newman recognized. Most were relatives who had visited Paul in Duluth at one time or another over the past few years.

He had been a popular man. Well liked, well respected. There were a lot of questions for Newman, who had been with him when he was killed.

"Have they caught the bastards, yet?" was the most common.

Afterwards, Newman had ridden to the house with an uncle from Buffalo who hadn't said a word, and who refused to be drawn into a conversation.

Janice seemed genuinely pleased that Newman had come to the house, and she personally fixed him a drink and made sure he had something to eat.

"Will you be staying in Atlanta tonight?" she asked him.

"I haven't decided yet," he said. He had been thinking about Dybrovik and the Russian deal. Paul had not had the chance to set up a meeting away from Geneva before he was killed. It was going to have to be somewhere on neutral territory . . . such as Athens, they had decided. He felt guilty thinking about it now.

"I'd like you to stay, Kenneth. We could have the day together tomorrow. There's a lot I'd like to ask you about my father."

"I'd love to, but I just don't know. I'll have to call my office."

She stared at him for a long moment. The house was filled with people, most of them standing around in little groups. "You can use the phone in the study," she said. "First door on the right, upstairs."

Newman went upstairs to her study, which had been made over from one of the smaller bedrooms. Its windows were covered in heavy, rich drapes. There was a small, leather-topped desk and a couple of matching file cabinets. The walls were lined with books. But there were no bits and pieces of memorabilia. The study was neutral.

He sat down behind the desk, picked up the telephone, and had the operator place a person-to-person call to Sam Lucas, the manager of Abex, Ltd., in New York.

Lucas seemed excited. "Am I ever glad you called, Mr. Newman. I was getting set to call down there, and I really didn't want to do that."

"What have you got, Sam?"

"We just received a telex from Dybrovik himself. Wants a meeting pronto."

"In Geneva?"

"No, that's the odd part. The telex originated in Moscow, and that's where he wants the meet. Immediately. Says your visa will be handled through their embassy in Washington."

"Impossible," Newman said without hesitation. "It'd blow everything wide open. I don't know what the hell he's thinking about."

"He says the meeting is 'most important.' His words."

"I'll meet with him, but not in Moscow. Telex him we'll meet in twenty-four hours in Athens. At the Grand Bretagne. He knows the hotel. Make the arrangements there for us yourself. Tell them we'll require adjoining suites, and absolute confidentiality."

"Yes, sir."

"And Sam, I want you to get a hold of Felix and tell him what's going on. He's going to have to cover for me in Duluth. He should be able to handle it with no problems."

"I talked with him this morning. Secretary Lundgren

wants to talk to you. Said it was urgent.''

"Tell Felix to stall him. Tell him I went to Buenos Aires or something. Anything. I'll talk to him when I get back from Athens.''

"Will you be needing any backup?''

"I'll keep in touch, Sam. It's up to you and Felix to keep things running while I'm gone.''

"How's everyone holding up down there?''

"About as well as you could expect. Janice is all right.''

"Give her my sympathies, if you would.''

"Sure,'' Newman said, and Lucas hung up. Newman was just taking the phone away from his ear when he heard a second click over the line. He left the receiver on the desk, and rushed downstairs. Janice was just moving away from the hall telephone. She looked up and their eyes met. No one else noticed that anything was going on.

"Don't worry,'' she said. "I won't say anything to anyone.'' She had a defiant expression.

"Why did you do that?''

"Because I wanted to know what's going on, and you wouldn't tell me. I'm not going to let my father's murder slip by. I lost my mother when I was five, and my husband two years ago. I've been through this before.''

"If and when I find out anything, Janice—anything at all—you will be the first to know. I promise you that. But my conversation just now had nothing to do with your father's death.''

"Do the authorities know that you're dealing with the Russians?''

"It has nothing to do with your father's death.''

"I want to believe you, Kenneth. God, if you only knew how I want to believe you."

"You won't be helping matters by—"

She cut him off. "I told you I wouldn't discuss this with anyone, and I won't."

He just looked at her.

"But I'm going to hold you to your promise. When you find out who murdered my father, you will tell me."

"I will."

She nodded sadly.

He needed Paul now, he thought, more than he ever had. He needed to bounce his concerns off someone whom he could trust entirely. At this moment there was no one on this earth who fit that description. No one.

Newman slept on the company aircraft; his crew timed their flight so they arrived at Athens a few minutes after noon on Saturday. The telex had been sent to Exportkhleb and acknowledged within two hours. Dybrovik would be there, no later than eight this evening.

He had a light lunch and half a bottle of wine by himself at the top Grille Room of the hotel, and then went up to inspect the rooms. They were on the top floor at the front of the hotel, overlooking Syntagma Square. It was the tourist season, but tourists rarely took suites, so only one other suite in that wing of the top floor was booked. They would have privacy.

Later in the afternoon he went for a walk around the square to put his thoughts in order. So much had happened to him in the past couple of months that it was difficult for him to put it in perspective. He had gained a wife, and then lost her. He had lost his best friend. There had been killings and kidnappings, and the Cargill elevator explosion. And overriding all of that was the Russian corn buy. So mammoth a deal that it went beyond surprise or awe. The numbers were so large as to seem unreal.

Paul was dead, and Lydia was gone from him. But thinking about them sharpened his desperate need to be with someone, so he put them out of his mind, thinking instead about Dybrovik.

The man was an enigma. Paul would have said he was a con artist, and Lydia wouldn't trust him. They'd agree that he was hiding something. Each time Newman had met with the man, he seemed just a little more desperate than the last time. Something was eating at him, and it had begun to eat at Newman.

Yet as far as the buy was concerned, everything was turning out exactly the way Dybrovik had promised it would. The Russians were taking the grain. They were providing the hard currencies with which to purchase more.

It was a straightforward corn buy. Except that the money was already in the hundreds of millions of dollars and would rise well above the two-billion mark, and the corn amounted to one-fourth the entire U.S. output.

He was torn. The Russians truly needed the grain. The Russians were playing some kind of market manipulation. The Russians were gathering a stockpile of food for a siege.

He had come around the square, opposite his hotel, where outside the American Express Building he bought a *Wall Street Journal* from the news vendor. He got a table at the sidewalk cafe, Papaspirou, and ordered coffee and a cognac.

It was six o'clock—two hours before Dybrovik was scheduled to show up. Newman was slightly hungry, but he decided against eating anything now. He wanted to be as sharp as he possibly could be for their meeting. There would be plenty of time to eat later.

As he sat sipping his coffee and cognac he unfolded the newspaper. There on the front page were photographs of Jorge Vance-Ehrhardt and his wife, Margarita, under the headlines:

INTERNATIONAL GRAIN TRADER AND WIFE DEAD
Found Strangled In Buenos Aires
Montonero Kidnap-Murder Plot
Blossoming Into Revolution

He was stunned. Lydia had expected this. She had felt all along that her parents would never be returned alive. He, on the other hand, had thought there was a very good chance that they would come out of it.

According to the story, Vance-Ehrhardt officials, who declined to be named, had agreed to the kidnappers' demands of one hundred million dollars in gold for themselves and for food and medicine for the peasants. But gunfire had been reported in a slum area of Buenos Aires, and when police investigated they found two gunmen and the landlady dead on the first floor, and upstairs the bodies of another terrorist and Jorge and Margarita Vance-Ehrhardt.

After he finished reading the article, Newman stared at the photographs. He could feel the fear beginning to work at his gut. Something was going on. Something that connected Cargill, Louis Dreyfus, and Vance-

Ehrhardt with Paul's death, and in all likelihood with the Soviet corn buy.

It went beyond coincidence, far beyond mere chance. For the first time in his life, Newman felt that he was not in control of the people and circumstances around him; that he was nothing more than a bystander, a spectator, an unwitting victim of some shrouded plot.

After awhile he paid his bill and went to his hotel.

"Ah, Mr. Newman," the desk clerk said, smiling. "There is a message for you." He handed Newman a slip of paper.

It was from Dybrovik.

> Kenneth,
>> Have arrived. Am ready for meet.
>> D.

Newman thanked the clerk, then took the elevator up to the top floor. The Russians were involved in all this, he was almost certain of it. It was what Dybrovik was hiding. It was what he had been so guilty about. Only now it was going to end, Newman thought. He was going to find out exactly what the hell was happening, or he'd stop all shipments and all futures buying. If they didn't like it, they could sue him in the Hague.

In his room, he telephoned Dybrovik's suite. The Russian answered on the first ring.

"It is Newman."

"Are you back?"

"Yes. I'm next door. Are you ready?"

There was a slight pause. "Yes. You can come over. I am ready to talk with you."

He sounded wooden, mechanical, as if he were talking in his sleep. "I'm going to want some answers,

Dybrovik.''

"I understand."

"The truth."

"I understand that too, Kenneth. You can come now."

Newman hung up, and stood there for a moment. There was something wrong with Dybrovik, something wrong with the entire setup. It didn't seem right at all. He had the sudden urge to quietly pack his bags and get out of there. The hell with the Russians. The hell with the deal.

He turned, went out to the corridor, and knocked at the next door. Dybrovik answered it immediately, as if he had been standing just on the other side. He was sweating profusely, and his eyes were bloodshot. It looked as if he hadn't slept in a week, or as if he were sick.

"Come in, Kenneth," he said in the same wooden voice.

Newman came in to the vestibule. The suite was nearly a duplicate of his own rooms. Dybrovik locked and chained the door.

"Go in, Kenneth. Please," he said, and Newman went on into the sitting room.

There was a dark, very intense-looking, small man seated in the corner by one of the windows, and he stood up, a slight smile on his face.

"Good evening, Mr. Newman. Permit me to introduce myself."

24

"Colonel Vadim Leonid Turalin."

"KGB?" Newman asked, just within the sitting room of Dybrovik's suite.

The little man nodded. "Welcome to Athens, Mr. Newman."

Newman suddenly became very conscious of his surroundings. The lights in the room were dim; the bathroom door was closed; the bedroom door was half open; the window curtains were drawn. He stepped back, but Dybrovik was there, and he turned around. "What the hell is going on here, Delos?"

"Please, Kenneth, we mean you no harm."

"Like hell!" Newman said. He felt cornered, and he wanted to get out of there.

"He wants to explain everything to you," Dybrovik was saying. "He wants to sit down with you—the three of us—and talk. That's all. Honestly.''

Newman turned back. He caught a fleeting glimpse of a large figure in the half-open bedroom door, and he flinched.

"I believe it will be to your advantage to sit down and listen to what I have to say, Mr. Newman. You will probably find that I make a lot of sense. I will be able to answer a lot of questions that must be plaguing you." Turalin paused. "Delos Fedor came to me and said that you were concerned by recent events."

"What do you have to do with all of this?" Newman asked. Every muscle in his body was tense. Would he be able to get past Dybrovik, and then unlock and unchain the door before the goon in the bedroom got to him?

"It was I who authorized Comrade Dybrovik to purchase corn."

"A hundred million tons of it?"

"Or more."

"Then it is a market manipulation? But why pick on me?"

"Two questions, actually," Turalin said, smiling. "Won't you sit down? I'll try to answer all your questions as fully as I can."

Newman didn't move.

"Please, Kenneth," Dybrovik said sadly.

"When we are finished with our little chat, you will be free to go. No one will stop you," Turalin said.

"If I'm not interested—if I want to leave this instant?"

Turalin just looked at him, a hard, flat expression in his eyes.

"Did your people kill Paul?"

"Paul Saratt? Your partner?" Turalin asked.

Dybrovik stepped out of the vestibule. He had a haunted look on his face. Newman glanced from Turalin to him and back. Then he nodded.

"No. We did not. It was your wife's people."

"Not Perés?"

"Not directly. But Perés is a very powerful man in Argentina. He has been making it very difficult there for Vance-Ehrhardt, Ltd. Even more so now that your father-in-law and his wife are dead."

"But you knew?"

Turalin shrugged. "We could guess. So should you have."

"Who kidnapped Vance-Ehrhardt?"

"The Montoneros," Turalin said. "Argentina is on the verge of revolution. Perés knows it. Your wife knows it. They are both struggling for the same aims, only from different directions. Perés wants to keep the country quiet so that he can retain his power. Your wife wants to keep the peace so that she can run the Vance-Ehrhardt empire. But it cannot last."

"How can you be so certain there will be a revolution there?" Newman asked, although he agreed with Turalin.

"The Malvinas defeat, for one. One hundred and thirty percent inflation for another. The exploitation of the pampas farmer." Turalin shook his head. "I'm certainly not going to argue socialism versus capitalism with you, but when people become as oppressed as the Argentines have become, then something must give."

Newman had more or less come to the same conclusions himself. They made his worry about Lydia all the more intense.

"Please sit down, Kenneth," Dybrovik said. "You

will be free to go when we are finished. He has given his word. I give you mine."

Newman came farther into the room, and sat on the arm of the couch. Dybrovik sat heavily in one of the easy chairs opposite Turalin. He still had the sad look in his eyes.

"You asked if this was a market manipulation," Turalin said. "It is not. If it were, we would have ordered you to purchase all the corn on margin. We would not have advanced your firm so much money. Nor would we be taking delivery of the corn we have already purchased.

"You've only taken eight million tons. The bulk of the corn is yet to come. Your ports can only handle forty-five or fifty million tons each year of all grain combined."

"*Our* ports, Mr. Newman. Soviet ports. There are Warsaw Pact ports at our disposal."

"I can answer your other question, Kenneth," Dybrovik said. "It was I who selected your company for the buy."

"Why?"

"Secrecy. When Colonel Turalin came to me with the order to purchase corn, I was told it would have to be done in total secrecy. Your company was the only one I felt could handle such a project. All the others were too large, staffed by too many people. Our secret would have gotten out."

Dybrovik's answer seemed well rehearsed to Newman. And although it was the answer he had expected, he found he was having a hard time believing it. Dybrovik was frightened.

"It's not a market manipulation, and you have had

nothing to do with the kidnapping of the Vance-Ehrhardts, or my partner's death, or the death of Louis Dreyfus, or the Cargill elevator explosion."

Turalin and Dybrovik looked at each other. "We had nothing to do with the Cargill elevator explosion, Mr. Newman," Turalin said. He too seemed uncomfortable now.

"And the Louis Dreyfus assassination?"

"Enough!" Turalin snapped. "It is time for you to answer a few questions. You indicated to Comrade Dybrovik that you were becoming concerned. Well, so are we."

It was so transparent. Newman wondered why this entire scene had been staged.

"We have given your firm a considerable sum of money with which to purchase grain futures. To date, what little corn you have purchased has all been on margin. Why is that?"

"Until I am convinced that this is not another Grain Robbery, I will continue to purchase on margin," Newman said. "That is, if I continue to purchase at all."

Turalin said something to Dybrovik in rapid Russian. Dybrovik replied tersely, and Turalin nodded. "You are still worried that it is a market manipulation such as happened in the early seventies."

"What about Louis Dreyfus?" Newman repeated. Turalin blinked.

Dybrovik suddenly seemed very nervous. "Kenneth . . ." he started, but Turalin savagely cut him off.

"You had him assassinated," Newman said. "It was your people . . . the KGB."

Turalin said nothing.

"Why, for Christ's sake?" Newman shouted.

"Kenneth, please, you have to understand that—" Dybrovik said, but again Turalin cut him off.

Newman got up. "If you kill me, your five hundred million becomes forfeit. It would be an expensive assassination."

"You don't understand, Mr. Newman," Turalin said. He remained sitting on the edge of his chair, his hands together.

Again Newman had the strong impression that all this was a put-on, some sort of an act.

"Did you kill Gérard Louis Dreyfus?"

"Yes," Turalin said softly.

"Why?"

"He found out about your deal with us, and he was moving against you."

Newman was deeply shaken. "You didn't think I could handle the competition, so you had it eliminated?" He glanced toward the bedroom door. The figure he had seen earlier was not there. "I'm withdrawing my company's participation in this thing. I will deduct for the corn I have already purchased and shipped, as well as for a reasonable commission, and the remainder of the fund will be retransferred to your Eurobank account."

"Wait," Dybrovik shouted, jumping up.

Turalin had also gotten to his feet. Newman backed toward the vestibule. At any moment he expected the bedroom door to open and an armed man to burst out.

"We couldn't take any chances with Louis Dreyfus. If he had ruined our deal, it would have meant . . . mass starvation," Turalin said.

For several long seconds Newman wasn't quite sure that he understood.

"It's falling apart on us. Albania. Poland. Especially Afghanistan."

Newman looked over his shoulder at the corridor door. It all fit together. It did make sense. They could not have gone to the American government, not without admitting defeat of their system. And yet it was all unreal. Bigger than life. What did they expect from him?

"You must believe us. We're quite desperate for grain."

"Why corn?"

"It's universal," Turalin said. "I mean, we can feed it to people as it is, it can be ground up into flour, we can make oil from it, or it can be fed to animals. There is no other grain we could have gotten in such quantities that would do so much for us."

It all seemed a little too glib to Newman, and yet, goddamn it, it fit. It was no less than he and a great many other people in the business had been expecting for a good many years. Still, Newman didn't believe it.

"And now I'm supposed to return home and continue working for you, knowing that you assassinated poor Louis Dreyfus?"

"We had no other choice, Kenneth," Dybrovik said woodenly.

"Good Lord," Newman breathed heavily.

Dybrovik suddenly turned away. He seemed all arms and legs.

"You must help us, you know," Turalin said. "We have no where else to turn at this date, without . . ." he hesitated.

"Violence?"

Turalin did not reply.

Alone in his room again, Newman stood by the

window looking down at the square. But he did not feel safe here. He felt like a soldier in the middle of a battle-field who had slipped inside a tent. Although he couldn't see the war raging around him, he was right in the middle of it, and very vulnerable. It was time to run. There was no way in hell he believed anything that Turalin or Dybrovik had told him. The story was so patently foolish that he was amazed they had even tried to foist it on him.

On the other hand, he had to ask himself, what would they have said or done differently had the story been true? If there was a lack of food, they'd have to either produce it or buy it. If they had been reduced to buying it, they would have gone about it this way.

It was no longer clear to Newman what his choices were, and he realized at this moment just how depen-dent he had become on Paul. They had understood each other, had respected each other. And above all, they had trusted each other.

With Paul gone, and without Lydia, he was truly alone.

He crossed the room, picked up the telephone, and started to ask the hotel operator to ring the airport, but then changed his mind. This phone was possibly being monitored by Turalin's people. Instead, he told the operator to send someone up for his bags, he was check-ing out.

He went downstairs. From a payphone he called the business aviation terminal, finally getting hold of Jacob, his steward, whom he instructed to ready the airport for immediate departure.

He was reasonably certain that his conversation with Jacob was safe, just as he was certain his next move would be monitored. At the bellhop station, he instructed the bell captain to have his bags sent over to the Athens Hilton.

"Is something wrong, sir?" the bell captain asked solicitously.

"Not a thing," Newman said conspiratorially. "It is a rendezvous."

"I understand, sir."

If Turalin had been telling the truth, he'd allow Newman to leave without interference. If he had been lying. . . .

Newman strode across the lobby, and outside hurried into the square, where he sat down on a stone bench. He had a clear view of a portion of the hotel lobby through the glass doors.

Several cabs came and went. A tour bus pulled up and ten or twelve couples got off and crowded into the hotel. Finally, a bellhop came out of the lobby with Newman's two suitcases and set them down on the sidewalk.

A very tall, husky man came out of the lobby, turned to the left, and then lingered there, watching the bellhop and the bags. From time to time he looked up; the bellhop placed the bags in the back seat, spoke to the driver, and watched the cab leave.

The big man watched the cab go, and then hurried back into the hotel.

"You have them confused," someone said from behind Newman and he spun around.

Dybrovik stood a few feet back, in the shadows of a clump of trees. He looked scared witless.

"Turalin wasn't telling the truth, was he?" Newman asked.

Dybrovik shook his head. "No. It was mostly all lies."

"Then it will be a market manipulation. Another Great Grain Robbery?"

"It's not that either. It's worse. It's . . ." Dybrovik stopped in midsentence. He was staring across at the hotel.

Newman turned. The husky man who had watched the cab take his luggage was starting across the street.

"It is Danilov. He is coming for me," Dybrovik said. He slipped farther back into the shadows, then took off running.

Newman hesitated a moment, then jumped up and started after Dybrovik. But he had waited too long. Danilov had spotted him; he shouted something and raced forward.

The park was fairly busy with tourists and lovers ambling hand in hand.

Newman made it to the other side. Dybrovik was nowhere in sight. To the left was Papaspirou; to the right, the park angled back toward a gathering of street vendors with their carts. Across the avenue was the American Express Building.

He sprinted to the right, toward the vendors. There was a small crowd of people there, and he hoped to lose himself among them.

He pushed his way through the knot of people and ordered a sweet tea from a vendor. As he dug in his pocket for money, he looked over his shoulder.

The big man emerged from the park at a run and pulled up short at the curb. Slowly he scanned the area across the street, and then looked directly toward Newman. But a moment later he turned toward the sidewalk cafe and started that way.

Newman paid for his tea, but left it there as he

sprinted around the vendor and hurried down the block, then across the street and down the avenue behind the American Express Building.

He'd take a cab out to the airport and get the hell away from Athens. Turalin had been lying to him. Even if Dybrovik had not confirmed it, the man chasing them had.

It was a lie, Dybrovik had said. Turalin was lying. It was worse than a market manipulation. But what did that mean?

Newman stopped about half a block away from the square and turned around. It wouldn't be so easy for Dybrovik to escape. He didn't have anywhere to go, and unless he had money he was in very big trouble. Turalin evidently had some kind of powerful hold on him. And yet he risked everything to come from the hotel and tell Newman that Turalin had been lying.

Newman started back toward the square. What the hell could he do against a large, well-armed Soviet secret service agent? Probably not a lot.

Someone careened around the corner, lost his balance, and scrambled to his feet. Newman frantically looked around, then stepped into the dark doorway of a small shop.

He could hear a man running toward him, and then he passed, and Newman almost stepped out. It was Dybrovik.

A second later there was a faint popping sound, and Newman heard someone coughing twice, and then for a moment nothing.

He pushed a little farther back into the shadows of the doorway. Someone else was out there. He heard the solid slap of shoe leather on the sidewalk. A minute later Danilov passed the doorway. He was holding a gun in his right hand.

Newman peered out of the doorway. Danilov was bending over Dybrovik's form sprawled out on the sidewalk. He raised his gun.

Newman stepped out of the doorway and, moving as quietly as he could, raced the ten or fifteen feet to where Danilov was hunched over. Clasping his hands together into one fist, he raised them high and slammed them down on the man's neck.

Danilov went down like a felled ox, but then started up again. Newman kicked him in the head, the point of his toe connecting with the man's temple, and he went down and stayed there.

Dybrovik's legs were moving as though he were trying to swim underwater, and Newman knelt down beside him.

"Can you get up, Delos?" he asked.

"It's Bormett. The Bormett farm. Iowa. Bormett. It's the key. The farm . . ." Dybrovik said, then he stiffened in Newman's arms, and slumped to the side, his eyes open, a great sigh escaping from his body. Then he was still.

Newman laid him down, then stood up. Danilov was beginning to stir. The Bormett farm. Iowa. What the hell did he mean?

Danilov began to rise, the gun in his hand. Newman stepped back, and with all of his might, all of his anger against Turalin and everything that had happened, he kicked out, connecting solidly with the man's temple. This time, Newman didn't think Danilov would ever get up.

25

Bormett stood at the edge of his east field, staring down the long rows of corn that marched away from him in military ranks. The sun was getting low behind the hill that stood between him and the house, leaving him very much alone. Catherine was preparing to go to church in Adel for Wednesday night choir practice, and she would not be home until after ten. When he didn't show up at the house to say goodbye, she would worry that he was working too hard, but she'd forget about it at church. He was always like this around this time of the year.

"It's finished," Joseph had said to him Friday night, and Bormett remembered now that he had almost replied, "It sure is." Of course he had said nothing of the sort; instead, he had thanked his old friend for a job well done, and they had had a couple of beers.

He stepped off the access road, into the first three windbreak rows of corn. It seemed as if he could see forever down the long, leafy green tunnel. It felt like home to him. He worked here. He hunted pheasant and rabbit here. And his existence and the pasts of his father and grandfather were tied up here. This place meant life to him, and growth, and all that was good and clean in the world.

Ten or fifteen yards into the row, he noticed the odor of rotten eggs. He stopped and fingered the large leaves. They felt substantial to him, already slightly moist from the beginning evening mist.

Five days ago this field had been sprayed. His spirits had sagged. He had waited for the fields to turn brown, for the stalks to droop, for the leaves to shrivel. But it hadn't happened. Each evening, after he finished his regular chores, he came out here to his favorite field, to where it had all begun, and walked up and down the rows searching for signs that he had killed his life. But there was nothing. Nothing that is, but good, healthy-looking corn.

He had also waited for the university to call him with their report, but they had not done so until late this afternoon. Then he sincerely wished they hadn't.

"Mr. Bormett? This is Dr. Murray Gray, from the University of Iowa, School of Agriculture."

"You've tested my samples?"

"Yes, sir, and to tell you that we are concerned would be the understatement of the year. We'd like to come out to your farm immediately."

"Come out to my farm? Why?" Bormett asked.

"The chemicals you gave us to test. They were all fine, normal pesticides, corn-borer poisons, rust and blight inhibitors. But one, the chemical in the milk jug. My God, Mr. Bormett, we still don't know what it is, but it's alive with bacterial organisms. If you sprayed that on your fields . . ."

Bormett's insides were churning. "Spray on my fields?" he asked, laughing. "Good Lord, Dr. Gray, of course I didn't spray any of those chemicals on my fields, at least not in years."

"I don't understand," the professor said.

"Those were chemicals that have been lying around the farm for years. I thought I'd clean them all out and find out just what kinds of things we had back there."

"Thank God," Dr. Gray said. "The chemical in the milk jug. Is there more of it out there?"

"Not to my knowledge," Bormett said, sick at heart. "It was just lying back there on a shelf with a lot of other junk."

"I'll destroy this, then. But you certainly gave us a fright, I can tell you that, Mr. Bormett. I was all set to call the Department of Agriculture and get your fields burned."

"Well, I'm sure glad you didn't do that," Bormett had said.

"I'd still like to come out and look around, sir, if you don't mind."

"I do mind," Bormett snapped, the fright rising in him like a dark monster.

"We just want to make sure there are no other contaminated sprays."

"I tell you that I cleaned out my chemical shed. You people got it all. The only other chemicals I have are fresh."

"If this organism had caught hold, it would have

spread like wildfire.''

"Just mind your own business, Gray, and let a man get to work."

Looking at his corn now, he could not see what all the fuss had been about. There was nothing wrong here. Nothing at all.

He turned around and headed back toward the access road. Bacterial organisms, Dr. Gray had said. So he wasn't out of the woods yet. But five days with nothing . . . well, it was heartening, that's all he could think. It was damned heartening.

Near the end of the cornrow, Bormett stopped again to examine one of the stalks. It looked good. Healthy. The ears were already more than six inches long, and from this point on they would fill out, and grow very fast to fourteen or even eighteen inches in length.

He pulled an ear off a stalk, and immediately knew that something was wrong. Drastically wrong. The ear was soft. And very light. He could dent it with only a slight pressure from his thumb and fingers. It was rotting on the stalk.

He dropped the ear, then pulled several others from neighboring stalks. But they were all the same. Soft to the touch, and very light.

Maybe it was just as this edge of the field.

He turned and raced down the row, stumbling to a halt a hundred yards along, where he snatched four ears off as many stalks. But it was the same. The cobs felt mushy.

Oh, God. It was happening. His fields were dying.

He pulled another ear off its stalk and raced with it back out of the row, up to the access road, where he could see better in the waning light.

This ear was as soft as the others. Whatever was

wrong with this one was wrong with the entire field.

He grabbed the husk and pulled it down, exposing the cob and kernels. A powerful smell of rot assailed him, and for several long seconds he stood there, staring at the terrible thing his corn had become.

Something had eaten at the corn. The kernels were blackened and rotted on the cob. Instead of beautifully even rows of kernels, there was nothing here but putrescence.

He made to throw the terrible thing down on the ground, but then he thought about Joseph and the others. They'd be out here in the morning. They'd see it lying here in the open. They'd know what was happening.

Instead, he turned and threw the infected ear back out into the field as far as he could, a noise like a wounded animal's cry escaping from his throat.

He stumbled back away from the field, as if it were a malevolent, living creature now, bent on destroying him.

"No," he cried, the sound strangely weak from a man so large, and he scrambled back up into his pickup truck.

He started the engine and spun the truck around in front of the tank farm, but stalled the engine before he could start up the hill. He managed to get it started again, then raced away from the field, up the hill, over the crest, and then down the other side into the farmyard. He parked behind the big barn.

He sat there behind the wheel for a long time, trying to understand. But there was no reason for it. Kedrov and the little man had no reason to do this to him. No reason at all.

He thought about the girl, Raya, but as hard as he

tried, he could feel no animosity toward her. None of this had been her fault. No doubt she had merely followed orders. If she knew what was happening, and how much it meant, she would feel guilty, he thought. But he was a foolish old man.

What had he done or said to attract the Russians to him? He had done nothing. He had done nothing. He was nothing more or less than an Iowa farmer. A successful corn farmer, but nothing more than a heartland farmer.

The United States has become the breadbasket of the world, he had told the Russians.

Was that what they had objected to? Could they have gone to such extremes out of mere envy?

He got out and started up toward the house. He could clearly see Kedrov's sickly sweet smile as well as Dr. Lubiako's sympathetic expression when he had introduced the farm journalist.

Well, I, for one, am worried about hybrids. I think we should move away from them.

Kedrov had not minced his words. Nor had the little man in the military uniform minced his words the next day.

"I've come to see you this morning because I would like to do a little horse trading with you," the little man had said.

"What do you want?"

"I need a favor, Mr. Bormett. Not a very large favor, and certainly nothing illegal by your own country's laws. I'm not, as you may fear, trying to recruit you to spy for the Soviet Union. But you can be of some small help to me."

"I don't know what you're talking about."

"I'm talking about an experiment that I would like you to help me with."

"What kind of an experiment?"

"Oh, it is harmless, I assure you. Harmless. But it does require your absolute cooperation."

Bormett said nothing. He was too frightened. He could only think of Catherine, and her reaction if she saw the photographs. It would kill her.

"Am I going to have your cooperation, Mr. Bormett?"

He had nodded. What the hell else could he do?

"Someone will be coming to see you. Follow his instructions to the letter. No questions asked. Do I make myself clear?"

Again he had nodded. The little man held all the aces.

"When you are finished, the negatives will be returned to you, and we will forget that we ever heard your name. Simple."

The negatives would be destroyed, the photographic record of his misdeeds erased. But what of the memory? It would endure. It was something he was going to have to live with for the rest of his life. That, and the fact he had killed his fields.

The porch light was on. As Bormett mounted the front steps, he had a vision of Katy coming out and saying, I've seen the pictures. What have you done? Why did you do it? What were you thinking about?

Inside, the house was quiet, except for the grandfather clock out of sight in the living room. He stood just within the vestibule listening, holding his breath.

After a minute or two, he went into the kitchen and turned on the light over the electric range. He got himself a drink of water at the sink, and then took down a bottle of bourbon from a cabinet and poured a stiff shot into his water glass.

He leaned against the counter, straightening up every now and then to take a sip of his drink as he tried to think this all out.

He had done what they wanted, because it would have been impossible to live without Katy. And he was sure that the pictures would have killed her or driven her off. So he had done what they wanted. He had sprayed his fields. But now he was faced with a second, and in some respects worse, dilemma. He had killed his corn. Dr. Gray would remember his tests. He would remember warning Bormett about the bacteria in the milk jug. When it was discovered that the corn was dead, they'd blame him. There'd be no insurance, no federal aid, nothing. He wouldn't go bankrupt, not quite, but his reputation would be destroyed. Next year, when there was a good crop, no one would bid on it. They'd be afraid of his corn.

Which meant he was ruined. How in hell could he explain to anyone what had happened? If the real reason for what he had done ever came out. . . . No matter the outcome, he was the loser.

He poured himself another stiff shot of bourbon, then left the kitchen and slowly trudged upstairs to his and Katy's bedroom.

He stood in the doorway, the only light in the room from the dials of the bedside clock radio. She'd be back in a couple of hours. He'd already be in bed, and she'd crawl in next to him and snuggle up close. They'd talk for a while, until they both drifted off to sleep.

It was a comforting routine that suited both of them. But it was based on trust, which in turn was based on truth, something he had been unable to tell his wife since Moscow.

Why? he cried to himself. What in God's name had he done?

He turned away in shame and stumbled back downstairs, where he stopped in the hallway, unable for the moment to decide what to do, or even in which direction to go.

The house itself seemed to be closing in on him. Katy was in every room. Her eyes were watching him, accusing him, and he had no defense for it, because he was guilty.

He let the glass slip from his hand and fall to the floor, where the liquor spilled on the carpet runner. Then he went outside, leaving the front door open behind him, stepped down off the porch, and headed toward the barn.

Albert Straub, one of the shift foremen, was just coming out of the lit machine shed. He waved when he spotted Bormett. Bormett didn't see him.

Straub called, "Got the gear box in number seven." Still Bormett did not seem to notice him. "Hey, Will," Straub tried once again.

Bormett knew that Straub was calling to him. But he just didn't give a damn. He went inside the barn.

"Well, I'll be damned," Straub muttered to himself, and went back into the machine shed.

A single light shone in the back of the barn, and Bormett walked toward it, only dimly aware of the hulking machinery stored in here. There seemed to be a humming in his ears, and it was getting louder and louder.

At the back of the barn he took out his keys and unlocked a small cabinet hanging on the wall above the workbench. On the shelves inside were several bundles wrapped in oily rags. He selected one, and put it on the workbench. Then he slowly unwrapped it. It was a military .45 automatic.

The gun gleamed dully in the overhead light. He had had it for a long time. Had used it occasionally for target practice. Couldn't hit a thing unless it was up close. But whatever one of those big 45-caliber slugs plowed into, it sure destroyed in a hurry.

A detached part of him was amazed at how calm he was as he reached up for the box of ammunition, removed the clip from the automatic, and began loading it. Amazed, because he was more frightened than he had ever been in his life.

He snapped the loaded clip in the handgrip, put the box back on the shelf, and then closed and locked the cabinet.

He could stop this right now, one part of his mind told the other. The thing to do would be to burn the fields. Get rid of the corn. Tell the truth to Katy. She'd understand. But even if she didn't, he'd be no worse off than he was right now.

He pocketed the .45, turned away from the workbench, and went outside to where he had parked his truck.

It was only about eight-thirty. Still an hour and a half or longer before Catherine was due home.

He wanted to talk to her now. He wanted to hold her in his arms, and hear her tell him that it would be all right, that everything would turn out for the best.

For a long time the Bormetts have been farming this land, Will, and they'll be farming it for a long time to come. So don't let one little setback bother you so much.

"I could have stopped it. It was my fault," he said out loud.

Katy would smile. *Don't you know, Will, that almost every bad thing that ever happens to us, we usually bring on ourselves? We're the cause of most of our own misery.*

"It shouldn't have to be that way."

No, it shouldn't, but it is. You just have to live with it.

"No," he said, holding his hands out in front of him as if to ward off a blow.

But Katy wasn't there. After a minute he blinked and looked around. Then he turned away from the house, climbed up into his truck, started the engine, and drove off.

He went back up the hill, then down the access road to the tank farm, where he stopped and shut off the lights and engine. He laid the ignition keys on the dash.

Dusk was falling. The crickets and cicadas were singing up in the stand of trees, and he could hear the big bullfrogs coughing in the creek on the other side of the hill.

He shook his head sadly that it had to end this way, then walked along the access road, pushed his way through the windbreak rows, and trudged down among the corn, careful not to touch any of the infected ears.

They'd find his truck, and then they'd come looking for him. When they found him, they wouldn't bother to look at the corn. Not then. Sooner or later, Albert or Joseph would be back out here, and think to check, and then they'd find out. But it would be too late. It was already too late.

He stopped about two hundred yards in, and pulled the .45 out of his pocket.

He didn't want to think about it. He didn't want to think about Moscow, or about the photographs, or about Catherine, or about what he had seen when he had shucked the ear of corn. He didn't want to think about anything ever again.

He levered a round into the chamber, clicked the safety off, and placed the barrel of the automatic to his temple.

"Katy," he said calmly. He pulled the trigger.

ALAS, BABYLON

And those who husbanded the Golden grain,
And those who flung it to the winds like Rain,
Alike to no such aureate Earth are turn'd
As, buried once, Men want dug up again.

—Rubaáiyat of Omar Khayyám

It was early evening, and Curtis Lundgren felt a smug sense of satisfaction as he rode through the west gate at the White House. The last time he had been here for anything other than a routine Cabinet meeting was shortly after the inauguration, when the President had offered him the job. Since then he had been a center-fielder in a game of very short hitters.

An aide opened the car door and helped Lundgren out. "Good evening, Mr. Secretary," he said.

Lundgren nodded and went inside. Michael McCandless was waiting in the outer reception room with a short, very thin man who looked as though he belonged on a college campus.

McCandless introduced them. "Curt, I'd like you to meet Raymond Yankitis, the President's special adviser on criminal justice. Ray, I think you know of Secretary Lundgren."

"I certainly do," Yankitis said, shaking Lundgren's hand. "And it certainly is a pleasure to meet you, sir."

Lundgren beamed. He liked being stroked.

"Bob LeMear will be joining us any minute now," McCandless said.

Yankitis took them back to his small office, where he sat down behind his desk. There were three other chairs. It was one of the smallest offices Lundgren had ever been in. Gave him claustrophobia.

"*You said you had something on Newman and Dybrovik,*" he said when they were settled.

"*Would anyone like some coffee before we get started?*" Yankitis asked.

"*Not for me, Ray,*" McCandless said. "*Curt?*"

Lundgren shook his head.

"*Well, we've certainly found out a lot about Kenneth Newman,*" McCandless said. "*And I'll tell you one thing right off the bat: until now I never had the slightest conception of how involved the international grain trade is. There are virtually no controls on those people. None.*"

Lundgren had to smile. McCandless was bright, but he didn't know the half of it. A two-hundred-year-old government was trying to oversee an industry that had been developing for more than two thousand years.

"*Is Newman involved with Dybrovik?*" Lundgren asked.

McCandless smiled. "*Up to his ears. Including the Russian's death.*"

Lundgren almost fell off his chair, he sat forward so fast. "*What?*" he sputtered.

"*That's right. Dybrovik was murdered four nights ago in Athens, Greece. It was a Soviet-style execution, but Kenneth Newman was seen shortly before it happened at the hotel where Dybrovik and several other Russians were staying. Greek authorities are keeping it quiet.*"

Lundgren sat back. He felt more than claustrophobia now, he felt as if everything were closing in around him. He also felt that he was missing some vital link between the startling news about Dybrovik and all the other things that had been happening over the summer.

"Newman flew back here immediately," McCandless continued. *"He's in Duluth for the moment."*

A young man with a short haircut, a button-down shirt, and a narrow tie appeared in the doorway. He was out of breath. *"Sorry I'm late, Michael. That fucking Pennsylvania Avenue should be made into a mall . . . no cars other than official government vehicles permitted on pain of death."*

"We were just getting started," McCandless said. *"You know Raymond, of course."* The newcomer nodded, then turned to Lundgren.

"Secretary Lundgren, I believe."

"That's right," Lundgren said.

"Bob LeMear, FBI."

McCandless motioned for him to take a seat. *"Bob is the special investigations coordinator for the Bureau,"* he explained to Lundgren. *"He and I have worked together on a number of other cases. The Agency's charter does not allow us to work domestically. So if one of our people heads home, Bob picks it up for us."*

"Newman is at home. We'll get a couple of our people on him as soon as possible. We got Reinke from the Sixth District to sign a wiretap order for us last night, and we just managed to get it in place before he showed up."

"To this point, as far as I can see," Yankitis said, *"there is nothing he can come back with. You're both clean. Well within the intent of the law."*

McCandless smiled. *"We've got him, Curt. All we have to do is wait for him to make a move."*

"I don't understand," Lundgren said. *"Are you saying he was involved with Dybrovik's killing? Lord, I can't believe that."*

"Involved, yes," McCandless said. *"We placed him*

at the scene at the time. But, as I said, it was a standard Moscow Center assassination. Newman definitely did not pull the trigger, but he was involved in whatever reason the KGB had him killed."

"Could you help us with that at all?" LeMear asked.

"Newman was selling the Russians grain through Dybrovik. I think a lot more grain that he had licenses for. I'm sure if you look a little closer at the Newman Company you'll find a string of subsidiaries that'll stretch from Duluth to Moscow and back."

"We've already set our accountants on that. They're not making much progress. At least not yet," Yankitis said. "But why would Dybrovik be killed?"

"I don't know," Lundgren said. "But I'm sure it's somehow tied to the other things I mentioned to Michael."

"You mean Cargill and Louis Dreyfus?" LeMear asked.

Lundgren nodded. He felt he was missing something. Something very vital. He just couldn't put his finger on it.

"So far we've found nothing."

"Nothing," McCandless agreed.

"Well, I think your answers are there."

"We'll get it out of Newman," LeMear said. "If anyone knows what's going on here, he does."

26

Kenneth Newman kept seeing Dybrovik lying on the sidewalk, the blood leaking out of his body in a widening pool. The Bormett farm in Iowa was the key, he had said. The key to what?

Turalin had apparently been lying; there was not much doubt of it now. It was to be some sort of a market manipulation. Dybrovik had apparently weakened, and Turalin had had him killed for doing so.

In the aftermath of Dybrovik's death, Newman had found himself torn between loyalties to his friends and his business and the desire to find out just what the Russians were up to. He understood that he had to arrange priorities, but he was having difficulties even trying to think about what was going on. That in itself was a new feeling for him. All his life he had been a pragmatic man; choice had consisted of weighing the facts versus his subjective judgments of personalities. Always before, he had managed to step back so that his own personality did not color the equation. Now, however he himself was a key part in the events surrounding his wife in Buenos Aires; his partner, Paul Saratt; the little KGB officer in Athens; and finally poor, hapless Dybrovik, who had trapped himself in something far bigger than his own life.

Throughout Lydia's pampered life, she had always been in control; in the important decisions it had always been Lydia and Lydia alone who had made the choice. That is, until she married Newman. It wasn't just that she had taken the title Mrs. Newman, thus forsaking (at least to the outside world) the Vance-Ehrhardt power, it was that she had bowed to decisions other than her own, and had acted out of concern for others, even though such acts ran contrary to her own desires. When she had taken over the Vance-Ehrhardt conglomerate, she had known her husband was in the middle of a large deal with the Russians, and that it would be to the best interests of her company, and therefore herself, to neutralize the Newman Company. She had warned her husband, though, and instantly, that there was a plot against his life. She had warned him.

Paul Saratt, on the other hand, had always been a follower, despite an expertise in the grain business that at times bordered on genius. "Whenever I have the urge to open my own operation, I begin to think of all the headaches it would bring," he had told Newman long ago. He had been happy being an employee, even though some of his ideas and deals were better thought out than Newman's. He had depended upon Newman to steer him in a straight line, never worrying about being let down. "Just like the frightened airline passenger," Paul had been fond of saying, "who calms his fear by telling himself that the pilot loves his life as much as me, and wouldn't do anything to jeopardize his." His involvement with Newman, however, had cost him the ultimate . . . his life.

Then there were Turalin and Dybrovik. As much as Newman wanted to balance them off each other, he could not. The match was totally unequal. Dybrovik had been a frightened man; an expert in his field who, beyond that expertise, had little if any stamina. He was like the head sheep in the flock—able to lead his charges quite well—whereas Turalin was like the wolf.

Which brought Newman back to his own conflicts.

It was night, and he sat in his study looking down at the harbor. He was alone. He had sent Marie, the housekeeper, away before he went to Athens, and she would be visiting her sister in Oregon for another ten days. But solitude suited him just fine. He did not think he could deal with anyone now.

Lundgren had wanted to talk to him before he left for Athens. Sitting here now, Newman had the urge to pick up the phone and call the Secretary of Agriculture, and tell him everything. Lundgren was a pompous, self-serving ass, but he did know the business, and he was in the administration. He'd have access to whatever information existed.

Yet, Newman supposed he was kidding himself after all. Clutching at straws. Twice he had met with presidents who had asked *him* for information and advice. So Lundgren and his cronies would probably not be able to help.

He considered contacting the FBI, telling them what had happened in Athens, telling them that he might be Turalin's next target unless he cooperated.

But what in hell would they do to protect him? Lock him up? Not an attractive proposition.

What should he do? Continue with the Russian corn contract? Simply cancel it and walk away from the entire mammoth deal? Or try to find out just what the hell they were up to?

After a while he got up and looked out the window. It was pitch black outside, although it wasn't very late . . . a few minutes before ten. He had not bothered to turn any of the house lights on; the dark house fit his mood.

Back at his desk, he set his wine glass down and picked up the telephone. When he got the overseas operator, he gave her the telephone number of the Vance-Ehrhardt estate outside Buenos Aires.

"Person to person to Lydia Newman . . . make that Lydia Vance-Ehrhardt," he said.

"Yes, sir," the operator replied. He picked up his wine as the operator talked with his trunk operator in Miami and rang the Buenos Aires operator, but without answer. "One moment, sir," the American operator said, and the line went dead.

Newman's gut began to tighten.

The operator was back a moment later; she sounded strange. "I am sorry, sir, but all calls to Argentina have been temporarily suspended."

"Suspended?" Newman said. "What the hell does that mean?"

"Service has been disconnected."

"Where?" Newman shouted. "Who pulled the switch?"

"The suspension has occurred from Argentina, sir. They are not accepting outside communications."

Newman broke the connection, then dialed Abex, Ltd., in New York. There was no one working here in Duluth, but Abex ran twenty-four hours a day.

The phone was answered on the first ring by the night supervisor. "McCarthy."

"This is Newman. What have you got on the wire from Argentina?"

"The spot market, sir? It's—"

"No, the news wire."

"I haven't seen anything all night. Let me check, sir," McCarthy said, and he was gone.

Newman remained behind his desk, looking toward the window. A flash of light passed the side of the house outside, then was gone. Someone had pulled up into his driveway. He opened a desk drawer and withdrew his .38 Smith & Wesson snubnosed revolver, checked to make sure it was loaded, then stuffed it in his pocket.

McCarthy was back on the line. "Not a thing, Mr. Newman. But there's something wrong with the spot-market wire out of Buenos Aires."

"It's dead?"

"Yes, sir. Since a few minutes after six our time this evening."

"I tried to telephone Buenos Aires, but the operator told me all circuits to Argentina were down."

"Jesus," McCarthy said. "They've talked about a junta down there for the past year."

"I know," Newman said. "Start checking around. Find out what the hell is going on. You might call the Associated Press, maybe they know something."

"I'll get it on right away, sir."

The doorbell rang.

"Have to go," Newman said. "I'm at home. Telephone me as soon as you find out anything."

"Will do, sir."

Newman hung up. Then, taking the gun out of his pocket, he hurried out of his study and downstairs as the doorbell rang again. If Turalin had sent someone to kill him, he surely to hell wouldn't stand out on the front step ringing the doorbell. On the other hand, that's just what the assassin had down when Saratt was killed.

At the front door, Newman cautiously looked out one of the windows. It was Janice Wilcox, Paul's daughter.

He pocketed the gun and quickly unlocked the door. She had a slight smile on her face when he opened the door.

"What are you doing here?" he asked.

"That's a nice hello," she said. She turned and waved toward the cab sitting in the driveway. The driver waved back and pulled away. "Didn't know if you were home, or in bed, or what," she said. "Aren't you going to invite me in?"

"Sorry," Newman said, stepping back. She picked up her suitcase and came in. She looked good, certainly a lot better than she had at the funeral.

They stood awkwardly facing each other in the vestibule for a minute or two, until at last Janice grinned and shrugged. "Surprised to see me?"

"What are you doing here, Janice?"

"I had to get away . . . after the funeral, you know."

"What the hell are you doing here?"

"I want my father's murderer," she snapped. "You

know something about it, and I'm not leaving until you point me in the right direction."

"Impossible," Newman said. He turned and went into the living room where he switched on a light. Janice followed him.

"I don't give up so easily, Kenneth," she said.

"No one will ever catch your father's killers. Not you, not I, not the police. No one."

"Maybe you didn't care all that much for my father."

Newman was stung. "That's not true."

"Then why aren't you going after his murderer? Why are you playing around with the Russians?"

"It's my business. Paul would have wanted it that way."

"Dad was working on this deal?"

Newman nodded.

Her eyes narrowed. "How did your meeting with Dybrovik go in Athens? You certainly came back fast enough."

"It went well," Newman said.

Janice stepped forward, an odd expression in her eyes. "You're lying," she said.

"Stay out of this, Janice. It's none of your business."

"What are you trying to hide? What is it about the Russians? Has it got something to do with my father's murder?"

"I said, stay out of it."

Janice looked at him for a long time. "If that's the way you want it," she said calmly. She turned and headed toward the vestibule. "Call me a cab, would you? I want to get downtown to a hotel."

"You can stay here tonight," Newman said going

after her. "I'll have you flown home in the morning."

She turned and smiled sweetly at him. "I couldn't stay here tonight, Kenneth. I'd feel like an ingrate."

He didn't understand.

"Don't you see? It would be bad form for me to use your telephone to call the wire services with the story about your meeting the Russians in Athens."

"You can't do this."

"Watch me," she said viciously. They were in the vestibule, and she snatched up her suitcase. "Are you going to call a cab for me, or am I going to have to walk downtown?"

"You're not going."

"Are you going to kidnap me?" she laughed.

"Goddamn it, Janice, you don't know what the hell is at stake here."

"What could be more important than my father's death?"

"The deaths of a lot of other people, a lot of people," he blurted.

Janice studied his face. "What are you talking about? What other deaths? And what do they have to do with my father?"

"Christ," Newman said. He ran his fingers through his hair. He felt completely out of control. On the one hand, he wanted her to go away, return to Atlanta and keep silent. On the other hand, she reminded him in so many ways of Paul that he found it difficult not to tell her everything.

She put her suitcase down and came closer. "What is it, Kenneth?" she asked softly. "What's happening between you and the Russians?"

"I can't tell you," he said. "You can stay here or go

and have your news conference. It doesn't matter. I have a lot of work to do, and I'm going to have to get on with it." He looked at her. "There's a phone in the living room. You can call your own cab if you want."

He turned and headed for the stairs.

"Who'd you hire to replace my father?" Janice called after him.

"No one," he said heavily.

"I want the job."

He stopped and turned back.

"That's right," she said, her face intent. "I want the job. I'm certainly qualified. I have my degree in business. And experience."

"You know nothing about the grain business."

"You'd be surprised how much I know. I'm my father's daughter. After my mother died, there were only the two of us, and he would sit and talk with me every night when he came home from work. I grew up in the business."

"Impossible," Newman said, although the idea was intriguing.

"Bullshit," she swore. "I have a feeling that at this moment I'm the only person you can trust. Are you going to pass that up?"

"In trade for what?" Newman asked.

"What do you mean?"

"You know goddamned well what I mean, Janice," he shouted. "You don't want a job with me. You want to pry into my business in the hopes it will lead to Paul's killers."

Her lower lip was beginning to quiver. "You can't understand . . ."

"Oh, yes, I can!" he shouted. "But if you want your

father's murderer you're going to have to go to Buenos Aires. You're going to have to talk to my wife, and to a man named Perés, the chief of police down there. They're working hand in hand.''

"Kenneth . . .''

Newman was hurting. He felt as if a Mack truck had run over his brain. "You want to know about the Russians? Last week in Athens, Dybrovik, the head of Exportkhleb, was murdered by the KGB. They're probably going to be coming after me pretty soon, unless I continue to play ball with them.''

She didn't move or say a word.

"You want murders? How about one hundred and forty killed in New Orleans when the Cargill elevator blew up? Cargill, you should know, is one of my competitors. Then we have Gérard Louis Dreyfus. I met a KGB colonel who admitted he ordered Gérard's assassination. Louis Dreyfus was also one of my biggest competitors. How about Vance-Ehrhardt? Even being married to one of them didn't help. Jorge and his wife were kidnapped. They found them dead in a Buenos Aires apartment.''

Still Janice said nothing. But her eyes were wide, and she was shaking.

"They were all my competitors for a corn buy the Russians have set up with me. So why was Paul killed? It was an accident, Janice. Simple as that. The Vance-Ehrhardt family wanted me dead. They figured I was behind the kidnapping. For all I know, my own wife ordered my assassination.''

"Christ,'' Janice said, and she started toward him as the telephone in the living room rang.

Newman took a deep breath, then went to answer it.

It was McCarthy from Abex.

"They're in the middle of a revolution down there, Mr. Newman! Half of Buenos Aires is in flames!"

"How'd it start? Who's behind it?"

"AP says it's the Montoneros in combination with low-level military personnel. The UPI and Reuters say it's a farmers' revolution."

Janice had come into the living room and was watching him.

"Anything on the Vance-Ehrhardt estate, or on Lydia?"

"Not a thing, sir," McCarthy said.

"Keep trying, then, and let me know the moment you hear anything else."

"Yes, sir," McCarthy said.

Newman hung up the phone and turned. Janice screamed, and the table lamp next to him exploded in a million pieces, plunging the room into darkness.

27

"Get down," Newman shouted to Janice as he lunged to the right and ducked down behind an overstuffed easy chair. Another shot was fired from the window, the sound soft and springy, like the noise an airgun might make. Newman had his pistol out, the hammer cocked back.

The house suddenly was very still. Newman peered around the side of the chair toward the window. At first he couldn't see a thing, but then he thought he caught a movement.

"Kenneth," Janice whimpered.

A third shot came from the window, and this time Kenneth caught the muzzle flash. He raised his own pistol and fired two shots, the noise deafening in the confines of the room. And then he waited, not at all sure whether he had hit his target.

The house was silent again for a moment, but then Newman heard a faint scratching sound. From outside. It was almost as if someone were digging outside the window.

"Janice? Are you all right?" he called softly.

"I'm all right. Did you get him?"

"I don't know," Newman said, relieved. He crawled over to where Janice was crouched down by the arch from the vestibule. She was trembling. "I'm going outside to have a look."

She grabbed him. "Oh, God, don't go out there."

"We can't just stay in here like this. If someone heard the shots, they may have called the police. I don't want to have to answer any questions just now. Besides, I think it's possible I hit whoever it was."

It was too dark for him to make out the expression on her face. She leaned forward and kissed him on the lips.

"Be careful . . . boss," she said.

He looked toward the window, but could see nothing except a lighter rectangle. He felt strange.

"Stay here," he said.

In the vestibule he got to his feet and hurried around the stairs and through the kitchen to the back door.

There was no one out there, as far as he could tell, but that didn't mean much. The wide back yard led into a long line of thick hedges, and trees separating his property from the place up the hill. Half the Russian army could have been hiding in the shadows.

He didn't think there was anyone else waiting, though, and after all he had been through the gamble didn't seem to matter as much as it would have a month or two ago.

He stepped through the kitchen door and, gripping

the pistol in his right hand, tiptoed down off the porch and hurried around to the side of the house, where he pulled up short.

He could see the street from here. At the bottom of his drive, across the street, a car was parked. He could not see if anyone was inside it.

He hesitated in the shadows at the corner of the house, staring at the car, wondering what would happen when he moved out to the front, into plain view. Then he decided he was being overly cautious. If there had been more than one person out here, then more than one person would have fired. Or one would have come into the house through the back door. There had been just one killer out here.

Newman took a deep breath in an effort to clear the tightness in his chest and started up the side of the house toward the front. Sweat was beginning to form on his forehead. He was a businessman, not cut out for this kind of adventure, and he wondered why he hadn't called the police after all, and let them work it out. But what would he have told them? That he had been with a Russian in Athens who had been killed, and now he feared the KGB was after him?

The living room window was just around the corner. A dark bundle was lying in the bushes beneath it. Crouching low, Newman moved closer until he could see that it was a man. He had apparently tried to crawl away, making the noise Newman had heard in the house. But, Christ, he was dead now.

He flipped the dead man's coat open, being careful not to get any blood on his hands, and pulled out his wallet. He fumbled in his own pockets for his lighter, and when he had it lit he opened the dead man's wallet.

Inside, he could just make out the Russian and English printing on a plastic laminated card. The name was Votrin. Sigorny something. A correspondent with Tass, the Soviet news service. There was a Washington, D.C., address.

Newman flipped the lighter off. Bullshit, he thought, looking down at the man. It was a safe bet his real employer was Colonel Turalin.

KGB here. It meant they were after him. Turalin's people had killed Dybrovik, and now they meant to kill him. He turned and looked toward the car. This one must have come alone, expecting no trouble. After all he was a professional in this business. Newman was a grainman.

Newman stuffed the man's wallet back in his coat, then stood up. "Janice?" he called through the broken window.

"Kenneth? Is it . . . are you okay?"

"I'm all right. I'm coming around to the front door. I want you to open it for me."

Janice stood at the open door, her eyes wide, her complexion pale. Her bottom lip was quivering again. "What happened?" she asked. Newman brushed past her into the house, and hurried down the corridor and through the side door into the garage, where he hit the door opener.

"What are you doing?" Janice asked. She had followed him.

"Upstairs in my study," he said. "First door on the right. On my desk, you'll find my car keys. Go get them, please."

"What are you going to do?" she asked. She was on the edge of hysteria.

"Do as I say," Newman said firmly. "I'll explain everything in a little while."

Hesitantly she stepped back away from the door, and then she was gone.

He hurried out of the open garage door and along the front of the house to the Russian lying in the bushes. Grabbing the heavy man beneath his armpits, he dragged him into the garage.

Some blood had leaked out across the driveway, so Newman uncoiled the hose and quickly washed the spots away.

He was replacing the hose as Janice came back to the kitchen door with the car keys. He took them from her, drove his car out of the garage, then came back inside and closed the garage door.

"Did you find whoever it was who shot at us?" Janice asked.

"Yes." The body could not be seen from where she stood. "We have to get out of here."

"What?" she said.

He stood looking at her. "You're going to have to trust me on this one, Janice. We've got to get the hell out of here tonight. Right now."

She didn't say anything. But she was obviously frightened.

"I'm going upstairs to pack a few things."

She stepped back, and he came into the house, closing and locking the door.

"Where are we going?" she asked, following him back into the vestibule.

"Wait here. I'll be right down," he said, and he hurried up the stairs.

"Where the hell are we going?" she called up to him.

At the top he turned and looked back down at her. "Iowa," he said.

It was about quarter to ten when Albert Straub pulled over to the shoulder, dimmed his headlights, and looked back the way he had come. He was less than two miles from his trailer in Dallas Center, but he just couldn't go on. It was as if something were pulling at him, yanking him back to the Bormett farm.

Will hadn't even seen him, although he had been standing there under the machine-shed light, as plain as day. Nor had he heard a thing. It was as if he had suddenly turned blind and deaf.

Will had been worrying around the place ever since he and Mrs. Bormett had returned from Russia. Cindy Horton had mentioned it just the other day. Said something about how Will had become snappish. It just wasn't like him.

Straub wasn't a bright man; he had never finished high school. But he did know farming, and he damned well knew Will Bormett. He'd been working on the Bormett farm almost as long as Joe and Cindy Horton. And he knew that something bad was eating at Will. The question was, would Will be needing some help?

In the distance, toward the east, there was a definite glow on the horizon over Des Moines. But back to the south, toward the farm and beyond it, there was nothing but the stars overhead, and darkness below.

Damned if he wasn't getting spooked, Straub thought. He eased his pickup truck in gear, flipped on his headlights, made a U-turn, and headed back.

Will might just have been preoccupied, but on the other hand he had never ignored a fellow before. That just wasn't the way Will did things . . . unless there was something really wrong.

He reached Highway 6 a few minutes later, and didn't

even slow for the stop sign as he squealed rubber around the corner. There was something wrong. Something badly wrong. The closer Straub got, the harder the feeling came down on him, almost like a crushing weight that took his breath away.

Straub pulled off the highway onto the access road that led down to the fertilizer tank farm. He'd take the east field road over the hill. It was a lot shorter.

The access road was heavily rutted, and twice his truck bottomed out on its springs. He swore out loud, but he didn't slow down.

About half a mile along, he could pick out the tanks, all clustered at the edge of the open field. Bormett's old pickup truck was parked there. Then Straub remembered. It was Wednesday night. Mrs. Bormett was at church. That meant Will had probably come out here to sort of look things over. Straub had always suspected the old man came out here on Wednesdays to hit the bottle, but he had never shared his suspicion with anyone else.

He parked alongside Bormett's truck and shone his flashlight into it. Bormett's keys were lying on the dash. That was strange.

Straub looked in the back of Will's truck. There was nothing unusual there. A couple of shovels and pitchfork, some rope, a few Lidacain mixing jugs. Nothing else.

Around the other side of Bormett's truck, Straub looked toward the cornrows. Had Will gone out there? He walked over, and there, just to the left, he could see where the first windbreak row had been disturbed. Will had gone out into the field. He was out there right now. Probably half drunk.

"Will!" Straub shouted. But there was no answer. He cupped his hands around his mouth. "Will Bormett! It's me, Albert! Will Bormett!"

Still there was no answer, even though Straub was shouting loud enough to wake the devil, and he started to get spooked again.

He looked over his shoulder, half-expecting to see Will coming around one of the tanks, a whiskey bottle in his hand, wanting to know what the hell was going on. But there was nothing.

"Will?" he shouted halfheartedly. Damnation. What if something had happened to him? What if he had drunk too much and fallen down or something? Farm work was dangerous. A man could get hurt pretty bad, or killed, just like that.

Straub pushed through the first windbreak rows and headed down one of the cornrows, the dark feeling rising up harder and harder inside of him.

Anything could have happened, he told himself. "Will! Will Bormett!" he shouted again. Damn, he could be lying there with a busted back or a heart attack or something. It had happened before.

About two hundred yards into the field, Straub noticed something large and dark hunched up between cornrows to the left.

He turned that way, crashing through the cornstalks, pulling up short at the last moment, the beer he had drunk earlier this evening coming up. It was Will Bormett. He was lying on his back. Half the side of his head was gone, blood and gore were everywhere on his shirt collar and shoulders. He still held a gun in his right hand.

"Oh, Jesus," Straub said, when he had finished

vomiting. "Oh, Jesus and Mary." He turned and stumbled back up to the trucks. He'd have to call Joe and Cindy, 'cause sure as hell he couldn't go to Mrs. Bormett.

Janice did not want to be left alone, so when they stopped around 3:00 A.M., about fifty miles south of Minneapolis-St. Paul, Newman registered them as husband and wife at the Faribault Holiday Inn. He had talked for the better part of four hours, ever since they had left Duluth, telling her everything that had occurred from the moment he had been called away from his honeymoon to meet with Dybrovik outside Geneva until tonight. He spared no details, neither physical nor emotional. And at times, speaking with her, he could almost believe that it was Paul seated next to him, and they were going over the entire project to date.

She hadn't said much during the telling, except to ask a question or two now and then when she didn't understand something. When he was finished they rode in silence, thinking their own thoughts.

"We'll stop soon," Newman had said finally. "If we get back on the road by eight, we'll reach Des Moines about noon tomorrow."

"Lundgren is probably going to be coming after you to stop you from dealing with the Russians, and Turalin is after you to force you to continue," she said.

"Something like that."

"What are we going to do?"

"Find out what the hell Dybrovik was trying to tell me about the Bormett farm."

"Somewhere in Iowa."

"That's right."

"I'm scared, Kenneth," she said. "Don't leave me alone tonight."

Inside the motel room he made sure the lock was secure, he flipped the deadbolt, and hooked the chain. If someone wanted to get in, he could; but he'd make a hell of a racket in the effort.

When Newman turned around, Janice was staring at him. "Why don't you go to bed, Janice. You look all in. Tomorrow will be a big day."

"What if you find something on this farm? What then?"

"Depends upon what it is," he said.

"But surely you're through dealing with the Russians?"

"Maybe," he said.

"Maybe? What the hell are you talking about, Kenneth? *Maybe?*"

"If there is starvation in the Soviet Union, I'll supply them with corn. I'm not going to let people starve to death."

"Dybrovik said that was a lie."

"As far as he knew. I want to make sure."

She hesitated. "I don't understand you," she said finally.

"No, I don't expect you do. It's the grain business."

"Doesn't it matter whom you sell it to?"

"Not at all, as long as it's used ultimately to feed people. That's why the farmers grow it, and that's why I buy and sell it. To feed people. Simple."

"It's not simple, Kenneth. Not when people start getting killed."

"Your father understood."

"My father is dead," she flared, and went into the

bathroom and closed the door. Almost immediately Newman could hear the shower running.

The Bormett farm in Iowa is the key, Dybrovik had said. Today they would know.

28

They crossed into Iowa about 9:20 A.M., after stopping for breakfast outside Albert Lea. Last night in Duluth Newman had been running on adrenalin, but this morning it was hitting him like a ton of bricks that he had killed a man. It was incredible. Things like this just did not happen.

It was a beautiful morning, bright and warm, only a few puffy clouds scudding across from the west. Once in Des Moines, he figured, he would check with the state Department of Agriculture to find out where the Bormett farm was located. Even if it was on the far western side of the state, they would be able to reach it by late this afternoon.

Dybrovik thought it was important. So important that his last words had been about the place. But Newman could think of no way a single farm could have any significant effect on Turalin's plans. It just didn't make any sense.

He tried to reason it out. The Russians wanted corn. A hundred million tons of it, or more. An unprecedented amount. Turalin claimed there would be starvation in the Soviet Union without it. Dybrovik, on the other hand, claimed that Turalin was lying.

Market manipulation was the first thought that had occurred to Newman. The Russians were purchasing corn now at low prices. When the market rose enough because of the heavy buying—and corn was already up more than seventy-five cents a bushel since spring—the Russians would resell, making a huge profit at the expense of the American consumer. Logical. But Dybrovik said it was worse than that, and he had hinted at some deep, dark plot.

"I'm sorry about last night," Janice said, breaking into his thoughts.

He glanced over at her. She had said little or nothing ever since they had left the motel this morning.

"I'm not," Newman said. He reached over to caress her cheek, but she pulled away.

Last night, after she had gone into the bathroom, Newman had lain down on top of the bedcovers and was just about asleep when Janice, wearing nothing, came out of the shower and crawled onto the bed with him.

"I'm frightened," she had said in a little girl's voice. "Please hold me, Kenneth."

They had made love, slowly, gently, as if they had been making love for years. Afterward they had fallen asleep in each other's arms.

This morning, when Newman awoke, Janice was already up and dressed, sitting in front of the TV, smoking a cigarette.

"It's late," she had said. "If you want to make it to Des Moines by noon, you'd better get up now." She stubbed out her cigarette and got up. "I'll be outside."

"Janice," Newman had said.

"I don't want to talk about it," she had said, and left the room.

It appeared now that she had changed her mind. And he was beginning to change his opinion of her.

"It'll never happen again, I promise you," she said, her voice far away as she stared out her window at the passing farm fields.

"Why?"

She turned to him. "You're married, for one. I don't love you. And I'm not in the habit of engaging in casual sex."

"I didn't think it was so casual last night."

"Forget about it," she snapped.

He shook his head. "No, Janice, I won't forget about it."

"Goddamn it, Kenneth . . ." She stopped and took a deep breath. "If you want to know the truth, I'm embarrassed. Embarrassed and frightened."

"That's quite a load to have to carry."

She looked sharply at him. "Let's just forget it. Okay?"

Newman started to say something else, but then closed his mouth firmly and concentrated on his driving.

They followed the Interstate straight south, through mile after mile of fields. They were in the heartland. Corn country. As far as they could see in any direction, the tassels atop the stalks waved in the gentle late-summer breezes. It was going to be a banner year. The weather had cooperated with just enough rain and plenty of warm, humid weather all across the Midwest. When the crops came in, they would flow outward by truck and train, by barge and ship, around the hungry world. It made Newman feel good, being a part of it.

They had been listening to the car radio all morning, and by 11:30 A.M., Janice found a Des Moines station that came in clearly. They hadn't said much to each other in the past couple of hours, and Newman was stiff from sitting in one position. They were getting low on gas.

"How about some lunch?" he asked.

"Are we far from Des Moines?"

"Twenty-five or thirty miles."

"Let's wait until we get there, and find out where the farm is. Then we can stop."

"Sure," Newman said. They were coming to an exit, and he began to slow down. "I'll just pull in for some gas. I want to stretch my legs."

Janice said nothing.

Just off the ramp was a Mobil station. He pulled up to the full-service pumps and got out, telling the attendant to fill it up. Then he went around the side and into the men's room.

He had been gone for less than three minutes when someone began honking a horn outside. He finished washing his hands and went back out. The station attendant was arguing with Janice. She was beeping the Mercedes' horn.

Newman sprinted across to them. She stopped honking when she spotted him. "Hurry up!" she shouted.

"I don't know what's going on here, mister . . ." the

attendant was saying, but Newman ignored him.

"What the hell is wrong?"

"Bormett," Janice sputtered. "It's Bormett. He's dead. It was just on the radio."

"Oh, my God," Newman breathed. He turned back to the attendant. "That's enough gas!"

"You said fill 'er up."

Newman grabbed the nozzle, flipped it off, and hung it up, then put the gas cap on himself. He pulled out a twenty-dollar bill, threw it at the attendant, jumped in the car, and headed back onto the Interstate as fast as he could go.

"What happened?" he asked.

"His name is William Bormett. His farm is west of Des Moines, near the town of Adel. They said he was found dead last night."

"Murdered?"

"He shot himself. They found him in his fields."

"Cornfields?" Newman asked. "Was he a corn farmer?"

"One of the biggest in the state," she said. But there was more, he could see it in her eyes.

"What is it, Janice? There's something else."

She nodded. "I can't believe this is happening," she said.

"What is it?" Newman shouted.

"Bormett and his wife . . . they just returned from Moscow a couple of weeks ago. He spoke about farming at a university there."

"Turalin," Newman said, half to himself, and suddenly he had a fair idea of what was happening, although it was so monstrous it nearly took his breath away. But it fit. It all fit.

"Turalin killed him?" Janice asked, picking up his mood.

Newman shook his head. "Unless I miss my guess, he didn't have to."

"What are you saying, Kenneth?"

"There's a map in the glove compartment. Get it out and find out how to get to Adel." His mind was racing far ahead. If Turalin had called Bormett to Moscow to set him up, and if he had done so, then the farmer's suicide probably meant he had done whatever it was he had been ordered to do. It gave Newman a cold feeling in the pit of his stomach. He hoped he was wrong. But if he was guessing right, it would already be too late to do anything about it. And then, God help them all.

There was no shortcut to Adel. The most direct route was around Des Moines on I-35, and then west on Highway 6. It was a few minutes past 12:30 P.M. when they turned onto the secondary highway. A sign said ADEL 12 MILES.

They passed through the small town of Waukee, and then a few miles beyond that the county road led up to the town of Dallas Center. They had just passed a sign that said ADEL 2 MILES when on the right, over a wide driveway, was a sign: BORMETT FARMS. Newman pulled up at the side of the road.

Cornfields stretched in every direction. The paved driveway curved around a low hill to the right, then dipped down into a hollow where there was a house and a collection of farm buildings. There were a lot of cars parked down there, and a number of people moving around.

Newman got out of the car, but he left the engine running.

"Where are you going?" Janice asked nervously. She didn't get out of the car.

"I want to look at something. Stay there," he said. He went around the car, walked a few yards down the driveway, then stepped off the road, over the drainage ditch, and into the cornrows. Instantly he was enveloped in a dark green, cool tunnel, which smelled faintly of rotted eggs. His heart was thumping against his ribs and his stomach kept turning over.

He stopped a few yards in, and looked at the corn stalks. They looked good. Healthy. He had seen a lot of corn in his life, and this looked as good as, or better than, anything he had ever seen.

He reached up and pulled an ear off a stalk, and immediately knew something was wrong. The ear was soft, almost liquid, to the touch.

Carefully holding the stalk away from himself, he pulled down the husk, and his stomach lurched. The ear was black and rotted. It had a very bad odor. He threw it down, and backed up a couple of paces.

He pulled another ear from a different stalk and shucked it, but it was the same.

Why in God's name had Turalin wanted this?

After a moment or two, he turned and went back to the driveway, where he looked down toward the house.

Something had happened to Bormett in Moscow. Turalin had probably set him up somehow so that he could be blackmailed. Then, back at home, Bormett had done something to his fields, probably sprayed them with something. When it began to develop, and he could no longer stomach what he had done, he had shot himself.

Newman realized that he was guessing, but he didn't

think he was too far off. Somehow, though, he didn't think Turalin's plan had been merely to ruin this one farm.

Janice had gotten out of the car, and she waited as he came back. "What'd you find?"

"I don't know yet," he said.

They got in.

"What do you mean, you don't know? What did you find?"

"Just exactly what I said," he snapped. He drove the rest of the way into Adel in silence, and then turned north. After a few miles he stopped the car beside another cornfield.

"Why are we stopping here?" Janice asked. "Christ, can't you tell me what's going on?"

Newman looked out across the field, conscious of his beating heart, of his aching stomach, and of his shallow breath.

Janice said something else, but he didn't hear it as he got out of the car. He stepped across the drainage ditch and entered the field.

There was no reason to suspect that whatever had gone wrong with Bormett's corn had spread to his field. Bormett's fields were at least five miles away from here.

The stalks and leaves all looked good, just as they had back at the Bormett farm. But there was that faint odor of rotten eggs.

Newman stopped about ten rows in. In the distance somewhere he could hear a crow cawing, and he thought he could hear the distant thunder of a jet airplane, probably taking off from the Des Moines airport.

He wondered whether Bormett had known all along

what was happening, or if he had found out about it just last night. Whatever the case, it must have been a terrible shock to him to see the devastated ears.

Newman reached out and touched one of the corn leaves. It felt good. Then, hesitantly, he reached out for an ear and pulled it off the stalk. It was bad. He didn't have to open it to know. But he shucked it anyway, exposing the obscene rotted mass.

He threw the ear down. Five miles, he thought, backing up. Fifty miles? Five hundred miles?

"Kenneth?" Janice called from back up on the highway.

Turalin had ruined the corn crops here in this part of Iowa. The same corn he wanted to buy. Much of this crop had, in fact, already been sold to Newman Company subsidiaries through Des Moines trading houses.

That meant Dybrovik was correct. There would be no starvation in the Soviet Union. Turalin had never wanted the corn. He wanted to ruin the Newman Company.

Newman rejected the thought. That wasn't it. That wasn't it at all. Turalin was thinking bigger than that. He wanted Newman to go on a buying spree as a cover. If everyone was watching Newman, no one would be paying attention to what the Russians were really doing. Which was growing corn . . . a lot of corn. A record amount of corn. Corn that the Russians would be able to sell to whoever needed it.

"Kenneth!" Janice called from the road again.

Newman started back, but stopped again as he looked down the cornrow. Why target a few fields around Des Moines, Iowa? If Turalin had planned this entire thing, why stop at just a few fields?

"Christ," Newman swore. He pulled an ear from a stalk, then bolted down the cornrow and out to the road.

A county sheriff's car was parked just behind Newman's. A uniformed officer stood with Janice.

"Here he comes," the deputy said, smiling. "Why don't you come on up here, Mr. . . . Newman?"

Newman came up onto the road, and crossed over to them. "Where's the nearest telephone I can use?"

The cop was taken aback. "In Adel, I suppose . . ." he started. "Just what the hell were you doing out in that field?"

Janice was looking at him, wide-eyed, her gaze flickering from his eyes to the ear of corn he was holding and back.

"And what the hell are you doing with that?" the deputy asked, pointing at the corn.

Without a word, Newman yanked back the husk to expose the rotted mess.

"Jesus H. Christ," the deputy swore.

"The entire field is like this," Newman said. "So is the Bormett field."

"Bormett?" the deputy snapped. "What do you know about the Bormetts?"

"This—whatever it is—originated on the Bormett fields, and unless I'm way off, it's airborne and spreading all over the place."

"Jesus H. . . ." the deputy said, and he let it trail off. "Just who the hell are you?"

"I'm a grain dealer. I came out to talk with Mr. Bormett, but we heard on the radio he was dead. Committed suicide. Now, will you get me to a telephone?"

"Who're you going to call, your lawyer?" the deputy asked. He couldn't keep his eyes away from the infected ear of corn.

"The Secretary of Agriculture in Washington, D.C. And I suggest that you get hold of your state Department of Agriculture and the governor. These fields are going to have to be burned off. Right now, before this spreads across the entire state."

The deputy's lips were working, but no sound came out. He glanced from the ear of corn to Newman and then out to the fields on both sides of the road. "Jesus H. Christ," he said again. Then he turned back. "You'd better follow me. We'll go back to the office in Adel."

"Right," Newman said. He laid the infected ear on the floor, in the back seat of his car, and as soon as Janice had gotten in, he made a U-turn after the deputy and took off after the flashing red lights.

"What is it, Kenneth?" Janice said in a weak voice.

"I don't know," he said. "Some kind of disease. And unless they sprayed this field as well as Bormett's, it's airborne."

"Bormett's field was infected?"

"That's right."

She turned in her seat to look at him. "Bormett went to the Soviet Union a few weeks ago."

Newman glanced at her. "That's also right."

"Colonel Turalin," she said, and she looked out at the cornfields. "But why would he do something like this? He wanted to buy the corn. Why kill it?"

"I don't know, Janice. I just don't know."

Curtis Lundgren was just leaving his office when his

secretary called him back. LeMear from the FBI had telephoned ten minutes earlier with some wild story about a dead Russian in Duluth. McCandless was coming over from Langley, and they were all supposed to meet at LeMear's office. It obviously had something to do with Newman, but LeMear had not been very clear. He had sounded very upset.

"What is it?" he asked his secretary, stopping in the doorway.

"It's an urgent telephone call, sir," the woman said.

"Tell whoever it is that I'll get back to them. I'm out now."

"It's Mr. Newman, sir."

"Newman?" Lundgren sputtered. "I'll take it in my office."

"Yes, sir," the secretary said.

Lundgren hurried back into his office, slamming the door behind him.

"This is Lundgren, now what the hell is going on and where the hell are you, Newman?"

"Listen to me, and listen to me closely, Lundgren, we've got a disaster on our hands out here, unless you move damned quickly."

"What the hell is going on?" Lundgren shouted.

"I'm calling from Adel, Iowa . . . just outside Des Moines. Does the name Bormett mean anything to you?"

"Bormett," Lundgren said. "Why of course. We sent him to the Soviet Union just . . ." He stopped. "My God. The Russians."

"That's right," Newman said. "Bormett's cornfields are infected with some kind of a disease. We're calling the university to send someone over here to try and identify it. Meanwhile the infection has spread to at least one field five miles away."

"I'll call the governor. You may need the National Guard to help burn off the fields. Where are you?"

"The sheriff's office in Adel," Newman said. "And listen, Lundgren. Last night in Duluth, a Russian tried to kill me. You'd better call the authorities. His body is in my garage."

"Right," Lundgren mumbled. "Meanwhile, sit tight. I'm coming out there."

29

Lydia Vance–Ehrhardt–Newman stood at the twentieth-floor window of the company building in downtown Buenos Aires, watching the *villas miserias* burn. The flames leaped high into the night sky, and the dense black smoke blotted out the stars toward the east. In other parts of the city she could see the flash of sporadic firing as Federal District troops continued to battle the Montonero freedom fighters.

"Libertad!" was their battle cry. Lydia shook her head. The *libertad* banners had suddenly appeared yesterday from rooftops, out windows, in the parks, along the beaches. It had been the signal for the revolution to begin.

She had been caught at work, and although the fighting hadn't gotten this far yet, it was coming close. Before too long, unless the federal troops got help, she and the others would be cut off here in the Vance-Ehrhardt Building.

Most of her chief executives had already left the city. Many of them had even left the country, taking boats across the Río de la Plata to Uruguay, and airplanes to Brazil and Boliva.

Even now there was a steady stream of aircraft leaving the airport southwest of the city. As long as the federal troops held that district, the planes would continue to leave. But the troops could not hold too much longer; the Montoneros were too well organized, and too well equipped, and had at least the tacit support of the army, whose lower ranks remained in their barracks.

When this was over, Lydia thought, lighting a cigarette as she watched the fighting, the new government would probably nationalize all the businesses, including Vance-Ehrhardt. But even if they didn't do that, they'd surely meddle with the pampas farm system, which was, of course, the lifeblood of the Vance-Ehrhardt conglomerate.

There would be little or nothing remaining in Argentina for the Vance-Ehrhardts, or at least there'd be nothing until the government stabilized and its leaders realized that a company is not merely a collection of buildings and a few employees. It needed leadership, expertise, and international connections. They would call back the executives, offering them certain advantages, and business would get back to normal.

Such a thing had happened before in Argentina, and it would happen again. Lydia was not overly worried. She was confident she could get to the airport before it was too late, and equally confident that she would return one day to resurrect Vance-Erhardt. But before she left Buenos Aires she wanted the answer to one question. She would not leave without it.

Grainex, their New York subsidiary, had first alerted her to the probability that not only was her husband dealing with the Russians, but that there was also a connection between Captain Perés and the Soviets. Perés had been seen on at least one occasion meeting with a known Russian sympathizer.

Also, Lydia had heard that Perés had meant to kill Kenneth, but that the operation had been botched and Paul Saratt had died instead.

She had heard about the plot from one of Perés' own people who was on the Vance-Ehrhardt payroll. But her informant did not know exactly who had ordered the assassination. Had it been Perés himself, or someone else? She was determined to find that out as well.

Someone knocked at her office door, and Lydia turned away from the window. "Come," she called out.

Francisco Belgrano, her father's personal secretary, came in. He was an older, distinguished-looking man who walked with a limp. Her father had trusted him implicitly, and so did she. "If I were to lose my mental capacities, Belgrano could step in and take over the entire business tomorrow," her father had once said.

During the past weeks she had relied heavily on his abilities and judgment.

He seemed distraught now. "You are simply going to have to leave this instant, my dear," he clucked, beginning to gather up papers from her desk.

"Has the messenger returned from police headquarters yet?" she asked. The telephone system was out; the revolutionaries had blown up the main exchange as one of their first acts. She had sent a messenger to ask Perés for a meeting.

"No," Belgrano said without looking up.

"Then we will wait."

"But his driver is back."

"His driver?" Lydia asked.

Belgrano looked up from what he was doing. "Your messenger was killed."

"The fighting has come that far?"

Belgrano shook his head. "No, madam. The driver informs me that Capitán Perés himself shot and killed poor Hernández."

Lydia's nostrils flared. She could feel the color coming to her cheeks. "Was there a message?"

"No, madam. None that I was told of."

"Where is the driver now?" Lydia asked, coming over to the desk.

"In the garage, waiting to take you to the airport."

Lydia opened a desk drawer and pulled out a .380 Beretta automatic. She checked the clip to make sure it was loaded, then levered a round into the chamber. "How about you, Francisco? Will you be coming with me?"

"No," the man said, straightening up. "I will remain. When the fighting dies down, they will need a maintenance staff here. Just until you return."

And if I never return, Lydia thought, you would do quite nicely as the head of Vance-Ehrhardt. But she didn't give voice to the thought.

She stuffed the gun in her purse, came around the desk, and gave Belgrano a kiss on the cheek. "I'm sorry it ended this way, Francisco," she said softly.

His eyes were suddenly moist. "I can understand the

revolution, but I cannot fathom the murders of Sir and Madam.''

"Take care," she said, stepping back.

He handed her the thin briefcase into which he had stuffed the papers. "You may need this," he said.

She took it, turned on her heel, and left the office. She went down to the brightly lit subbasement parking garage. The electricity was off in much of the city, but this building had its own emergency generating system, as did many buildings. Her father had had it installed years ago.

The young driver who had been leaning against the hood of her Citroën sedan straightened up as she approached.

"Are you sure it was Capitán Perés, and no one else, who shot Hernández?"

"*Sí*, señora," the frightened young man said.

"But then he let you go. Why?"

"He told me to come back and tell you . . . and you alone . . . what happened. He said you would understand his answer to your question."

The answer was loud and clear. Perés had killed Saratt, after all. But what else? How deep did his involvement with the Russians go? And would he try again to kill Kenneth? "Let's go," she said, climbing in the back seat. The driver jumped in behind the wheel, started the car, and headed out.

"The main highway out to the airport is still clear, señora," he said.

"First we will stop at Police headquarters," Lydia said.

The driver looked at her in the rearview mirror.

"I'll only be a minute or two. Then we will go straight

out to the airport."

"But señora, Capitán Perés . . . he is still there."

"I hope so," Lydia said, smiling. "I hope so."

It took less than five minutes to reach the police building, but already the fighting was closer. As the driver parked at the side of the building, Lydia could hear gunfire less than two blocks away. The driver was obviously frightened half out of his mind.

"If they come too close, take the car and drive like hell," she said, getting out. "I'll find a ride out to the airport with one of the policemen."

"But, señora."

"Wait only as long as you can, then get out of here," Lydia shouted, and she strode across the sidewalk and entered the building.

Just inside were three wide, marble steps that led up to the lobby. Sandbags had been placed across the steps, and she stood at the bottom looking up into the muzzles of a dozen rifles.

"Do not fire!" someone shouted.

"I want to see Capitán Perés," Lydia called up.

A police lieutenant with greasy hair stood and waved her up the stairs. She picked her way through the sandbags; at the top he helped her over.

"I am Lieutenant Martínez. I will escort you up to the capitan."

"I can find my own way, thank you," Lydia said.

"I will escort you," the lieutenant said firmly. He took her arm and led her across the lobby to the bank of elevators. Only one, apparently, was working. There were sandbags everywhere. They were waiting for the siege to begin.

They entered the elevator, and when the lieutenant

turned his back to Lydia to press the floor button, she quickly opened her purse and pulled out the Beretta.

He turned around and his eyes went wide. He started to reach for the pistol at his side.

"I will shoot you without hesitation, lieutenant," Lydia said. The elevator doors closed and they started up.

"What do you want?"

"How many people does Perés have up there with him?" she asked.

Something flashed in the lieutenant's eyes. "A dozen soldiers. Maybe more. Give me your gun."

"If you are lying to me, I will kill you the moment the doors open."

He stepped back. "There is no one there with him. He is alone."

"No one is watching the elevator?" Lydia asked. Something was wrong. The lieutenant was hiding something. She raised the gun so that it pointed at his head. "Quickly," she said.

"Whoever comes up must call on the elevator telephone. Otherwise the doors will never open. He has the master switch up there."

"Call him!"

He picked up the telephone.

"Make a mistake and I will kill you," Lydia said. "You have a message for him that must be delivered in person."

"Capitán, it is me . . . I, we must talk, sir," the lieutenant said. He was sweating. "Yes, sir, I am alone." He looked at Lydia, then shouted, "It is Lydia Vance-Ehrhardt . . ."

Lydia fired, the shot hitting him just above the right

eye. His head snapped back, and he dropped the phone and crumpled to the floor.

Perés' office was on the fifteenth floor, and they were already coming to the twelfth when Lydia hit the button. The elevator lurched to a halt, and slowly the emergency doors came open onto a corridor with office doors on either side.

She jumped off the elevator; a split second later an explosion shattered the silence. The car rattled in the shaft, and then suddenly dropped out of sight, crashing to the bottom. Perés had evidently placed an explosive charge on the elevator cables.

She raced down the corridor to the stairwell, and then up three flights of stairs to the fifteenth floor, where she opened the door a crack and looked out into the wide corridor. No one was in sight. She stepped out and hurried toward Perés' office, which was off a side corridor to the left. She came around the corner as the large man was turning away from the open elevator doors, where he had been looking down the shaft. She raised her pistol as he started to bring his submachine gun up.

"Don't!" she shouted.

He stopped, the gun halfway up. "Your husband is not dead," he said. He was very nervous. She could see that he was sweating.

"But you ordered him killed, didn't you?" she snapped.

"A lot of people will die for Argentina before it is right."

"Why do the Russians want my husband dead, Perés? He has been working with them."

"The Russians? How would I know that . . ."

"You've been seen with them, goddamn it! Don't lie to me or I will kill you this instant." She raised her gun a little higher.

Perés backed up a step. "It is a lie."

"It's not a lie," Lydia said, advancing.

"You have to believe me. I'm not working with them. Please," he pleaded.

Lydia said nothing.

"Look . . . the Russians ordered the kidnapping of your parents so that your husband's deal with them would go through unhindered."

"What?" Lydia cried.

"Yes, it's true. We caught one of them who had been left for dead at your parents' mansion. One of the terrorists. We gave him drugs. He told us everything."

"Then you were involved with my parents' kidnapping too!"

"No," Perés shouted, backing up another step. He was very close to the open elevator shaft.

"Why, you dirty bastard? Why kidnap my parents, and then try to kill my husband? Why both? What are you trying to do?"

"Ask Belgrano. He knows everything."

"Belgrano . . ." Lydia started, but then it hit her in a blinding flash. Jesus. Belgrano and Perés had been working together to take over Vance-Ehrhardt when the revolution came. They had used the Russians, but then doublecrossed them. All the killing would not stop. Her parents were dead, and they meant to finish by killing Kenneth and then her.

"Bastard!" she yelled. She pulled the trigger. The hammer snapped, but the shell didn't fire.

Perés laughed and started to bring his weapon up.

Without hesitation, Lydia leaped at the man. Only in the last instant did he realize what was about to happen, and he fired wildly, the shots ricocheting off the floor, as Lydia slammed into his chest with every ounce of her strength. Perés was driven backward, through the open elevator doors. Lydia tried to jump back, but he reached out and grabbed her arm. She could feel the bottom going out from under her as she tumbled into the shaft with him.

"Kenneth," she cried, "Kenneth," over and over, as she and Perés fell to the bottom.

Colonel Vadim Leonid Turalin stood at the third-floor window of the Lubyanka prison looking down at the preparations in the courtyard. He wore a pair of heavy gray woolen trousers and an open-necked cotton shirt. He shivered. It looked cold outside. A thin drizzle fell from a leaden sky, and the tall lights on the walls threw long shafts of yellow that glinted off the wet slickers of the men standing around the canvas-covered truck.

Actually it was old fashioned and somewhat melo-dramatic, he thought, taking a deep drag of his cigarette. If they had given him a choice, he certainly would have put a pistol to his own head and accomplished the task with a lot less fuss.

He sighed deeply.

The fool Dybrovik had been the key to his own un-doing. Dybrovik had known what he was doing in the grain business, and, surprisingly, he had handled him-self brilliantly, in the end, with the bankers of Geneva. All the money—all the Soviet money—had been neatly transferred into a numbered account in Turalin's name.

The fool had made it look as if Turalin were stealing the money. And the Internal Affairs Directorate had believed it.

It had all come down to a matter of control, Turalin thought. He had made a tactical error with Dybrovik's wife. Perhaps it would have been better to have controlled the nagging woman, rather than killing her. But at the time it seemed to be clear. The control of Dybrovik had been keyed to his wife, with whom he had a somewhat complex relationship of love and hate. She had been his wife as well as his domineering mother. And he had deeply resented her absolute control over him, while at the same time finding comfort in it.

Again Turalin sighed deeply. Could have beens. But it didn't really matter. He had won after all. The American corn crop was ruined, the Soviet wheat and corn crops mammoth. It was all going to work.

He turned away from the window as a key grated in the lock. The heavy steel door opened and Brezhnev's aide, Anatoli Andreyevich Shumayev, stooped as he came in, a sad expression on his face. He closed the door behind him, and Turalin could hear the guard turning the lock again.

"Good morning, Vadim Leonid," the large man said. He looked around the small cell, then pulled a wooden chair away from the table and sat down. He lit himself a cigarette, taking his time about it.

"You have come to gloat, comrade?" Turalin asked. He really didn't care. The man was an incredible fool. Fortunately, the Soviet Union would survive despite him and his kind.

Shumayev shook his head. "No, my friend, merely to pick up the pieces. We have to know where we stand, you know. Policy and all that. Brezhnev meets with the American President in a couple of weeks. And he is very angry. He thought that since you and I had an understanding, perhaps I could talk some sense into you."

Turalin had to laugh at the pompous fool. And yet Shumayev was sitting there, and he, Turalin, was waiting here to be escorted outside in the rain, to be stood up against the wall and shot to death.

"They called you 'the little man,' " Shumayev said.

Turalin raised his right eyebrow. "You've seen the intercepts, listened to the tapes."

Shumayev nodded. "We've seen it all."

"Then what do you want with me?"

Shumayev looked disdainfully around the room. "I personally don't want a thing from you—you disgusting *little man*—but Comrade Secretary would like an explanation."

They were locked in here. Turalin had heard the key. It would take the guards several long seconds to make it in, even if they were watching, or even if they were alerted immediately. A lot of damage could be done in that time.

But he held himself in check. Just for a minute or two more.

"What have you to offer me, you disgusting *obese* fool? My life?"

Shumayev stiffened. Turalin had heard that he was sensitive about his weight.

"Let's just say, a more perfect aim by your executioners, to eliminate any suffering."

Turalin laughed. "And in return, what do you want? Specifically."

"Comrade Party Secretary tells me that there were

three operational phases to your scheme. The first was a surplus of grain. Our farmers, I am told, will provide that, mostly in wheat. The second was a surplus of Western currencies. From what I have learned, you managed somehow to amass more than one billion American dollars. In itself quite a feat. And third, you wanted to manipulate the world market for vast personal gain.''

"You have an understanding of what I was trying to do," Turalin lied.

"I submit to you, Comrade Turalin, that the facts, as we have come to know them yesterday and today, simply do not support the third phase of your scheme."

"I see," Turalin said noncommittally.

"What Comrade Brezhnev would like, then, is a clear explanation."

Turalin laughed again. He moved over to the table and stubbed out his cigarette.

"Don't be a fool," Shumayev hissed. "In less than five minutes you will be marched out of here and executed. Have you no concern for the welfare of your country?"

"None," Turalin snapped. His hands shot out and grabbed Shumayev by the throat. The man's eyes bulged; almost instantly his face began to turn purple.

Actually, it didn't matter one whit whether or not the entire world knew of the ultimate plan. One part of Turalin's demented mind understood that. Turalin didn't care.

Shumayev was beating on Turalin with his fists. In an effort to avoid the blows, Turalin lost his balance, and both men fell to the floor.

Bormett had done what he was supposed to do. Although Turalin had heard nothing since the initial green light, he could envision the damage being done out there. Once the BTP-12 had been sprayed on the field, on any field, there was nothing that would stop its rapid spread. Across an entire continent.

Someone was at the door, and Turalin could hear the lock turning, but Shumayev's face was almost blue-black now and his tongue protruded grotesquely from his mouth.

The corn crop across America was composed of half a dozen hybrid varieties. BTP-12 attacked them all. A natural strain would have been immune, but not the hybrids.

Someone was shouting behind him, and then there was a thunderclap in his head, and everything began to go dark.

But that didn't matter, either. He had won. After all, he had won.

THE VALLEY
OF THE DYING STARS

Ah, make the most of what we yet may spend,
Before we too into the Dust descend;
Dust into Dust, and under Dust, to lie,
Sans Wine, sans Song, sans Singer, and—sans End!

—Rubáiyát of Omar Khayyám

It was a few minutes after three in the morning, and Michael McCandless was dead tired. His eyes felt as if there was sand in the sockets, and his mouth tasted like a dirty old sock. He had come down to TELEMETRY AND ANALYSIS around ten last night. Now he sat at one of the monitor consoles, sipping coffee as he looked across at the satellite display maps.

The tracking chart showed that SPEC-IV was coming up over Novosibirsk. Something new had been added to the display. Infrared and heat-sensing equipment aboard the satellite, hundreds of miles above the Soviet farms, had been switched on. Vast areas of farmlands showed up bright pink, the cooler mountains in dark blue.

"Heat," the chief analyst, Joe DiRenzo, had explained when they first began noticing a change. "Certain forms of root rot, stem rust, and other crop disorders produce abnormal amounts of heat. We're picking it up as pink."

That had been one week ago. Then the pink areas had been confined to a small corner of the Ust-Urt Plateau. But all through the week they had spread, like some insidious monster creeping across the land.

"No chance of a mistake here, Joe?" McCandless had asked hopefully.

"I'm afraid not. We showed Williams the heat traces.

393

He was the one who came up with the enhancement idea. We took the heat readings of normal crops and compared them, in the computer, with what we're coming up with over central Europe. There is no mistake."

"The temperature difference has to be minute,"
McCandless argued, even though he knew he was beating a dead horse. But he felt he owed the President an explanation.

"In each plant, yes, the temperature rise is minute,"
DiRenzo said. "But cumulatively, over tens and hundreds of thousands of square miles, our instruments can easily detect it."

All week they had watched the pink spread, until there could be no doubt in anyone's mind that they were witnessing a complete failure of the Soviet wheat crop.

Coincidence? McCandless wondered. There had been no operation by the Central Intelligence Agency to damage the Soviet crop, he was one hundred percent sure of that. He and General Lycoming had told the President so, as well.

"But how about a Chinese operation? Or a British deal? Or some other independent?" The President had asked yesterday. "Christ, this could end up in a war."

Gene Wilson, who was head of the Department of Agriculture at the University of Illinois, and who had worked on government analysis projects in the past, had sat forward. They were in the Cabinet room. "From the information I'd been given—if it's accurate—I'd say their problems were foreseeable."

"Could you be more specific, Gene?" the President had asked. He had looked very old; all used up. Everyone in the room had been concerned that he would have

a heart attack in the middle of all this.

"Inadequate soil preparation, for one. And a general lack of chemical pesticides and blight inhibitors," Wilson said. He looked around, taking the pipe out of his mouth. "They may have had the hybrid seed, and certainly they have the land. But they simply have not committed the money they need for proper chemical farming."

"Then you suspect their entire crop will fail?" Lundgren had broken in, incredulously.

Wilson had turned to him. "Hard to say, Curtis. But if I had to give an educated guess, I'd have to say yes. A major portion of the Soviet wheat crop will fail, and a lot of the corn as well."

He had leaned forward for emphasis. "It's not like our problem, one of an airborne bacterial organism spreading on the wind. With the Soviets it's simply lack of pesticides. A lack of treatment across the board is producing similar results across the board."

Everyone in the room was silent for a long time, all eyes on the President, who finally nodded. "We're going to have to come up with a solution, of course," he said.

"We have the money," McCandless said. "We can buy the grain."

"Where?" the President asked. "We have to keep our wheat to start to compensate for the failure of our corn."

"That's a question better asked of someone like Newman," Lundgren suggested. Everyone looked at him. "After all, he was right in the middle of all this from the beginning. He was the one dealing with the Russians."

"He is a grain merchant," McCandless said hopefully.

"One of the best," Lundgren said.

"That may be true, gentlemen," the President said, *"but where the hell is he going to get the grain?"*

30

The Newman Company 707 touched down for a landing at Washington's National Airport, its golden flanks and red twin-eagle logo on the tail flashing in the sun. Near the end of the runway, the pilot expertly turned the big plane around and brought it down the taxiway toward the business aviation terminal.

Newman had spent the past week and a half talking to agronomists and plant pathologists, and reading everything he could lay his hands on. During the flight east, he brooded about the grim picture he had built up.

The disease that killed Bormett's corn was, as Newman had suspected, caused by a bacterium that the scientists were still working to identify. Much hinged on their findings. All cornfields throughout the Heartland were being burned, but the bacterium—depending on the strain—might be one that could survive for a fairly

long time in the soil. Chemical controls would help, but
they waited upon identification of the disease. It might
be several years before the land was again healthy for
corn.

In the meantime, the nation's seedsmen would be
working at top speed with university researchers to
develop new, resistant hybrids. That, too, could take
time.

States outside the Corn Belt grew corn, but only
enough for their own needs; they would not be able to
supply the large feedlots, where corn and silage consti-
tuted the main diet of beef cattle. Dairy cows, too,
depended on stored feeds for ninety percent of their nu-
trition, and a large portion of that was corn. All would
try to bring their cattle through the winter on hay, and
next year ranchers could put some cattle to pasture—if
they were lucky enough to live in an area that provided
good pasturage. The value of beef cattle would, of
course, be reduced by the inability to feed them the
twenty to twenty-five pounds of grain a day they usually
received during the last hundred days before slaughter.

There was no question that herds were going to have
to be drastically reduced. Beef would be abundant
briefly as both beef and dairy herds were decimated, but
then it might all but disappear from the table.

Killing off the herds was also going to mean a serious
decrease in such items as milk, butter, and cheese.
Newman knew that the United States sat on mountains
of dairy surplus, as did the European Common Market.
But the mere anticipation of the loss of so many cows
would cause prices to soar. And even the surpluses
wouldn't last for the several years it might take to purify
the fields, develop new hybrids, and bring in a corn crop

that would make it safe to begin to rebuild the herds.

Ninety to a hundred percent of the ration of hogs was made up of corn; that's why the corn-producing states were the primary hog-producing states. Experiments with substitutes for corn in hog production had not, thus far, proved commercially feasible.

The feed given to chickens was 2/3 to 3/4 corn, because corn constitutes such a cheap, complete source of energy, protein, and fiber. There had been discussions of the need to work on soybean-type substitutes, but very little had been done in that area so far.

The American way of life was going to be very different for a long time to come.

The intercom chimed, and Newman, who had flown alone except for the crew, picked up the receiver. "Yes?"

"There's quite a crowd by the terminal building, Mr. Newman, just as you suspected there might be. Would you like us to call a police escort?"

Newman looked out the window, but he could only see the edge of the crowd. "How many out there?"

"Maybe fifty or sixty. There are a lot of cameras and lights. Most of them look like television people."

"Don't call the police," Newman said, resigning himself to the battering he was going to get. It had been the same at the airport in Duluth. "Can you see if Hansen is out there?" John Hansen was the company attorney.

"Yes, sir, he is. He called from inside after we touched down. He's there with the car."

"Fine," Newman said. They had come to a halt, and he unbuckled his seatbelt and rose.

Jacob came from the galley and helped Newman with his coat, then went forward and popped the main hatch.

A set of boarding steps had been pushed up.

Newman grabbed his briefcase. "Thanks, Jacob," he said.

"I'll have your bags sent over immediately, sir," the steward said. "And, good luck, sir."

Newman stepped off the plane.

A reporter at the foot of the stairs shouted up, "What are you going to tell the Senate subcommittee in the morning, Mr. Newman?"

Newman started down as John Hansen pushed through the crowd. He was an older man, with gray hair and wide, honest eyes. He wasn't smiling.

"Mr. Newman, can you tell us where we're going to buy corn to replace the crops that have already been lost?"

Newman looked at the man who held a microphone out. Behind him was his cameraman. "No, I can't."

"Will you tell the subcommittee?" another reporter asked.

Newman shook his head. "No," he said.

"I have a car around the side," Hansen said in his ear, but the reporter was persistent.

"Why not, Mr. Newman?"

Newman had been edging forward, away from the boarding steps, and he stopped now and faced the newspeople. "Simply because there is no corn available worldwide to replace the corn we have lost."

"How about our wheat, sir?" another reporter asked.

Newman turned to her. "What about our wheat?"

"It's all right. Can't it be used to replace corn?"

"No," Newman said. "We can make bread with it, but it cannot be used effectively to feed cattle or pigs."

"You're saying there will be a meat shortage?"

"Meat," Newman said, "along with milk, cheese—all dairy products."

Hansen took Newman's arm and forcibly hauled him away from the journalists who were screaming out questions, and hurried him around the building to the attorney's chauffeured limousine. The reporters were right on their heels, and only stopped shouting when the driver finally pulled away.

"Jesus," Hansen said, breathing a sigh of relief.

Newman didn't really care. He had felt a sense of unreality since last week in Iowa. None of this could or should be happening.

"We have less than twenty-four hours to get ready for the hearing. I hope you realize that, Kenneth," Hansen was saying. "Between Sam Lucas and a few of the others from Abex and Duluth, I've managed to put together an organizational chart for your business interests that should hold them at bay. At least until we can figure out a way to back out of our subsidiary committments without causing any more waves."

Newman was staring out the window, not really listening. It did not matter what he told the Senate subcommittee tomorrow, because nothing would alter the facts, among them that Lydia was dead.

He had found out about her death yesterday. The revolution was over. Argentina had a new government. The fighting had all but stopped, although the farm-fields on the pampas were still burning. The farmers had set them on fire.

Francisco Belgrano, Vance-Ehrhardt's private secretary and now apparently the head of the conglomerate, had telexed Abex in New York, asking about grain supplies. And he had included in his telex that Lydia's body had been found at police headquarters. She had evidently died in an elevator accident. Capitan Perés had died in the same accident.

"Are you listening to what I'm trying to tell you, Kenneth?" Hansen asked.

Newman turned to him, and shook his head. "Not a word, John, but it doesn't matter any longer. I'll answer any questions the Senate puts to me."

Hansen looked at him for a long moment. Then he shook his head, too. "You do realize, of course, that if you do such a thing, you definitely will be leaving yourself open for criminal prosecution."

"The administration knows most of it already," Newman said. Lundgren had told him as much last week in Iowa. They had met at the Sheraton in Des Moines where they had watched, from Newman's eighth-floor room, the burning of the fields to the west around Adel. It had seemed like the end of the world.

"You're not above the law, you know. You can't just deal with whomever you like, whenever you like," Lundgren had said.

Newman had turned tiredly to him. "What difference does that make now? Or do you think I had something to do with that?" He pointed toward the reddened sky.

"Right up to your ears, Newman. You were with Dybrovik when he was killed in Athens."

"The FBI was watching me?"

"The CIA," Lundgren said defensively. "Why was Dybrovik murdered? What did he do?"

"I don't know."

"Did he have something to do with Bormett?"

"He knew about him. But I don't think Dybrovik was

a part of it. He was just a grain man. Nothing more."

"A Russian grain man with a Swiss bank account. A little unusual, wouldn't you say?"

Newman said nothing.

"Sooner or later, it will all have to come out," Lundgren said. "We know that you met with Dybrovik in Geneva a couple of months ago. And we know that you've set up quite a network of subsidiaries, although we haven't got it all unraveled yet. And we know that you were selling the Russians a lot more than one million tons of corn. We know for a fact that you committed for at least five times that in futures. And I have a feeling that's just the tip of the iceberg. What we don't know, yet, is how all of this fits together."

Newman was surprised at the extent of Lundgren's knowledge, but then the man had the help of the FBI and CIA.

"I don't know if it all does fit together," Newman had said. "So if you are looking to me for answers, don't."

Lundgren had looked from the western sky to Newman and back, and he finally shook his head. He was angry. "I'm meeting with the governor in a few minutes. You wouldn't care to come along and help out, would you?"

"There's nothing I can do right now. But when you are ready to ask me some serious questions, and ready for the answers, I'll be there."

The subpoena had come thirty-six hours ago, and Newman had ordered Hansen not to seek a delay.

There were a few reporters at the Watergate when they pulled up. "Do you want to go around to the back?" Hansen asked, but Newman shook his head.

"I'll see you in the morning, John."

"I thought you'd come over for drinks and dinner tonight," Hansen said.

"Not tonight."

Hansen touched his arm. "I'm sorry about Lydia. We all are, Kenneth, but unless you pull yourself together, you may very well lose your business."

"Maybe that would be for the best," Newman said. "See you in the morning."

"There's a message for you at the desk, sir," the doorman said.

Newman nodded, then crossed the lobby and stopped at the desk.

"Good afternoon, Mr. Newman," the building security manager said. "You had a call on your personal service." He handed Newman a slip of paper.

It was from Janice. She had telephoned about two hours ago.

Kenneth,
   I'd like to see you this evening. Am here in Washington at the airport Marriott. Please call.

                               Janice

He took the elevator up to his apartment, then telephoned the Marriott. Janice answered immediately.

"It's me. Just got your note," Newman said.

"I'd like to see you tonight."

"I'm tired, Janice. Tomorrow is going to be a trying day."

"I'm sorry about Lydia," she said hesitantly.

"Where did you hear about it?"

"Sam Lucas. He told me. I *am* an employee, remember?"

Newman's entire body ached. He could see Lydia standing in her office telling him to leave. He would never forget that scene.

"I'd like to talk to you before your hearing tomorrow morning," she was saying.

"There's nothing left to be said," he snapped.

"I want to apologize . . . for the things I said when we were in Iowa. I . . . didn't mean them."

"Leave me alone . . ."

"Goddamn it, Kenneth, let me help," Janice shouted.

"Christ," Newman said, under his breath.

"Kenneth?"

"Can you take a cab over here, or do you want me to send a car?" Newman said.

"I'll take a cab. Be there in ten minutes flat!"

Newman slowly put the phone down, wondering just what the hell he was doing. But then he thought back to another scene with Lydia . . . this one on an airplane on their honeymoon. He had stared at the stewardess, and Lydia had asked him if he didn't prefer a simpler woman. He had told her no, at the time. But he had been lying. To himself, as well as her.

He took a quick shower, changed his clothes, and opened a bottle of wine. The security manager rang as he was laying out the glasses and said there was a Ms. Janice Wilcox to see him.

"Send her up," he said, and he went to the door a minute later.

She got off the elevator, and when she saw him standing there she hesitated.

"Are you going to stand out there all night?" he asked.

Her face lit up, and she hurried up the corridor. "Oh, Kenneth." She smiled. "I'm glad to see you."

He didn't know exactly what it was he was getting himself into, but it felt good, at last. Damned good.

For the rest of that busy fall and through the hectic, often grim months of winter, Newman recalled in detail those final hours preceding what came to be known as the Great Food Depression. Afterward, nothing was the same, nor would it ever be.

"We're going to want the truth here, this morning, Mr. Newman," Senator Abrahamson from New York said. "And if you don't feel as if you can give that to us, then you might just as well get up and leave."

Newman sat next to Hansen at the witness table in the crowded Senate hearing room. Janice had remained at the Watergate to watch the proceedings on television. Every few seconds a camera strobe would flash, and there was an almost constant murmur of conversation in here and out in the corridor.

Senator Abrahamson banged his gavel several times. "There will be order, or I will clear these chambers of spectators."

The noise level dropped, and Abrahamson covered the microphone as he leaned over to talk with one of the other senators. A messenger had just come.

They seemed to argue, and a moment later the other four senators got up and came closer so that they could take part.

The noise level in the room rose even higher.

Finally Abrahamson turned forward and took his hand away from the microphone. "Mr. Newman, if you would step away from the witness table, there is someone in the private chambers who would like to consult with you before we proceed."

Pandemonium broke loose in the room. Hansen grabbed Newman's arm. "Stay here, Kenneth. I don't know what's going on, but stay here until we find out."

Newman pulled away. "It's all right, John. I have an idea what this may be about."

"If you will just follow the page, Mr. Newman, he will direct you," Abrahamson's voice boomed.

All the reporters were talking and shouting at once, and Abrahamson was hammering his gavel.

Newman followed the page around to the back of the hearing chambers, down a short corridor, and into one of the conference rooms.

The President was there, perched on the edge of the table. Lundgren sat to his right, and to his left were two men whom Newman did not know. The page closed the door, and Lundgren made the hurried introductions.

"Bob LeMear, FBI, and Michael McCandless, CIA."

Both men nodded in turn, but Newman said nothing. He had expected Lundgren and perhaps the CIA and FBI. But not the President of the United States.

"Let's get quickly to the point," the President said. "We don't have much time." The others nodded. "Mr. Newman, I'm going to ask for your complete cooperation. Do I have it?"

Newman barely nodded.

"Good," the President said. "To begin with, nothing that's said in this room will get out of here," he said. "Do I make myself clear?"

Again Newman nodded. He knew what was coming. Or at least he felt he did.

"We need grain, Mr. Newman. Our corn shortfall

will be in the range of two hundred million tons.''

"We've been set up, Mr. President,'' Newman said. "It was a Soviet KGB plot. I'm sure the Russians are ready and able to help us out.''

The President looked directly at him. "Then you don't know yet.''

Newman straightened up. "Know what, Mr. President?''

"About the failure of the Soviet crops, mostly wheat.''

"My God,'' Newman said. "How extensive?''

"Very.''

"Then it backfired on Turalin,'' Newman said. Turalin understood that his people could live on little more than wheat alone. Americans needed meat for their way of life. But Newman was also thinking now about the only other major corn producer in the word: Argentina. Her fields had been burned. Another Turalin plot?

"We want you to reorganize your company,'' the President was saying.

Newman interrupted. "You don't understand, Mr. President. With our corn gone, and the Russian wheat failed, there is no other crop in the world.''

"Argentine corn,'' Lundgren started.

"The pampas farmers burned off their fields.''

"Canada?'' the President asked.

"Wheat. Won't replace our corn.''

"Europe?'' McCandless asked.

"Europe can hardly feed her own people,'' Newman said. "I can get bits and pieces here and there, Mr. President, but not two hundred million tons for us alone. The Soviets will need help, and so will the

Argentines, as well as the countries they normally supply."

"We're certainly not helping the Russians," Lundgren said, jumping up. "Christ, they brought this all on themselves."

"We're going to have to," the President said calmly. The others looked at him. "Or it will lead to war."

Newman heaved a sigh of relief. The President understood. At least one man understood.

Lundgren was clamoring about something, and the President finally turned to him, and said, "Shut up, Curtis. Just shut the hell up."

"I . . ." Lundgren sputtered, but he clamped it off.

The President turned back to Newman. "Go ahead and tell Abrahamson and his bunch anything you want, except the truth. I don't want to start a panic. When you're finished, we'll talk again."

"This is going to have to be organized through the United Nations," Newman said.

"What will be . . ." Lundgren started, but he shut up again when the President glared at him.

"It's the only way we'll be able to keep it fair."

"Just one question," the President said.

"Sir?"

"Is there enough food for everyone?"

"I don't know, Mr. President. I don't know."

ABOUT THE AUTHOR

DAVID HAGBERG is the author of *Last Come the Children* (Tor Books, 1982) and, as Sean Flannery, the author of *The Hollow Men, The Trinity Factor, The Kremlin Conspiracy,* and *Eagles Fly,* among other novels.

A native of Duluth, Minnesota, David Hagberg lives with his wife on the Gulf Coast of Florida and spends as much time as possible aboard their twenty-foot sloop.